PRAISE FOR *GRIM ROOT*

"In this acidic meta-horror novel, the inherent horror of reality TV mixes with more otherworldly terrors as a dating show descends into madness. This is gory fun."

—*Publishers Weekly*

"Ask me to watch a single episode of a reality TV dating show, and I'll tell you to get out of my face. But set it in a haunted estate, where gruesome curses and death await the players? I'm in. Bonnie Jo Stufflebeam fires up her penchant for pulp, served dry on a platter of her trademark wit, while still managing to invest the reader in the plights of her well-drawn characters. Mystery, love triangles, haunted fruit, oozing walls, and yes, death—that's *Grim Root*."

—Chris Panatier, author of *The Redemption of Morgan Bright* and *The Phlebotomist*

"A delectable dark cocktail of a novel, *Grim Root* is a heady mix of macabre humor and full-on horror, pure delight for fans of literary supernatural fiction."

—Elizabeth Hand, author of *A Haunting on the Hill* and *Generation Loss*

"As incisive and clever as it is humorous, *Grim Root* explores the tangled web of female competition, sexuality, and the ways that women destroy each other."

—Drew Huff, author of *Free Burn* and *The Divine Flesh*

"Whether you love or hate reality TV dating shows, don't we all wish the contestants would be subjected to strange and dangerous paranormal forces? In *Grim Root*, Stufflebeam expertly interlaces reality dating dynamics and misogyny with classic gothic madness and decay. You'll refuse that final rose and beg for the embrace of these grim and deadly roots."

—Angela Sylvaine, author of *Frost Bite* and *The Dead Spot: Stories of Lost Girls*

"Conceptually brilliant, eerie, and entrancing, *Grim Root* challenges readers to examine societal and Hallmark depictions of love. Stufflebeam masters this close-up of dark intentions in yearning for courtship, status, and the risks for conformity, revealing what is left behind as the flowers of romantic love wilt. Sure to haunt readers long after the final page."

—Belicia Rhea, author of *Voracious*

GRIM ROOT

CONTENT WARNING

This books is intended for mature audiences.
Reader discretion is advised.

Edited by Rob Carroll
Book Design and Layout by Rob Carroll
Cover Art by Dan Fris
Cover Design by Rob Carroll

ISBN 978-1-958598-36-8 (paperback)
ISBN 978-1-958598-70-2 (eBook)

darkmatter-ink.com

GRIM ROOT

BONNIE JO STUFFLEBEAM

DARK
MATTER
INK

GRIM ROOT

BONNIE JO STUFFLEBEAM

DARK
MATTER
INK

For William.

CHAPTER ONE

LINDA

EVEN BEFORE COMING on the dating show, Linda knew she'd need to refer to herself as broken; it was the only way a vague Iowa boy like The Groom would accept a divorcée with a tendency for distant expressions.

For their first solo date, Tristan took her to a taxidermist's oddity shop. When he removed the blindfold, she yelped. Before her, a stuffed bobcat raged, teeth bared, tongue an ungodly shade of pink as it lolled from its mouth. Then Linda laughed, remembering the camera behind her and the people wielding it.

"This is where you take a lady?" she asked him.

"What can I say?" His drawl was too much.

She followed him, meandering so the camerawoman, Jazz, could keep up, to a glass case that held several jars of eyeballs in viscous fluid, carved wooden monsters, and skeletons of different animals glued together to make stranger beasts.

"Any wife of mine can't be scared of weird stuff," he said. "Want to know a little secret? I love horror movies. Growing up, I wasn't allowed to watch them. But I did. They're my guilty pleasure."

Tristan wasn't the most eloquent man, but, to her surprise, Linda found herself entertained by the young airline pilot whose foremost redeeming feature was his pocketbook. Before coming on the show, she had expected to be bored by the sight of his broad chest, and eager to leave his presence, but she didn't hate his company after all. He was easy on the eyes, just not her type. Sometimes, though, she wondered if the producers hadn't slipped something in her champagne, some kind of mood-altering drug that made her flirtatious and eager for the dates. Except she wasn't eager, and that was exactly the reason those producers accepted her application in the first place: she was the token divorcee. She understood her role. She understood her lines. It soothed her to have a script, however unwritten.

"I love horror," she said. "The bloodier, the better."

She didn't watch horror, or movies of any kind. These days, she thrived on reality TV shows, where broke dreamers begged rich people to fund them—and sometimes got what they asked for. She liked the wish fulfillment, and a dating show was a similar animal. Linda's most prescient hobby, however, was her garden.

Tristan watched her with the doe eyes he could switch on in an instant. He reached out and tucked her hair behind her ear. "You couldn't be more perfect," he said.

"Hold there," Jazz said. "I want that from another angle."

Linda chewed her lip. She'd known the shoot would be long when the big wig producer assigned Jazz to it. The camera-woman moved to the other side of the couple and set up her rig. Linda adjusted the scratchy microphone clipped under her clothes. "Again," Jazz said.

Linda stood still, waiting to repeat the scene.

"Linda, your hair," Jazz said. "Needs to be untucked."

"Oh, right." Linda grimaced. The reality show experience was a strange one. She untucked her hair. "I love horror," she repeated. "The bloodier, the better."

Tristan's eyes went full doe as he re-tucked her hair. "You couldn't be more perfect," he said. "Shall we?"

When he extended his hand, she clasped it, and they weaved through more glass cases with eerie items. Tristan stopped in the back of the store. Linda paused beside him and discovered the object of his entranced gaze: the dried brown hide of some viscerally upsetting creature. It was five feet taller than they were, with a gaping mouth, knotty lips, hands like branches, and feet like roots. It had no eyes. "I love creepy shit," Tristan said.

Linda's stomach twisted. The thing was too uncanny to appreciate as a curiosity. It made her want to stop looking, to forget it ever existed. But Tristan had said something about it, and she was expected to reply. She pulled his words back to the forefront of her mind. *I love creepy shit*, he had said. But how was she supposed to respond? She knew that already; he told her ten minutes ago. Her life these days was a series of déjà vu, if not from repeating her lines from different angles, then from having the same conversations over and over with the handsome dreg.

"You're cute," she said. She kept herself from adding, *thank God*.

After the taxidermist's shop, Tristan took her to a courtyard between two hotels. At the courtyard's center, a convocation of gargoyles hunched over a spurt of water, their backs to whomever was unlucky enough to stand beside the fountain. The crew had draped a round table with a red cloth. On the table, the producers had placed two plates with green beans, mashed potatoes, and two cuts of rare steak. A decanter of red wine was set between two glasses.

Two cameramen joined Jazz. They set up one camera across from the table and one on either side of the couple. The setting sun chilled the autumn air. The producers had kindly set up two outdoor gas heaters.

As Linda settled into a Gothic wrought iron chair, she inhaled the steak's sweet blood scent. It was a damn pity that The Groom and his potential brides were discouraged from eating on camera. While getting ready for the date, Linda had scarfed a protein bar, but she adored a good steak.

"We're rolling," Jazz said.

"You passed the test!" Tristan said as soon as the camera lights went red.

"I didn't even study," Linda said.

Tristan guffawed. "You're smart," he said. "I like that."

Linda wanted to readjust in the chair—it was too hard on her ass—but she didn't want to reshoot.

Tristan poured two glasses of red and passed her one. "Shall we?"

"We shall," Linda said.

They clinked glasses. "To our future," Tristan said.

"To our future," Linda repeated. She sipped the wine. At least they were allowed, nay encouraged, to drink.

"So, Linda Meadows, is there anything I should know about you?"

Linda longed to glance at the cameras, but she kept her gaze focused on The Groom. These situations and conversations weren't scripted, but they were part of a set of calls-and-responses ingrained in anyone who had ever seen even one episode of the show.

"As a matter of fact, there is," she said.

Tristan set down his glass as if on cue. "You can tell me anything." He smoldered.

Linda fidgeted with her pinky ring. She wasn't nervous to tell him; she was worried she might get it wrong and have to redo the conversation, and she was tired, eager to be alone at the mansion while the other women went on their group date the next day. She needed to get it right. It was expected of her: second one-on-one dates always ended with a tearful confession.

"I was married for five years," she said. "But it didn't work out."

"Wow," he said. She was never sure if he feigned his surprise. "What happened?"

Linda took another sip of wine and paused for dramatic effect. She had decided what she would say when she accepted the invitation to appear on the show. "We were too young. We didn't have the same values," she said. "He didn't value family. Or romance. And all I wanted was love."

The truth was she had met him at a time when she was financially broke and emotionally broken, and he offered her a job with his landscaping firm and a hand to hold when she felt darkness closing in. At first, her work slowly healed her, and he soothed her worries: he assured her that she was a good person deep down, no matter what she'd done in her past. But as the years elapsed, he stopped looking at her through his oxytocin-tinted contacts and decided that her healing wasn't happening fast enough. She was cold, he told her, and sometimes, the glints that gleamed in her eyes frightened him.

Linda wasn't exactly lying to Tristan: she did want a person of her own, someone to see her in a warm light, but it wasn't her ex-husband who kept her from it. Rather, she didn't know how to crack open the cage of her ribs and offer her insides for viewing.

Tristan placed his hand on hers. "I understand. Family's so important."

"I feel like I'm broken," she said. She let her voice catch in the middle. "How could you ever want me?"

"Linda, no." Tristan took the wine glass from her and set it on the table. He got up from his chair and stepped over to her. He wrapped his arms around her shoulders and kissed the lobe of her ear.

"I'll make you whole again," he said. He smelled like aftershave.

"I know you will," she said.

And maybe he would. She wasn't broken, but she wasn't whole. Unlike many of the other women vying for his attention, she understood, through the strength of age and subsequent experience, that someone could house two opposing forces within the same body.

His voice hummed in her ear, and she laughed as a shiver shot down her spine. It had been a while since she'd allowed herself to let go, and letting go surrounded by cameras was more difficult. The wine helped. She felt at ease as he kissed her tenderly. She understood the appeal: of him, of the competition, of romance on camera, where the world could see the best parts of you. The lovable parts. Her body buzzed with unknowing. The future was hers for the taking. She kissed him back as the cameras and the gargoyles watched.

AFTER HER DIVORCE, Linda moved on. She felt little for the dalliances with strangers she met through dating apps, but to hold and be held by people who didn't know her secrets made her feel like she might be worth the love she craved.

The night Deja invited Linda to appear on the show, Linda was supposed to meet a young man named Nick, with blazing blue eyes and a similar love of gardening. He was her type: nurturing, gentle, naive. She nursed a martini near the door of her favorite local bar; a love of vodka ran in her blood, and she embraced it in her weaker moments. She scanned each person who entered. Instead of Nick, a thick woman in a tight red dress slid into the seat opposite her and snatched the martini from the table, downing it in one go.

"Excuse me?" Linda said. "That's my drink."

"You don't need it," Deja said. "Alcoholism runs in your family."

As the woman bit into the olive, she winked at Linda like they had known one another for ages. She set the glass back down, now marred by a blue lipstick print.

"I know all about you. Your divorce. Your secret past." She swallowed the last bite of olive and flicked the toothpick across the bar. "Your dead father."

Linda's stomach dropped. "How?"

"It's all online, if you know where to look. I follow you."

"On Instagram?" Linda had a lot of followers; she didn't know most of them.

"Listen." Deja leaned forward. "I need a contestant for a TV show. You can leave everything behind. Be a new person. Find love! Money, too, if you make it far enough."

"Wait, a dating show? Like, reality TV?"

"*The Groom*. It could be a fresh start."

Linda raised her eyebrows. It was the most well-known dating reality TV show out there. A bevy of past contestants went on and did things divorced from the lives they'd lived before. It was on the verge of being canceled, or so Linda had read.

"Nick isn't coming, is he?" Linda gestured to the bartender for two more martinis.

"I'm your date, honey," Deja said. "But not for long."

Linda chewed on her olive. "A fresh start?"

"Our network has a lot of money. With money comes power," Deja said. "Your bad credit? I can make it go away. The same goes for files that hold powerful information. They can be deleted. We don't just have a lot of money. We have great lawyers, too."

"And if I don't want to?"

"Secrets have a way of getting out," Deja said.

Linda inhaled the botanical scent of gin: juniper, coriander, lavender. She'd grown all of those herbs herself. After her divorce, she tried to take out a loan to open her own nursery, but every bank shot her down.

"I'm listening," she said.

AS HAD HAPPENED after her one other solo date with The Groom, Linda returned to the mansion and two waiting women in the living room. Twenty-five women had started their journeys there. Five competitors remained. One of the women, Marion, was sunk into the cushions of the white leather couch, her expression sullen. She held a glass of white wine but took no sips as Linda stood before her and waved with a flopping hand.

The other woman, Sabrina, lit up. Long yellow pajamas hugged her wide hips and round belly. She looked good in yellow; it was her signature color. She'd tamed her wild curls with a scrunchy, but several tendrils had sprung free. She looked relieved to see Linda again. She patted the cushion beside her and grinned.

"Tell me everything," Sabrina said.

"Not so fast," said Deja. "Confessional."

With a flourish, Linda reached one hand out toward Deja and sighed. "Take me away."

"If you hate it so much," Marion said, "just leave."

Deja lingered, unwilling to remove Linda from the scene of a potential drama. The cameraman who'd been filming the ladies-in-waiting perked up.

"You're going to let her talk to you like that?" Deja said, smirking.

"Yeah, where's that firecracker energy?" Marion said.

"I'm not lowering myself to her level."

Marion slammed her body back into the couch.

Deja scowled as she gestured toward the confessional room. "After you," she said.

IN THE CONFESSIONAL, Linda squinted as she adjusted to the intensity of the lighting on all sides.

"Did you have a good date?" Deja asked. "Tristan said it went well."

"Did he?" Linda grinned. "I was wary at first, but the curio shop turned out to be interesting."

"You like looking at dead things?"

"No. Not particularly. But I like going places I've never been before."

Deja twisted her lips to the side. "Tell us about the date, then."

Linda recounted her date to the three cameras. She waxed poetic about Tristan's love of scary things. "It's a layer of depth I didn't expect."

Deja remained stone-faced. She was good at that.

The uncanny creature with roots for feet flashed in Linda's mind. Its sallow skin had reminded her of her dead father. She shivered.

"Something the matter?" Deja prompted.

"Nothing." Linda faked a smile. "Tristan is everything I could want in a husband."

"How did he respond to the revelation that you've been married before?" Deja's eyes glinted.

"When I told him I've been married before, he said exactly the right things. He has a true heart." Sometimes it surprised Linda how well she'd learned these lines.

"What did you tell him about it?"

"We were young, my ex-husband and I. We thought we'd stay the same people we were when we were twenty. We didn't."

"And you want to get married again?"

"I loved being married. I loved the idea of going through life with a partner, building a life with the love of another person. I loved being a wife. Taking care of a house. Thinking of another person and how we could make it, together. I just want someone who will care about taking care of a house with me. I want to be equals in all things."

"You think Tristan can give you that?"

Linda paused. "I know he can," she lied.

Deja glared at her. "You don't have to bullshit me here," she said. "Sometimes, honesty makes for the best TV. And what we're creating here is the best season in all of this show's history."

But Linda shrugged. "I'm not lying," she said. "You know me, Deja. I'm an open book."

LINDA'S PARENTS HADN'T been equals. Linda's mother had worked herself to exhaustion taking care of a home that Linda's father never appreciated. Before coming on the show, Linda visited her mother to let her know that she wouldn't be stopping by for the three months it might take to film. Linda signed herself into the mental health facility and asked the orderly if she could take her mother for a walk.

Linda met her mother at the back door and offered her an arm to hold. Linda's mother refused the gesture, opting to walk on her own down the three concrete steps that led into a yard surrounded by forest.

It was about to storm, a fall rain that appeared with the changes in temperature. The cooling air fought with the cruel Texas heat, and in the distance, Linda glimpsed sparks of lightning in a gray cloud. She heard no thunder, but the wind picked up as they walked, blowing the limbs in the woods with a violence that made Linda uneasy.

"I won't be around for a while," Linda told her mother as they walked along the tree line.

"Okay," Linda's mother said.

"Do you want to know where I'll be?" Linda asked.

From the door to the institution, an orderly kept a close eye on them.

"You want to tell me," Linda's mother said. "I have no choice but to let you."

"I'll be in California. I'm going on a show." As she said it, Linda felt the faintest spark of excitement.

Linda's mother smirked. "What's the show?"

"It's a dating show," Linda said. "One where you compete with other women for the heart of some rich bastard." She forced a laugh, trying to show her mom levity even as she longed to hear a message of congratulations leave the woman's lips.

"That man better watch out," Linda's mother said, no hint of cheer in her words.

Linda frowned. "What's that supposed to mean?"

Linda's mother sighed. "Have a nice trip, I suppose. I'll just be here, all alone. It's not like I have a husband to keep me company. That's no thanks to you. But you go compete for one, dear. That's lovely for you. Truly."

Linda said nothing. Instead, she led her mother back to the door and the orderly stationed there.

"Everything all right?" the orderly asked.

"Fine," Linda said, and she handed her mother off.

As she drove away, the storm moved in, leaves rushing across the country road that led from the institution back into the city. Linda let the nothing settle over her, a comfort.

AFTER LINDA'S CONFESSIONAL interview, Deja ushered her back into the tense living room. Linda understood that she was expected to engage, no matter how tired she felt, with the other women. She smiled with her mouth and not her eyes at Deja as the producer settled into the background.

Sabrina patted the space beside her again. "Tell me everything," she repeated.

Linda fell back into the couch cushions beside the warmth of her friend. Marion's arms were still crossed over her chest, her wine glass half-drained. She didn't look in their direction, feigning a lack of interest.

"He took me to see taxidermy," Linda said.

Sabrina raised her eyebrows and paused for dramatic effect. "What?"

Marion let out a snort.

"Some sort of curio shop." She remembered that woody skin, the empty space where the eyes should have been. It wasn't even the look of the thing that unsettled her the most; it was the idea of its texture, ridged skin both hard and soft to the touch. But, of course, she hadn't touched it. "He said he likes spooky stuff—and he wants someone who likes that shit, too."

"Gross," Sabrina said.

"How romantic!" Marion said sarcastically. She rolled her eyes.

Linda side-eyed Marion as a fire lit in her belly. "It was cool. Then we went to this old courtyard with stone statues. Cute little table and chairs. Steak. Wine. A perfect end to a great evening."

"Looking at dead shit," Marion said. "I'm sure."

"Better you than me, girl," Sabrina said. "My mother used to have a taxidermy bear. Like this full-size black bear. She kept it in the entryway to ward off evil intentions."

"I'm sure your sister loved that," Linda said.

"She did." Sabrina set her empty glass on the coffee table. "She believes in all that stuff."

"What stuff?" Linda asked.

"Omens. Wards. Curses. Manifesting your destiny."

"And what about you?"

Sabrina swallowed hard. "Of course not."

Linda smiled, a genuine gesture this time. "Your family sounds special."

"They are," Sabrina said. "My sister's still alive, but my mom died when I was in middle school. The taxidermy bear, though—I had nightmares about that thing. I hate the way their eyes are glossy. It's like they're alive but trapped in this dead body."

"The eyes are usually fake." Linda poured herself a glass of wine. She tapped it with her nail. "Glass."

Sabrina let her head fall back. "Oh, that makes so much more sense."

"You two are messed up," Marion said. "This is morbid."

"You don't have to be here." The wine fed Linda's fire.

"Where else would I go?" Marion said. "I live here, too."

"Wherever," Linda said as Sabrina said, "Literally anywhere."

"Where's Charity? Go hang with her," Linda said.

"She's sleeping or sulking or something," Sabrina said. "About your date."

Linda pressed her lips together. She didn't like being the object of Charity's disdain. "So, what's on the agenda tomorrow?" she asked.

"Elimination ceremony in the evening," Sabrina said.

"Are you sure?" If she were expected to party tomorrow, she'd need to pass out right away to feel fresh and have enough energy to be charming.

Marion stood and set her glass too hard on the table. The clink of glass on glass rang out in the room. "Why would we make that up?" she said. She threw her hands up, then stormed past the camera and up the stairs before Linda had a chance to respond.

"Great," Linda said. "She'll be pleasant tomorrow." Linda tried to laugh, but she was too tired. "Want to swim in the morning?"

Sabrina glanced at the camera operator, then waited a beat, as they'd been instructed to do before discussing logistical information that wouldn't air.

"Can't," Sabrina said. "I have to reshoot my date."

"Redo the whole date?" Linda balked. "What the fuck?

"That camera guy, you know the one, he messed up the footage big-time."

The camera operator in the room half-grinned. "Dumbass."

"Fired?" Linda asked.

"Oh, yeah. Deja showed him no mercy."

Linda peered into the shadows, where Deja stood, a silhouette with no face. Deja stirred, aware of Linda's attention. Linda considered making a face at her producer—sticking out her tongue or giving her the middle finger—but that would only make Deja pick on her during the next outing.

Instead, Linda's body relaxed into the idea of a day to herself. On her way to bed, trailed by Jazz, Linda crossed in front of Charity's open door and peered in for a single second. Charity was sprawled out on her bed, her back propped against her headboard, reading some thick book. Even after her temper tantrums, the woman looked flawless, her short silky black waves never out of place. Her skin never seemed to betray her with a blemish. As a flush spread over Linda, she blamed it on the wine.

Linda had only paused at the doorway for a moment before moving on, so she was surprised to hear Charity's faint laugh behind her, followed by the utterance: "Don't spy."

If Linda had been Marion, she would have returned to the door and engaged Charity in an argument. She would have advised Charity not to open her door if she didn't want people to look into her room. She might have torn the book from Charity's hands and read the coveted title. What was she always reading at night? The question had burned inside Linda for all the weeks that she had known Charity—or not known her, as was the more accurate description.

But because Linda was not Marion, because Linda was Linda, she stayed the path to her bedroom, where she settled into an uneasy sleep plagued by nightmares of the dead.

CHAPTER TWO

SABRINA

"BET YOU CAN'T guess where we're going," Tristan said as he swept Sabrina into an embrace outside the mansion's gaping front doors. Sabrina couldn't help but feel like a fairy tale princess when she examined the backdrop she'd been living against for the past six weeks.

"Bet I can't!" Sabrina said, which was what she had said the first time they'd gone on the date, four days ago, unaware at the time that the cameraman had ruined the footage. Internally, she laughed. *I know where we're going, what we're going to say, and how you will respond to everything.* She didn't mind. These recorded dates made her nervous, and knowing the outcome was a gift. During this go-round, she could relax into Tristan's kisses. She could expect him to prove himself a decent man.

When Tristan offered his hand, she took it. Together, they strode out to the red Corvette parked in the drive. He opened her door for her. She slid across the cool leather seats. He offered her the radio dial, a formality since they weren't allowed to play music, but she fiddled with it like it mattered while Leo, the cameraman in the backseat, caught every slip of small talk.

When they arrived at their destination, Sabrina peered out on the decorated field with renewed appreciation. The first time she'd gone on the date, she had been too nervous to take in all the details. The production team had strung colored gold bulbs from poles, creating a walkway of light that led to a golden circle altar hung with glittering glass shards. They caught the light as they spun in the breeze. Several chairs sat on either side of the altar, and red rose petals covered the ground.

"Wait a minute," Sabrina said, repeating her line from the first date, "But we still have several weeks before you choose."

Tristan took her hand. "This is a trial run." He moved his hand from hers and placed his palms onto her shoulders, turning her to face another direction. "A dress rehearsal, if you will."

Sabrina moved toward the gown that hung from the make-shift dressing room as though it called to her. She ran one hand down the cream fabric, and the shining pearl beads on the bodice tickled her hands.

"It's beautiful," she said.

"It'll be more beautiful when you're wearing it."

"And what will you wear?"

"That's a surprise." He winked as he gestured toward a suit in a bag. "See you soon."

Sabrina dressed in the middle of a tent. Four days ago, she had tripped over the dress as she struggled into it, but this time, she slipped into it with ease. She emerged from the tent to find Tristan in the same Navy-blue suit he'd worn the first time.

"Wow," he said, breathless, as he took her in.

"Wow, yourself," she said.

He offered her his arm. "Are you ready?"

Down the aisle, a priest in a traditional collar waited. "As I'll ever be."

"Can we get that again?" one of the cameramen said, and Sabrina jumped at the sound of his voice. She considered the decorated field, reminding herself that they were surrounded by onlookers watching their every move. It was easy to forget. Sabrina had a lot of practice at forgetting.

SABRINA'S SISTER MORGAN nominated her as a contestant on *The Groom*. Morgan didn't tell Sabrina until after she'd been asked to audition, shoving the packet that contained the NDA and other information into Sabrina's chest. Sabrina had returned from a long shift at the hospital and didn't have the energy to consider significant life changes, so she melted into her mother's old cozy chair, letting the cushions soak her up, and let the packet fall to the floor.

Morgan bent and picked it up, then slid out the paperwork and read it off.

"I don't want to be on TV," Sabrina said. "Right now, all I want to do is watch it."

She leaned forward and grabbed for the remote, but Morgan snatched it away and shoved it into her bra. Behind her, another reality TV dating show blared: five women and five men humping on a dance floor in the middle of some island.

"If you win, you get all kinds of contracts," Morgan said. "Money. More money than you make as a nurse."

In the next room, Sabrina's father coughed and wheezed as if on cue.

"You know we need that money," Morgan said.

"You go," Sabrina said. "You're the one obsessed with this shit."

Morgan scoffed and stood, pacing back and forth on the threadbare rug beneath her. "You know they'd never take me." She stopped and leveled a jealous glare at Sabrina. "You got the looks, Sabrina. I got the brains. Thanks to Mom. You know that." She knelt again at Sabrina's feet. "Come on. White men love you. You're a damn shoo-in."

"But that's the other thing. I don't want to date some rando who just wants to be famous or whatever."

"You mean a nice man? Face it Sabrina, your taste in men is awful. You know I can pick them better. You know you shouldn't be trusted to find a man on your own."

Sabrina massaged her temples as her headache intensified. She ran through a quick list of her last three boyfriends: a pothead who thought he could solve world hunger just by getting high, her superior at the hospital (bad career move), and a self-obsessed professional who never even tried to make her come.

"You're right. I'm shit at dating."

Morgan held out the papers, and Sabrina took them, looking them over.

"You owe this to Dad," Morgan said and placed her hand on Sabrina's knee. "You owe this to Mom." She dug her nails into her sister's skin until Sabrina squirmed.

Sabrina's mom, back when she was alive, had plans for her daughters. The woman harbored an obsession with new-age miracles and therefore frequented the local occult stores, making friends with the crystal healers and tarot card readers there. While pregnant with Morgan, her spiritual intention was to bestow the girl with brains, but she regretted her decision after Morgan failed to blossom physically. So, when pregnant with Sabrina, she set her intention for beauty. She used to brush Sabrina's soft, curly hair and tell her that she'd never have to worry. With looks like hers, fame would find her. As a child, Sabrina's mom enrolled her in acting school. Sabrina didn't take to it, though, and in her elementary school play, the school cast her as a cactus. Her mom died before seeing her failure.

"Fine," Sabrina said, yanking her hand out from beneath Morgan's nails. Blood beaded in the scratch marks left behind. "I'll do it."

AT THE ALTAR, Tristan swept Sabrina into his arms and dipped her to the ground as the priest intoned, "I now pronounce you…committed to the journey of finding love!"

As Tristan peered into Sabrina's eyes, he breathed the words she was born to hear. "How are you so pretty anyhow?"

Sabrina's face warmed at the compliment, then remembered the work it took to get here. Morgan had been poking and prodding at her since the time of her first pimple. When Sabrina was thirteen, Morgan enrolled her in a weight loss program; when she was fourteen, she plucked her eyebrows nightly; at fifteen, she highlighted Sabrina's hair; at sixteen, she bleached her teeth; at seventeen, she waxed her legs and bikini; and, finally, when Sabrina turned eighteen, Morgan took her shopping for the priciest lingerie. All for the sake of Sabrina's destiny. The girl would one day shine her light upon their family and deliver them from darkness.

"I was born this way," Sabrina whispered up to Tristan, and he engaged her in a kiss that made her head spin.

BACK AT THE mansion, Sabrina settled into the comfiest chair in the living room and ate her dinner—a single protein puck and a diet soda. As the other women grabbed their food from the kitchen, variations on the same meal, Sabrina judged their every move. Charity would never win. She was too tall, too aggressive. Tristan needed a woman who let him win on occasion, and Charity rode each fight to its worst conclusion. Amy had a fair shot. She was quiet but gorgeous and when she moved, her body's sultry walk seduced the room. Marion was a shoo-in for the final three. A southern girl, she slid easily into Tristan's arms. Sabrina was the less safe pick but still an acceptable choice. Like Tristan, she appreciated tradition. She was raised in the south, albeit on the other side of the tracks: the tired outskirts of Atlanta. Still, she was willing to cook for the man and charm him with the drawl that came out when she cussed.

Sabrina's gaze landed on Linda. Since their first night, they'd bonded over a mutual distaste for Marion's clinging and a shared appreciation for black coffee at any hour. In the mansion, friendships had been formed from less. As Linda stood over the sink and bit into a peach, letting the juice dribble down her chin, Sabrina frowned. Linda was a dark horse. Sabrina shared a room with the woman, and in her sleep, she moaned slowly, steadily, as though experiencing a great pain—or pleasure. Sabrina had asked her about it during their first week, and Linda had confessed to nightmares. Sabrina thought little of it at first, but as the weeks wore on, she understood less and less Linda's reasons for coming here. The woman was divorced and unemployed, coming off a job working for her ex-husband's landscaping company. They'd listed her job as *influencer*, on account of the landscaping company's social media profile she'd commandeered out of spite. Without being allowed her phone, Sabrina couldn't look up Linda's page, but Marion claimed to have sneaked a peak from a cameraperson and said it was all close-ups of Linda snipping red buds off plants, slow-mo visions of the dead leaves falling to the floor, and gardening tips delivered in monotone as Linda walked, dressed in a designer dress and stilettos, through her garden. Linda claimed that she was here because she wanted to start a family, but even mentioning the word *family* made her eyes darken. But opposites attract, and Tristan had thus far seemed fascinated by the woman.

"Deep thoughts?" Linda said as she leaned on the arm of Sabrina's chair.

Sabrina forced herself to smile. "Just wondering who's getting cut next."

"We'll find out soon enough." Linda pursed her lips. "It's not you, by the way. It's anyone but you."

"And Marion."

"Yeah, and Marion."

Linda glanced across the room at Amy, then Charity. A jealous twinge twisted in Sabrina's belly, but she pushed it away. Sometimes, Linda looked at Charity like she'd rather be by her side than Sabrina's. "It'll be her over you," Sabrina said. "I promise you."

Linda chewed her lip, but before she could respond, Deja swept into the room in her nice pair of black slacks and black button-up blouse, the outfit that signaled to the contestants that they were about to film a formal event.

"Ladies, the ceremony starts in an hour," she said. "Time to put on your faces."

Marion squealed and dropped her protein-puck wrapper, then darted up the stairs while the rest of the women cleaned up after themselves and ascended calmly, even if inside their chests, their hearts pounded like war drums. At least, that was what Sabrina's heart felt like. She thought of her sister waiting by the television, skipping from show to show, waiting for Sabrina to return either empty-handed or with a blazing ring on her finger. Sabrina couldn't let her down.

DRESSED IN THEIR sparkling ball gowns, the five remaining contestants stood in a line in the mansion's living room. In front of them stood a shelf with all their photos displayed. Flickering candles cast shadows across the images of their grinning, airbrushed faces. Sabrina tried to keep her eyes away from the photographs ruined with giant red "X"s. She smoothed the belly of her dress and hoped that the cameras missed the spot where several beads had fallen off. The contestants had to supply their clothes, and she'd found hers in a local thrift store. It had been some teenager's prom dress, once upon a time.

Brandon Fuller, the show's host, strode through the front door. Marion shrieked when she saw him, running to throw herself into his arms. Brandon's hair was streaked with insistent highlights, his face thick with Botox, and when he smiled down at Marion, Sabrina could hardly see the shift in his lips.

"Darling girl!" Brandon cooed as he spun her around by one hand. "Oh, what a delicious gown. And I came hungry!"

Marion swatted his hand playfully. "I'm here for Tristan, and you know it."

Tristan stepped in the door behind Brandon. "My ears are burning." He clapped a hand on Brandon's shoulder. "Don't worry, bud. I'll introduce you to my sisters soon as I get the chance."

Unfazed, Marion threw her arms around Tristan next.

"What a welcome!" he drawled. As they let go, he stepped down into the room. He wore his Wranglers and a dress shirt, while Brandon donned his token white suit, with its hint of pink lining peeking through. "Ladies, are we ready for the ceremony?"

As one, they all answered: "Yes!"

Sabrina shivered at the chorus.

"Well, well, well, don't y'all look fancy tonight?" Tristan paced back and forth in front of the line of women while the cameras tracked him. "Making my job hard, you know."

Marion fell into line with the others, waiting her turn for an inspection. When Tristan said nothing specific to her, she pouted. Sabrina tried not to roll her eyes. As Tristan passed her by, he winked. Her stomach flip-flopped.

"Tonight's a big night," Tristan said. "Tomorrow, we've got a little road trip ahead of us. But there are only four seats on the bus."

He stopped pacing and crossed his arms across his chest. "Unfortunately, I can't take all of you with me. I've got to pick. And that's what we're gathered here for. To pick."

Brandon stepped next to Tristan with a basket of red ribbons. "Here you are, Tristan. Give a ribbon to the four women who you want to accompany you on this next stage of your journey."

Tristan took the basket and set it on the podium beside him. "Thank you kindly." He paused for effect as he ran a ribbon through his thick fingers. "The first name I'm going to call is…" He held the ribbon out as if in offering. "Marion."

Marion shrieked as she ran forward.

"Will you accept this ribbon?" Tristan asked.

"I will!"

He tied it onto her wrist, and she stood behind him, facing the other women.

Tristan picked up the second ribbon. "The second name I'm going to call is…Linda."

A thin smile spread across Linda's face as she moved toward him, offering her hand.

"Linda, do you accept this ribbon?"

"I do."

"I enjoyed our spooky date," he said.

"Me, too." She stepped beside Marion.

Tristan took the third ribbon. "Charity," he said, and Charity made her way across the room to him like she was ready to eat him alive. She towered over him on her heels as he tied the ribbon to her wrist.

Sabrina and Amy shared a nervous glance. Amy had never been mean to Sabrina, and she wished the woman no ill, but she'd be damned if she was about to lose to her.

Brandon waved from the sidelines. "Last ribbon," he said. "Make it count, old boy."

Tristan took the final ribbon into his hands. "There's only one name I'm going to call. And that name is…Sabrina."

Sabrina let out a sigh of relief. "Damn right," she said before she realized the words were on their way out. She covered her mouth as she stood before Tristan.

"Do you accept this ribbon?" he asked her.

She nodded as he tied it onto her wrist. It stretched tight against her skin.

"Watch that mouth, you hear?" He was grinning, but Sabrina felt the shame course through her.

"Of course," she said as she joined Linda in the line of chosen women.

Amy stood silent across from them. Tristan held out his hands to offer her a hug, but she fell to her knees in tears. As she pounded the floor with her fists, Brandon walked over to the shelf of photographs and drew an "X" across her face. "Why?" she called out, but no one moved to help her. Instead, Deja ushered the camera people closer.

"Zoom in on her face," Deja said, loud enough that they all could hear.

Tristan turned to face the remaining women. "Congratulations!" he said as Deja ushered Amy into a different room, where she could no longer ruin the soundtrack. He reached into his pocket and pulled out a white envelope. He handed the card to Sabrina.

"A date card?" she said.

He nodded as she slid her fingernail along the crease and pulled a white card with words scrawled across it.

Fear makes the heart grow stronger.
Who will be able to stay longer?

Across the bottom of the card were all four women's names. Sabrina read them aloud: "Sabrina, Marion, Charity, Linda."

Marion's face fell.

"Linda?" she said. "But Linda just had a one-on-one..."

It was protocol for any woman on the one-on-one to be excluded from the next group date, for fairness' sake.

"I need all my ladies on this one," he said as Marion crossed her arms. "You understand."

"I do," Sabrina said, wanting to please him.

"What's with all the spooky shit? Did I miss something?" Linda said. "Halloween was two weeks ago." She had a point. The show made no mention of the holiday because the actual airing would take place in the summer, and the producers usually worked to imbue the show's activities with a sense of timelessness. The production team would edit out Linda's comment.

"It's bullshit," Marion said. "You shouldn't get to go on two dates in one week."

"Now, ladies," Tristan said, frowning. "Let's not fight. I don't like it when girls fight."

Charity rolled her eyes. "It's bullshit. And I'm not going to take it, not tonight!" She stomped her feet and, like a child, ran up the stairs to her room. Tristan stepped to go after her, then stopped and glanced back at the other women.

Sabrina reached for Tristan's hand and squeezed it, seizing the moment to comfort him. "I can't wait...for whatever it is."

Tristan's frown relaxed. "Good," he said. "Now head on up and pack your bags. We're going on a road trip in the morning."

CHAPTER THREE

SABRINA

IN HER HALF-SLEEP, Sabrina felt a hand creep across hers. Her heart hammered as she began to scream, but a palm cupped her mouth.

"It's just me," a male voice said. She'd recognize the voice anywhere.

"Tristan," she breathed from behind his hand. He uncovered her mouth. "What are you doing here?"

"Wondering if you wanted to take a walk," he said.

She grinned. "I'm in my pajamas."

"So am I." He gestured to his sweatpants and sleeveless shirt. She could make out the bulging outline of his arms in the dark.

Together, they sneaked across the room, then out the door. Leo, the cameraman posted outside, eyed them, but Tristan slipped the guy a bill, and he turned his head and camera in another direction. Sabrina giggled as they tiptoed together down the stairs. He was a fun man. She'd never been with a fun man, not one with a job and goals and no ring on his finger.

Outside the mansion, Tristan breathed out loud. "I don't know how they think I can meet my forever-lady if we're never alone long enough to ask the real questions."

"The real questions? Like pineapple on pizza?"

He laughed. "Other questions." He took her hand as they ventured farther out into the woods. "Like, do you want kids?"

"Of course." Sabrina pushed at his shoulder.

"Speaking of tongues." He stopped, pulled her to him, and pressed his hand to her back. The way he maneuvered her, it was like she weighed nothing when she was, in fact, a curvy woman.

"I didn't say anything about—"

He bent and took her bottom lip between his teeth, giving her a playful nip before his tongue slipped into her mouth. He was a good kisser. She felt lost in him. Then, she heard the branch snap.

She pushed him, but he laughed at the fear on her face, visible as the moon swept through the breaks in the trees. Leaves crunched as she stepped back.

"Probably an animal," he said.

"That's what I'm afraid of," she said. "Bears, coyotes..."

"You're scared of little animals? Wait until we get to where we're going tomorrow." He laughed, then mimed zipping his lips. "Oops."

Sabrina's heart jumped. "Where are we going?"

"A fricking haunted house!" His voice lifted like an excited child. "In the middle of nowhere. For a whole week."

The blood drained from Sabrina's face. "Ghosts?"

"Yeah, ghosts. What else?"

"I was being hopeful." She shivered in the cold night air. "Tristan, ghosts aren't to be messed with."

"You believe?"

"Sort of. I try not to, but...yeah. I don't want to chance it." She tried to step away, but he pulled her back into him and hugged her close.

"I'll keep you safe from bears, coyotes, and ghosts. You'll be there with me, and I'll keep a special eye out to make sure nothing bad happens."

Sabrina relaxed into him once more at his words, his assurance, his request that she stay calm. Sabrina understood herself: reluctant to make decisions, make significant steps, to do the things she should—until the important people gave her that sweet permission. Like her sister and the show. Like her decision to become a nurse in the first place. Her school guidance counselor pushed Sabrina in that direction, and when Sabrina floated the idea to her sister, she agreed, it was a good career path that would offer some opportunity. Sabrina might meet a doctor, her sister said.

Tristan was no doctor, but his hands were steady as they slunk up her shirt and cupped her breasts.

"You like that," he said, and Sabrina let out a little moan of pleasure. She liked it. He had told her so.

Sometimes, in the back of her mind, Sabrina wondered about her impressionability. That other people might know what she wanted more than she knew, that her thoughts about herself might be wrong. But his hands were gentle, and his lips were sweet, and she did like it. She just hadn't realized it until the words left someone else's lips.

Sabrina had never formed plans for herself, after all. As a little girl, she took seriously her mother's life plan: Sabrina's superpower would be her good looks. She was smart, but her sister would be able to mine intelligence, not Sabrina. Sabrina's excellent science scores were inconsequential until the school guidance counselor brought them to Sabrina's attention. Would she like to be a doctor, the woman had asked. But no. She realized that after Morgan reminded her about the pain she would feel when a patient was too sick to recover. Sabrina's heart was too soft.

She let Tristan press his hand against the space where her soft heart lay inside her chest, and her skin erupted in goosebumps at his tender touch.

"Would you like me to make you scream?" he asked.

"What do you mean?" she asked, remembering the sound in the woods. She had been on the verge of screaming already.

"Make you come," he said. "You've come before, haven't you?"

Warmth spread through her body. "Yes! I've come before." And she had. In high school, she and her best friend had practiced their orgasm faces by pleasuring one another and recording the results before her sister found out and told the girl's parents. In nursing school, one of her sweeter boyfriends had ensured that she was satisfied, but he was keeping other women satisfied, too. A couple of other boyfriends had succeeded, as well. Sabrina counted them in her head. "Like, at least twenty times."

"Twenty times?" Tristan pulled his hand away. "You've only come twenty times in your whole life?"

She shrugged. "It's hard for me."

"The choice is yours, Sabrina: do you want me to be your numbers twenty-one through twenty-five?"

Her stomach twisted at the sight of that mischievous grin.

"Do *you* want to be my numbers twenty-one through twenty-five?"

"I do," he said.

She flashed back to their fake wedding in the woods less than twenty-four hours ago. "I do, too."

The air was cool on her bare skin, the bark of the tree rough against her back as he pressed her into it. She gasped into his ear as he rubbed circles between her legs, letting each wave of pleasure wash over her, one after the other until, finally, she begged him to slide inside. He pulled a condom from his pocket and met her eyes for an answer.

"Yes, obviously," she said, and he ripped it open and slid it over himself.

It had been so long since she was opened up, and as they writhed together in the amber dark, she felt as though she had taken this moment, this one breathless instant, all for her own.

A single red camera light blinked on and off in the blind distance.

CHAPTER FOUR

LINDA

IN THE MORNING, Linda woke an hour before everyone else. It was her little custom; she needed those thirty minutes to herself, even if the cameras remained on her as she fixed a cup of coffee and a cream cheese bagel and ate breakfast wrapped in a blanket on the patio. Tatum, the camera operator assigned to the morning shift, was kind enough not to ask her any questions, and once or twice he'd set up his recording rig then left with a wink.

The morning of the group date, she was not so lucky, but the cameraman half-dozed behind his set-up as Linda let the steam from her coffee tickle her chin.

The mansion sat at the top of a hill overlooking a valley, and Linda gazed on the rooftops below and wondered about the morning routines of the families who lived inside the affluent houses. Even though her father had been an alcoholic, she had loved waking on weekend mornings to the sound of bass pounding her ceiling. Upstairs, her father cooked biscuits and gravy, spun Pink Floyd on his record player, and downed Bloody Marys. She remembered sliding into consciousness, wrapped in a blanket on her family's couch, while her older sister moped in her room like Charity did every day.

Linda smiled to herself. Charity loved throwing fits, but Linda minded them less than Marion's. They were more fun to play off, for one thing. Charity was cuter than Marion, for another.

Tatum's walkie-talkie beeped. "Charity's on her way down," the voice in the walkie-talkie said.

"Speak of the devil," Linda muttered.

The cameraman snapped back to life. "Were you saying something?"

Linda shook her head. "Just thinking."

"You know you're not allowed," he said.

Linda laughed. "I'll go in now." She stood and waited for him to pack his tripod, then moved into the kitchen, followed by his camera. She took a seat at the marbled bar. Charity breezed down the stairs in a long white robe. Linda nodded a greeting, but Charity didn't look her way. Instead, she filled a cup of coffee, grabbed a protein bar, and disappeared back up the stairs.

"She's mad at you," Tatum said, provoking.

It was too early to play along. "Nah," Linda said. "Charity's not a morning person." But she ached in her belly. Despite her negativity, Linda wanted the woman to like her—and only her.

LINDA AND THE other women shared two bathrooms, so Linda and Sabrina took turns with the mirror. They had bonded over their love of makeup and playing with new techniques, but for the show, they kept it simple, classic: foundation, eyeshadow, winged liner, mascara, a hint of blush, powder. Cream under the eyes. A touch of color on the lips—long-lasting, in case of kissing. Setting spray, because the days were long, and the body aches and subsequent sweating were real.

Because Charity did little to get ready, she was always the first waiting in the living room, so it was no surprise when Linda and Sabrina went downstairs and found her there. The producers had advised that each woman pack a bag with multiple changes of clothes, and Linda shifted her heavy duffel into her other hand and leaned against the wall. After this morning, she didn't want to sit next to Charity. It was best not to engage, or they might be goaded into a fight by the people behind the cameras.

Marion was the last to arrive. The women had been told to dress casually, which translated in reality show speak to jeans and a flattering blouse. Linda wore a black sweater with three-quarter sleeves and pockets, and three dangly bracelets on her wrists. Marion wore a tube top covered in sparkling studs. When the morning sun hit her, she was blinding.

Brandon and Deja surveyed their choices. Brandon was part producer, but he wasn't around as much as Deja. Rumor had it that he'd received a promotion over her and been given another show to run. When he reached Marion, he gave her a thumbs-up. "Love the look," he said. When he reached Linda, he shook his head. "You didn't have a nun costume?"

"It's called a habit," Charity said.

Brandon moved to stand in front of her. "You shouldn't be talking," he said. "You should be changing clothes, too."

Charity tugged on her shirt, revealing a small slip of cleavage. "That better?"

Brandon grinned as he held his hands out to the sides. "That's all I ask, ladies. Is it too much? I don't think so."

Deja moved in front of him, blocking the view of his terrible suit. "We need confessionals on all of you," she said. "Linda, you're with me." The other producers, Becca and Tatum, gestured to their girls as Brandon looped arms with Marion. Linda followed Deja to one of the confessional rooms, where she sipped from a champagne glass full of orange juice.

"Mimosa?" She shoved the drink into Linda's hand.

"I'd rather not this early," Linda said.

"Nonsense. You aren't driving anywhere! Besides, you're going to need it where we're going."

Linda set the glass on the ground. Her stomach lurched. "And where are we going?"

Deja downed the rest of her juice, then sat in the chair across from Linda, assuming a relaxed stance: legs spread open, arms splayed out across the back of the chair.

"A haunted house," she said, as though it were the most normal thing.

"A what?" Linda laughed, suspecting some fuckery. Deja loved to make the contestants cry; it was producer gold. And she was always trying to break Linda down by bringing up family troubles or her divorce.

"You believe in ghosts?" Deja asked.

"No." Linda picked up the mimosa and took a sip. It was mostly champagne, and she nearly gagged.

"You want to know what happened there? At the place where we'll be staying?"

Linda relaxed into her chair. "No, but you'll tell me anyway."

Deja leaned forward. "This house used to be inhabited by generation after generation of spoiled rich assholes. They were in the lumber business, not that that's important, but it was long hours and lots of hard work running all those crews, bribing all the forestry services, and the family's patriarch, well he took to downing whole bottles of vodka when each day was done."

Linda's chest tightened. She stopped drinking, but she didn't dare move for fear that the camera would catch her shaking hands.

"The father came home one day to a bad scene. His kids had really messed the place up. Troublemakers. He was smashed out of his mind. Tired of them and tired of his terrible life. So, what he did was he took one of the axes used to cut down those trees...and he cut each child to pieces."

"Jesus." The glass slipped from Linda's hand, shattering on the ground.

"Oops," Deja said. "Did that story bother you?"

"You knew it would." Linda bent to collect the glass shards, but one of them sliced into her finger. She gasped at the sudden shock of pain.

"Blood everywhere, but that wasn't the worst smell. It was the father's body. It stunk of vodka from the inside out when they found him. And I do mean *inside*, because guess what? His body had been twisted into pieces, too. And they never knew who, or what, did that to him."

The smell of the champagne floated, reminding Linda of her father's breath every time he hugged her. She felt like throwing up. Shook her head. "You're trying to freak me out." She wiped a drop of blood on her pants, then stood with all the strength left in her trembling legs. "That stuff's not real."

"Murder isn't real?" Deja stood to her level.

"Of course, murder's real. But ghosts aren't. It's just an old house in the woods, with an unfortunate history, but you're using it to try and manipulate me, like you always do. But you know what? It's not gonna work this time, because according to the show's rules, I'm not supposed to be on this group date, so I'm not going."

Deja laughed. "You're not? You don't need this show?"

"I don't need this *date*. I'll finish the show."

"Funny," Deja said. "Your contract states that you're in breach if you refuse any activity we ask you to do. And if you're in breach of contract, we don't have to fulfill any promises we made to you, either." Deja stepped forward until she was right in front of Linda. Linda's lungs quaked. "No future for you, Linda. That's not what you want, is it?" Deja's breath hit her right in the nostrils; she stank like alcohol. "All those secrets coming to light? Be hard to start a nursery with things like that hanging over your head."

"No," Linda whispered.

"Then I guess I'll see you on that bus."

Linda turned and ran from the confessional to the bathroom, where she locked herself inside and slid to the floor, heaving as she tried to arrange her thoughts.

Deja was always manipulating them, but she'd never sounded dangerous before. Why was she threatening Linda on camera? Maybe it was a drunken lapse in judgment, a power play to get better footage than Brandon. Either way, that's just what Linda had given her: a freak-out and some broken glass. It probably made Deja's day. Linda wasn't proud of herself in that moment, but it wasn't the worst thing that she could have done. Still, she hoped to finish the show without a total mental breakdown on camera. She needed to showcase her best self. Needed the camera, the audience, to love her. She had too much to lose otherwise. She couldn't back out now.

DAY ONE AT
MATRIMONY MANOR

CHAPTER FIVE

LINDA

"LET'S GO, LADIES," Deja said, her face betraying no hint of what went down in the confessional. Linda joined the women as they formed a line and exited the mansion, then piled into the van that production used to transport them from date to date. The conversations they had inside the van were filmed, but it was unlikely they'd be used; the show liked to give the illusion of a life where pretty women moved like magic, appearing one place, then another, with no need for boring in-betweens. In-betweens weren't sexy, and Linda had never felt more aware of the ways people avoided transition and the uncertainty that came with it.

Linda dozed as the van merged from a packed California freeway to a less-traveled highway surrounded by tall trees. She dreamed of eyes: jars full of them, glass and plastic and wood. She peered into each jar packed into a curio case, then realized that she had to pee. She looked for the cameras, but there was only one giant bulbous camera, like the kind shops used to catch shoplifters, that watched her. She waved two crossed fingers in the sign for bathroom and searched for a door. Inside, she sat on the toilet and tried to let go. She felt watched. She looked about the room for signs of a camera; they weren't supposed to watch her in the bathroom. She frowned in a tight thin line. *Get out of here*, she said, and that's when she noticed them: a hundred eyes blinking at her from every wall.

Linda jolted awake as the van pulled up to a building on the side of the road. A faded orange sign proclaimed GAS by the service lane, while a weathered wooden sign proclaimed STORE atop a faded white shack.

"Last chance to use the restroom before we arrive, ladies," Deja said. "I'll be chaperoning each of you in, one by one."

"Me first!" Linda jumped from her seat. She did need to pee—and to gulp some fresh air, untainted by the perfume of hair products.

"Come on, Meadows." Deja ushered her forward. Together, they climbed from the bus into crisp air infused with the smell of coming rain. Linda walked on legs that creaked from a couple of hours' disuse. As they entered the tiny store, a gas attendant hurried past them to the van.

"Shit," Deja said. "I forgot about Oregon's pump laws. Get into the bathroom. I need to take care of this. I'm trusting you, Meadows. Don't you dare go sneaking a phone call or a newspaper, yeah?"

Linda gestured to the empty store. It seemed that the gas attendant was in charge of everything. "Who would I borrow a phone from?"

"I'll be right back, you hear?" Deja hurried out, and Linda breathed a sigh of relief at being unobserved for what seemed like the first time in a year, though it had only been a month and a half. She'd made it farther than she thought she would when she signed on, and the fact that Tristan had gone for both her and Sabrina made Linda think there may be more than met the eye with him. And Charity had her charm when she wasn't causing a stir. His decision to keep Marion, on the other hand, reflected poorly. Marion was the frontrunner, which Linda forced out of her mind when she needed to be attracted to him.

In another week, the final women would take Tristan to meet their families. Linda pushed the thought out of her mind; she hadn't prepared Tristan for that yet.

Linda made her way to the bathroom door in back. At first, she averted her gaze from the newspaper display, then she laughed at herself and snuck a peek. Who would know? UPSET AT MATRIMONY MANOR, the headline of the little local paper read. MAJOR TV NETWORK PURCHASES ABANDONED HISTORICAL SITE. Linda read the article's first line: "TV network ABS is rumored to be using the infamous Williams family manor as the location of a ghost-hunting series." No mention of the place being haunted. Linda scoffed. Deja had been trying to scare her with baseless history.

Linda heard the ding of the bell on the door and jumped away from the newsstand.

"Ready?" Deja said.

Linda hurried into the bathroom. Before sitting, she checked the walls for eyes. There were none to be found.

Once Linda finished, Deja ushered her out of the store. She'd turned the newspapers around on the stand. The gas station attendant was re-hanging the nozzle.

"I know who you are," he said to Linda and Deja as they approached. "I know where you're going."

They stopped. The attendant was the type of man who seemed ageless, with a face that had weathered years of a nebulous quantity. He grinned at them and handed Deja back her credit card. "Here you are, Deja." He'd slid a business card underneath. "I examine TV credits religiously. You're headed out to the manor. I read about it in the paper."

"Shhhhh!" Deja shoved at Linda. "Back on the bus, Linda!" As Linda followed her orders, she heard Deja saying, "They're under embargo, and if you had any experience in—" She read the man's card. "TV writing? You'd know that. Now, please, I don't need any more gas, and I've got to get the rest of these women fixed up. If I catch you saying one more word to them, I'll pass your name on to every exec I know so you never get any work, you hear?"

The man straightened his posture. "Sorry!" He turned around and rushed back inside.

Linda waited on the bus for the rest of the women to head inside, then back. Despite her curiosity, she had an uneasy feeling about the situation. Sabrina returned to the van and took the seat beside Linda.

"Do you ever feel like something's catching up to you?" Linda said. "Something bad?"

"I'm worried about you." Sabrina rested her hand on Linda's knee. "Since your weird date, you've seemed weird, too. Did the taxidermy possess you? Do I need to learn exorcism?" She shivered. "Scratch that. I don't mess with supernatural shit."

Linda pinched her lips. "I'm just tired, I think." She pushed away the unfamiliar sensation of fear. "This process is difficult."

"I think you mean *journey*," Sabrina said. They laughed. The producers required them to utilize the language chosen by the network—words that masked the truth. "We're going to have fun," Sabrina said. Her skin had taken on a happy glow in the morning light. "No matter what wild-ass scheme Tristan cooked up for us."

From the front of the van, Charity glanced back. Her expression seemed filled with longing, like she wanted to come back and laugh along with them. Marion paid them no heed. Linda wished she could tell Sabrina what she'd read in the gas station, but she didn't want to break her contract. The network could sue for any breach, and Linda didn't need more financial woes.

"Yes, please, to fun." Linda rested her head on Sabrina's shoulder. Charity turned back around to face the front. The van moved forward, onto the highway, then into the woods.

THE TOWN CALLED Matrimony was a ghost town. One dirt road led up a stout mountain, and as the van crept along it, Linda watched the rundown buildings pass. There was no telling what they used to be with their rotted signs.

At the top of the mountain stood the manor. As they neared it, Linda made out its roof reaching toward the sky and walls of gray stone with wood accents. A giant iron gate surrounded it, and through the thin slats, Linda took note of the heavy woods that formed a natural fence. She scanned the gate line, which faded into trees, at one patch of forest that looked like it led from the manor to a path down the mountain. When the van rolled to the gate, Deja removed a clicker from her pocket and aimed it at a keypad. The gate crept open with a meandering squeal. The driver rolled inside, and Deja clicked the device again, closing the gate behind them.

"Where are we?" Marion said.

"You know I can't say until we've got a good shot." Deja bumped back into her seat. The driver took them up a long dirt driveway flanked by un-manicured bushes. Off to the side, a vast orchard sprawled. The van parked in front of the manor. The women gathered their things, disembarked, and waited by the driveway while the camera crew hurried outside.

A fine mist came down. Linda had never been so far north, but she understood that rain was a common occurrence in certain parts of the world, and she'd often wondered why people had ever used wood at all on their houses there. An abundance, she guessed, peering into the thickets that surrounded the place and obscured the mountains.

As Linda waited to be summoned, queued, lined up, and prompted, she stepped closer to the woods. The fence that protected the estate from the poor people who once lived below—or their ghosts—threaded through the dense forest. The trees seemed to bend toward her.

"The trees," she murmured, partly to Sabrina, but primarily to herself.

"Kind of like this place I saw in a magazine one time." Sabrina stood beside her. "The crooked forest? Something like that. In Poland."

"Yeah? What made them that way?"

"Man-made, I think?" she said. "I didn't get to finish the article. Got called over to do a patient. The magazine got tossed."

"I didn't think hospitals ever tossed those mags." Linda felt dueling urges to run into the woods and away from them, to run toward the manor and away from it. Linda shook her head; she was letting the spooky vibes get to her.

"What are you nerds talking about?" Marion came up beside them. "I never know what it is you two are saying."

"We're talking about twisted forests," Sabrina said.

"Is that some kind of euphemism?" Marion said.

"Big word," Charity said from behind them. Her voice was silk, and a quiver traveled down Linda's body. "They're ready for us, by the way."

"You know, I did hear that a certain bachelor has a twisted trunk," Linda said as they walked back over to the camera crew. Sabrina snorted, and Linda took note of Charity trying hard not to laugh. It made her want to make another joke, to force the levity from Charity's lips whether she liked it or not.

"What's funny?" Deja said as she moved from woman to woman and straightened their shirts. "No jokes until the cameras roll."

"We were just talking about wood," Sabrina said. Deja raised her eyebrows. Sabrina motioned to the forest. "The trees, Deja."

"Yeah, yeah. They were shaped that way by the prior inhabitants of the Matrimony Manor. The Williams family. They were loggers, and they experimented with growing trees into bendy shapes to make it easier for furniture builders, et cetera." Deja waved her hand as though that were the end of the explanation. "We're on network TV, so act like the ladies you're not."

Linda grimaced. "Yes, ma'am."

"We're rolling in three…two…" Deja held up one finger.

Brandon Fuller strode from the front of the manor, Tristan by his side. They both wore simple suits as they took their places in front of the line of women.

"You're probably wondering why we brought you to an isolated manor in a ghost town in the middle of nowhere," Brandon said. "Well, ladies—you're here to be tested." He paused for dramatic effect. "Tristan, why don't you tell these lovely ladies what this test is all about?"

"Sure," he said. "This big old house here is haunted. It's got a lot of history. As you all know, I like scary stuff. But more than that, I need a woman who isn't afraid—of haunted houses, tough conversations, a kid's temper tantrum, or of new adventures. I do a lot of scary stuff. I need a lady who can be by my side, from bungee jumping to jumping from a plane. Man, I need a lady who can handle a haunting."

Linda wanted to laugh; in ordinary circles, she would be sure this was a joke. With Tristan, she knew it wasn't. He honestly thought he needed a wife who could handle a ghost. She desired to break character and ask, *You see a lot of ghosts, Tristan? Something you want to tell us about your family's farm, Tristan?* But instead, she kept her determined face front-and-center—the face that said instead, *No haunting is going to keep* me *from true love.* And maybe she'd say those words out loud later, in the confessional.

"That's right, ladies," Brandon said. "Next week, the remaining three women will be taking Tristan home to meet their families, to spend a night in the homes where they grew up. You might end up in some uncomfortable conversations with loved ones who don't understand this journey. Tonight, and for the next seven days, you'll all be spending your days and nights in what's certain to be an uncomfortable situation: a haunted mansion in the middle of nowhere. Not all of you will be able to handle it. The ladies who *survive* all the way to the final day will be the ladies who move on to next week. Those who buckle under the pressure?" He made a slashing motion at his throat.

"As you can see, the van is leaving." He frowned, a momentary lapse of his staged facade. "There will be no way to leave this place unless you decide to leave the show." On cue, the van pulled away down the long drive. Brandon tapped his watch. "Your week in this house starts...now! Good luck, ladies. You're going to need it!" He relaxed and nodded at Tristan, no longer the focus of the cameras' gaze as they shifted to cover the women's reactions. "Be seeing you," he said to Tristan. "Have fun!"

"I sure will!" Tristan said as Brandon jogged around the manor to his waiting helicopter. Deja frowned and followed after him, but Linda couldn't hear what she was saying.

"Well, what do you think?" Tristan said to the contestants.

Marion ran up to Tristan and threw her arms around him for the thousandth time. "It's gorgeous!" she said. "I can't wait to spend the next week here. Is there an Ouija board somewhere?"

Tristan laughed. "Maybe? We can check."

"Yeah! Marion, we can call on the ghosts of your fashion sense," Charity said. She squeezed his hand. "How many beds are in that fancy house?"

Tristan blushed. "Enough," he said.

Sabrina turned on her reserved charm and smiled her killer smile. "I love a challenge." But her lips shook as they fell back into their standard line.

"I'm not scared of ghosts," Linda said. "I've seen worse."

Sometimes, uttering her lines gave her a sense of belonging, of completion. Other times, they were too close to the truth.

Tristan nodded. "I know you have." He sounded so serious, referring to her divorce like it had battered her, but her divorce was not what had haunted her, not by a long shot.

Tatum exited the manor's front doors, tall and ornate with delicate stained glass. "We're ready for you inside," he said. The stained glass depicted a gruesome scene: a naked woman, her skin transforming to bark, her limbs sprouting, and as they poked forth from her flesh, they speared the man who chased after her. On the other door, a group of men felled a forest.

"What the fuck?" Linda said as she passed through.

"It's a take on a Greek myth," Charity said. "Daphne and Apollo."

"Oh, the woman who turns herself into a tree to get away from that asshat?" Linda shivered. "I've never much liked the woods, to be honest."

"I love the forest," Tristan said. "I thought you said you did a lot of camping?"

Linda swallowed as she ducked inside and away from the illustrations. "Used to."

"And why don't you go anymore, Linda?" Deja's voice echoed as she faced the group filing in. Linda marveled at her ability to be everywhere at once—and to make Linda feel like the floor was falling away from her with a single question.

Linda pursed her lips. She wouldn't play this game. "Just don't."

When Tristan stopped inside the grand foyer, the women stopped behind him. They stood on an uneven wood floor of deep purple grain. An elegant wood stair reached in twists and turns to the second story. Upon the ceiling, someone had painted a family history—people, marriages, funerals, and bloody births—all surrounded by a frame that resembled the bark of a tree. The whole room smelled like freshly cut lumber.

"It's gorgeous," Linda said, clutching her chest.

"Wait until you see the rest of the place!" Tristan said.

He led them through the manor. "The whole thing was built from wood from the old-growth forests around us." He stomped against the floor with his boot. "You don't see wood floors like this anymore. The same goes for the furniture. Most of this is original to the house, but some of it had to be replaced—and it's not all pristine." He put his foot up on an ornate, carved chair at the dining table and pushed until one of the legs collapsed. "Watch where you sit, is what I'm saying. Wouldn't want any of you ladies to get a sore ass from a fall."

"He's already talking sore asses?" Charity whispered. "But we've hardly even kissed!" She feigned surprise, holding an open palm over her mouth in a scandalized gesture.

Linda smirked. Charity's snark was out in full force, as though she'd decided to throw caution to the wind.

On the second story, the group walked a hallway of empty bedrooms, followed by the cameras that were their consistent companions. Tristan assigned each bedroom to one of the women, grouping them in the hall despite the ubiquity of rooms. Marion got the Sequoia Room; Charity the Pine; Sabrina the Cherry Blossom; and Linda the Redwood. Linda set her bag on the bed, which was decorated in a thick quilt of red patches. "What kind are the trees around the manor?" she asked Tristan.

Tristan shrugged. "Beats me." He stepped out to check on the other women. Linda pushed her hand into the mattress; as it creaked, a musty smell rose from it. The room was sparsely decorated with an armoire of redwood and a redwood vanity with a small round mirror. Linda went two doors down to check on Sabrina, passing Charity's room full of green. Sabrina's bed was decorated in a quilt of pink squares.

"They stuck to the themes, didn't they?" Linda ran her hand along the quilt. Unlike Linda's room, Sabrina's walls had been covered in oppressive baby-pink wallpaper. "I lucked out with redwood."

"You did." Sabrina lifted her folded clothes out of her overnight bag and placed them on the nightstand. "Want to make a bet on how long before Marion freaks tonight?"

As if on cue, Marion screamed. The three women rushed to her door, where she stood staring at a squashed daddy longlegs.

"They're harmless, you know." Charity bent and scooped the dead thing into her hand. It was as big as her palm. "They have enough poison inside to kill you, but their mouths are too small to bite."

"Whatever," Marion said. "I'm not letting anyone, or anything, stand in my way."

Linda let the beat pass before she turned to glance at the cameraman who stood in the corner of the room. He was hiding a smirk.

"Okay, Marion, slayer of spiders," Linda said. "Why don't we make our way to dinner?"

"I'm not prepared for dinner," she said.

"They did tell us to get gussied up, Lin," Sabrina said.

"Oh, right," Linda said. "I guess we do have an hour." She returned to the hallway. She didn't need a full hour to refresh her makeup and slip into a dress. She bit her lip. The hall was lined with portraits. The coloring of the people's faces was uncanny. Family portraits, but she failed to understand why the artist had painted the skin with weird veins like vines. She reached out to the glass and traced the lines that formed the face of an angry-looking matriarch with piercing black eyes and wild black hair. The artist had covered the hair with pieces of leaf matter.

"I'm going to get a better look at that forest," Charity said beside her.

Linda jumped. "Neat?" she said, startled by the closeness of the woman who wanted nothing to do with her. Charity smelled like rosemary.

"I'm inviting you." Charity stepped back from the creepy portrait. "Take it or leave it, Meadows."

Linda watched Charity walk halfway down the hall. She was weirded out by the woods, but she was intrigued by Charity. She chased after her.

"It's still weird to hear my new name," Linda said as they descended the long stairwell. "I went by my married name for so long, but I changed it when I got divorced. Fresh start all around, you know."

Really, she had hoped that changing her name would help her hide from the reputation that preceded her, but it hadn't worked: Deja, at least, had found her anyway.

"What was your married name?" Charity's voice was calm, unfazed by the admission that Linda was a divorcee.

"Wallace," Linda said. "I always liked it."

Charity said nothing, and as they exited the manor's front door, the cameraman from the manor's interior traded off with one perched outside, leaning against the manor's stone wall in waiting. He hefted his portable rig onto his shoulder. Linda was grateful that the show had gone with rigs that only required one person—camera and mic in one. Even if it meant that everyone was required to wear microphones pinned to their clothes, it was better this way. Being followed around by two or more production people, like some similar shows, would have felt like a circus.

At the edge of the woods, Charity paused. "I like Meadows more," she said.

Linda smiled. But then her gaze returned to the trees. Linda had always thought that leafless trees looked like people, with their reaching branches as many arms and their upper crowns as wiry hair. These trees leaned forward like eavesdroppers attempting to hear the goings-on of the elite inside the manor.

"I have an app on my phone," Linda said. "It lets you identify plants. I wish I had it right now. I'd love to know what type of trees these are. I've never seen anything like them."

"Me neither," Charity said. She smoothed a hand through her hair, and the gesture made Linda's stomach jump. "Though I'll be honest—my garden at home is all like herbs and vegetables and stuff. Inedible plants? Not so much my bag."

"Oh?" Linda said. "You do a lot of gardening?"

"I do a lot of cooking," Charity said. "Gardening is a support hobby."

Linda laughed, and her stomach flip-flopped again. This was the most Charity had talked to her since they met on the first day of filming.

THE SHOW'S FIRST day had been at the mansion cocktail party, where every woman arrived for the first time in a white Cinderella-style horse-drawn carriage. It was their first meeting, and the producers placed Linda and Sabrina into the same carriage and sent them on their brief journey from the staging area to the front of the mansion. Linda watched first as Sabrina performed her shtick, stepping from the carriage in her emerald-green silk gown and making her effortless way to Tristan, who stood in a suit in the mansion's front courtyard. Sabrina pulled out a pair of syringes filled with clear liquid and handed one to Tristan.

"Oh, shit," he said, smiling wide. "Did I forget a check-up?"

"I'm a nurse," she said. "And I plan on nursing your heart, so I wanted to introduce myself with a toast."

"I don't drink bodily fluids, I'm afraid." Tristan laughed his easy laugh, and Sabrina matched his good humor.

"It's champagne," she said.

"Oh, I drink champagne." He bumped his syringe into hers. "What do you want to toast to?"

"To new love!" she said, and together, they squeezed the syringes into their mouths.

Linda had prepared no such theatrics. When Sabrina disappeared inside, and it was her turn, Linda stepped from the carriage, navigating her heels on the cobblestone path. Her sparkling purple dress dragged behind her, and when she reached Tristan, she stood before him with her arms flat at her sides.

"Hi," she said.

"Well, don't you look gorgeous," Tristan said, and for the first time in a long time, Linda felt like a new person.

"What's your name?" he said.

"Linda Wall—" She laughed. "Sorry, my name is Linda. Linda Meadows."

"If that isn't the sweetest name I've ever heard," Tristan said, and he grabbed her hand and kissed the back of it. "I look forward to talking with you, Linda Meadows."

She bowed a little, a strange urge, then wobbled inside the mansion to the room full of women. All of them were decked out in elaborate ball gowns, teetering on tall heels. Linda scanned her surroundings; she could beat most of them in the game of wits and beauty. Then her gaze landed on a woman leaning alone in a corner. She was the only woman wearing a suit, and the crimson jacket and pants hugged her every curve.

Excitement flooded Linda. Now this was a woman she wasn't sure she could beat.

BACK IN THE woods, Linda smiled at Charity in the soft green light.

"Wait, you said that gardening is a support hobby? What's a support hobby?" Linda said.

Charity laughed, too. Her laugh was warm. "I just meant— fresh veggies make for better cooking. I wouldn't garden, I don't think, if I didn't love to cook."

"I have a huge garden," Linda admitted. "What do you cook?" Linda took a step deeper into the woods.

Charity pointed out a patch of purple weeds as she followed. "Don't cook with that," she said. "Poisonous as fuck."

"Oh, I know. That, too." Linda pointed to a red berry.

"I would cook with that, though." Charity bent and pulled a wild onion from the ground, then stood and kept walking. As she spoke, her face lit up as Linda had never seen it. "To answer your question, I cook all kinds of things. My mom taught me a lot. I make my own kimchi with cabbage that I grow myself. It lasts me the whole winter. I make stews when it's cold."

"It doesn't get cold in Texas often," Linda said, "but you better believe that when it does, the chili pot comes out."

"It doesn't get cold in LA either," Charity said. "But isn't it all relative?" She motioned to Linda, who shivered in the breeze. "I've never made chili," Charity said. The leaves crunched beneath their feet. "Growing up, on the first frigid day of the season, my mom always made us Hobakjuk."

"Were both your parents Korean?" Linda asked.

"My mom. My dad was white as Tristan."

Linda bent to pick up an acorn the size of a golf ball; it was a pale-peach color, and it felt to the touch like rubber.

"This is cool," Linda said, studying the weird texture. She pocketed it. "What's Hobakjuk?"

"Pumpkin porridge? We ate it as a snack. It's not filling." Charity stopped. "Hey, watch out." She pointed at a cluster of green plants spread on the ground before them.

Linda stepped back, stunned by the presence of the patch. She stuttered as she spoke. "I'm allergic to poison ivy."

Charity frowned. "We better get you inside," she said.

"Almost time, anyway. Got to get all dolled up for our date!"

Linda jumped as the cameraman moved to allow them to pass him. She'd forgotten that he was there. His presence was cursory; the two women getting along offered little for the show to work with. As the rivals re-traced their steps backward, he followed close behind. The sun set, and with its bowing, shadows danced with their shadows—three became four became a mess of moving darkness on the forest floor. It smelled like old leaves and something more pungent, not altogether pleasing. The scent reminded Linda of when she found a dead possum in the woods. Like decay. Maybe it was the leaves rotting where moisture caught underneath them. She shrugged it off and focused on the calm she felt beneath the unease, a peace that came from the company of the woman beside her. Charity was different than Linda had thought she might be, and Linda felt lucky that she might emerge from the competition with not one friend but two.

"Hey, can I ask you something?" Linda said, seizing the moment.

"You can try," Charity said.

"What's the book that you're reading?"

Charity laughed. "It's this weird ghost story. *House Ghosts.*"

"Oh, my God." Linda paused for a moment. "You're kidding."

"I am not."

"Did you know we were coming here?" Linda asked, but Charity smirked.

"What do you think?" she said.

At the door to the manor, Charity gave Linda what seemed a punctuation mark to their time together as she pursed her lips and heaved a hefty sigh. As they passed the threshold back into the manor, Charity stiffened. She didn't glance again at Linda as she strutted upstairs, followed by a lonely cameraman and his camera.

Linda ached in her chest. And elsewhere. Her camerawoman zoomed in on her stricken face. Back in her bedroom, Linda tried to shake it off, but as she freshened her makeup, she thought only of the soft-looking hood above Charity's eyes. As she flat-ironed her hair, she thought only of Charity's hair, the cute bounce of it, the one stubborn curl that crept out from behind her ear. How when Charity walked in front of Linda, Linda couldn't help but focus on the curve of her neck to shoulder—how soft her skin looked there. As Linda stepped into her sparkling black dress, she thought of the fabric in another room, moving over another body. She wondered what Charity would be wearing.

CHAPTER SIX

SABRINA

SABRINA DIDN'T FUCK with ghosts. As she shut the door to her Pepto-Bismol-pink room, she shivered in the chilly old-house air. Falling in love had nothing to do with haunted houses. Nothing good had anything to do with haunted houses. Not that Sabrina had been inside many, but her mom had instilled the fear of God in her when it came to messing with violent forces. Her mother believed that your thoughts formed reality. If that were true, then her mother's thoughts had ended with her mother's death, her father's illness, and her world crumbling to its barest essential: Sabrina and her sister, alone, with her sister caring for Sabrina the way they knew how.

Growing up, Sabrina's home had stunk of sage and had been littered with crystals and rocks. Her mother had tucked a new stone into Sabrina's pocket each morning, usually the ones she claimed brought love or beauty.

Sabrina understood none of it, and when her mother died, Sabrina buried her nose in science books and forgot the smells of the cleansing herb.

THE HAUNTED MANOR didn't smell like burning sage. Instead, it smelled like mildew, pine, old quilts, mothballs, and something sour and unnameable. Sabrina scrunched up her nose as she lay back in the bed she'd been assigned. In the hall, she heard Charity and Linda talking. The pang of jealousy that moved through her belly made her laugh at herself. The way that Linda looked at Charity wasn't the way Linda looked at Sabrina; it was more similar to the way that Sabrina looked at Tristan. As their voices drifted down the hall, a knock sounded on Sabrina's door.

She shook herself awake and answered. Deja stood on the other side. "Can I come in?" the woman asked as she breezed into the room. For once, she wasn't followed by a camera. For once, Deja shut the door to the eyes of other people. She sat on the edge of Sabrina's bed as Sabrina sat up.

"Make yourself at home," Sabrina said.

Deja tilted her head. "You're not the funny one. That's not your role."

"My role?"

"Surely, you've thought about your role?" Deja reached out and smoothed Sabrina's hair at her part.

"I was about to take a nap," Sabrina said.

"You can't sleep on this opportunity." Deja sucked her teeth. "You know, I worked my ass off to get here. You understand? I started as an assistant to some other producer. Real gem of a man. An ass-man, thank God. Ask me how I know. And it took years to get a camera gig. It took more than I thought I'd ever give a job. Now, I'm producer. Ringleader of this circus. I didn't climb. I clawed. But it was my dream. What's your dream, Sabrina?"

Sabrina frowned. "I want to find love."

"No. Your real dream."

"That's real," she said. "It's what my sister and I—"

"You aren't going to win this. You do realize that?"

Sabrina's stomach turned. She had as much of a chance as anyone else. Her sister wouldn't have sent her to a task that she was incapable of completing. Tristan wouldn't have kept her if he didn't see something in her.

"Oh, honey. You're here because it looks good for you to be here. Makes Tristan look less shallow to consider someone with hips. You think the people higher up than me care about you?" Even though Sabrina tried to move back, Deja's fingers wrapped around her chin before she could. "You're not going to win. But you can make a name for yourself. This kind of exposure? It leads to things. Money things. Money's the goal. It should be, anyway. That's all we've got, women like us."

"So, you want me to leave?" Sabrina said. "If I'm not going to win?" She choked back a cry. She didn't want to be the kind of woman who cried in front of powerful women.

"No. I want you to fight. You're not going to win, but you can show these producers that you're worth investing in. Be bold, Sabrina. Cause trouble. Give us some damn good TV." As Deja let go, a grin spread across her face. "Earn me that big, final promotion, yeah?"

After Deja left, Sabrina stared at the empty space her body left behind. Deja was a powerful woman; her absence registered in a room. Sabrina would never be that kind of powerful, but, like her mother, she could exude intention. She could sneak her way into his heart. She could start a little fire, unnoticeable until it burned the whole house down. And when Tristan came to her rescue, she could kiss him so hard it sucked the air out of his lungs.

CHAPTER SEVEN

LINDA

FOR DINNER, DEJA had forced the two camerawomen to dress in long muted-green and ocher dresses, with high lace collars. They served the four cast members and Tristan while the two cameramen and Deja filmed.

"This ghost town was founded in the 1880s," Tristan said, glowing with the expulsion of knowledge. "We thought it would be fun to eat like pioneers."

"I love it," Marion cooed.

"This butter here was made at the ranch ninety miles south." Tristan picked up the butter dish and displayed it to the table—and the cameras.

"You know, my uncle has a ranch in Texas," Marion said.

Linda's annoyance with Marion was tripled by the fact that she was from the same state: a region worlds different from the vibrant college town where Linda grew up. Marion's Texas was oil fields, mudding, and babies right out of high school.

Tristan handed the butter to Marion. Marion's face twisted in confusion; the bread hadn't been passed around, and it seemed as though Tristan forgot that butter was meant to go on top of something else. Marion nodded at the dish, as if in approval, and continued nodding, unsure of where to go from there.

"Here, honey." Charity placed a slice of bread on Marion's plate. Marion looked relieved.

No one ate. A camerawoman arrived with a tray of steaming pork, then sides: green beans, a bowl of baked beans, and a tray of corn on the cob. Linda's stomach ached, and even though she knew that eating wouldn't fix her particular butterflied affliction, she spooned generous helpings of meat and beans onto her plate. She grabbed the tray of corn, and as she stabbed with her fork at the juicy kernels, her fellow contestants stared her down. Did she dare? She requested the butter from Marion, slathered a thick glob across her cob, and bit in. The inside of a kernel squirted across the table, and a mixture of corn juice and butter dripped from the corner of her mouth down her chin.

"I love a girl who isn't afraid to get messy!" Tristan said, and Marion snatched the corn tray and piled high her plate with cobs. Sabrina ate like a normal person, and Charity didn't give in to animal temptation. She fixed a dainty plate and nibbled at a green bean.

"I heard you two took a walk." Tristan pointed with his fork to Linda and Charity. "Are we becoming friends?"

"No," Charity said. Linda's body heated from head to toe.

The ground vibrated. It was enough to stop Linda's train of thought, but not enough for her to be sure that the rumbling was real. But her dinner companions also wore puzzled expressions.

The ground shook, harder this time.

"Do you guys feel an earthquake?" Linda said.

Before her eyes, the wood seemed to quiver. This time, the floor didn't stop moving. Tristan jumped from his chair and rushed to shelter inside a door frame.

"Ladies!" he yelled, motioning.

Marion sprung up after him, and together Tristan and Marion clutched at the frame. Sabrina dropped to the ground and scurried under the dining table. "The door frame thing is outdated," she yelled, but Tristan didn't hear her. Linda copied her friend. Charity followed. The three women lay balled up beneath the table, their dresses hiking, their knees pressed against the hardwood. The floor moaned and shivered, and Linda felt it against her knees. For a moment, it felt like flesh against her skin.

"Is this normal for an earthquake?" she said.

"No," Sabrina said. "This is haunted shit."

In that moment, Linda believed it. She was kneeling against the evidence of ghosts. Again and again, the floor shivered, its texture changing beneath Linda's bare knees.

"Do you feel that?" Linda asked, and Sabrina shook her head in a silent yes. When Charity squeezed her eyes shut, Linda wished she could reach out and comfort the woman she'd thought incapable of fear. On the table, the dishes rattled as the wind outside picked up and whispered against the windows.

From the doorframe, Tristan screamed.

The house creaked like it was letting free one long sigh—then went silent. Linda waited, crouched beneath the dining table, palms pressed into wood that now felt like wood.

"It's over." Linda saw Tristan's feet move as he took one tiny step away from the doorframe. "We're safe now."

Linda's skepticism rushed back. She was on a reality TV show, in a house purchased by the network for a show about hauntings. A world constructed from romantics who thought of love as a game culminating in one life-changing ceremony that signaled the beginning of your actual life. For the next week, she would live in a constructed nightmare.

"I'm going to kill these producers," she muttered, but when she tried to find the camera operator filming them hiding, she didn't see anyone. She crawled from under the table. Tatum and Leo, the evening's crew, hid beside Tristan and Marion, their cameras abandoned across the room.

"They spooked the camera dudes," Sabrina whispered.

"Talk about unprepared," Linda whispered back.

Linda wanted to ask Sabrina about what she'd said under the table; did she really believe in hauntings? Maybe Sabrina was a planted contestant, there to legitimize the spooky occurrences. Linda bit her tongue.

Tristan and the rest of the contestants returned to the table. When Linda bit into the corn left on her plate, the kernels' hot juices dripped like sap from a tree, and she licked it from her fingers until nothing more remained.

CHAPTER EIGHT

SABRINA

AS SHE STOOD from the floor on shaky legs, Sabrina excused herself. In the bathroom, she splashed water over her face, letting the cold droplets soothe the skin that burned from embarrassment. She had freaked out and given into superstition.

Her mother's obsession with hippie intentions and manifestations had expanded to fill her entire self, until Sabrina, then an impressionable child, couldn't help but cling to the power that it promised. If Sabrina wanted it bad enough, it would happen—and Sabrina wanted what her mother wanted for her: for her beauty to win over the world. In her older age, Sabrina's mother's soul pickled until it was too bitter to taste. Instead of gifts, she manifested curses.

It wasn't the curses that killed Sabrina's mom, but Sabrina wondered if the cancer started from those awful impulses, lodging itself in her throat until it grew to take her over head-to-toe. No matter how badly Sabrina wanted it, not even her fierce desire kept her mother alive. At first, she blamed herself; maybe, deep down, she wished her mother dead. As she grew older, she clung to rationality like a life raft.

Sabrina licked a finger and swiped below her eye where her mascara smudged. She reached into the drawer where she had hidden several lipsticks and pulled out her favorite shade of all-day pink. As she dabbed the stick against the areas that dinner had ruined, she remembered how her mother, then her sister, taught her this and all the rest. They bought her books on makeup application, weight maintenance, and sex appeal, alongside children's adventure novels. Her mother wanted her to use her looks. Sabrina learned to do just that.

. As she stared into the mirror, something shifted behind her. She turned, but it must have been shifting light. She pressed her hand to the wallpaper. Beneath her palm, a heartbeat that was not her own. She shivered as she ran through all the normal explanations: plumbing, electricity, a prankster on the other side of the bathroom, the earthquake's aftershocks. *I'm a god- damn nurse*, she whispered to herself. *I'm a rational woman.*

Her sister, however, believed it all, and sometimes, Sabrina craved that surety. If manifesting were real, then her mother's birth spell was real, and Sabrina's purpose really was to win the heart of an eligible man, to exist for others to see and love.

. Sabrina hadn't told Tristan about her mother's blessing, but his keeping her around suggested that he believed her purpose to be physical, too.

She removed her hand from the wall and shook herself back to reality. It had to be an aftershock. And there would be more. Mother be damned, there was no such thing as ghosts.

AFTER DINNER, THE group convened in a parlor with an expansive ceiling of exposed beams. Two couches covered in coarse floral fabric flanked a giant glass coffee table. They took their seats: Tristan, Sabrina, and Marion on one couch, and Charity and Linda on the other. Tristan poured fresh glasses of red wine from a decanter while the camera operators filmed.

"I'm not used to earthquakes." Linda swirled her glass like she knew jack shit about wine.

"That wasn't an earthquake," Tristan stretched an arm across the back of the couch. "Don't you believe in ghosts?"

"No," Charity said.

"Yes," said Marion.

"Sabrina?" When Tristan caught her in his gaze, she remembered the secret conversation they shared in the woods. Off-camera, so did it really happen?

"No. And yes."

"What does that mean?"

"It changes, I guess." She shrugged, but in her belly, stomach acid roiled.

"I don't," Linda said. She and Charity shared one of their annoying secret glances.

"I have a ghost story." Tristan rubbed at the back of his neck. "You guys want to hear it?"

"Yes," they all said, in unison now.

"Well now." His lips were stained red from the wine. "I grew up on a farm, and we weren't necessarily believers in the supernatural, my family, but we weren't ones to tempt any spirits either. So, my mom didn't allow tarot or Ouija or any of that." The way he pronounced Ouija—*oh-ee-jah*—made Sabrina smile. "But one of my friends, now he was a troublemaker, and one night he brought over the leg bone of a murder victim his dad dug up. This kid said that a long time ago, someone in his family was murdered by a vengeful lover, some well-to-doer. Rather than turn the bone in to the police and get on the bad side of some powerful people, this kid's ancestors buried the body and tried to forget this person ever existed."

Sabrina frowned. The story was familiar; it was almost the same as the family ghost story she told Deja about when prompted during interviews. At the time, Sabrina thought it was an off-color question to gauge her storytelling abilities. Now, she felt like Deja was testing her, trying to make her accuse Tristan of lying. It would make him hate her, but it would be good TV. She pressed her lips together, her chest tight. She'd do no such fucking thing.

"That's awful," Marion said.

"It is! And this kid brings this bone over and tells us this story, and that his farm has been haunted for years by the ghost of this young man."

"The vengeful murderer was a woman?" Marion said. "How could a woman do such a terrible thing?"

"You'd be surprised," Charity said.

"Sometimes, a little lady goes over the edge, just like men do," Tristan said, nodding. "That's feminism."

Sabrina searched the room for a hint that Deja might be trying to push her into acting up. Deja had told her she could make a name for herself but that Tristan was off the table, that she'd never win. But Sabrina had one thing Marion didn't: a deep need. Her sister had laid out all the reasons why it was a good idea for Sabrina to find fame and carry her family on her coattails. Marion came from money. Sabrina came from dirt.

Tristan took another sip of wine. It seemed that he'd been talking, but Sabrina had zoned out. "So, this bone—"

"The haunted bone," Charity said, deadpan.

"The haunted bone. Our friend brought it to our farm, for some forsaken reason, and he told us that he wanted to do a séance with the thing. My brother and I didn't want to, but this kid and my older sister overruled us. So, he set up a circle of candles, with the bone in the middle, and we joined hands and chanted."

"What did you chant?" Sabrina asked.

"I don't remember now," Tristan said. "Something about 'speak to us,' or some basic séance shit."

Her mother and she had chanted words from a poem about death: *And death does follow, but we bid it wait / For we aren't prepared to leave this place / But you, the spirit, please go free / And take with you all the lessons you have gained.* They soothed her in the face of death, but even the chant hadn't been enough to stop her wailing at her mother's grave.

"The standard," Charity said. She and Linda shared yet another glance. So much of this experience was small glances between women. Sabrina wondered again: why *was* Charity here? She seemed to disdain everything Tristan said, and she had no qualms about letting that disdain show. She was the weakest link. Maybe Sabrina could take her out first.

"If you can't say something nice," Marion said. "Then please shut up."

"I'm providing commentary," Charity said. "Just because I'm clever doesn't mean you have to jump down my throat."

"You're not clever," Sabrina said. "You're sarcastic. There's a difference."

Charity smirked. "Tristan likes it."

"I doubt that," Sabrina said. "Everyone knows you're at the bottom of the totem pole."

Marion pursed her lips, her eyebrows drawing down her face. "That's what I was thinking," she muttered.

Tristan set down his glass. "Ladies, are we not getting along? Is there something going on in the house?" He meant the mansion, but *house* had become a pseudonym for group, coop, collection—however he thought of the remaining women vying for his attention.

"Charity isn't here for the right reasons," Sabrina said.

"She won't shut up, and I want to hear your haunted story!" Marion said.

The camera crew exchanged glances. Charity stood up. The full height of her was alarming, like an Amazon demigod. Marion stood four inches shorter than Charity, but she squared off against her, arms on her hips. The stance reminded Sabrina of her mother, who stood like that in every photo. Sabrina stayed seated beside Tristan, seizing the opportunity to scoot closer. She closed her eyes and imagined the future she wanted: the wedding dress, the man.

"I'm here for the wrong reasons?" Charity's voice shook with rage. "You have no idea what I feel for Tristan. I'm not about to let a dumbass like her steal him from me."

Sabrina opened her eyes and leaned to whisper in Tristan's ear, letting her lips vibrate against his lobe. Distracting him, she snuck her hand onto his upper thigh.

"That was a scary story, Tristan," she said. "Is it true?"

"Every word," he whispered. "I'd never lie to you."

She imagined him repeating those words—*I would never lie to you*—for the rest of their lives, like a promise greater than *I love you*, and because she believed it, it would be real. He would never again lie to her.

CHAPTER NINE

LINDA

IN THE PARLOR, the couch's frenzied floral pattern attacked Linda's eyes, so she kept her gaze trained on Charity instead. The women were fighting again.

As Charity lunged toward Marion, Tristan rose.

"Whoa. Ladies, you're both here because I care about you. There's no need to fight over me."

Charity displayed her palms. "Fine," she said, falling back into the couch in a huff. "She started it."

"Oh, that's mature," Marion said, then seemed to catch herself. She grabbed Tristan's hand. "I want you to be happy. I worry about women who might be here, you know—"

"For the wrong reasons," Tristan said. "I get it. You don't have to protect me."

Linda kept her expression nonplussed, like she'd practiced in the mirror again and again in preparation for the show. She pursed her lips tight. Unlike the other women, she didn't want to fight over him. Tristan was a decent man, but Linda watched the other women fawning over him and scoffed.

All in all, he was average. Below average when it came to smarts, even if he did know the ins and outs of running a farm, which was something. Maybe his appeal was that he delivered what he promised. Even though her reason for being here wasn't him, she might have been given a worse fate. Linda glanced again at Charity. Linda didn't want to leave the show yet.

"Hey, let's have a friendly competition!" Tristan gestured at a dartboard on the other side of the room.

"Yes, please," Sabrina said, not bothering to hide the exasperation in her voice. She rushed to Tristan's side, seizing another opportunity to stand close to him.

The camera crew readjusted their shot and checked the cast's personal microphones. Linda stood still as Leo replaced hers with a fresh one. "Less static," he explained.

"Maybe that's the ghosts," Linda said, smiling.

He winked. "Probably so."

The crew finished. "Play away," Becca said as she peered into her eyepiece.

"I'm going to sort y'all into two teams," Tristan said. "Charity and Marion, you're together."

Marion groaned, then turned it into an unconvincing cough.

"Sabrina and Linda, you're the dream team." He beamed. "I know better than to break up two besties. I've got sisters!" Tristan winked at Charity and Marion. "Let's let the grumpy ladies go first." As Tristan moved beside the other women, Sabrina stewed beside Linda, who ignored her friend's rotting mood.

Tristan explained the game. "Each team gets three shots per turn. The goal is to hit all the numbers in reverse sequential order, from twenty to one. Then you have to hit the bullseye. First team to get every number plus that bullseye wins."

Marion stepped to the piece of tape placed on the wooden floor. The producers must have examined the house for potential activities beforehand and put it there—the work of making preplanned events look spur-of-the-moment. Marion glanced at Tristan.

"Go ahead now," he said.

When she threw the dart, it landed in the inner area of the twenty. She jumped and yelped.

"Good job, cowgirl!" Tristan slipped an arm around her waist.

Charity and Marion both landed their next shots.

"Damn," Linda said. "We're fucked."

"Speak for yourself." Sabrina stepped to the line.

Sabrina landed a nineteen and cursed. "Here, have the next couple turns, too," Linda said. On the second try, Sabrina sunk a twenty. Linda cheered. Tristan laughed and sipped his wine, observing the members of his harem.

The women played for twenty minutes before Tristan forced Linda to take her turn. "We want to see what you're made of!" he said.

Linda chewed her lips. She stepped up to the tape. She'd played darts once or twice with her father in some bar with lax rules. He took her there without her mother knowing, and his friends cooed over the child in her big-girl britches, drinking a Shirley Temple while her dad downed bottles of Shiner Bock. When her father drove her home, he swerved all over the road. The thing was, she hadn't known better then. For the longest time, that night playing darts at the bar was one of her favorite memories. She had loved the feel of the car jerking over the pavement, like the kiddie coasters at Six Flags. It was later, once she learned about the world and its dangers, that she realized her father had endangered her life. She felt like a fool—and as though she could never trust that feeling of joy again.

Linda focused on the bulls-eye. She tossed the dart. It lodged in the wood paneling of the wall behind the dartboard.

"Better luck next time," he said. "But you can't get better if you don't practice!"

Linda stepped forward to retrieve the dart. She yanked it from the wall. She started to turn, but Sabrina gasped behind her.

"What's that?" Sabrina said. Linda turned back. The hole the dart had pierced oozed, a pink line of goo trailing down the wall in a single stream.

"Ew." Linda leaned closer. The slime smelled like rotten meat, some old takeout left in the fridge too long, but also sweet. The pink liquid frothed, the bubbles hissing as they popped. Linda started to touch it, but Sabrina grabbed her hand as it neared the substance.

"You touch every weird thing you see?" Sabrina said.

Linda lowered her hand. "What the hell is this?"

The others gathered round, studying the goo with wordless interest.

"It smells like pus," Sabrina said. "Might be a fungus. Or something that rotted in the walls?"

The others made noises of disgust. Linda felt like she might barf. She stepped back and tried to take in a fresh breath, but all she could smell was rot. Suddenly, the whole room was filled with it.

She felt a hand on her back. "I'm okay, Sabrina," she said, but it wasn't Sabrina.

"You look green," Charity said. "Here, sit." She motioned to the couch.

"I need air," Linda said.

"Sure." Panic infused Charity's voice. "Come on." Charity didn't wait for a cameraman, so the one who followed them scrambled to gather his gear. Together, Charity and Linda walked a long hall to the foyer, then exited the manor through the front door. Outside, Linda leaned against the building's stonework. She took several deep breaths. The rotting smell wasn't gone, but the outside air minimized it.

"This house needs some repairs, huh?" Charity said.

"It's silly to be freaked out by that, right?" Linda said. She'd never seen or smelled anything like the goo, and its presence had chilled her to the core.

"It's an old house," Charity said. "Old houses do weird shit sometimes. Especially when they've got producers setting them up for maximum spook." She shrugged. "It's not silly," she said. "It's never silly to feel something."

"You think the producers did that?" Linda said. "And the earthquake?"

"They've been manipulating us this whole time. You know that Brandon Fuller tracks our menstrual cycles, right? And then Deja tries to make us do wild shit when we're on our periods. This is more manipulation. You'll see."

"God, this show is fucked up."

"But adored by millions." Charity gave Linda a fake winning smile. "That's why we fame whores put up with it, right?"

The cameraman grunted. "Change the topic," he said. "You know I can't air any of this."

"That's the point, numb nuts," Charity said.

Linda didn't want to break her contract or risk Deja's wrath. She wiped at her forehead. She was covered in sweat. "That smell fucked me up."

"It was a bad smell, dude," Charity said.

Linda tried to think of something, anything, other than the smell. "You're good at darts."

"Thanks," Charity said. "You're not." Suddenly, Charity laughed, and like a whirlpool, Linda found herself pulled into the unexpected glee. Together, they cackled until finally, Linda steadied herself.

"I warned y'all." Linda nudged Charity. "And yet, you made me throw one anyway."

"I didn't make you do anything, Meadows." Charity threw her hands up in the air. "No one controls your actions but yourself."

"And the contracts we signed," Linda said. The cameraman coughed. The mention of contracts, too, was forbidden. It ruined the magic, the producers said. Or in the case of this manor, this challenge, this journey—whatever the correct language was—the horror.

CHAPTER TEN

SABRINA

SABRINA WATCHED CHARITY lead Linda outside and turned back to the room. Deja had told her she had no chance of winning, but two of her competitors kept sneaking off and ignoring the man they were supposed to be fighting for. Sabrina glared at Marion, who dangled from Tristan's arm like a sloth. Deja thought Marion was going to win, so Marion would be the hardest to beat. Sabrina thought of her sister; she would beat the bitch for her.

Sabrina startled at the thought. It felt like someone else speaking through her. She didn't use words that brought women down. She shook herself off and did what she'd been taught to in order to chase away the dark parts of herself: she focused on her man.

"Tristan, you look tired," she said. Leo had followed Linda, and Tatum had ventured off to find Deja. Becca and Jazz were filming them now. "Not much for secretions?"

Tristan grinned. "I don't mind a good secretion."

"Ew!" Marion slapped him on the shoulder, but Sabrina had caught his attention. His eyes remained trained on her.

"Your feelings on the matter?" he said.

"I deal with nasty shit all day, every day," she said. "The walls are oozing? At least I'm not the one who's supposed to clean it up."

The words ignited something else in Tristan. He shook Marion off. "Wait, can we even use any of this footage? Like, are y'all getting the nasty wall in these shots?" he asked the camera operators. "Where's Deja?"

Sabrina sighed, the moment lost.

"Honestly? Tatum probably got lost looking for her," Becca said.

"Himbo," Jazz said.

"I bet Sabrina wouldn't get lost." As Tristan gave her his boyish grin, her skin flamed.

"Fine, I'll find her." Sabrina winked at Tristan and strode out of the room as though she had any idea where she was going.

The halls were dark, the gas lamps turned down for the evening. "Deja," she whispered into the vast empty space, then tried it louder. When she got no response, she moved along the wall toward the hint of light: what she assumed was the entryway.

"Deja!" she called, louder this time.

"What the hell do you want?" Deja appeared at the stairs like a statue come to life.

"We need you in the parlor," Sabrina said. "Clean-up on aisle Tristan."

"He pissed himself?"

"What? No. There's weird ooze coming from the walls."

Deja's face fell. "What does it look like?"

"Like something gross. Puss…or molasses?" Sabrina wondered what Deja was getting at. "Is there asbestos in this house?"

Deja composed herself. "No, of course not. You think I'd put your lives at risk?"

"I don't know what you would and wouldn't do. You fed my haunted story to Tristan. Why not throw a bunch of beauty queens into a house ruined with asbestos? Sure sounds like something a producer would stoop to."

Deja took two fast steps, then was right in Sabrina's face, her hot breath coming down on Sabrina's wine-warmed cheeks.

"I wouldn't hurt you," she said. "That's a step too far."

"And the story?"

"Tristan is dumb as a doornail. I give him good stories. So what? If you married him, he'd steal your stories all the damn time."

Sabrina relaxed. "It wasn't to provoke me?"

"Oh, honey." Deja grinned like a madwoman. "That's all anyone in this business is ever going to do to sweet women like you. Your only way out of being poked and prodded? Give in to the wild side on your own. No prodding necessary." She winked. "Unless you'd like a little prodding. I hear he's not so bad in bed, that low-rent John Wayne."

"John Wayne was a terrible racist."

"Ha!" Deja gestured for Sabrina to follow down the hall. "Your boy Tristan has his fucked-up ideals, I'm sure."

"The fuck?" Sabrina said, but Deja was too far past to hear as she disappeared around a corner. Sabrina followed, but all the doors were closed, and no light peeked out from underneath. The hair rose on her arms. The weird old place was getting to her. She touched a doorknob, ready to turn it and see if the door led to the parlor, but instead of laughter, inside she heard a high-pitched whine, like a scream turned to too high a frequency. She pushed the door open and stepped inside, ready to rescue Marion from whatever spider had crawled across her chest, but the room was empty and dark.

She started to turn back when the lights flickered on. They were electric. She breathed a sigh of relief at the hum of electricity. Some areas of the house were wired, but they'd been instructed to rely on the gas lamps for ambiance.

The room was a blank expanse of wood walls and floors. Sabrina spun in its center. If a camera entered, it would capture a brilliant shot of her: carefree, a perfect specimen of femininity. Strong-willed enough to hold her own against the cowboy, but demure enough that she'd make him feel special. She imagined the teaser for the season, her spinning right in the middle. The room moved around her as her thoughts traveled from the idea of being watched until she was just Sabrina. She laughed out loud. For one moment, she didn't want to be a wife. She wanted to be this: a woman spinning in a room of her own.

She stopped, shook herself, and uttered a silent apology to her mother's memory, to her sister back at home waiting for her to win this thing.

The air thinned, and she doubled over to keep herself from falling dizzy to the floor. When she stood back up, a woman stepped out of the wall.

Sabrina screamed, but she was still alone. She narrowed her eyes; the woman hadn't stepped out. Instead, her outline pressed itself from inside the wood, as though she was trapped inside. By the time Sabrina pressed her shaking hand to the wall, the wood was smooth again.

She pursed her lips until all the blood fled from them. She was seeing things. Hallucinating. She'd need to be more careful. The last thing she needed was to faint in front of Tristan. Weak women couldn't work farmland with the man of their dreams.

But as she flexed her fingers against the wall, they sunk into it. A panicked wave moved through her, followed by her mantra: *I'm a rational woman. I'm a rational woman.* On shows like these, producers did everything in their power to control situations. Determination settled in her twisting gut; there had to be a trick to it. Some secret compartment behind the wall where the producers stood and made puppets of themselves. She stepped back. Deja would be cleaning the goo for a while yet. She needed to find the trick.

SABRINA WAS NO architect, but she understood that the wall had another side somewhere. She opened the door to the hall and peeked out. She didn't want to be scolded, but the coast was clear. As she snuck through the passageway, she kept one hand against the wall, feeling her way along. Finally, her hands landed on a part that felt less than solid. When she knocked, a hollow echo answered.

As she pressed her palms to it, it flexed like plywood painted to match the surroundings. When she pushed in harder, it met its stopping point, refusing to budge farther. She pressed into it again, pushing up, and the panel slid away from the floor into a secret slit in the ceiling. She ducked under and into a deeper dark.

Relief flooded her at the implication; trap doors meant tricks, and tricks meant that her rational mind was right. She felt her way through the secret area, wall surrounded by wall, until her fingers curved around a corner. She turned into another long stretch, then followed a straight, claustrophobic line until she felt a handle.

"Holy shit," she muttered, then twisted it open.

It opened into a crawlspace. As her eyes adjusted, she noted the dirt floor. She climbed down a little ladder, and her feet landed on soft earth full of footprints. She made her way on hands and knees through the crawlspace, her back brushing against the underside of the floors, until suddenly, she felt air. She unfolded herself, standing at her full height, and took in the trick: someone had cut into the cross-beams a little hideaway, and as Sabrina stepped onto the platform inside the wall, she felt the softened give of something other than wood. Her hand left an imprint in the strange material.

She laughed as she listened through the thin substance; a mechanical hum, like the hum in the empty room. She was a rational woman after all. As she pulled away, she heard another sound: voices, Tristan's and Deja's and Marion's, an echo. Her heart rate picked back up. She stepped away, back into the dirt, then hurried back through the secret passage.

"EVERYTHING OKAY?" TRISTAN asked when Sabrina entered the parlor.

"Fine," she said. "Just fine." And she let him wrap his arms around her shoulder and pull her to him. Together, they fell back onto the couch as Deja ordered Tatum to throw away the rags she'd dirtied while cleaning and then patch the hole in the wall.

"Old pipes," Deja said to the cast, shrugging as she shut the door behind her.

CHAPTER ELEVEN

LINDA

BACK IN THE parlor, Sabrina and Marion had seized the opportunity granted them by the absence of two competitors to get an edge in with Tristan. They sat on either side of him on one of the raggedy couches, sipping wine and giggling.

"What did we miss?" Charity said as they entered the room.

"I'm calling the game," Tristan said. "You and Marion win."

"Yes!" Marion yelled.

"Congratulations." Sabrina pursed her lips.

"No surprise there." The pink goo had been cleaned off, the wall patched good as new. "Did you guys figure out what that stuff was?" The smell had dissipated a little, but Linda would have to suck it up for the evening.

"No clue," Sabrina said. "Maybe you hit a dead mouse trapped in the wall? Maybe it's weird sap. Deja said old pipes."

Charity ran her flexed shoe across the floor, a graceful ballerina move. "The wood floors in these rooms look like they were re-done recently. I took a peek in the kitchen earlier, and the wood flooring in there is, like, knotty and old. Kind of warped. It would make sense if the walls hadn't quite dried out." She shrugged. "I'm no renovator, though."

"Ya'll are delusional," Marion said. "We're in a haunted house. It's trying to tell us something. Don't you know anything about ghosts?"

"What's it telling us?" Linda asked.

"That's what we have to find out!" Marion said. "It's some spirit who didn't get to profess his love—or some child who misses her mother. That's common."

"What if it's evil?" Charity said. "A man who didn't get to exact the vengeance he desired."

"Or a woman who hated the color of curtains here but never got to change them," Linda said.

"Exactly." Charity walked to the red velvet curtains and ran them between her fingers. "These are hideous, if I say so myself."

"I think they're charming," Sabrina said.

"Ladies, I doubt this is the last we'll hear from this house," Tristan said. "From what I've read, stranger things than oozing walls have happened here."

"Like what?" Linda asked.

"Noises, apparitions," Tristan said. "Your standard haunted fare."

"Yes, yes," Charity said. "The starter pack."

"Deja told me a man murdered his family. Chopped them up into little pieces." As Linda said the words, her stomach twisted, remembering the description of his drunken rage.

"That's not what she told me," Tristan said. "Told me it was used as an orphanage for troubled kids, and they died here."

Linda's body froze, a cold tremor shooting down her spine.

"Told me a story about a mom who drowned her baby…" Sabrina fiddled with her fingers, a nervous habit that left them in need of nightly repair. "Sounds like she gave each of us our own cliché."

Tristan laughed, but the women didn't crack a smile. Linda forced a laugh, but it sounded more like the beginning of a choke—and her breath was heavier than usual in her chest. Deja's stories were meant to provoke, and in her case, they had succeeded.

"Stop making it a joke! It's always the ones who don't take it seriously who get fucked up first," Marion said, pleading. "Do y'all even watch any scary movies?"

"I love scary movies," Linda said.

"Me too," Sabrina rushed to add.

"I love the good ones. Not the same ones that you love, Tristan," Charity said, looking at him from the corner of her eye. It was like she understood that she was moving farther away from him with every conversation they had here. What was she doing? She'd be sent home if she weren't careful. "But I'd watch them to make you happy."

The air in the room stood still and silent. Linda was glad for a break, though she wished the pus smell would go away, that her lungs would open and let her deeply inhale clean air.

Tristan slapped his hands on his thighs, the way he did when he was done with a conversation. "I think it's time to have a little one-on-one time, don't you?" Tristan stood and offered his arm to Marion. "My lady?"

She giggled as she joined him, and together they made their way from the parlor.

"Do we have to stay in here?" Linda asked. She examined the closed window; outside, there would be air, and even if it smelled like the creepy woods, she longed for it. The cameraman nodded. They had to stay. She slouched.

"Do you think she's the frontrunner?" Sabrina stared at the doorway through which Tristan and Marion had disappeared. She tore at her cuticles until Linda placed a gentle hand on hers.

"Do you care?" Charity said.

"Of course, I care," Sabrina said. "Tristan's kind and funny and interesting. He makes me excited when I see him."

"He's cool." It was the only thing Linda could think to say.

"Anyone can be kind and funny and interesting and *cool* if they've got money." Charity laughed.

"Do you have money?" Linda asked, then reprimanded herself for the intrusive question.

"I'm tired of sitting around like this," Charity said. "Let's play a game."

"What game?" Linda said, relieved.

"Light as a feather, stiff as a board!" Charity laughed again. "It'll be like old middle school slumber parties. Which is exactly what this experience has been like, to be honest."

Linda hadn't experienced middle school slumber parties. She had been closed off from those worlds. Like any child in a turbulent home, she clung to her mother's hand long past her youngest years. The one sleepover she went to ended with her calling her mother halfway through the night, begging her to take her home. Her homesickness was like a stomachache that could only be cured by the presence of her mother and father. If she didn't keep watch over her family, if she allowed herself to be distracted by friendship, bad things might happen.

The women knelt on the floor, and it was Linda who lay on her back with her arms crossed over her chest. Charity and Sabrina sat on either side of her body and shoved their fingers under her back. Together, Charity and Sabrina chanted: light as a feather, stiff as a board, light as a feather, stiff as a board. Linda relaxed under their shadows. She felt safe—and light. She breathed in and out, unbothered by the smell of pus so long as she was being touched.

The image of the taxidermy creature flashed before her closed eyes.

She coaxed herself to chill out, pushing the nightmare fuel away. She breathed in, then out, and time stilled for her.

The women's fingers left the back of her dress. She jerked back into the reality of the room, the smell, the manor, the situation.

"Who's next?" Tristan said. When her eyes flew open, he stood above her. "You look comfy."

Linda sprang up. "We were playing a silly game."

Marion held a pink apple in her hand. She held it up. "There's a gorgeous little orchard out there. You can see the moon all big in the sky. Apples everywhere!" She took a crunchy bite, then spit it out onto the floor. "Ugh, that's rotten." She blushed, searching the room. "Is there a napkin somewhere? Sorry. It surprised me. It didn't seem rotten."

Linda looked down at the chewed remains of Linda's bite; tiny red seeds had fallen with it, more like a pomegranate than an apple. Linda bent to inspect them. They weren't like pomegranate seeds at all. She squished one between her fingers. It felt like caviar.

"Why are you digging around in my trash?" Marion said. Sabrina produced a tissue from a fancy gold box on a side table. Marion let it flutter to the floor, where it covered the apple bits. Linda picked it up for her.

"Linda, why don't we go for a walk?" Tristan said uneasily. He probably thought she was weird for inspecting it, but why did no one else notice how bizarre—how wrong—the fruit was? She'd heard that apples were different in the northwest— wild varieties were unlike the store-bought ones—but she'd yet to see anything as odd as this one.

"I'd love to see this orchard," Linda said, more curious about the weird fruit. "It sounds lovely."

"Get your own special place," Marion muttered.

"I'd love to take you there." He looped his arm with Linda's.

Outside the manor doors, Linda dropped the apple guts onto the ground. Tristan watched as they tumbled out of the napkin.

"You ever seen an apple like that?" Linda said as the cameras closed in on her face.

"Nah," Tristan said. "But once, when I was little, my mom took me to this new grocery store, and you wouldn't believe the fruit they had! Spiny little things. Things that looked like weird red tongues."

Leaves crunched underfoot, though Linda realized with a start that they were still nowhere near either the orchard or the woods. "How'd you get here?" she said to the leaves.

"I got here because I'm looking for love," Tristan said. He moved to hold her hand. It felt nice to hold someone's hand. "I'm ready to settle down. Have a family." He stopped at the edge of a paved path. "This is the path that leads to the orchard, by the way. If you squint, you can maybe make it out, where that big archway is."

They made their way down the pathway made of little stones.

"Speaking of which, if you make it through this week, and I hope you do, who will I meet when I come home with you next week?" When he smiled, the moonlight glinted in his perfect teeth. "What's your family like?"

Linda tried to shove her hand into her pocket, then realized she didn't have any pockets in her dress. Damn women's fashion.

"My cat," she said. "His name's Salmon."

"Salmon, nice," he said. "I like cats. Who else?"

"My sister won't be around. She moved away when she turned eighteen and never called, never wrote. I've tried to look her up online, but she must be off-the-grid or something."

"I'm so sorry. That's awful." Tristan paused and grabbed both her hands as though to lead her in a sudden dance. "How did that affect your parents?"

"My dad died when I was in middle school," Linda said. She swallowed hard and felt her chest try to close. "My mother— well, she's locked up." She pulled Tristan along the path.

"In prison?"

"An institution." Linda pinched her lips. They reached the archway, and the moon shone on a circle of what looked, at first, like apple trees. The loop had a break down its center, a pathway through the trees. "She broke after my dad died. There's no talking to her anymore." Linda dragged her lip between her teeth. "What I'm saying is, you won't be meeting any of my family. You'll be visiting a broken home, with a broken woman. The only one around me who has it all together is Salmon."

Tristan squeezed her hand again. "I can't wait to meet Salmon."

Linda forced herself to smile.

"Let's walk," he said, and Tatum leaned over and flipped a switch. The orchard lit up as the ornamental lights that the producers had installed popped to life. Tristan and Linda took two steps forward, and Linda got her first good look at the trees.

The trees in the orchard had similar bark to the trees in the forest, waxen and thick with a rubbery look, but they were different, too. Their leaves were like great big ears, complete with curves and folds. Linda held a leaf between two fingers. It was squishy to the touch. Linda pressed her hand against the tree trunk; it felt like skin stretched over muscle, but harder, more like the rough areas on Sabrina's hands from where she picked herself raw, half-healed. The trees bore the fruit that Marion had brought inside the house. The fruit was fuzzy on the outside, like a peach. Linda shivered to be in the presence of its wrongness. The previous owners of the manor must have been horticulturists with wild vision.

All she could think to say was, "Wow."

"Wow indeed," Tristan said. He beamed out at the courtyard.

"Don't these trees eek you out?" she said.

"Nature does freaky things."

"This is man-made," she said. "Someone bred these."

"This doesn't frighten me. It's when things that aren't supposed to be alive, come alive—that's what gets to me."

"Like a haunted bone?"

"Like a haunted house."

Linda pulled away from the tree. She wanted nothing more to do with it.

"Thanks for being so understanding about my family," she said, and she pulled at Tristan's hand, tugging him closer to her.

"Everyone has their demons," he said. He bent to her, and their lips met for an instant. Linda felt no spark.

The lights cut off all at once.

Linda jumped, then felt Tristan's hand closing over her upper arm. He grabbed her too firmly, but she attributed it to fear. Still, it made her even uneasier.

"We blew a breaker," the cameraman called out. "The lights overloaded the circuit."

"What the hell is happening here?" Deja's voice was tinged with annoyance. "I told you to make sure we didn't trip it."

A flashlight shone across Linda's eyes.

"Get back inside, lovebirds. We can't film out here right now." The flashlight moved closer until Deja's hand brushed against Linda's hair. "Here, I'll lead you."

"We could've adjusted to the dark if you didn't shine that thing at us," Tristan said.

"You can adjust to my ass if you get testy with me again, country boy." Deja shoved the flashlight into Linda's hand. Linda aimed it in front of them and walked forward. Tristan huffed into the wet air and followed. "That's right, Linda. Now there's a woman who knows what's good for her."

Linda's body flamed, but she kept moving. The misty rain on her skin annoyed her, and Tristan's presence beside her was even worse, especially when he looped her arm with his.

"These producers," Tristan whispered once they were far enough away. "Is it a California thing? Southern folk don't ever talk so rude."

Linda relaxed as a laugh overtook her, fake at first, then real as she pushed away the terrible orchard. "Yeah, they do," she said, remembering the old phrases her mom used to spew toward her, words that looked on paper to be coated with honey but when spoken dripped with poison: *Oh, honey; Thanks for sharing; Bless your heart.* "Maybe you didn't notice them." Tristan tensed beside her, but she didn't regret the snarky comment. The dark brought out the worst in her.

THEY REJOINED THE others in the parlor, but the night had withered and died on the vine. Charity rose when they entered as though she were greeting a judge. She was, Linda realized. A flash of the elimination ceremonies they'd all been forced to endure appeared behind her blinking eyes. Even outside of competition shows like this one, relationships were nothing but daily judgments until one or the other party found someone unworthy of continuing on.

"Back so soon?" Marion perked up.

"Blackout," Linda said. "Spooky." She waved her fingers like tentacles.

Tristan laughed uneasily. "Producers forced us back in here. I'm beat, though. What do you ladies say to calling it a night?"

"Call it like it is," Charity said. She faked a yawn. "I'm surprised we lasted this long."

"I've got a wild day planned for you all tomorrow," Tristan said. "Can't wait to see what you ladies are made of."

The women said their goodbyes to Tristan and filed out of the room. As Charity smoothed past Linda, Linda heard her mutter: "Skin and bone, country boy. Women are made of skin and bone."

THAT NIGHT IN her bed, snuggled under the red quilt, Linda turned the phrase over and over. Women are made of skin and bone. Linda shivered despite the blanket's insistent warmth. If she asked Tristan what women were made of, he'd give her a saccharine answer: sugar and spice, and you give me that sugar right here on my lips, little lady. Skin and bone was closer to the truth, but it withheld crucial information. Linda was made of more than that; she was made, too, of cellulite and follicle, brittle nail and aching ancient injuries. Blood that often betrayed her with its pressures high and low, hormones that waxed and waned like a stupid moon in her pineal gland. She was made of fear and longing and the dirt on the bottoms of her feet from walking barefoot. She was made of roots that stretched as veins through her body, and as she lay trying to sleep in a house in the middle of nowhere, she imagined those veins pushing out through the bottoms of her feet and climbing down into the wooden floors, drilling through to find any substance that might hydrate her. She listened as the house made its old-house noises, something like a desperate sucking sound, and imagined that it was her body seeking what it came for.

CHAPTER TWELVE

SABRINA

AFTER WASHING HER face and applying six creams—under-eye, face, hair, skin, foot, and cuticle—Sabrina sunk into her pink bed. She sighed into the feather pillows, but as she rolled to face the wall, she remembered the woman's outline in the walls downstairs and rolled to face the ceiling instead. It had been a nasty trick.

The wood bed frame creaked with each of her movements, so she tried to move as little as possible to keep her mind off haunted thoughts. Her creams' floral scents mixed with the other creams' smells of mint and rose, and she breathed in the concoction that kept her soft enough for stray men to stroke.

She had barely dozed off when she woke to a hand tugging at her blanket.

"Care to be possessed?" Tristan whispered into her ear as she suppressed a scream. He stuck his nose into her hair. "You smell amazing, you know. And your hair." He ran a hand through it.

Despite herself, a glow warmed in her belly. When his hands traveled to rest against her belly button, she ached between her legs.

"Possessed?" she whispered as sleep cracked in her voice. "You know I don't believe in that."

"You said yes and no," he said. "Those kinds of answers confuse a man."

"Yes," Sabrina said as she wrapped her arms around him and pulled him into her. "Possess me."

They made love like two planes of glass, trying not to break one another, legs straightened out, her thighs tightening as she gripped him inside of her. He rocked on top of her in his quiet thrusting. She grabbed the tender skin of his ass, guiding his every movement. Their cheeks grazed one another as they let their tiny moans vibrate in each other's ears. Sabrina broke apart beneath him, her body trembling as he pressed it into the mattress.

He kissed her goodnight and slipped out of her room, leaving her to the squeaking bed frame.

THE FIRST TIME Sabrina had sex, she was fifteen. Her sister had brought a boy home from school, a friend from the junior swim team. Morgan set them both down and issued her command: "Alex, remove your shirt."

Like so many people, Alex listened to everything Morgan told him. He pulled his shirt off over his head. He was all muscle and sinew, a pale, lean boy, with a handsome flop of black hair. "You're going to take Sabrina's virginity."

He clutched his shirt to his chest and balked. "I thought this was a date."

"It is," Morgan said. "You're dating my little sister. It will look good for her."

"Like, at school?" he said, but Sabrina understood: it would look suitable for the story of her life. Lost it to a swim team boy at the age of fifteen. It was a little younger than most women— but lots of pretty girls who developed first lost it early—and not late enough to make her seem frigid. It would give her a hint of wildness, while the fact that the boy was athletic, older, the friend of her sister, would show that she was wanted, lucky even, from a young age.

"But I like *you*," the boy said to Morgan.

Morgan cackled. "No, you don't. My sister's the pretty one."

"She's fine." He glanced at her as though appraising her for the first time. "I mean, I guess you're right. She's hot."

"Good. Then I'll leave you to it." She tossed him a condom. He caught it before he realized what it was. His jaw hung open as she shut the door behind her.

"Your sister's crazy," he said to Sabrina as the door clicked into its frame. "Fucking nuts."

Sabrina shook her head, beaming. "She's not. She was born to be brilliant. She looks after me."

Alex set the condom beside him. "No, dude, she's bonkers."

Sabrina's stomach twitched. She hated hearing him diss her sister like that, but she wasn't supposed to talk back to men in a way that would turn them away from her.

"Maybe you're bonkers," she whispered.

His laugh was a loud sound. She laughed in time with him, until they were both cracking up and rolling on the floor.

"We're all bonkers," he finally said. "Isn't that the lesson of high school?"

"I guess." Sabrina blushed. She didn't feel crazy. She felt pretty and lucky—and eager to kiss the boy in front of her.

"Hey, I didn't mean it as a bad thing." He rolled closer to her and rested his hand on her outstretched leg. "I meant it as a compliment."

Before she lost her nerve, she leaned in and pressed her lips to his. He pulled back, surprise registering on his face.

"You want this?" he asked.

"I do." She waited, and he hesitated only a moment before he returned to her, his hands cupping her cheeks as his lips tangled with hers. They breathed into one another until her body relaxed, and the rest was eager and rushed, but at the same time, it was intoxicating in its adultness. The strange sensations were otherworldly if unsettling. After he fell apart, he folded into himself, then pulled back on his clothes as though in a hurry.

"Well, thanks," he said as he hurried from the room, then from the house. Sabrina peered out her window at him waiting for his brother's car. She imagined their life together: they might hold hands as they sprinted down the hallway; kiss under the football field bleachers; rub their feet together under the lunch tables. They might be known as *cutest couple*, voted *homecoming king and queen*. Sabrina pressed her palms to the window until her sister came in and pulled her away.

"Now you forget him," she said to Sabrina, so Sabrina did.

DAY TWO

DAY TWO

CHAPTER THIRTEEN

SABRINA

AT THE BREAKFAST table, Sabrina waited for Tristan to come down. When he ventured into the kitchen, he poured a scoop of protein powder into a glass of water and downed it in one gulp. Sabrina pushed a bowl of cereal and the bottle of milk toward him, but he ignored it and left.

"For me?" Linda slid into the chair behind Sabrina and poured the milk, then frowned at the colorful cereal loops. "No wonder he ignored you. These colors are against nature." Her gaze gleamed, then faded. "Or maybe I'm too tired to be hungry."

"Late night?" Sabrina asked her, imagining Tristan climbing into her bed, then going down the hall to Linda's. Her stomach twisted at the idea that they might be tunnel sisters already, before the private nights for three of the women in the penultimate episode: the sanctioned bedding of the potential brides. People fucked outside that episode—rumors abounded about prior seasons' Lotharios—but it was frowned upon. This year, Tristan had chosen her to take off-camera. Sabrina smiled at the thought.

"Nah. I was out like a light." Linda ran her hand through her hair. "Why? Were you up until the wee hours?"

Sabrina folded her hands in her lap and lay her head against the table. She closed her eyes. "I tossed and turned."

"Did you now?" Linda raised an eyebrow.

As Sabrina breathed in, she caught the scent of wood, but something else behind it: the smell of sweating skin, odor after a long, frightened run. It was a particular smell: fear. She knew it from those moments in her life she didn't wish to recall. It was the smell that she caught from her armpits after sweating out a fever; waiting on a pregnancy test; pulling to the side of the road when she saw those flashing lights; walking home alone at night; running home alone at night. Her head spun as a nervous trill moved through her. She lifted her head and scowled.

"Do you smell something?"

"Like what?"

"I don't know. Skin? Blood?"

Linda's eyebrows bunched together. "You should make sure you sleep," Linda said. "We'll need our energy to fight off all these ghosts." Sabrina tried to smile, but Linda's expression portrayed something that Sabrina didn't like: a brief meanness that flashed in and out. It was that judgment that irked her: *Sabrina shouldn't eat the cereal, and she should get more sleep, and under no circumstances should she let Tristan into her room.* As competitors, it was their curse to judge everyone. Thus far, Sabrina and Linda had formed an alliance, but Linda wanted to win, and eventually, they would need to tear each other apart.

CHAPTER FOURTEEN

LINDA

AFTER BREAKFAST, THE production team gathered the contestants and lined them up outside the manor. The only information that Deja had given them was to dress for activity, and Linda shivered in her gym shorts and tank top.

Tristan removed his hands from the pockets of his cargo pants and paced back and forth as the cameras followed him.

"Growing up on a ranch, I learned to be active at an early age. Fitness was instilled in me, and I expect any lady of mine to follow me on adventures of a physical nature." He winked. "Today, we're going to rappel down the side of the manor!"

One of the cameramen leaned over the roof's edge and waved.

"How the hell are we getting up there?" Charity said. "There is no fucking way."

"I'm glad you asked! Inside Matrimony Manor, there's a secret staircase that leads up to the top of the roof there. Ladies, to get to the top, we climb!"

Marion jumped up and down, while Charity's face drained of its color.

"I'm afraid of heights," she said, and flexed and unflexed the hand that lay at her side, beside Linda's steadier hand. Linda let her skin brush Charity's, sharing a brief warmth that Linda hoped might calm her. Charity didn't seem to notice.

"Well, now is your chance to face your fear. This is an important challenge, because tonight—you guessed it!—is an elimination ceremony." Tristan tried to look somber, but it was like a puppy dog pretending at guilt.

Linda's stomach tensed as the cameras cut on Tristan's final word.

"Shit," Charity muttered, but this time Linda didn't ache to comfort her, too preoccupied with thoughts of elimination. She didn't love Tristan, but the thought of her new life formed a blank expanse ahead. She should be excited about the idea that he might draw that red X across her photo, that she might leave the manor and its awful smells and weird noises, but as the prospect hit her for the first time, her heart skipped a beat. If she went home now, Deja would have to give her what was promised: a clean slate. But she had never been without the skeletons in her closet. They had become like old friends, an excuse to remain rooted and refuse forward momentum. Going home meant a reckoning with herself. Her palms sweated.

Sabrina chewed her fingers, probably more nervous about the ceremony then the rappel, while Marion preened in preparation for the challenge.

As Tristan chatted with Jazz, Deja ushered each contestant into a makeshift confessional to record their impressions on the challenge ahead. Linda took her seat and tried not to let the goosebumps all over her arms give her away.

"Scared?" Deja said. She held out a shot and winked. "Need some liquid courage?"

"You know I don't," Linda said.

Deja pursed her lips. She knew both the power of silence and the benefit of a well-timed nudge.

"I'm a little scared," Linda said, deciding to give her something. "I'm not an active person."

Deja grinned. "Now I know that isn't true. You went on a lot of camping trips as a kid."

The color drained from Linda's face. Here she was again: facing Deja's attempts to make her spill, when Deja had promised not to go there. It made Linda mad, but she remembered the harm that anger could cause. Never again.

"That's right, but it was so long ago." Linda forced herself to shrug. "The muscles lose their memory."

"Do they, though?" Deja said. "I'm not so sure."

"I'm a different person now," Linda said.

"Of course, you are." Deja let her smile diminish. "You've been through so much. Your family. The depression that kept you from working for so many years, racking up all that bad credit. Your divorce."

Linda tapped her finger on her hand, hoping the kinetic movement would keep her from lashing out. "I've been through a lot, which is why I know I can handle this challenge." She cocked her head and smiled with only her lips. She wasn't about to slip up. The show had stolen her divorce and made it their own, and she was willing to pay that price, but anything else negated Deja's promise. A clean start. A new road.

"Do you expect to be the one sent home tonight?" Deja said, sighing as Linda refused to say more.

Linda swallowed once, then pushed the fear she'd let enter her back down where it belonged. "No," Linda said. "He'll pick me."

"Good girl." Deja looked out from behind the camera. "That's the spirit."

AS LINDA STOOD, waiting for the confessionals to wrap, the air changed beside her. Charity stepped into her range of recognition. Linda softened to see her there.

"Be glad not to do those anymore," Charity said.

"The confessionals?" Linda said.

"Yeah." Charity fluffed her hair, which had fallen flat from humidity. The air near the manor smelled of rain. "Deja can go fuck herself."

"I wish she would. She might be more pleasant."

"There's something creepy about her, yeah?" Charity peered over to where Deja interrogated Sabrina.

"She's from LA." Linda shrugged.

"I'm from LA, remember?" Charity crossed her arms.

Linda laughed nervously. "Must be why you're creepy, too."

Charity playfully pushed her. Where Charity's hand touched her, Linda's skin, even beneath the clothes, blazed.

"Why are you talking to me all of a sudden?"

Now it was Charity who shrugged. "Guess I stopped caring."

"I thought you were one of the contestants who aren't here to make friends."

"I'm not." Charity smirked. "I'm not trying to make... friends."

Linda flushed, then hurried to change the subject. "Are you really scared of heights?" She looked up at the top of the manor with its backdrop of gentle mountains.

"I am."

Linda grinned at her. "Guess I'm beating you in the challenge today."

As Charity frowned, Linda regretted her words. "Guess so."

THE STAIRWELL WAS located on the west side of the manor. To get to it, Tristan led the contestants through a kitchen with uneven wood floors and a wet stench, then through a long hall of closed doors, to an archway with the stairs visible through it, anchored to concrete. The stairs were wrought iron, a spiral that reached above the contestants' heads. Linda stared up at the winding steps and the endless darkness and shivered.

"I'll go first," Sabrina said, pressing her foot onto the first stair. "Feels sturdy to me."

"Be my guest," Marion said, her voice quivering.

"I want to go last." Tristan laughed. "I like the view."

Charity delivered a faked laugh. Linda leaned in. "Hey, want me to walk behind you? Will that help at all?"

Charity grimaced. "Yeah, it might. If I fall, you can catch me."

"I wouldn't be so sure," Marion said. "Sabrina's a better bet with those man arms."

Charity rolled her eyes and took the first two steps, then made her steady way up the rest. Linda hurried to catch up, and behind her, she heard Marion and Tristan giggling as they ascended.

Charity's response to fear seemed to be to get the scary thing over with as soon as possible, and Linda had to admire the commitment. She tried to call up and engage Charity in conversation, but the woman was long-gone ahead of her. Linda walked alone.

As she took one stair at a time, her breath rushing out quicker and quicker, she kept one hand on the wrought iron rail and ran the other along the stone work at the stairwell's sides. Whoever had built it hadn't left much space to look at the floor from on high. But it wasn't the sense of claustrophobia that unsettled Linda as she climbed, and she puzzled over the reason why the stairwell shook her so. Then, it hit her: it was the only place in the whole house that wasn't made of wood.

She laughed at herself; if that was spooky, she was in for a long rest of the week.

LINDA EXITED THE stairwell through a door that seemed to perfectly fit her. Tatum waited on the top of the roof, and he helped keep her steady as she emerged onto a rooftop made of weathered wood tiles coated in moss. Linda breathed a sigh of relief.

She settled onto a flat area cleared of moss—where the cameraman had set up a space for rappelling—and looked out at the tree line that surrounded them. From up high, she could see the tops of the tallest bent trees, but from her angle, they seemed as straight as Tristan always advertised himself to be. She squinted at the sparse patches of green that clung to some of the branches, while others seemed to have dropped their leaves.

"Make up your damn mind," she muttered. "Are you evergreen or not?" She shivered in the autumn chill.

Tatum gathered up the cords, which were secured at the roof end around a chimney flushing, and dropped the loose end down the side of the manor. He moved back and forth from preparing the rappels to helping people through the tiny door. Linda leaned back as much as she could against an area of exposed fascia and watched as the man helped pull Tristan through. Charity sat curled in a ball in a tight corner of roof, but Linda didn't want to bother her after she'd raced up the stairs away from Linda.

"Well, isn't this a sight!" Tristan said as he unfolded himself and peered out at the tree line.

"It's gorgeous!" Marion said and did a little jump. Her foot slipped out from under her. She flew forward, catching herself on the flat, dry area of roof. Tristan rushed to her side and wrapped his arm around her waist.

"It's slippery," the cameraman said in a monotone, testing the cords.

"You know she could sue the network if she got injured," Tristan said.

"She cannot," the cameraman said. "These ladies signed waivers."

Linda pushed herself off the fascia and took her first glance down the side of the manor. It was a long way.

"Now, why would you ladies go and do a thing like that?" Tristan said.

"To date you," Sabrina said. "We're here for you, Tristan."

"Camera isn't even on you," the cameraman said. "No need to bullshit."

Linda's gaze darted to Charity. She was shaking even worse than before.

The cameraman spoke into his walkie talkie. "Should I make the scared one go first, Deja?"

The static crackled.

"Yeah, I'm down," Linda said, stepping forward. She'd take a page from Charity's book and get it over with while doing Charity a favor. Maybe Charity would throw her one more minuscule bone before the show was finished. Linda presented herself, arms extended.

"Tie me up!" she said.

"Color me impressed," Tristan drawled. "Let's go, Linda! So, you got a little sense of adventure."

"I sure do!" Linda put her hands on her hips.

The cameraman scurried behind the camera. "I'm going to need you two to do all of that over again."

LINDA AND TRISTAN repeated their lines word-for-word, then the cameraman strapped them up and set them loose. They perched on the edge of the roof, feet teetering half-on, half-off, waiting for the cameraman's signal.

"Would have been nice if they had someone here for like, safety, or someone who knows what they're doing when it comes to rappelling," Linda said.

"That would cost too much," Tristan said.

"Don't I know it."

"Hey!" the cameraman said. "No talking like that. You'll fuck with the audio track. Don't make me do more edits than I have to." He positioned himself to film downward as they went, but he'd also suited them up with GoPros for some close-up, adventure-style shots. "Also, I'm a certified rock climber, I'll have you know."

"Okay, okay!" Tristan said. "Can we get this rolling? We're kind of hanging off the building here."

The cameraman explained what they needed to do once the shoot began. Then he grinned and held up his fingers: three, two, one. *Action*, he mouthed, and Tristan looked over at Linda. "You ready for this?"

Linda took a glance down the building at the ground so far below. Deja waited at the base of the manor, hidden in the shadow of a door's arch.

"I'm not going to get any readier!" Linda said.

"Slow and steady," Tristan said, and he took his first shaky step down the stone that formed his wall, the outside of the stairwell they'd climbed to get to the roof. Linda found her footing against the wood paneling that formed the bulk of the manor's exterior. Her foot pressed into the wall, and it seemed to flex inward like memory foam. She shrieked as she took a hurried next step, hoping to bypass the rotten spot, but her foot landed once more in a soft spot. She hurried down three more steps, giving herself too much slack on the strap that held her steady, and she lost herself in the momentum, falling, her legs struggling to catch up, until they slipped and missed the wall, and she hung suspended in the rope, spinning around to face the forest.

"Are you okay?" She heard Tristan's harried voice to her left. "Linda! Are you all right?"

Linda closed her eyes and breathed, letting herself be cradled by the straps. "I'm okay," she whispered. When she opened her eyes, she glanced below. Deja hadn't stepped out of the shadow, but even through the gloom, Linda thought she could see the white of smiling teeth in her face.

"Are you sure you're okay?" Tristan asked. "What happened?"

Linda shivered while recalling the sensation of her foot sinking into soft wood. As her body spun to face the wall, she inspected the wood paneling. It looked no different than it should, and as she pressed her hand into it, it didn't seem to flex.

"Nothing," Linda said. "Lost my footing. That's all."

She rappelled to the closest window and grabbed hold of the ledge to slow her spinning. She put her feet once more onto the wall. This time, they didn't sink. Tristan followed, keeping a careful eye on her. His concern was obnoxious. She sighed as she felt her world return to normalcy—or as normal as it had been of late, anyway. She closed her eyes and inhaled, and when she opened them again, she saw something move behind the window glass.

She looked more intensely, but the glass was dirtied on both sides. She swiped with her hand at the exterior, and the scene inside became marginally more evident: the room was full of houseplants, their leaves overgrown to form a baby canopy. The nursery looked peaceful, like a place she'd enjoy exploring when she got a moment alone.

"Is something the matter?" Tristan asked. "You look haunted."

I've always been haunted, she should have said. It would have made for good TV, and it was true. But in that moment, she didn't want to play along with the broken idea Deja had of her, the idea that Tristan had clung to: a woman in need of fixing.

"I'm fine," she said—and she made her eager way down to the bottom.

SHE PEERED UP as Tristan re-emerged onto the rooftop. As the Groom, he had to climb the stairs a total of four times. Linda didn't envy him. Instead, she smirked to watch him tiring from the repeated exertion. He was usually so fit, so up for anything, but when he landed at the bottom of the manor with Sabrina, then Marion in tow, his hair was stuck with sweat to his forehead, and little bags had formed under his eyes.

He tried to smile at Linda as he passed her once more to disappear inside to the stairs, but his mouth faltered. It was almost endearing.

Sabrina planted herself beside Linda as they peered up for Tristan's final descent.

"How's Charity?" Linda asked. "Anymore ready than before?"

"Not so much," Sabrina said. "But she said she's determined to do it."

Sabrina crossed her arms over her chest, then glanced at Linda before returning her gaze to the roof. "What happened?"

"What do you mean?"

"I was watching, and you tripped or something? You sounded freaked."

Linda scowled. "I lost my footing, slipped on some moss or something. The wall was super soft." She forced herself to smile. "No biggie."

Sabrina's mouth fell open. "Those bastards didn't."

"Who? What?"

Sabrina clicked the OFF button on her mic, then leaned in and gestured at Linda to do the same while Deja's back was turned. Linda clicked hers off.

"I found this room," Sabrina whispered. "And I saw a woman step out of the wall! I thought it was real…"

"Were you on drugs?"

"Linda. You know I don't. Don't interrupt me."

"Sorry," Linda said. "Go on."

"Anyway, I freaked the fuck out, but then I explored the hall and found this secret hallway. They hid it behind some crap fake door. When I walked back there, I found a spot where producers could stand and make impressions in this soft material they replaced the wall with."

Linda's stomach twisted. The implication went beyond the manipulation Linda had come to expect from the show.

"So, they really are planning on messing with us?"

"Not planning to. They're already doing it."

"And you're sure you weren't on drugs?"

"Linda, I swear to G—"

Deja stuck her face between them.

"You can gossip with your mics on," she said. "Turning them off is against the rules. You both know that."

Linda pressed hers back on as fast as she could. "Accident," she rushed to say.

"Don't let it happen again."

Deja stared at Sabrina until she, too, flipped hers on, then beckoned Linda to follow her. When Linda stepped away, Deja handed her a wireless earpiece.

"I talked to Tristan, and he said that sometimes you say weird things when you're together," she said.

"Weird things?" Linda scoffed. "Weirder than telling us he needs a woman who can handle ghosts?"

When Deja shrugged, her shoulders cracked. "I'm only trying to help you win."

Linda turned her lip up at the edge. Deja knew she wasn't there for Tristan, but Linda wasn't about to let Deja catch her on camera saying it. "What are you saying I need to do?" she asked.

Deja reached into her pocket and pulled out a wireless ear piece. "Keep this in today, so I can guide you. I know what he likes, so I can help."

"And, bonus, you can reprimand me when I do things like turn off my mic?"

"That, too."

Linda took the ear piece and shoved it in. "Happy?"

Deja spoke into her microphone, producing a terrible echo of her voice. "Very."

As Linda rejoined Sabrina, her mind buzzed. They were manipulating them, sure. Linda had been dealing with manipulation during the entire process. But goading Sabrina to call Marion a bitch, then recording it, was worlds different than what Deja was trying to do to Linda. They had a goddamn contract. Wasn't that worth something?

Linda fingered the piece in her ear. She'd have to be more careful than ever. She'd have to live inside her part: the cool, unassuming Linda who wanted nothing more than love. She'd have to swallow every ounce of anger as though it were a glass of top-shelf Glenlivet, aged and smoky on her tongue.

THE TWO WOMEN watched in silence as Tristan coaxed Charity to the edge. He helped her settle herself and prepare to rappel, and even from below, Linda could tell how fiercely she gripped the strap.

Charity made her first few steps, then screamed as her strap loosened too quickly. Rather than tighten it, she pulled the wrong way, sending herself flailing to the ground. She let out a yelp as her foot twisted against the manor wall. Sabrina rushed to her first, hands extended to catch her as she fell. Sabrina eased Charity to sit on the ground. Linda stood off to the side, unsure how the cameras would want her to act.

"You okay?" Sabrina said.

Deja glanced up at the cameraman on the roof. He gave a thumbs-up to signify he did indeed get a shot of the fall from above. Satisfied, Deja moved to Charity's side. "What's the damage?" she said as Charity flexed her foot back and forth.

Tristan touched down as Charity waved Deja away. "I'm fine enough," Charity said.

"Seems like a sprain," Sabrina said. "Should be okay with a little rest, but it'll be vulnerable to further injury. She shouldn't re-do the rappelling, or do any more extreme sports." Sabrina shot Deja a dirty look. "Charity, does it hurt to move it?"

"Only a little." Charity moved the ankle in a circle. "I'll be okay."

Sabrina looked up at Deja while Linda wrung her hands. "Do we have an ankle brace?"

"Oh, sure." Deja placed her hands on her hips. "In the full-service medical facility."

"An ACE bandage then? And maybe a small length of metal to stabilize?" Sabrina said.

"Do you need me to get something?" Linda asked, but her voice was lost to the air. Deja nodded to Sabrina and called into her walkie talkie for assistance. Linda's eyebrows drew together, flexing her own feet in her shoes, wincing at the pain Charity must feel. It wasn't like her to feel someone else's pain. The sensation surprised her, and her mouth went dry as she struggled to find her lines.

"This will look great in my heels," Charity said.

"No heels," Sabrina said. "Flats only—and I doubt you'll be able to get into those."

"I was kidding," Charity said. "Everyone knows I'm going home tonight anyway."

Tristan frowned, then leaned into Charity's already crowded space. "Don't say that."

"Yes, don't say that," Deja said.

"Wait, we aren't going to do the elimination when Charity is injured, are we?" Linda spoke loudly this time, determined to gather an answer, any answer. That old heart was rising again into her chest, and she clenched her fists as she failed to let it go.

"You bet we are," Deja said. "We're on a schedule here, Meadows."

"But she can't stand!"

Deja shrugged. "Then she'll sit."

"I'm right here," Charity said as she held out her hand for Sabrina to help her up. She steadied herself on her feet. "And I can stand fine."

"Careful," Sabrina said. "You don't want to injure it more."

"Help me inside," Charity said. "You have filming to do out here."

Sabrina nodded at Linda, Marion, and Tristan, before helping Charity to hobble inside the manor, away from the camera's prying lenses. Tristan pulled his GoPro off his forehead and tossed it at Deja's feet.

"What is your problem?" Deja said.

"I'm tired of performing," he said.

"You're being paid to be here," Deja said. "You agreed to perform for us."

Tristan glanced over at Marion, tossing his head as the cords of his neck bulged. He wove one hand through his hair, gripping it at the root, silent as he waited for Marion to back him up.

Instead, she buried her hands into her pockets. "She's right."

Tristan's mouth opened and closed as his posture stiffened. He snatched the microphone from his chest and threw it into the dirt, his breath forceful as he turned from them.

Linda watched the scene unfold and understood at once: Tristan and Marion were fucking. As her head went light, she laughed at the fact that she didn't notice before now.

"What's funny?" Tristan asked, kicking dirt over the microphone like a child throwing a fit. "Why is everyone always laughing at me?"

"Oh, I don't even know why I care." As Linda spoke, her hands traveled to her mouth, tracing her lips as they moved free from the script. Even as she tucked her elbows into her sides, she tightened her fists, her knees shaking as fear and anger warred inside her.

"Care about what?" Marion said, moving toward Tristan as though he might protect her from the tension that hung in the air.

"That you're going to win. That this thing is rigged. That you're already together in every sense of the word." Linda leaned on this last phrase, letting it form an innuendo. "Why are we, the others, here?"

"Hey, hey." Tristan stepped forward, palm outstretched, and Marion pouted as their shades uncrossed on the ground. He placed one hand on Linda's shoulder, but his grip was tighter than usual, his knuckles white. "It's not rigged. I care about you. My affection for all y'all girls is different, sure, but my attraction to you is no less strong than my attraction to the other ladies here."

When Linda shook her head, her hair slapped against her cheeks. It wasn't his lack of affection that irked her. When she studied Tristan, she felt a whirlpool of emotions, but none of them made her want to press herself into him until she disappeared. Sabrina's eager hands healed wounds and deserved the simple comfort she sought in the country boy, and Charity must want Tristan if she stayed on this long And didn't she deserve whatever she longed for? What was making the vein on Linda's forehead pulse was concern for them, not herself. Linda hoped these two women could have everything they desired, but they were being set up for heartbreak, and with broken bones to boot.

"You don't even care about him!" Marion said, stepping forward in a cat-fight stance, hands on hips, head cocked in challenge.

"She's right. You don't give a shit about him, do you?" Deja said in Linda's ear.

"I do, too." Linda slid back into the game.

"Prove it," Deja said. "Tristan needs a woman who can fight for him."

Linda stood off against Marion and made a conscious decision to let down the gates that held back her rage. She cracked her knuckles. "You don't get to tell me who I do and don't care for!"

"You talk more to that fat nurse and the lesbo than you do to Tristan," she said.

"Excuse me?" And without thinking, Linda lunged forward, and in a single flash she remembered how good it felt to let fury take over. She pushed Marion backward, and Marion stumbled, landing on her ass in the patchy grass. She cried out. "Calm down!" But Linda was ready to do whatever she needed to do to shut the woman up.

Stepping between them, Tristan pushed against Linda with one outstretched hand. His force kept her back, and the distraction of his hand landing on her tit morphed her fury into twisted confusion. She moved away from him, repulsed by the display of masculinity and disappointed by his insistence that she calm.

Without another word, Linda turned on her heel, tossed the ear piece into the grass, and trudged back into the manor.

CHAPTER FIFTEEN

LINDA

LINDA FOUND SABRINA wrapping Charity's foot in a living room full of antique chaise lounges and couches with curved arms. She flopped into a dusty red chair as the gravity of her behavior settled over her. Leo rotated the camera, zooming in on her face. "You're not going home anymore," Linda said to Charity, her head lolling back, her neck stretching so long it felt like her air was restricted. "That honor is mine." As she said it, she felt bigger, longer, her reclining form insisting on its space like a lion in the sun-drenched savanna.

"Nah, it's me." Charity propped her jaw on her folded hand. "I guarantee it."

"Did you attack Marion?" Linda shifted her head back in line with her spine and took in her friends with the sides of her eyes. Charity touched Linda's arm as Sabrina whipped her head around. "Didn't think so."

Charity's mouth had been stuck in a grimace, but now her grin showed all her perfect teeth. "You didn't!"

Outside, Tristan's loud voice met its upper pitch as he yelled at Deja about *something safety something*. The others paused to eavesdrop, too.

"Shit, you might be going home," Sabrina said.

"You guys, no way. I bet if we went into the shrine room, my photograph would already be turned the fuck over and marked with that X." Charity shook her head, then winced at her foot. The two gestures were unrelated.

Linda frowned. "The shrine room?"

"You've seen the show, right?" Sabrina said.

"Of course," Linda said.

"The shrine room—the room with all our photographs lined up with candles, where Mr. Farmer's Tan decides which wifeys he wants to kick to the curb."

"Oh, the interview room?" Linda's stomach fluttered even as she barked a laugh. "Where the traveling shelf lives. Where the host and the groom chat."

"Uh-huh. That's the one." Standing, Sabrina offered her hand to Linda. "Let's have a look in the light of day, shall we?"

As Linda grabbed her hand, she was unsure whose was clammier. The palms slid against one another as Sabrina pulled her to her feet. Linda let go and wiped the sweat onto her pants.

"There's not a whole lot of that light-of-day stuff to go around in this place, though, is there?" Charity's crumpled body still pulsed against the faded room. "Are you coming?" Her breath caught as she spoke.

Charity moved her ankle in a circle, lips pursed. "I guess."

"I'd advise against it," Sabrina said.

"I take your advisement and raise you an *I don't care.*" When Charity began struggling to her feet, Linda rushed to help while Sabrina assisted from Charity's other side. Charity laughed at their concern, pushing them away. "Don't fuss over me! I'm okay. Seriously." She stuck out her foot and put a little weight on it. "It doesn't feel worse than it has before. I'll be fine."

Charity waved Leo in front of them. "A shot from the front seems advisable, yeah, cameraboy?"

He stood at attention and slid the camera from its standing rig. "I don't even know where you people are trying to go."

"We're going to the shrine room, aren't we?" Charity winked at Linda.

"Right, okay." He backed into the foyer, then stepped into a hall Linda hadn't noticed. Charity strode elegantly despite her injury, and time slowed as Linda followed behind, watching each gentle sway of Charity's hips. As they crossed the threshold into a hall, the wood flexed beneath them but didn't creak, creating an eerie quiet. They traveled in a line as the cameraman showed them the way without realizing they didn't know it already—through the narrow hall and to a small stairwell with five steps. He backed up until he was pressed into a doorway, then chewed his lip and lowered the camera.

"I need to readjust." He scooted along the wall and back down the stairs, aiming the lens at the women's backs as they ascended. The landing wasn't large enough for all three of them to stand, so Sabrina remained on the penultimate stair while Charity grabbed for the doorknob.

"Wait!" Leo yelled.

Linda jumped.

"What?" the women said at the same time.

"I want to get your reactions from the inside. Pretend to open the door, pause, then shut it."

Charity rolled her eyes, but she did as the man asked. Once she clicked the door shut again, he elbowed his way back through their throng. "Don't mind me, no need to move to let me through, I'm just the guy who makes this all happen for you, no biggie."

Charity grinned. "Feeling snarky today?"

"I hate the fucking woods," he said beneath his breath. "I didn't sign up for woods." As he pushed through the door, he flipped on a light and called out, "Action!"

The room looked like a funeral home with dark green wallpaper and two antique chairs set side by side in front of wood shelves lined with photographs of the season's contestants. The ones who had been sent home had X's drawn across their faces. Linda gravitated to them without realizing she was walking. She ran a finger down one of the X's and felt a pang for the girl, who had been so eager to please that she arrived at the mansion on the first night with several ears of corn strung together and placed on her head like she was a demented May Queen of the fields. If Linda were here for the right reasons, maybe she should have sacrificed herself to the elimination ceremony so that poor girl could stay.

Linda let her gaze settle on the middle rows, where the current contestants' photos sat amongst several flickering, battery-powered candles. She and Charity lined one shelf, while Sabrina and Marion took up another. Linda glanced back to see if anyone was watching her, but Charity peered at the wallpaper, inspecting a network of tiny lines. Blushing, Linda ran a finger down the glass of Charity's portrait, swallowing hard as she traced her chin and neck. Quickly, she pushed her photograph a couple of inches toward Charity's then joined the woman at the wall.

"What's up?" Linda folded her hands behind her back. It was unreasonable, impossible, but she needed to hide them, lest the evidence of her actions show on the tips of her fingers.

"It's just...someone drew all over this wallpaper." Charity reached out as though to touch the wall, then withdrew. "I wonder if some little brat got his hands on a pen and went wild."

Linda faked a laugh. It didn't look haphazard. The green design on the walls seemed like a map through the woods.

"Obsessed," Linda whispered.

"What, the tree people?" Charity said. "Yeah, I'd call them tree-huggers or something, but they seemed as obsessed with cutting them down as they did with depicting them all over the damn place." Charity waved her hand around to indicate the copious amounts of wood in the room, as it was in every room. "Should we do an interview?" Charity gestured to the two chairs set in front of an army of cameras. She fell back into one of the chairs and crossed her legs. "Do you think your future wife is here, Mr. Farmhand?" she said.

Linda eased herself into the other chair and made a contemplative hum. "I do. I think she's in this room, in fact."

Charity leaned forward and gasped. "Is it...Sabrina?"

"No."

"It's Leo!"

Leo scowled as Linda shook her head.

"Oh!" Charity's cheeks went bright red, but she raised her eyebrows in mock emotion. "It's the ghost!"

One of the photographs fell over. Linda jumped and shrieked as the glass shattered all over the floor. Once she realized the source of the sound, she checked on Charity, who had drawn her feet into her chest and curled into herself. Across the room, Sabrina stood frozen beside the altar of photographs.

"My bad." Sabrina grabbed another frame and bent down, trying to sweep the glass into a single pile with it.

"Goddamn you," Leo mumbled. "Quit making a mess! You're not even supposed to be in here."

"Then why'd you let us in?" Sabrina said.

"Good TV," he said. "Duh."

Linda shivered as she calmed. "It's okay."

As Charity stood, she scrunched up her face. "What else can we get into here? It's my last night. I want to go wild!"

She ran, leaping over the broken glass pile and a shocked Sabrina, and stopped before a big metal cabinet. It was the only metal furniture Linda had seen in the whole manor. Charity pulled open a drawer. "Ooo," she said. "A blast from the more recent past!" She pulled out a black VHS and held it aloft, then started to open another drawer.

"Hey, stop it," Leo leaned over his camera, his voice pitching. "You're not supposed to go through that. Not even crew goes through that stuff. It's in our contracts and everything. Belongs to the previous owners of the manor, okay? Please. Charity—please!"

"Well!" Charity finally turned and acknowledged him. "Give me something better."

"God, you're impossible." Leo pointed at a laptop connected to a projector aimed at a white wall. "Go through the dailies. I don't care."

Charity dropped open her mouth and placed her hand across her chest. "Well, I never!" She mocked Marion's accent.

"You wouldn't." Sabrina stood from the glass wreckage and inched closer to Linda and Charity. Linda's stomach jumped at the idea that she might see herself on the screen in all her reality TV glory. She'd lain awake at night re-imagining herself, making up the comments that her fans might leave her once they watched the show. Deja had failed to make her crack, excepting the single incident with Marion today, and the camera would show Linda as a caricature, a woman with a story plain and straightforward, none of those confusing layers that threatened to peel away at any moment. Another person. Warm, happy. In love. Not only would the show erase her sticky past from the endless search results that defined her, but she would be remade within those results: one of the final women on *The Groom*. An exalted position. A darling of this modern world.

"Hurry up before I get Deja in here," Leo said.

Charity bounced her shoulders as she shifted to the laptop. She fiddled with the buttons until she figured out how to project the film onto the wall. Linda imagined Deja and the other two producers reviewing film stuffed in the little interview room, picking apart their contestants as they searched for areas of weakness to exploit, mistakes to call back to. Again, Charity sunk into the chair beside Linda and offered her an imaginary bag of popcorn. Linda smirked, her head spinning at the attention as she faked taking it from her. She liked chopping-block Charity, and a brief pang cut through the pleasant fog: she might have to say goodbye, one way or another, tonight.

On screen, Tristan held hands with Sabrina at a little table in the back of the mansion. Sabrina's face was soft with affection. A few scenes from their dates played out: he'd taken her parasailing, then tight-rope walking between two skyscrapers. Linda noted the moment before each feat that Sabrina puffed out her chest, the moment she dropped fear from her repertoire. The same look Linda saw when Sabrina rushed to Charity's rescue. Sabrina was demure, but she had something strong-willed inside her that always threatened to release.

The next scenes showed Deja and Tristan outside of what looked like a medical building.

"She isn't going to want to do this," he whispered.

"She doesn't have a choice, lover boy." Deja patted him on his broad shoulder. "Go meet your lady, Mr. Big Balls in Cowtown."

Charity guffawed, but Linda's attention was on Sabrina, who stood rapt as she watched herself, gaze glittering with the film's reflection.

"I look like I love him," Sabrina said as the TV version of her rushed into his arms. "What are we doing today?" her televised self said.

"I thought you could show me what you're made of!"

The lovebirds entered the nondescript building, and TV-Sabrina's eyes widened as she realized what she was in for. He'd brought her to a butcher.

"What the shit?" Charity revisited her earlier crouched-up posture, gathering her whole body into the chair, her knees pulled against her chest. "What the actual fuck?"

Slabs of meat hung from the ceiling, and TV-Sabrina shivered as she stepped into the room.

"Fast-forward, please," the real Sabrina said, cringing away from the images.

"What is this? What kind of season are we on?" Curio shops, butchers, and haunted manors. *The Groom* seemed to have gone off the rails, and Linda didn't want it to take her down with it. She tugged at her shirt not because the room was hot—it was—but because she was suddenly feeling con- strained. "You never told me about this."

"It was weird, okay?" Sabrina covered her eyes. "They wanted us to pick a pig and then cook it over a pit. Stuff its mouth with an apple."

"And did you?" Linda said.

"Well…yeah…"

"And you like this sick fuck?" Charity said.

"He grew up on a farm. His parents still run it. I'll have to get used to livestock if I want to be with him." Sabrina's voice went small.

Charity poked her finger into the keyboard to fast-forward.

As Linda watched, too intrigued to look away, the camera remained zoomed-in not on Sabrina's face while she chose her meal, not on Tristan's while he struggled not to gag, but on the carcass as the butcher cut her choice down for them. Maybe Deja knew what she was doing. The wet slap sound of the pig's body flopping onto the floor evoked a sick satisfaction.

Finally, Charity reached the end of the recorded date and let the dailies resume. It was more of Sabrina, so Charity clicked away to search through the files for someone else. She found the file labeled LINDA and pulled it up.

Linda leaned forward in her chair. She expected to see lingering glances and sweet, sloppy kisses. She expected to see herself fawning over Tristan while he offered drawled-out platitudes in return. She didn't expect to see shot after shot of her face, lost in fevered stares . She watched as the lens caught her eyeing Marion with bared teeth.

"Wow, you hate her," Charity said.

"But I don't..."

The dailies cycled through more shots of the veins on Linda's neck pulsing as Linda leered at Marion, at Deja, at every minor inconvenience. In one scene, she dropped a glass on the kitchen floor, and they cut the footage to show Marion cutting her foot on a shard, followed by Linda laughing at her bleeding foot.

"That's not how that went..." Linda muttered as bile rose into the back of her throat, leaving a sour taste on her tongue. "I was laughing at a joke she made. She was being a good sport."

In another scene, Linda narrowed her eyes at the back of Tristan's head as he sauntered in front of her into a restaurant.

"The sun was in my eyes," Linda said. She gulped a breath as panic tremored through her. She rubbed her hands over her legs, wiping the sweat across the goosebumps rising up over her skin. She wasn't that person, but the proof was recorded. She'd made those faces.

Charity shifted uneasily in her seat.

"Keep going," Linda whispered.

"Are you sure?" Charity asked.

"Yes."

Charity fast-forwarded from scene to scene: Linda clinking glasses and grinning when women were eliminated; scenes cut together to make Linda look gleeful at their failure; Linda teasing Tristan, with his laughing response chopped off so it looked like a serious insult; Linda in the interview room, shaking as Deja asked her about her past.

"I don't want to talk about that," Linda said, referring to her meltdown on screen. That one was uncut, a brutal truth.

"They make you look like a psycho," Sabrina said, a nervous edge to her voice.

"Is that who I am?" Her stomach twisted. She didn't feel like a psycho, not here, not in this room beside Charity, even if outside of the manor she may have wondered from time to time if she held the capacity for evil. But worse, Deja had promised Linda she would emerge from the other side of this with a clean slate. The dailies were anything but clean. She felt her mouth mirroring the grimace projected on the wall— those veins, like some supervillain, popping.

Sabrina rested her hands on Linda's shoulders. "Of course not, sweetie." But her hands squeezed too hard, digging into the tender muscle.

They watched Deja sit Linda down for an interview and ask her one prying question after the next. She mentioned Linda's family whenever possible. *Your father, your father,* she said, until Linda shut down and refused to answer. "You said you'd make that go away," Linda hissed on camera.

"Turn it off," Linda said to Charity. She stood and reached to exit out of the video herself. "I don't want to see anymore of me."

"What happened with your father?" Sabrina said.

Linda felt a different haze come over her. It was the one she lived inside as a kid, the one composed of tobacco smoke. The one that made her feel like some other person trapped inside her child body. "My father died when I was young," she said, but it was like another person speaking.

Charity frowned. "It's like she's trying to get you to break. Like she wants you to lose it."

"Kind of like you lost it today," Sabrina said.

Linda's chest ached. They were right, and she'd done what Deja had wanted.

"What did Deja promise you?" Sabrina narrowed her eyes.

"Nothing! I was frustrated with her, that's all." She wrung her hands in her lap.

"I mean, she promised me stuff, too," Sabrina said. "I think that's how they get you."

"We'll tell if you'll tell," Charity said.

Linda tried to keep her voice steady. "She promised me the same kinds of things she promised you, I imagine. Money. Fame. Glory. That she'd show my good side."

"Fine, keep your lips zipped tight then." Charity clicked into a folder titled MARION, opening something new. The three women gasped in chorus. On screen, Tristan and Marion writhed in the half-dark of a bedroom. It wasn't the manor.

"That hussy!" Charity laughed. Linda tried to laugh, too, but her mind was on her own footage, and something about the intimacy of the on-screen couple's connection paired with the nakedness of the camera on them stirred pity in her.

"He slept with her, too?" Sabrina's voice was tiny, her face fallen.

"*Too?*" Charity said.

"You shouldn't worry so much about so-called infidelity," Leo said. "Becca, Jazz, and I don't worry about any of that."

Linda ignored Leo and stared at the screen until Charity turned it off, and only then did Linda realize the implication. Only then did she shake herself out of her fog, turn, and place a hand on her friend's hand. Sabrina's bottom lip trembled while Linda froze with indecision. She didn't know the script here, and the cameras were still rolling. Was she supposed to act angry or understanding? She looked to Leo, a question in her eyes, but he didn't notice. Instead, he grinned at the prospect of drama, a fight, a raise when he got the perfect shots. He aimed his camera at Linda's face in that moment, and later, the dailies would register her disgust.

CHAPTER SIXTEEN

LINDA

SOME OF THE contestants longed for a career as a reality star, increased followers on their social media accounts, a chance at being The Bride when that show's next season rolled around. In the video Deja made her send in, Linda had told the other producers that she curated her own social media account, where she posted photographs of plants and landscaping techniques for her husband's business, but she found no pleasure in it. She gained followers, and it meant nothing to her, the way her marriage had meant nothing to her, the way losing her virginity meant nothing, the way every big event since middle school meant nothing to her, at all.

But she wanted to be seen by the masses, to be judged decent. She wanted to hear the words from tabloids that she never heard from her mother: *You're a good person. What happened to you wasn't your fault.*

When Sabrina ran from the shrine room, giving her an out, Linda seized the moment. As Leo followed after, trying to catch the meltdown, Linda ambled, dazed, in the other direction.

"Where are you going?" Charity called after her, but Linda needed to be alone. It was an urge as simple as breathing.

To locate any degree of privacy, she'd have to open doors the producers demanded remain closed. She felt her way in the half-light, finally choosing a door in the hall outside the parlor. It led to yet another hall that stretched unlit into the distance, devoid of shadows. Linda took her first tentative step inside.

The floor beneath felt knotted. She wondered if she might be walking to the servants' quarters, an area of the manor that the owners had perhaps spent less money on, leaving the floors uneven. Linda scoffed. She was tiring of being beholden to rich people. Or even just people who hadn't made the same terrible decisions she had.

AFTER GRADUATION, SHE'D needed to get as far away from her foster family as possible, so she signed up for her first credit card on her eighteenth birthday, checked herself into a hotel, and drained the mini bar while she slept in a room all her own, for the first time in her life. It was intoxicating, to feel safe and unbothered, and when she woke the next morning, she thought she might finally be on the road to happiness.

After she maxed out the first card on nights at the hotel and meals ordered in, she sought out waiting jobs. Her first was at a steakhouse, where she served people in fancy suits, on dates and for business dinners. She felt okay as she ferried top-shelf whiskey to their tables, like she might become a useful member of society, until her first drunk and irate customer went off on her over a wrong order. Instead of speaking calmly to the man, like her supervisor had taught her, she shrunk to the floor as her body shook and her vision blurred. Her supervisor rushed in, soothed the man with freebies and promises to do better, then led Linda into the backroom.

Linda told her supervisor it would never happen again.

It happened again, and Linda found herself fired.

She tried other jobs: warehouse gigs, where panic overtook her at any hint of pressure; retail, where the customers' anger seemed fiercer than the drunk men at the steakhouse; and administrative work, where frequent absences made her an unlikely candidate for retention. Finally, she relied on credit alone, racking up one hundred thousand dollars of debt before she met her ex-husband.

He met her on a bad day as she carried a box of personal belongings from the real estate office that had canned her. He ran into her on the street, paying attention to his phone instead of the sidewalk. He helped her pick up the meager items the box contained: a box of business cards, a couple books, a jar of peanuts, and a hyacinth in a terracotta pot.

"My favorite flower," he said as he scooped dirt back into the pot.

"It was ugly when I bought it, but then the flowers sprung free, and I was smitten," Linda said as sweat gathered under her armpits.

He smiled. He wasn't a pretty man, and he was nothing like her father, who had been big and round, with jet black hair and a clean-shaven face. The man who smiled at her was small, with angular features and a red beard to his chest. His long red hair was braided down his back. When he offered to buy her a cup of coffee, she agreed.

At dinner, she told him about her troubles with employment. He was easy to talk to, and he sympathized with her inability to keep a job and the looming weight of her monstrous debt.

"I might have the perfect job for you," he said. "No angry customers. No rush jobs. Come work for me at my landscaping firm." He slid a waxy postcard across the table.

"Landscaping?"

"I do all the designing, but you can help me with installation. You'll work with plants, get physical activity. Trust me. My other employees are relaxed as hell, sometimes too much." He laughed. "But I swear: as your boss, I'll never yell at you."

Linda had no other choice. She took the job. She let herself fall into the hard work, and she found a surprising amount of peace handling roots, planting flowers, digging holes for trees, laying grass. She enjoyed the way the plants she tended didn't care about her credit score or her past, and for a little while, she felt that old feeling return—she might be on the journey to happiness.

Her new relationship with him didn't hurt, the flooding of all those love chemicals that left her in an ecstatic daze.

For the first year of their life together, Linda thought her ex was non-judgmental. She told him everything, *everything*. He soothed her worries, reassured her he loved her, and then proposed to her.

They were married for four years. Each year, he pulled farther away. Finally, he admitted she wasn't the woman he thought she was. She was too cold, he said, and sometimes, she got this look in her eye that scared him.

The one thing she never told him was it scared her, too.

And Deja had caught it on camera, again and again, and turned it into a story.

LINDA'S STOMACH TURNED with rage. Deja had sworn to show her in a positive light, to not only wipe clean her slate but to help her build a new reputation. Linda wanted to confront her, to quit, to tear things apart, to hurt her, but that would only give Deja more fodder for the villain narrative she had constructed. So, Linda walked, hoping one of her steps would slow her speeding pulse.

As Linda arrived at the first door, she expected to find a servant's bedroom on the other side. But when she opened the door, she found a room full of sticks. She could hardly see into it. She reached one hand inside and felt the closest branch. It was slick, like the trees in the orchard. Someone had filled the room full of wood, cut from outside. The room reeked of rot, like mold on an old trunk. She sneezed.

Linda tried to adjust to the dark, but she couldn't make out the contents of the room beyond the ocean of branches sticking up in every direction, as tall as the ceiling. She shut the door and moved on.

The next room was also full of sticks piled to the ceiling—and so was the next, and the next. Linda's knees shook as she stood in front of the fifth and final door. She opened it. It was full of sticks. They were all the same. She turned and sprinted back down the hall, shut the door behind her. She leaned against the door and wheezed.

Even if ghosts didn't haunt the eerie manor, it was haunted by the memory of a family who didn't behave as other people behaved. Linda understood that kind of family. It didn't feel safe, but it felt familiar, and there was a comfort in that. She stretched, letting her shoulders pop as she lifted them above her head, and when she brought them back to the floor, they were once more clenched into fists.

Her goal hadn't changed: she would rise above and refuse to give Deja the breakdown she hoped for. She sat there until her nails dug into her palms hard enough to leave little half-moons of blood, then finally let her fingers uncurl. *She wouldn't give in*, she repeated. *She wouldn't.*

CHAPTER SEVENTEEN

SABRINA

AFTER SEEING TRISTAN rolling around with Marion on video, Sabrina rushed from the shrine room, aware of the way her hair blew behind her, a cinematic touch she wasn't unhappy about, even if she was running too quickly for the single cameraman to follow. As her feet pounded the floor, the house moaned in response. She wasn't sure where she was headed, only that it was away from the video playing against the wall. Away from her friend. How had she missed the signs that Linda was the villain? Maybe it was editing magic, or maybe the woman she had trusted held inside her a darkness that came out only when Sabrina wasn't looking. Maybe the man she had trusted was a slut.

She broke into the silent room near the parlor, the one with the electric lights that buzzed overhead. She was less scared of seeing that form in the walls again than she was of her own mind feeding her false information. Her sister had told her, over and over, that she was a terrible judge of character. Why couldn't her sister be here with her? Sabrina needed Morgan to advise her. She needed Morgan to tell her what to do.

As she fell to her knees in the middle of the floor, she let herself cry. She had thought that sleeping with him meant she was his number-one, that he was most likely to choose her at show's end, but he had chosen Marion, too. Maybe Sabrina was the exotic second place.

The lights flickered. Sabrina ignored it. She lay on the hard floor and recalled the soft touch of Tristan's hands on her shoulders, his big hands massaging her when she needed it most. She'd been an idiot. Worse, she'd branded herself as one of the slutty ones.

Suddenly, hands closed around the edge of her shoulders. She screamed as she struggled away.

"Sabrina, it's me," Tristan said. He sat crouched on the floor, his hand suspended in the air where he had groped her a moment prior.

"What are you doing here?" she spat out.

"I heard crying again," he said. "Has it been you the whole time? Since we got here?"

"You think so little of me?"

"Crying isn't weakness," he said. "What's so wrong that you've been sobbing every night?"

Sabrina screwed up her forehead. "I haven't been crying every night. Just now."

Tristan chewed his lip. "And what has you so sad right now?"

Sabrina folded her arms. "You."

"Me? What did I do?"

"Slept with Marion." Sabrina swallowed hard.

"What? How—" Tristan stuttered. "Why do you think that?"

"I saw it, Tristan. In the footage."

Sighing, Tristan stood. He held his hand to her, but she refused to take it.

"I saw you. I thought I had a chance of winning, but Deja was right, wasn't she? I'm here to be drama fodder."

Tristan stroked his chin. It wasn't a typical gesture for him. "Yeah. I did sleep with Marion." He checked the room for cameras. Sabrina wondered how he was alone. "You have to understand, I can't choose a wife without knowing if we're compatible in bed. So, yes, I slept with you, and I slept with Marion, but it's because I know it's going to come down between you two. Not because I've already chosen her."

Sabrina's stomach twisted. He seemed genuine.

"No modern man in his right mind is going to choose a wife without sleeping with her first. That would be crazy, Sabrina. Don't you think?"

"Sex is important to you," she said.

"Duh," he said. "It's important to you, too. I've seen it. You're as sexual as I am." A boyish grin spread across his face. "Admit it." His voice was strong, dominant. Her cheeks grew warm. "It is," she admitted.

"Then what's the problem here?" He offered his hand again.

This time, she took it, letting his fingers trap hers. "Nothing," she said, and she meant it. Her anger, her jealousy—they had faded the instant he told her she was a serious contender. "So, you really like me?"

"Sabrina, I'm falling in love with you." When she rose to her feet, he clamped his hands once more on her shoulders, forcing her to remain still as his eyes bored into her. "You're a smart girl. Surely, you know that."

"I don't," she whispered.

"Then you don't know men as well as you think you do."

He pulled her to him, his lips catching hers in a feverish embrace. As he forced his tongue into her mouth, she yielded to his strength. Holding her against him, she felt like he might be her fate, after all.

When the lights flickered again, he pulled back.

"What's with this room?" he said.

"You haven't seen anything," she said, then took his hand in hers. "Let me show you something wild." She tugged him through the hall to the secret door, then through the hidden hallway to the crawlspace.

"Is this wise?" he asked as he peered into the sandy ground. "Haunted house and all?"

"It's tricks," she said. "Come on."

He raised an eyebrow, but he followed her nonetheless down the ladder, then crawled behind her as she made her way up through the musky air to the platform where the producers made their spooky magic. When they reached it, they both stood up, and she explained the vision she had seen of the woman stepping out of the wall. Tristan ran his fingers up and down the squishy surface.

"Holy shit," he said. "This looks like wood, doesn't it?"

"Hollywood and its illusions," she said, and they shared the laugh of two flyover-state people who had been taught not to trust the coasts.

"I wonder if there's anyone in there now," he said.

"Probably not. I don't think anyone else has discovered it yet."

Tristan smirked. "But I wonder... If someone were in there, what would they see happening between us?"

He pushed her back into the wall, and it contoured to her body like a foam mattress, wrapping around her curves. She pressed the palm of her hand into it to steady herself, but Tristan wrapped his arm around her waist, alleviating the need. He bent his head and nipped at her neck with his teeth. When she let out a yelp, he bit harder.

"You like that," he said, and she moaned in agreement, then bit her lip.

"What if someone hears us?" she said.

"They won't if I cover your mouth," he said.

"Do it."

He cupped his hand over her lips as he worked himself out of his pants, then yanked off her shorts and slid into her. She gasped against his life lines, his love lines, her hot breath warming his skin as he took her. Their bodies formed twisting, eager shapes in the wall, and Sabrina let her head roll back as Tristan commanded her to come.

She did as she was told.

HER SISTER HAD trained her in the art of submitting. She hired a man to come over and left him with Sabrina alone in the house they now shared as adults, where their father stayed secluded and sick in the back room.

"So, what are you wanting from me?" the man asked.

Sabrina shrugged. "I thought you were supposed to tell me."

His laugh was warm and gentle. "We have to talk it out first, doll, or else we won't know how far is too far."

She stepped toward him in a way that she suspected was seductive. "Do whatever you want to me."

He held up his hand. "Your limits?"

"None," she said, even as she shuddered to think of the things she'd seen in pornography. She didn't want to be difficult. Men didn't like difficult women.

"We'll start small," he said. "A little spanking. A little rope play. How does that sound?"

"You're the boss."

"If that's your fantasy, yeah, I am."

He stayed true to his word, and every time she let out a moan of discomfort, he stopped and eased up on his ties, or hit her a little softer. By the end of the session, her ass was red but not bleeding, and she wore no imprints of ropes in her skin.

"That's it?" she said.

"That's all I'll do for someone as green as you," he said. "But you call me if you need more."

He slid her his card, and the second he left, she handed it to her sister.

Over the next two years, her sister forbade her from having sex with anyone but the man she paid. She forbade her to set up her own meetings and told her she needed to learn obedience, that she needed to go as far as he would take her.

When Sabrina asked him to torture her, he refused. "You don't want that."

"How do you know?" she said, anger building in her belly. She pushed it down.

"Because, when you're uncomfortable, your shoulders tense. When you asked me that, they tensed bad. Pick something else."

After he tied her up for the hundredth time and fucked her until she could no longer take him, he drew her into his chest and hummed in her ear. She melted into him, and in her chest, she felt the first hot glow she'd ever felt. She knew its name, and she had memorized her script.

"I love you," she said.

The man groaned as he nudged beneath her chin. "You don't," he said. "You don't even know me."

But she was so sure. It was what was supposed to happen, falling for the man, and she lifted up off his chest and looked into his face and saw what she thought must be loneliness there. She felt the first tear fall, certain she was reciprocating the message in her gaze: *I'm lonely, too. We're two of a kind.*

He said nothing more as he pulled her back to his chest and stroked her hair, letting her cry into him. When she was drained, he moved out of her bed and knelt before her as she sat at the edge of her mattress. "This has to be our last meeting," he said. "I'll take my payment now, and I can refer you somewhere else, but I can't let my clients get attached."

As his hands folded into hers, she wanted to beg him, to apologize, to ask what she'd done wrong, to understand the way men and women worked, to feel like she was more than a lost girl who seemed to scare men away, but her sister's lessons had worked their magic: a good woman didn't pry. A good woman stood by while her man did what he thought was best for them both.

AFTER TRISTAN CAME, pulled out, and tossed the condom to the ground, they sat on the platform, where he tugged her into his lap and stroked her hair. It reminded her of the aftercare she'd received from the Dom, those gentle moments that formed her fantasies more often in older age than the whips and ties and paddles had. A slow peace settled over her.

"I knocked the breath out of you, huh?" Tristan said.

Sabrina laughed. "Guess you did."

They sat with the steady sound of Tristan's soft wheezing for a time before Tristan spoke once more, his words laced with concern. "Seriously, though, are you okay?"

Sabrina startled back awake. "I'm fine," she said. It was the truth. "Are you okay? Are you allergic to dust or something?"

"You're the one wheezing over here." Tristan laughed.

"That's not me." Sabrina said, a cold shiver running through her.

"Then who the hell is it?"

They stopped talking, listening for any hint of where the sound was coming from. Sabrina heard a little moan, and then more heavy breaths.

"Oh, my God," she said. "It's someone having sex."

"Who's having sex?" Tristan snorted. "Besides us."

Sabrina remembered Leo and his weird advice. "Apparently the whole crew." She giggled. "They're in a throuple or something."

"But there's four of them," Tristan said.

"Yeah, they're leaving Tatum out."

"Poor dude," Tristan said. "I'll be extra nice to him from now on."

As Tristan returned to stroking her hair, they listened to the feverish sounds of lovemaking, trying not to laugh.

CHAPTER EIGHTEEN

LINDA

WHEN LINDA RETURNED to her room, she found Charity waiting in the hallway, leaning against the wall. Linda hid her bloody hands behind her back as she approached.

"Where did you go?" Charity asked, her eyebrows drawing together.

"Cleared my head," Linda said, making her voice even and sure. "Sorry to run off."

"Do what you have to do."

The floor creaked, and they turned to see Sabrina padding down the hall toward them, her mascara smeared underneath her eyes.

"You okay, hon?" Charity asked Sabrina as she approached.

"Huh?" Sabrina said.

"Your mascara ran," Linda said.

Sabrina wiped her finger under her eye, then inspected the black smudge on the skin. "I was crying," she said. "I'm better now."

The ladies did as ladies do and escorted Sabrina to the bathroom to tidy her face and dress for the evening's elimination ceremony. The bathroom assigned to them was on the same hall as their bedrooms, and Linda and Sabrina had already littered the countertops with the contents of their makeup bags.

"What is all this stuff?" Charity picked up a bottle of finishing spray and shook it up.

Linda grabbed a sheet of makeup remover and wiped under Sabrina's eyes until all the mascara was gone. "It's poison," she said.

"I bet, you calculating Jezebel."

Sabrina chewed at a nail as she sunk onto the closed toilet seat. "This place makes me feel like I'm losing my mind."

"All women lose their minds when it comes to men," Charity said. "That's why I date women."

Sabrina frowned even as Linda's stomach jumped, her face flushing as her pits broke out in sudden sweat. It was an almost comical reaction. Linda would have laughed at herself if her best friend weren't hurting. "Why are you here if you date women?"

"I date men, too?" Charity said.

"Huh." Linda leaned into the mirror and swiped her eye-shadow brush across her eyelid.

"Hey, show me how to do that." Charity scooted next to Linda.

The heat inside her intensified. "Okay." She grabbed hold of Charity's shoulders and studied her face, hyperaware of how long she inspected each feature. "What color are you wearing tonight?"

"Blue. Suit."

"Then let's do a winged eye."

"Will that look okay on me?" Charity ran her finger along her hooded eye. "It won't get all smudged?"

"Nah. You have to make it tight and curve it a little more. Close your eyes." Charity closed her eyes, and Linda leaned into the canvas. Charity's skin was smooth and pale. Linda picked up Charity's hand by the wrist and studied the veins. As she traced her finger along a deep blue one, it pulsed under her touch.

"What are you doing?" Charity whispered.

"You have cool undertones," Linda said. "I have the shade of eyeshadow for you."

Linda opened her berry palette and grabbed a new brush, swiping it through the color. She added dark at the outer edge, light at the inner edge, with a brief shadow of rose. Then she took a black liner that matched Charity's hair and ran it a couple of times along her eyebrows. She uncapped the liquid liner and held it at the edge of Charity's eyes.

"Stay very still," she said even as her own hands trembled.

As she worked to give Charity her wings, she felt Charity's hot breath along the edge of her hand. Linda had missed out on middle school makeup sessions, on the giggling overnights her sister never invited her to. There had been no time for them by the time Linda was old enough, her mother too frail, her father already gone. Linda had spied on her sister and her friends, how they snuck to the liquor cabinet and took tiny sips of vodka, then rolled around on the floor, leaving lipstick stains on the carpet. Their father scolded them when he woke from his permanent place on their couch. One time, Linda's sister and her friends held a cut-out of a jack-o-lantern over his face and took photographs of him with his tongue lolling out. The whole house reverberated with his snoring. Once, Linda snuck in for a sip of her father's liquor, but the taste hurt her throat, and for the whole next day, she smelled it rising from inside her.

Charity's breath smelled like coffee and chocolate.

"All done." Linda finished the points of the wings.

Charity opened her eyes and peered into the mirror. "Wow." She ran a hand along her lips. "What about lipstick?"

"Right." Linda grabbed a deep pink, her favorite color. She would have to go with red on her own lips tonight, but it was worth it for the hint of smile on Charity's face. She uncapped the lipstick and ran it along Charity's mouth. When she finished, she wiped at an uneven line, slowly, letting her finger pull Charity's lip, revealing the smallest hint of the deep pink insides of her mouth.

On the toilet seat, Sabrina blew her nose. "Hate to interrupt," she said, and when she stood, she stood tall, resolve hardening her features. "You're hogging the mirror."

Sheepishly, Linda stepped back from Charity, and Linda noted from the corner of her eye the movement reflected, a loss as the two women separated, their shadows uncrossing from one another. She imagined them moving toward one another instead. Her chest blazed between the ribs, like the kiss of fire on an icy day. Then, she turned and left the bathroom to dress for the evening ahead.

DEJA WAITED ON the other side, her shoulders stiff as she tapped her foot. She waved a hand at Charity's face and shook her head.

"Nope," she said. "Take that shit off."

"I just put it on…" Charity said.

"Doesn't matter." Deja held up a clipboard like it explained something integral about the situation. "Marion isn't feeling well, so we can't do the elimination until later. We're going to do some reshoots instead, ladies, so get out your old clothes and your old looks." She mimed scrubbing her face. "That means no makeup for you, tomboy."

Charity rolled her eyes, but Deja ignored it.

"I need all three of you downstairs to reshoot the first-night dinner scene. Crew didn't get a single shot of any of y'all freaking out on the floor under the table." She shook her head. "And I want it. I want it badly."

No one moved.

"Go! I don't care how smelly your dirty dresses are. Pull them out, iron them out, and get down to your fake dinner. Now, ladies!"

Linda's heart picked up speed, and together, the remaining contestants rushed off to their separate rooms, scurrying like frightened rats.

BECCA WAITED FOR Linda in the dining room, where Linda was supposed to crawl under the table and look terrified. Becca gnawed at her bubble gum as she pointed to the spot where Linda should sprawl.

"Right there," she confirmed, snapping, as Linda crawled under. "We don't have all day here." Then Becca knelt and aimed the camera at Linda. "Fix your lapel mic. Your levels are low."

As Linda fiddled with her lapel, Becca blew a bubble and let it pop over her mouth. "Any day now!" she finally let out as she picked at the skin of bubblegum on her lips.

Linda paused. "What is wrong with you?"

"Listen, we're in a fucking haunted-house horror, and everyone knows the slutty ones and the Black ones and the gay ones die first." Becca made a circular motion with her hand, like the movement of a clock. "Let's get this finished already."

"I have so many questions," Linda said, but a brief reminder of the flexing floor that first night whispered through her. "First, you believe in the haunted thing?"

Becca shrugged. "I'm not the only one who keeps hearing the walls cry."

Linda lay on the ground like she had that first night, positioning herself to face Becca and the camera. "You did, too?" She fiddled with an old green bean under the table.

"Now, look freaked," Becca said.

Linda didn't have to try too hard. Becca was one of the producers, the Oz behind the curtain. If she was scared, then there was something to be scared of. She widened her eyes and tried to call up every noise-with-no-cause she'd heard over the past few days. As her hands shook, she forced the tremor to move through her until her whole body vibrated. Becca ordered her to make a few adjustments as she shot, then leaned back. "You're all great at this lying shit, you know. A bunch of actors."

"I'm not an actor." Linda scowled. These shows always hired an actor or two, in case the real-life contestants were duds for drama, but Linda never imagined someone might accuse her of being hired. Then again, Becca had to know who the real actors had been. It wouldn't have made sense for Deja to keep her in the dark. But a lot of things about Deja didn't make sense.

"We're done here," Becca said.

"Wait." Linda crawled out from beneath the table. "Are you the slutty one or the gay one?"

"Both, I guess."

"Who are you sleeping with?" Linda asked, trying to keep the conversation going in the hopes that it might keep her mind off the cornucopia of errant noises.

"Jazz, Leo. It's not just sex, though, despite what Deja says."

"Deja knows?"

"She found out. She finds everything out."

"Does she care?"

"Shit yeah, she cared. Threatened to sack us." Becca huffed. "I'm so done with her bullshit."

"If it's not just sex, what is it?" Linda glanced down at her hand and traced a blue vein.

"We're in love. Like you."

Linda barked a laugh as she pushed herself to her feet. "Sleeping with Tristan is the last thing on my mind."

Becca rolled her eyes. "I'm not talking about him."

CHAPTER NINETEEN
SABRINA

AFTER RESHOOTS, SABRINA dressed. There was a ceremony to attend and a man to impress.

Sabrina wasn't about to out anyone, but the next time she got private time with Tristan, she had to tell him: two of the women weren't invested in him. She had seen it in that bathroom with Linda and Charity.

Her sister had warned her that other women cared for their friends only when it benefited them. Sabrina had doubted this the way she had doubted the reality of the destiny bestowed upon her at birth—doubting was a way to stave away the fear that she was, in fact, alone in the world of women. When she reached the mansion on her first day of the show, and Linda had swept her underneath her wing and promised her not even The Groom could come between them, Sabrina ached for the missed memories of slumber parties and shopping dates.

When Sabrina met Linda, she felt like she saw clearly, for the first time since her sister's advice had confused her. Friends, other women, could exist even within that inevitable competition for a man. But as Sabrina sat ignored while Linda cooed over Charity in the bathroom, understanding crept in. Linda wasn't a loyal friend. She just didn't care for Tristan. She would probably drop everything for love, even her friends, just like Sabrina's sister had taught her.

It was small, the realization. Sabrina had her suspicions after the dailies that Linda's secrets might come spilling out, that they may be the kinds of secrets Sabrina couldn't look past, that Linda might indeed be the villain of the competition, and that had made her wary, if unsure. She felt no conviction yet.

But this small thing, this tiny slight, hit Sabrina clear as day. Linda had forgotten her wounded friend the moment Charity stepped into the light of that bathroom mirror. And if her sister had been right about women, what else might she have been right about?

Sabrina zippered the back of her dress, feeling once more part of a true-love fairy tale. Tristan was the man for her. Right? And hadn't this all been decided years ago, anyway—back at her birth, when her mother blessed her with beauty, so that years down the line, Tristan could look at her with his wanting gaze?

THAT NIGHT DURING the ceremony, as Tristan slipped the corsage onto Sabrina's wrist, she would lean over and whisper into his ear, "Charity and Linda aren't here for the right reasons." Then, she would let her smile spread once more across her face and fade again into his background.

CHAPTER TWENTY

LINDA

ONE BY ONE, the women swept down the stairs and lined up in the lobby of the manor. Rain pelted the windows from the outside, leaving smears of water, and only Deja and Tatum stood behind cameras on the floor below.

Charity wore her suit, the same shade of blue as an abandoned pool left to fester, but the shade brought out the cool tones of her blood. She radiated untouchable calm. Sabrina had cleaned herself up, but the skin around her eyes was puffy from crying. In the dim light from above, her yellow dress sparkled. Marion wore red with a split down the belly that showed her button. Though her skin was paler than usual, she seemed in good spirits, ready as ever for the cameras.

Linda dressed in her best outfit of the season, twisting her hair into an effortless braid that now hung over one shoulder. As she descended the stairs, tiny step by tiny step in a clinging mermaid skirt, her sky-blue tail moved around her white heels like sea waves. The glitter she smeared onto her chest gave the illusion of a reflection in crystal clear water. She claimed her place in line beside Sabrina. She reached for her friend. When Sabrina squeezed her hand, she squeezed it back with a sweaty palm. Sabrina let go.

Tristan stood in his blue suit in front of a table set with crisp white corsages. Linda wondered if production chose the color to calm everyone after the day's quarrels. Outside, a motorcycle growled into the drive. The cameras glared at Tristan and the women from every angle as Brandon threw open the door and made his rainy entrance.

"Can I get a towel?" he boomed. No one moved. "Damn it, where is everyone? Why are we running a skeleton crew?" He turned on his heel toward Deja. "What the hell?"

Coolly, her gaze slid toward him. "We're filming, dipshit."

"And I'm part of that, aren't I?" Below him, a puddle had formed and was spreading out into the foyer.

"It's me and Tatum tonight," Deja said. "Get your own towel."

Linda shifted her weight from foot to foot. She'd never seen them struggle so openly for power. According to her research, they were both top-tier producers for the show until Brandon was given *The Bride* franchise to lead, leaving Deja with the graying original.

"Why are there only two of you?" he said as he stomped through the room on his way to the hall bath. When he emerged holding a towel, he thrust out his hands as though he'd been waiting an eternity for an answer, then toweled his hair.

Deja sighed as she finally stepped away from the camera. "Three of them ran off together earlier this evening. So, if you wouldn't mind, please do tell the big guns to send me more fucking crew when you get back. My cell phone hasn't worked since we got here."

"So that's why you haven't been responding to me," Brandon said. "I thought you were just being pissy again."

"Where are Becca and the rest?" Linda asked, her stomach turning. She'd taken to Becca and Leo. Not so much to Jazz, who was a pain in the ass perfectionist despite the music note tattoos covering her whole body—but Linda didn't wish terrible things on the woman. And it was terrible things that popped into her head at the news that they were missing.

"Ran off together." Deja sounded exasperated.

"Ran off where? We're in the middle of nowhere?" Sabrina pursed her lips, her eyebrows rising.

"Don't worry your pretty heads about it." Brandon chuckled. "Deja runs them off every year. Don't you, dear?"

"It's not me. It's their goddamn loins. They get tired of the sacrifices required to work a job like this—"

"The manipulation," Charity said, earning her a side-eye from Deja.

"And they're not supposed to be having sex with one another, but they always do, and it always gets in the way, and then they quit together in some big, romantic gesture. It happens every season."

"Triads run off together every season?" Charity smirked.

"No, the triad thing is new. Usually, it's two of them. But the times, they're changing," Deja said.

Brandon tossed his towel into the hall and marched into the room's center. He examined the line of women, then motioned to Marion's bare stomach. "Tatum, I want the center of your camera on Marion here. She knows how to dress for these." He grabbed hold of Charity's shoulders, moving her like a poseable doll to the end of the line. "Much better. I'm ready to start now." He turned toward Deja's camera, and Deja squeezed her lips together as she adjusted the tripod. "What an entrance, am I right?" He paused to give the sound engineers a clean cut. "Ladies, Tristan, let's begin." He folded his hands at the level of his dick and faded into the background.

"I knew today would be a challenge," Tristan said. "But I also knew that you ladies would be up for it. Some of you performed well today." He glanced at Marion. "Others left something to be desired." His gaze slid from Charity to Linda. "In more ways than one."

He picked up the first corsage. "I need a woman who takes challenge head-on. Who doesn't let the stresses of life get to her. A woman who gets along with other women." He paused for effect. "But I also need a woman who's honest. And there are women here who are keeping secrets from me."

He raised the corsage. "Marion, will you stay with me on this romantic adventure?" he said.

She gasped as she bounced out of line. "You bet I will!" When she held out her hand to him, he slipped the corsage on her wrist. She soothed back into line but stood forward a step from the other women.

Tristan huffed, then took another corsage off the table. "Sabrina, will you stay with me on this romantic adventure?"

Sabrina yelped as she rushed forward to snatch the corsage. She slipped it on her wrist, lifted onto her tiptoes, and whispered into Tristan's ear. Tristan frowned as his gaze pinpointed Linda, then Charity. When Sabrina pulled away, she kissed Tristan on the cheek before retreating back into line.

Brandon stepped out of the shadows as though he were the rotting host in an old *Cryptkeepers* episode. "Tristan, you have one choice left," he intoned. They were the exact words he used every time, and Linda wondered if he grew tired of them, or if they were the most comforting words he ever uttered.

Tristan picked up the final corsage. He breathed in and out, flaring his nostrils. He looked at the corsage, then up at the remaining two women. He pursed his lips. He ran a hand through his hair. He glanced from Linda to Charity, then caught Linda's eye. "I have my suspicions about some of you not being here for the right reasons," he said, "but I need to follow my heart. And my heart tells me…" He paused to press his hand over his chest, let his breath catch, then said, "Linda, will you remain on this romantic journey with me?"

An icy dread traveled down Linda's throat as she opened her mouth to speak. No words came out. When she stepped forward, he lifted her arm from her side and slid on the corsage.

"Let's reign in the temper, okay, Linda?" he said. "I know you're not that kind of girl."

Linda's brain buzzed. *Was* she that kind of girl? The kind of girl who let a man call her girl, who wore corsages in her thirties, who stood in a line of women and let someone choose her. The kind of girl who yelled, and who enjoyed it—yelling at Marion had exhilarated her. The kind of girl who wanted to be picked and seen and loved by complete strangers behind their television sets?

"Yes," she whispered and faded into the line.

"Charity," Brandon said, holding back a grin. "Pack your bags. You're going home."

Charity crossed her arms, delivering one final smirk to Linda. Linda's chest swelled. Ever since day one at the mansion, Charity had thrown her little fits—Linda had been the subject of them on more than one occasion—but this time, Charity had let her in on a secret: they had never been real. Just like Linda, she'd been reciting unwritten lines, playing the part her producers dreamed up for her.

"You think you're better than me?" Charity said, her voice rising.

"You know what you did," Tristan said.

She threw her head back and stuck out her tongue. "Do I now?" She stomped toward him, the threat of violence in each step. "You're going to keep *these* bitches?"

"Don't you dare call them that." Tristan flexed his hand like he might make a fist, but he didn't. He wouldn't. It wasn't chivalrous to make a fist in a woman's direction.

Charity marched forward another step. "They're a bunch of no-good rich girls."

Linda frowned. She wouldn't consider herself, or Sabrina, a rich girl. Charity had informed her that the fit was coming, but that didn't mean Linda had to like the contents. As Charity's friend, shouldn't she now be exempt from rough words? Her stomach twisted.

"Now, that's enough." Brandon pressed his palm to the middle of Charity's chest.

"What are you doing, old man? Trying to cop a feel?" Charity jerked away from him and turned, snarling, to her fellow competitors. "You're never going to be good enough for him," she said, then turned and ran all the way up the stairs.

With Charity gone, Linda stood, reeling, in the flickering foyer light. As her stomach sank, she felt nauseated—too much happening at once. First, she felt relief that she was chosen, followed by sadness that Charity was not. Then a strange sense of camaraderie that she might be the one chosen by Charity, not Tristan, the only woman Charity had opened up to throughout the whole experience. She felt wounded by the woman's words even though she wanted more than anything for her to remain at the manor, just she and Linda— no one else. An impossible wish.

Once Charity returned, Brandon escorted her out of the door and into the rain, with her one packed bag in tow. Linda stood in the parlor with her gleaming glass of champagne and listened as the motorcycle drove away.

"You okay?" Sabrina rubbed her hand against Linda's back, but her nails were strangely sharp against her dress. "I was the final choice in week two. Hurts, doesn't it?" Her voice was silken, like an impractical bandage.

"Yeah, it sucks." Linda sniffed her champagne. The bubbles jumped into her nose. She sneezed.

"What stick was up Charity's ass?"

"The rough kind." Linda drained her glass. "I can't believe she's gone."

"I can. It was always going to be the three of us."

"I guess so." She let her gaze fall on Tristan and Marion giggling in the corner of the room. It was rude as fuck, especially as Sabrina stood within hearing distance.

"Can you believe they fucked?" Sabrina said.

Outside, the rumble of a motorcycle returned.

Linda's shoulders straightened. "Did you hear that?"

In the corner, Tristan and Marion broke apart, and Linda set down her empty glass and ran to the foyer. Brandon panted as he dripped through the door. Behind him, Charity stood, illuminated by a single flash of lightning. She pushed forward into the room, and the cameras moved to capture her there.

"We're back," Charity said, and without thinking, Linda reached out to pull her friend close, taking the rain smell into her body. "You don't hate me," she whispered. "Right?"

"We're blocked in," Brandon said. "There's a fucking mudslide on the road."

"Wait... A mudslide?" Linda pushed back from Charity's embrace. "You can't go around it?"

Brandon ran his hand through his perfect, wet hair. "Would I have come back to this hellhole if we'd been able to go around it? No. I would be dropping this chick off and heading back to my private cabin."

"What about Becca, Leo, and Jazz?" Linda said. "Did they get out okay?" She chewed her lip. "Will it be open by the time we're supposed to leave?"

"What am I? Nostradamus?" Brandon said.

Deja swept her hand against Brandon's shoulder. "It'll be fine, Brandon. We've got an extra room. I'm sure the forestry service will start clearing that up as soon as possible."

"You let them know we were going to be up here, yeah?" Brandon said.

"Of course." Deja's voice came out reassuring, kind. Not at all like Deja. "I'll have Tatum show you to a room."

Tatum stepped out from behind his camera and motioned for Brandon to follow him up the stairs. Once they disappeared beyond the view of the stairwell, Deja folded her hands and turned to the contestants.

"This doesn't change a thing. We'll make this part of the show. Charity, do your thing." Deja winked. "I know you will whether I tell you to or not." She turned to Tristan. "Why don't you take your ladies into the den to celebrate?"

Tristan forced his face into a smile that didn't reach his eyes. "Of course. Ladies, let's go." He reached out toward them, and both Sabrina and Marion stepped forward to take an arm. They shared a glower, so Linda looped her arm in his instead. Deja advanced ahead of Tristan, with a portable boom and camera. Linda gave the lens her best bullshit smile, too.

In the parlor, Tristan filled shiny pewter goblets with champagne. "To love!" he said as they clinked their cups and swigged. The champagne tasted metallic, but Linda swallowed it before her throat had a chance to react. Tristan patted the two spots beside him on the couch. Sabrina and Marion rushed to fill them, leaving Linda standing.

"Now, I need you ladies to get along," he said. "We're going to be here a while longer, it seems."

"You already told us we'd be here a week." Marion counted on her fingers. "It's been, like, two days."

"Mud isn't permanent or anything." Sabrina clapped her hand on Tristan's thigh. "I can last longer than a mudslide."

Staring out through the parlor door into the hall, Linda frowned as she tried to parse the weird conversation. A hand reached around the frame. Linda started to call out, but Charity's face followed the hand as she peeked into the room. She caught Linda's eye and held one finger up to her lips. Linda smirked. Charity placed a hand against the air of the door, mimicking a mime pressing at glass. She fake-pounded, her face straight even as Linda lost her composure and laughed out loud. In the eerie manor, laughter felt wrong as it echoed, but it helped her chest lighten.

Tristan, Sabrina, and Marion looked up at the same time.

"It's nothing." But when Linda stuck out a hand and leaned into the wall, her hand sunk through the wood, just like her foot had done. She shrieked, and Charity rushed forward to grab hold of her waist and keep her from falling into the house. Linda yanked free her hand as Sabrina jumped up to help. The wood popped back to solidity.

Linda examined her hand; it was covered in the same pink slime the dart had set free. Charity pulled her jacket off and handed it to Linda.

"Wipe that shit off," she said.

"What is it?" Linda's lip curled. It reeked of rotting meat.

"Probably fungus. We'd better get you cleaned up."

"Could be the same material the producers used to trick us elsewhere," Sabrina muttered.

"We did no such thing," Deja said, but Linda ignored the protestation.

"I'll do it," Tristan said, and he took hold of Linda's elbow and led her out of the parlor, through the long hall to the downstairs bathroom before she could utter a single word. He stopped before the bathroom sink and examined her.

"Sorry you were last." He ran the creaky water faucet. "I don't mind a catfight, but those ladies would never forgive me if I let fighting stand." He grabbed a hand towel and wet it under the cold water. Linda dropped Charity's jacket to the floor, a blue puddle, and Tristan wiped at the slime.

"That's fine." Linda glanced to the bathroom door. "I shouldn't have attacked her." But unlike her prior scripts, her heart wasn't in this one. Something had ignited in her out there, faced with Marion's rude words, and it was then she realized: she felt more natural when lunging toward the woman than she did when playing nice, like she had done the rest of her time on the show. Her stomach flip-flopped as a thought passed through her: *Is that what I am*? She blinked, and her father's face, bloated with death, appeared. Her eyes flew open.

"I know tensions are high," he said. "I couldn't sleep a wink with all the crying you ladies were doing."

"Is that what was keeping you up?" Linda said, then held back her desire to say more. "What crying?"

"All night. Weeping." Tristan finished wiping away the mess and dropped the towel into the sink, not bothering to clean up after himself. "Was it you?"

Linda imagined herself weeping in bed as she had done as a little girl on so many of her father's whiskey nights. She hadn't cried when her father died, nor since.

"I don't cry," she said. "I didn't hear anything."

The color drained from Tristan's face. "Then who?"

"Marion?" The most probable person, the one Linda had seen cry the most.

"No, she was with me." He said it without meaning to.

Linda felt her mouth lift into a knowing half-smirk. "You think we don't all know that?" It was a cruel thing to say, but Linda was glad she said it. She watched Tristan's expression morph from planned smolder to confusion, then to fear, then to anger, his nostrils flaring.

"Were you spying?" he whispered, his voice tinged with red.

Linda leaned forward. "We're being watched all the time. If you think we have any modicum of privacy, then you're more stupid than I thought." She found again a straightness of posture and affixed a glamorous nonchalance to her demeanor.

"Lovely," he said, and his lips turned down in the first genuine frown she'd seen on him. "You're a gem. Glad I chose you." His lips flattened. "You don't have the friends you think you have. You know that, right?" With that, he turned and slammed his way out of the room, disappearing up the stairs, while Linda stood, stunned, the water running pink down the drain behind her.

LINDA CHEWED HER lip as she started back toward the den, but she was stopped in her tracks by the echoes of confrontation. She headed toward the sounds at the other end of the manor until she reached the kitchen. In the dark, shadows crept through the single window, spilling across the floor as the rain pounded the glass. She paused outside a closet and pressed an ear as close to the wall as she dared. She didn't want to encounter any residue the walls might make.

The voices were clear and easy to identify.

"You left me on this show like a captain abandoning a sinking ship. If you've got such big ideas about how things should be done around here, why'd you disappear to run your own show?" Deja said. "You fucked me over, knowing I could have your head on a platter for all the harassment complaints I field about you."

"Don't you threaten me," Brandon's voice wavered. "I know that you grew up in this house."

Silence stretched out before Deja spoke again. "What?"

"You thought you could keep it a secret?" Brandon cackled. "They did their research, you know. They told me to use it."

"Use it how?" Deja asked, an edge to her voice that frightened Linda more than the haunted house.

"They want me to fire you, Deja. On camera. The haunted manor thing is played out. It hardly works for ghost-hunting shows. You thought you'd make it work on a romance? They knew the season would suck, so they want to go meta. Next time I come up here, I'm supposed to reveal that you grew up here. I'm supposed to play some of those tapes you tried to hide away. And then, I'm supposed to fire you for lying."

"They want to go meta?" Deja stuttered. "That's a desperate move. That's some late-stage franchise bullshit."

"They're desperate. That's why they promoted you. You're supposed to take the fall for the show losing money."

"I was promoted, Brandon, because I get the best out of these girls. I'm good at my job."

"That may be, but you and I both know that means nothing. Say the wrong word, do the wrong thing, and you're out, whether you're good at your job or not."

Linda's forehead scrunched up. She had read about the show doing poorly: numbers down, profits down, lawsuits up. Tristan wasn't their most exciting Groom, likely pulled from some trash heap somewhere. And the dates this season had been strange, lower budget. Butchering pigs and going to curio shops weren't break-the-bank excursions. Still, she'd trusted Deja to follow through on her promise to erase Linda's record when the show was through, even if she now doubted the producer's intentions. She thought the woman had power. Was that another lie?

When next Deja spoke, her voice was further inflamed. "So, they know that I grew up here? What difference does that make? That just means that I had the inside scoop for how fucked-up this place is."

"A couple of gooey walls and an earthquake? Deja, this place is falling apart, not haunted. You know how it looks? Like you convinced some network to buy a family home no one else wanted. It looks like embezzlement."

Linda's stomach twisted. Weren't the walls a trick of production?

"I have no ties to my family anymore."

"Be that as it may, you fucked up. And now I'm stuck here." Brandon hacked what sounded like a hairball. Linda tried to hold back an involuntary noise of disgust.

"The mudslide is my fault, too?"

"If it is, then I'm not going easy on you, no matter which room you put me in," Brandon said.

"Fine. You want the room closer to the ladies? It's yours. Now get the hell out of my sight before I fuck you up." Deja's words were tinged with venom. Linda shivered as she tried to parse what she'd heard.

All at once, a theory moved through her, making her hair stand on end. Deja was the producer. She knew everyone's secrets, their inner lives, their weaknesses, their sore spots. If the show was failing, if she needed ratings, she might do everything in her power to make her contestants implode. Linda understood that desperation called for darkness. And she felt Deja's target burning its mark into her forehead. How far was Deja willing to push her?

She remembered the dead thing in the curio shop and shivered.

"Hey, listen, you're my friend," Brandon said, softening his speech. "Aren't we friends?"

"Don't you touch me." Something hit the wall, and Linda jumped. She'd heard enough. She turned and ran as quietly as she could back to the den where the other two remaining women waited for her and Tristan's return from the bathroom.

"What happened?" Sabrina asked, while Marion crossed her arms at the appearance of Linda alone. "Where's Tristan?"

"Went to bed. Said he hasn't been sleeping." Linda shrugged. "Says one of us has been crying." As they shared accusatory, confused glances, an ache spread from her foot up her body. She yawned as she felt the floor pulling her toward it, her eyelids dragging. "I'm afraid I'm in the same boat." After saying her goodnights, she made her long way up the stairs, followed by no cameras, no operators.

CHAPTER TWENTY-ONE

SABRINA

THAT NIGHT, SABRINA lay beneath her blankets and waited. During the elimination, she'd whispered to Tristan that Linda wasn't there for the right reasons. He'd chosen her anyway, but his hand was likely forced. Producers did that, Sabrina had heard: forced The Groom's hand when it made for better drama. Sabrina had piqued Tristan's curiosity. All night in the den, she had caught him glancing her way. She was ready to tell him everything she knew, or didn't know, about Linda. All she had to do was wait for him to climb into her bed.

Some time later, she rolled over and out of the bed, frustrated to still be alone in the chilly dark. When she opened the door and peered out into the hallway, it was empty. Tristan's door seemed closed, but Sabrina figured he'd left it unlocked. If he wasn't ready to come to her, she would go to him, play demure, claim that her reason for sliding into his private space was to make sure he'd caught her warning. She tiptoed down the hall.

He answered the door before she knocked, and his mouth opened in an "O" of shock. "Sabrina," he said.

She shifted her weight to one foot and crossed her arms. "Now, how the hell did you know I was outside your door?"

He laughed as he checked for onlookers, then yanked her inside. "Got a sense for you, I guess." He killed her grin with a hard kiss to her mouth, and they fell together to the floor, where their limbs twisted together in a confusion of garments and skin. The floor smelled like old, unwashed carpet, and Tristan's body smelled like sweat and sex. Had he failed to shower after their prior encounter, or after Marion, or after—? Sabrina tried to push the thought out of her head as Tristan's fingers delved into her, but she squirmed at the discomfort.

"You're dry," he said as he pulled his hand away and sat up, his dick going limp.

"It's nothing," she said. *Men need to do the things men do.* She imagined her sister's voice telling her that, though she was unsure if that was ever the subject of a lesson. Maybe Sabrina now attributed all life's lessons to her sister. Surely, she had learned something, anything, on her own.

Tristan folded his hands over his groin. "Something on your mind?" He frowned. "Is this more about Linda?"

More about Linda. It was a safer subject, the one she'd come here to discuss. "Yeah, about Linda." Sabrina trembled as the manor's cold air washed over her. Her bared nipples throbbed. She wrinkled her nose. "Something's weird with her. She's not here for the right reasons."

"Right reasons, sure. You mentioned."

"She's not interested in you." Sabrina paused. She was here for a dalliance with another woman, for one thing, but Sabrina wasn't the kind of person to out someone like that. She'd been presented with the opportunity multiple times at the hospital, and she understood the implications even outside HIPAA. "You're going to get hurt."

Tristan cleared his throat. Silence took its beat. He unfolded himself from the floor and stood up, then perched on the edge of his bed. "I don't like drama." He glanced around the room, and Sabrina realized he was looking for a camera. "Linda couldn't hurt a fly."

Sabrina screwed up her forehead in thought. The evidence was in brief words, a frightening flash in Linda's eyes when she angered, that temper that trickled out on occasion, and some secret promise that kept slipping out. Sabrina's brain felt foggy.

"Is this some jealousy thing?" Tristan asked, his voice soft and sweet. "I know it's hard for women. You all get pulled in so easily to competitions like this. You take things personally. Linda is a good woman. She's gone through a lot."

"Her divorce?"

"Her divorce. She doesn't have any family. She's had it rougher than us, you know."

Sabrina considered this, then tilted her head as she looked up to Tristan's naked, hulking form. Even with his penis hanging like a worm between his legs, he was commanding, his voice solid, rough at the edges, that southern lilt like a spell. "I lost my mom," she said. She needed him to transfer his sympathy to her. If he felt too sorry for Linda, he might choose her out of pity, and Sabrina couldn't have that. "My dad is sick."

"You're stronger than her." Tristan reached out his hand, and as Sabrina took it, she knew he was right. Linda was the one to pity. Women were slaves to their competitive natures. He'd said the words. They were real. She shouldn't have tried to backstab. It wasn't what a good woman did. She remembered the fight, and Tristan's stern words as he chose Linda last. She needed to make him see that she was sorry. That she was a good woman. As she let Tristan pull her into his chest, and as she listened to the thump of his heart, she made herself cry, and through the walls, another woman's sobs formed a harmony.

CHAPTER TWENTY-TWO

LINDA

LINDA HAD CRAWLED into bed when a knock sounded on her door. She groaned and rolled out of the covers, but as her feet hit the floor, her stomach turned. It might be Deja on the other side, demanding more reshoots or trying to pull her into a confessional, to catch her tired and likely to crack. She hesitated at the door. But it could be Charity. She yanked the door open.

Charity stood on the other side, her hair in a spiky bun on top of her head. "Wait until you see what I found," she said, extending a hand.

The twists turned to butterflies as Linda took it, lacing their fingers together. She needed a break. She needed to unwind, to engage in whatever adventure Charity had in store for them.

Charity led them through several halls on the second floor, then up a miniature staircase so small they could only ascend one person at a time. The floors creaked, but Linda decided not to worry. Deja had her hands too full to care about Linda and Charity sneaking off into forbidden areas of the mansion.

At the end of the hall, they came upon a closed door that had been wallpapered over. Inside, the hallway that stretched out before her was darker, not even a window light at the far end to be seen. As Linda crept down it, her eyes adjusted. The gas lamps had been removed, leaving behind shadows of themselves in the faded wallpaper. She breathed in. The air smelled wet, like mildew, with a hint of something animal. She took the hall step by step, imagining herself on camera, though no camera followed them, a rarity that had become more common with the skeleton crew.

Charity glanced back and grinned, then pointed to one of the doors lining the hall. Linda stopped outside of it.

"Ready?" Charity said.

"I have no idea. You haven't told me a thing."

"That would ruin the surprise."

"You're about to show me anyway, aren't you?"

Charity laughed, then opened the door. The far wall was made of glass, and through it, moonlight leaked across the floor. When Charity flipped on the switch, the room filled with light. Potted plants lined each wall and hung from the ceilings. Linda gasped.

"It's the room I saw when we were rappelling," she breathed.

"I had some time on my hands," Charity said. "Being fired and all."

Linda stepped close to one of the plants and touched the broad green leaf of a Monstera. It was nice to touch something green and familiar. "I can't believe you found this place." She breathed in the fresh air.

"I found it for you." Charity moved beside her and reached once more for her hand. This time, her touch felt different, softer, more vulnerable. Heat spread from her hand through her body. "You had a rough day. With the shrine room and everything..."

Linda's breath hitched. "Yeah..."

Charity reached her other hand to Linda's cheek and pulled Linda to face her. "It must have hurt to see yourself edited like that."

Linda swallowed and forced herself to ask the question lodged in her throat. "Do you think that's me?" she said. "The way I seemed in those edits?"

Charity's smile was kind. "Of course not."

"Then what was that?" Linda felt herself choking.

"Manipulation." Charity brushed her fingers across Linda's cheek, her touch so much gentler than Tristan's, and so much more welcome. "That's all any of this is."

"It doesn't feel like manipulation here. Now."

"No. This might be real." Charity hooked her finger under Linda's chin and pulled her face up, then leaned in so their lips were nearly touching. "This might be the only real thing."

As their faces moved closer, eyes meeting across the divide, wide and wanting, Linda's knees shook, but her hand in Charity's stayed still. Linda had never kissed a woman. She breathed in Charity's smell, like lavender and mint. Their lips pressed together.

Outside, a loud crash, followed by shouting.

"Damn it." Charity pulled back.

Brandon's voice slammed through the window. Together, Charity and Linda pressed themselves to the glass and peered into the yard. Brandon and Tatum stood across from one another, a camera downed between them.

"What the fuck, dude?" Tatum screamed.

"An accident," Brandon slurred, stumbling forward in the mud and swinging.

Charity and Linda shared a questioning glance. Should they do something? Linda didn't want to. In fact, she desired nothing more than to turn away from the window and forget the world outside of the nursery. But she wanted to be that good person, so she would go to the lawn with Charity and try to help the clueless cameraman. Maybe his lens would catch something they couldn't edit away.

AS CHARITY KNELT to pick the camera up, Linda stepped between the brawling men.

"Chill," she said.

"That's what I was doing!" Tatum yelled, backing up. "Having a smoke. Trying to relax before bed. Then this psycho came out and fucked up my camera."

"Accident." Brandon tried to lunge forward, but his steps were sloppy, and he tripped over Linda's foot, sprawling to the ground.

Charity frowned over the broken camera.

"Probably doesn't want all that shit he said earlier to be on camera," Tatum muttered. "Fucking lawsuit in a suit, that's what you are."

Brandon didn't seem to hear Tatum. Just laid, legs and arms akimbo, in the dirt. Linda breathed a sigh of relief.

"I don't know anything about cameras," Charity said, "but he may have succeeded." She handed the bundle to Tatum, with all the gentleness of passing a baby, then winced. "Sorry, man."

"Shit." Tatum's scrunched-up forehead softened, his eyes rounding with sadness. "My girl. They're gonna take her out of my check."

Linda placed a hand on Tatum's shoulder. "Lucky for you, there's like four more in there, at least."

"You're right." He exhaled, then attempted a smile. "Thanks, bros."

Linda and Charity helped Tatum inside, leaving Brandon to his drunken sleep in the dirt.

He'd ruined Linda's moment. He deserved it, and worse.

DAY THREE

CHAPTER TWENTY-THREE

SABRINA

SABRINA HAD NO clue what the activity of the day was supposed to be, only that Deja instructed the women at breakfast to wear clothes they didn't mind getting dirty. When Sabrina entered the kitchen again that afternoon, she found a table full of random ingredients: eggs in a carton, flour in an unlabeled canister, a bag of grits, a softening stick of butter, and various fruits and vegetables. The three remaining women lined up as Tristan took his place in front of them. Tatum aimed a camera at him as Deja smoothed a few of his hairs away from his face.

"Where's Brandon?" Sabrina whispered to Linda, hoping that Tristan would see them speaking and believe her redemption.

"Probably sleeping off the hangover."

"No shit?" Sabrina said. "You see him last night?"

"Heard him, and saw him. He was fucking with Tatum in the yard."

Deja turned to them and placed her hands on her hips. "Are we done gossiping?" She gestured to the table. "I thought we were here to win Tristan's heart."

Sabrina mimed zippering her mouth while Linda scowled and shut up.

"We're go on three, Tatum." Deja stepped out of the shot, then counted down.

On three, Tristan beamed. "Ladies, the way to a man's heart is through his stomach. It's the God's honest truth. Today, we're going to have a cooking competition! I want all y'all ladies to cook me your best brunch, and I'm a lucky bastard cause I'll be eating all of them."

Sabrina's heart jumped. She was a good cook, but Marion was such a southern belle that there was no way she didn't know her way around a kitchen. Sabrina glanced in her direction. Her skin had warmed again in color, no longer its sick sallow, but she seemed skinnier, weaker. Sabrina's confidence rose.

"The winner gets to go on a picnic with me." Brandon glanced to the lone window in the room. "And even though it's sprinkling out there, we'll make the most of it!"

As Tristan stepped back, Tatum turned his camera toward the women, who rushed forward to grab their ingredients.

"Is there a cookbook or something?" Linda said.

"There is not," Tatum said, grinning on the sideline.

"Well, shit. I'm out."

"Try, Linda." Tristan sounded annoyed. Sabrina struggled to keep her lips from spreading into a smile. "Pretend to care."

Linda grabbed a handful of fruit and got to chopping it.

Sabrina knew exactly what to make: biscuits, grits, sausage, and gravy. She eyed Marion, who was going for the eggs. She'd scramble them, or make an omelet. It was too easy to overcook an egg, and Sabrina had no idea how Tristan took his. Grits were easier to manage: the more butter, the better. For the biscuits, she poured her flour and baking powder into a bowl with some salt, cut in the butter, then stirred it all together with a splash of milk. She was careful not to over-knead as she rolled the dough out, then used a rocks glass to cut them into perfect circles. After she shoved them into the oven, she heated the sausage and cooked the grits and gravy, taking in the sweet and salty smell. When her biscuits were risen and ready, she arranged them on a plate, poured the gravy on top, and added the sides.

She was the first one finished, and as she carried her tray full of food out of the room to the dining table, she caught Marion's glare. The woman was only a few minutes behind Sabrina, but by the time Marion carried out her omelet, Tristan was already poised with his fork over the steaming gravy, about to cut into a biscuit.

"Damn," he muttered as he chewed, then swallowed. "Damn," he repeated as he dug in again.

Marion pouted as she pushed forward her plate. "Don't fill up."

He grinned up at them as he wiped his mouth with a napkin. "Oh, I can put the calories away."

Behind them, Linda stepped out with her bowl of scrambled eggs and added her offering to the table. Tristan barely looked up at her as he sampled Sabrina's grits and sausage, then moved onto Marion's meal. The omelet was perfect, with the little yolk pouring out as his fork found it, coating the plate with a pleasant orange glow. But Tristan returned to Sabrina's plate as soon as he had his bites of Marion's and Linda's.

"We have a clear winner," he said, pointing to Sabrina. "This dame can cook, damn it."

Sabrina's whole body lit up as Tatum aimed the camera to capture her elated expression. She jumped up and down, then rushed to Tristan's side and threw her arms around his shoulders.

"Will you do me the honors of a little picnic in the rain?" Tristan said.

"Duh." Sabrina stepped back beside Marion the Linda. When Linda reached out to high-five her, Sabrina made herself meet her hand, and the sound of the slap reverberated through the room.

When Sabrina turned to Marion, there was fire in Marion's eyes, but she stuck out her hand to shake Sabrina's. Sabrina took it, a gesture of goodwill, and Marion held tight to Sabrina's hand, pumping it up and down, her grip tightening. "Strong shake," Sabrina said, laughing nervously, but as the grip grew stronger, Sabrina's bones complained. "Ow!" Marion didn't let up. Sabrina tried to pull away. "Quit it! That hurts."

Deja glanced at Linda. "Are you going to stand there while your friend needs help?"

Sabrina didn't have time to puzzle over the words, but Linda didn't move from her spot, her mouth frozen in an "O" of shock. Marion kept squeezing, until finally, Tristan stood and slammed a fist on the table. "Enough!"

Marion let go of Sabrina's hand, then turned and stormed out of the room. Sabrina held her hand up to the light. It was bruised with the shape of Marion's fingers.

"For someone sick, she's still strong," Linda said. "You okay?"

When Sabrina didn't answer, Tristan reached for her hand. She winced as he held it softly in his.

"I'll never understand you women." He gestured out the window. "But I understand a picnic. Come on, Sabrina. Let's make the most of this time."

THE PICNIC CONSISTED of the rest of Sabrina's breakfast biscuits, strawberry jam, and mimosas. They trekked through a patch of mud to reach the blanket production had laid out for them, then settled into cross-legged positions across from one another. Tatum held an umbrella over them while Deja operated the camera. Mist crept sideways into their hair and across their clothes, and as Sabrina bit into her first biscuit, she shivered.

Tristan unbuttoned his flannel and slipped it over her shoulders. "Can't let a pretty gal like you suffer, not even for me," he said.

Sabrina smiled. It felt right being out here with him, as right as anything had ever felt. Maybe destiny was as simple as that, intentions or no intentions. She was meant to be here. She was meant to be his. She felt it as certainly as she'd ever felt anything before. "Thank you," she said. Tristan flicked a speck of crumb from her lips. "This time means a lot to me."

"Me, too," he said. "So, tell me: what do you really think of this place?"

Sabrina shivered again, this time not from the cold. "It's creepy."

"It is," he said. "Are you starting to believe in ghosts?"

Was she? "Unsure." She'd discovered weird walls that could be production tricks, and heard about weird cries in the night, but had anything unexplainable happened? She thought of her mother and the intentions that seemed, on the surface, like weird oils and pretty crystals. Maybe that was how the supernatural worked; it disguised itself. Or maybe life was as simple as it seemed on the surface.

"My mom fancied herself mystical in some way," Sabrina said. "I didn't tell you that before, because I thought you might find it off-putting, but now, I feel comfortable telling you."

Tristan raised his brows. "Mystical? What does that mean?"

"She made intentions and recited chants. Wore charms. Burned a lot of incense and sage. Cursed people who did her wrong, which was like wishing them ill and stuff. It seemed the same as make-believe was with the other kids. Some of them believed Santa was real, and it was the same with us, only we also believed our mom could make things happen by wanting them bad enough."

"But she died when you were young, right?" Tristan touched her thigh, giving her a gentle supportive squeeze.

"Yeah. Cancer. She couldn't wish herself well."

"Is that when you stopped believing her?"

Sabrina shook her head. "It wasn't all at once. It was kind of like how some people come to no longer believe in God. It happened year by year. For a long time, I believed that we could still make things happen by thinking about them. My sister believed, and she lived to carry out my mother's wishes. I did what my sister wanted me to. First, because I believed, too. Eventually, I followed her because she's smart, and she always knew what was best for me. At least, she did then."

"And now?" Tristan asked.

"I'll follow *you*. You know what's best for me." As she said it, she relaxed into him. Even in the middle of a strange place, in a relentless mist, she understood that Tristan could take care of her the way she needed. The way she wanted.

"That's right." He kissed her, capturing her lips and forcing her to surrender to him. "I know what's best."

CHAPTER TWENTY-FOUR

LINDA

WHEN LINDA TASTED her scramble, she tried not to gag. The eggs were both watery and overcooked. Tristan had left them on the table when he and Sabrina went for their picnic—and she didn't blame him. She took the bowl into the kitchen and dumped it in the sink. She'd woken ravenous, and the kitchen was full of uncooked food.

"Didn't win, huh?" Charity said, breezing into the kitchen, her hair a tangled mess.

"I'm a bad cook." Linda shrugged. "There's worse things."

Charity glanced over the leftover ingredients. "I can whip something up." She grabbed a couple of eggs and stepped to the stove, pulling a pan off the drying rack. "Sit."

Linda sat. When she considered the events of last night, she came back again and again to the almost-kiss. Her cheeks warmed as she fiddled with her necklace. She wasn't about to bring it up, but Charity peered over her shoulder as she tossed the eggshells aside.

"Crazy night, huh?"

Linda's stomach jumped. "Wild."

"Brandon is a mess."

Linda opened then closed her mouth. "Yeah…"

Charity frowned. "Everything cool?"

Linda passed a hand over her forehead, which was covered in perspiration. "Fine." Her palms were damp. "Actually, I'm not feeling so hot." She had to get away from Charity, from the uncomfortable conversation that threatened to emerge. "Thanks for the offer, but I'm going to sneak in a nap."

Charity turned from the stovetop, confusion knitting her brow. "What's the matter?"

"Maybe I caught what Marion has. I don't know. Sorry." Linda stood up and wobbled on unsteady feet toward the door. "Really, sorry."

Charity stepped forward, but Linda was faster backing away. "You don't have to apologize. Do you need help?" Charity said.

Linda shook her head. "No help." With that, she turned and left the kitchen.

Pausing on the stairs to her bedroom, her sweating diminished as her heartbeat slowed. She hadn't felt anything for anyone since her ex—not even Tristan. She'd forgotten how overwhelming it could be. To hope for a touch or a kind word. To feel a wanting in her skin. As she took the first step, Brandon appeared at the top of the stairs.

"Looking pale," he said. "Something wrong?"

Linda shook her head as she climbed. "Just tired. Didn't sleep much."

Brandon made no sign he remembered their altercation. "It wasn't you crying all night, was it?"

"Nope." Linda tried to bypass him, but he stuck his hand out.

"I've got a proposition for you, Lin." His grin was monstrous, full of too-white teeth. "What do you say we have a chat?"

"Not interested," she said, eyeing the path to her room. She'd heard about his come-ons.

"What do you say you step into my room here?" he said.

"What do you say you let me go get some rest?"

Brandon moved his hand away. "Do what you need, I guess. I thought you'd be interested to hear I can make your problems go away."

Linda's gaze slid to him. "What do you know about my problems?"

His smile fell as he shrugged one shoulder. "Deja told me everything, of course."

"And I suppose you want—what? Some kind of sexual favor?"

He let out a quick laugh. "Ha! Nothing so crude. I want you to help me give people something to talk about. A nip slip at the live finale interview. Show the world yours, and I'll make sure no one finds out about your youthful indiscretions."

"And my bad credit? Deja said she could clear that up for me."

"Deja's a liar," he said. "But I'm not."

"What-the-fuck-ever," Linda said. "You're no better than she is."

"But I'm not about to lose my job," he said.

"And if I refuse?" A sharp cold flowed through her body, but she forced herself to say the thing she'd been wanting to say to him all along. "Your time is coming. Someone's going to catch you harassing someone soon, you know.

Brandon formed a fist. "Watch yourself. You wouldn't want your new friend Charity to find out about who you really are, would you?"

The cold fear thickened, settling in her gut. "Fine," she said, her voice small and defeated. "I'll be your puppet. You. Deja's. I'll do whatever the fuck you want, okay? Just let me go to my room." Even on her feet, she felt as though she were on her knees. The idea that Charity would never speak to her again was worse than the world knowing her secret. "Don't tell anyone. Don't tell her. I'm yours. Jesus fucking Christ. Can I go now?"

Brandon stuck out his hand, and as Linda shook it, she realized she was shaking harder than she'd ever shook before.

AS BRANDON WENT downstairs, Linda closed her door and slid to the floor. Her heart hammered against the back of the door. Her heavy breathing echoed as a knock sounded.

"Go away," she whispered, then repeated it like a mantra. "Go away, go away—"

"Linda. It's me." Charity's voice drifted through, soothing and sweet.

What if she saw the truth in Linda's eyes? Did Linda really want to answer? But as though compelled, she stood and let Charity inside. Charity held Linda, one hand wrapped around each of Linda's lower arms. Linda felt trapped, but it was the kind of trapped that made her feel safe, like a hug or the missionary position. She searched Charity's face but found no hint Charity had heard anything Brandon said.

Suddenly, she wanted nothing more than to go. Charity's touch brought to her a surprising clarity. She was being manipulated from all sides, her reputation and her hard-fought new life threatened. She couldn't trust Deja, whose aim seemed to be making her crack, and now, she couldn't trust Brandon and his weak promises. Maybe, she thought, if she could go away with Charity right now, she could get ahead of the nightmare. She'd tell her everything, on her own time, on her own turf. "Let's get out of here," she said.

Charity looked deep into her eyes. "Why?"

Linda shook her head, then she found she couldn't stop. "They're making a villain out of me, Charity. I don't know how long I can do this."

"You can do this. I believe in you. All you have to do is watch what you say. Be mindful of every facial expression you make. They'll cut your sentences together, so refuse to speak whenever you can. Or—"

"I'm afraid I *am* the villain," Linda said. It felt freeing to voice the worry. "That it's like my nature or something."

"It's okay," she repeated. "You're okay."

"We have to go," Linda said, her voice tinged with desperation. "The mudslide."

"It's not real," Linda said. "It's more manipulation, that's all. It has to be."

Charity's brow knitted. "I was there. I saw it, remember?"

Linda reshuffled her thoughts, coming up with a new scapegoat, another reason they weren't actually trapped. "It has to be cleared by now."

"Brandon would have left if it were."

"Then we'll clear it."

"You didn't see the thing, Lin."

Linda broke all at once. She shook in Charity's arms, her tears soaking Charity's shirt as she clenched at the legs of Charity's pants. Charity ran her hands through Linda's hair, shushing her like a child.

As Linda's heaving slowed, Charity pulled back. "Let's go. It's worth a shot."

"THERE ARE NO towns for miles," Charity said as she shoved a sweater into her backpack. "We need to find Brandon's hog. We're not equipped to go that far on foot."

"Where did he put it?"

"It's parked on the side. With the keys left in it."

"Why would he do that?"

"He was mad when we came back and just stormed in. But I've got a keen eye." Charity grinned.

Together, Charity and Linda finished packing their necessities into two bags and slung them over their shoulders. They slunk through the hall and down the stairs, but the crew were busy with the picnic, and they encountered no one on their way out the front door. Once they stepped foot into the mist, however, they realized their issue: the producers had set up the picnic within view of the front doors. No one looked up as they opened the door, but it was only a matter of time before they were caught in the corner of Deja or Brandon's eye.

They ducked back inside.

"Back door?" Linda said, and Charity nodded as she grabbed Linda's hand and tugged her through the manor to the kitchen, and out through the servants' entrance.

They pressed their bodies against the exterior walls and found the motorcycle leaning against the building. Charity tapped at the keys left in the ignition.

"Thank God for morons."

"In this context," Linda said as she peered out, trying to suss out a path to escape.

The back and sides of the manor were closer to the forest than the front with its flat, mowed expanse and apple orchard. If they drove around the manor, they'd encounter the same issue as before. As they stood squashed against the wall, the truth dawned on Linda.

"They're going to hear us," she said.

"But they won't be able to catch us." Charity climbed up and straddled the cycle. "Hop on, lady."

Linda had never ridden before, but she didn't want to admit as much to Charity and risk losing the illusion of cool she'd somehow emitted in Charity's direction. As she struggled to mount, Charity grabbed hold of her hand and helped her over, then passed her a helmet.

"Hold on tight to me," Charity said, and without another word, she started the engine.

Before Linda could worry, they were zipping through the mud toward the edge of the woods. Linda glanced over her left shoulder to see a kerfuffle of bodies rising, then racing toward them—Sabrina, Deja, Brandon, and Tatum, nearly the whole damn gang—but then their bodies became smaller and smaller as the motorcycle carried them forward to the gates, which opened at the cycle's approach. Linda thought for one moment about Sabrina being stuck at the manor, then let it go. Sabrina was a show darling. They'd never let anything bad happen to her as long as Tristan was around.

Linda was soaked, but through the rain, she saw Charity clicking a handheld button to close the gates behind them.

As the gates swung shut, the wind whipped her hair. She understood the appeal of hogs, and in her elation, she imagined Charity and her weaving through the streets of Los Angeles, the perma-sun beaming down on them, the world watching them go—always go—nothing, no one, to stop them.

Charity braked. Linda slammed forward into her body. When the whiplash subsided, her eyes focused through the rain. They'd traveled only a few miles down the only road, and before them, the path was covered with rocks and mud so tall she couldn't see to the other side. The whole side of the cliff had disintegrated onto the road.

"Fuck." It was all Linda could say.

Charity stood with her feet balancing the bike, hands still on the bars, mouth twisting. "We have to turn back."

"No." Linda let go of Charity's shirt, tumbling over the edge of the bike into the dirt. "We can't do that."

Charity kicked the stand out and dismounted, then reached a hand to help Linda back up, but Linda scurried away in the dirt like a frightened rodent.

"No," she said again, and she turned so her hands and knees struck the soil as she crawled, slowly at first, then faster, eagerly approaching the mudslide, scrambling for purchase in the slick of the ground. "Damn it, no." She tried to find a handhold. Her hands closed over a rock, but the rock slid, taking her with it. She tried to find a foothold, but every hard surface was surrounded by mud. There was no way over. No way through.

Charity's hand closed over her shoulder and yanked her back. She felt her body behind, safe and warm, as Charity wrapped an arm around her shoulder.

"It's a few more days," Charity said. "We'll get through it. Together."

Linda tried to believe, but when she looked at her hands, the mud covering them looked like blood through her blurred vision.

CHAPTER TWENTY-FIVE

LINDA

BY THE TIME they returned, the picnic had ended. Deja waited at the gates for them, but they sped past her on the bike to the front of the manor. Tatum aimed his camera at them as they entered.

"Damn it," Linda said. "I look like the fucking villain again."

Charity shook her head. "You're okay."

Sabrina leaned against the wall of the foyer, arms crossed. "You were going to leave without telling me?"

Linda stood, dripping onto the floor.

Deja burst through the door. "You didn't think that was going to work, did you?" she said, anger rattling her words. "There's a fucking mudslide."

As Charity stepped forward, her footsteps tracked mud. "Linda didn't believe it was real, so I wanted to show her."

Deja came so close to Linda that Linda could smell her wine-breath. "You thought I'd fuck with you about being trapped here? How little you must think of me."

Linda pursed her lips together, willing herself to remain a level above Deja's prodding. She wouldn't give her the outburst she wanted. She couldn't let the camera see.

"Is she so off base?" Charity stepped between them, moving Deja and Linda apart with outstretched palms. "You've been messing with us all from day one."

Deja's gaze traveled down Charity's body to the floor beneath them, then flicked her irritated stare to Linda. "We'll deal with this later. Right now, you're making a mess of my set. Go get clean."

CHARITY AND LINDA took over one bathroom in the hall. Charity laid down a flat carpet of trash bags for them to lay their muddy clothes on.

Linda couldn't help but smile as she removed her jacket. It clunked as it landed on the pile of discarded vestments, and she crouched to search its pockets. She pulled out the acorn she'd pocketed during her first walk in the woods with Charity. For some sentimental reason, she wanted to keep it. She placed the acorn on the counter top, and the two women stared at it as though it were a talisman of first connection. Then they looked back at one another. Linda struggled with her blouse. It caught halfway off her left arm. Charity stepped forward.

"Do you need some help?" she whispered.

Linda's stomach flipped. "Please," she said.

Charity placed both her hands on the edge of Linda's shirt and lifted it, obscuring Linda's vision with black fabric. She pulled until Linda came free.

"Thank you." Linda let herself smile.

"You know that I'm attracted to you," Charity said. "Even if it's a terrible idea."

Linda swallowed. "Even though I'm the villain?"

"You're not," Charity said. "That's smoke and mirrors." She hesitated. "You're attracted to me too, right?"

"Yeah," Linda said. "I am."

Charity reached a hand to the rim of Linda's jeans. "These look difficult, too."

"So difficult," Linda said. Charity smirked as she popped open the button. She slid down the zipper. She shimmied the jeans past Linda's considerable hips, bending as she slipped them down farther to the knees. Linda was aware of the placement of Charity's head, at level with her covered cunt, and Linda felt as though she might drown in the anticipation of pleasure that washed over her and left her wet between the legs.

"I've never—" she started to say, but Charity shook her head.

"You don't have to set my expectations low," Charity said. "Or confess like it's a crime you've never loved a woman before." Charity tugged at Linda's jeans until Linda stepped one foot, then the other, out of the cuffs. Charity pressed her lips into the front of Linda's underwear.

"But we haven't even kissed," Linda said.

Charity pulled back. "You're right." She laughed softly. "I forgot that part." Charity stood. She grabbed hold of Linda's hands and placed them at the first button of her nightshirt. "Do you want to undress me?" she said.

Linda nodded.

"Do you want to kiss me?" she asked.

Linda nodded.

"Take these off me. Let's get in this shower." Charity led Linda over each button, then shrugged the shirt off. She led Linda's hand to the band of her shorts, then wiggled her way free. She turned, the globe of her ass lit by a single recessed light, and turned the knob. Thank God the manor had installed modern plumbing. As Charity stepped into the shower, Linda followed suit.

Charity washed Linda with a bar of soap left over from some earlier time. The bar was cracked down the middle, but it sudsed back to life as Charity stuck it under the water. She ran her hands over every part of Linda, pausing to touch between her legs. She knelt at Linda's feet and soaped her knees, her calves, her ankles. Then she rubbed a finger against the soap and pressed it against first Linda's then her mouth.

"Better get every crevice," she said as she let the shower water run over their lips. When the soap had washed away,

Charity pushed her mouth against Linda's, and Linda's body gave up its ghosts.

When Charity pulled away, Linda could do nothing but drag her back in again.

After, Linda washed Charity, marveling at how her curves felt when Linda traced them with her soapy hands. She paused at the space between Charity's legs long enough to test slipping one unsoaped finger inside Charity's fold. She felt as slick as Linda was sure she felt. Linda's body trembled.

They traded washing one another's hair with leftover shampoo and conditioner. They rushed through the cleaning of the hair, eager now more than ever to test one another's tastes. But Linda found the experience of hands on her scalp more erotic than any sex she had yet experienced.

They climbed out of the shower and forwent the towels, dripping water all over the wooden bathroom floor. It felt, in a way, like letting all the day's fuckeries trickle off of them, without the harshness of rubbing it away. "Sit on the edge of the bathtub," Charity said, and as Linda settled her ass on the thin edge, she wondered at the fact that she hadn't seen this coming from the moment she stepped foot inside The Groom Mansion. There, Charity had stood in that yellow suit, and Linda passed her over in favor of the milquetoast Tristan. As Charity pushed apart Linda's legs, Linda realized she had been a fool to think, even for a moment, that he could have excited her the way Charity was exciting her now.

Charity's face disappeared between Linda's legs, and Linda struggled to hold onto nothing, for nothing was within the grasp of her shaking hands, as her body abandoned itself. Then they traded places, and Linda let herself dissolve into Charity's sour-salt tang and the all-consuming sound of her moaning.

After they were both satisfied, their bodies covered in goose-bumps and their muscles loosened, Linda grabbed a towel from the stack on the bathroom counter and bent to clean the mess of water they had made. She scowled as she came face to face with the floor.

"What's the matter?" Charity asked, toweling her hair dry.

"The wood grain." Linda laughed uneasily. "Look at it."

As Charity bent down, her knees popped. She made a face of discomfort, which then shifted to confusion. "What the—"

Beneath the spilled water, the wood grain had opened several small holes, like tiny mouths. The water was disappearing into them, and as Linda and Charity watched, small limbs emerged and stretched from the old boards.

"Wood dies, right?" Linda said. "It shouldn't be able to grow after it's…dead, right?"

"I think so." Charity frowned. "Should we let someone know?"

"Let them know what?" Linda said, her head fogged and light. "Yeah, we should tell someone. Deja, probably. This property belongs to the network."

"I'm not willing to believe this house is haunted," Charity said. "For all I know, this could be another trick set up by production before we arrived. But if not, it can't be good for the house to be absorbing water. Like, structural integrity and all that?"

"I'm with you." Linda squeezed Charity's hand, and Charity winced as she let go. "Let's tell Deja."

AFTER THEY DRESSED, they found Deja. Once Tatum was ready to follow, Linda and Charity dragged Deja into the bathroom to have a look at the floors. The mouths had disappeared, though the new limbs remained.

"This is normal," Deja said. She placed a hand against a smooth part of the wood. "You've heard how trees sometimes keep their dead alive? There's a lot of that in this house, I'm afraid. A result of the fungal and root networks that travel deep under the manor. They pump energy and sugar and all that into the wood that forms the floor, and as a result, the floor tries to return to its living state. That's why some of the weird things happen here. It's a natural phenomenon we planned to milk for drama." Deja scowled. "It was my great big idea, and I'm likely to be fired or demoted or resigned to the most minor of decision-making from here on out for it." Deja stood, her knees creaking, and faced the women. "I'm sorry for the way I've been acting. I've been worried about my job, my livelihood. You ladies understand." Her eyes flashed.

Linda shuffled her feet as she forced herself to respond. "No worries."

"So, the wood is living?" Charity drew out the words, her jaw set firm.

"It's living dead, more like," Deja tugged at her clothes, revealing more of her neck and chest, which she forced out proudly. "This old manor has to have major renovations every year when these limbs appear. I'm sure you've noticed some rougher spots and some newer floors. That's why we got the place so cheap. That's why we brought you all here. This whole thing is a silly confluence of nature's fuckery and humanity's frugality." She shrugged. "Maybe try not to get the floors wet next time. Now, maybe we should get back on track with this show?"

"Yes, of course." Linda started to frown, then shook it off and smiled instead. "Sorry." It was the least she could do to placate Deja after her runaway attempt. Deja was too calm. Linda flashed back to the argument she heard between Brandon and Deja. Deja's family had owned the manor. That's why she knew so much about it. Linda chewed at her lip until she tasted blood. It was Deja's blood who had constructed these walls, this floor. She swallowed down the copper taste and did what Deja wanted.

LINDA WOKE IN the night to Deja looming over her bed, a camera poised to capture Linda's startled gasp as her eyes popped open.

"What the fuck?" she said, her breathing rushed.

"You didn't think I'd forget about your indiscretion earlier, did you?" Deja set an earpiece in the center of Linda's chest. "You've been misbehaving, Linda, and you know what's at stake if you don't do what I say. Now, put this in and follow me."

Linda rubbed the sleep from her eye with one hand while she picked up the earpiece with the other.

"Where are we going?" Her heart hammered. Deja had never woken her in the night like this. In the moment of escape, she hadn't thought of punishment, too consumed with the hope that she was on her way to uncover one of Deja's lies. Girls who disobeyed the rules had been sent home before, but there was always a confrontation with The Groom before they went. After the show, women were publicly shamed when they were found to have boyfriends beyond the mansion, or when they refused the ring they were supposed to accept at show's end. The manor, though, felt like a different playing field. Linda doubted that Deja would lead her to Tristan and ignite an argument. At least the camera was on. Linda popped the ear piece in and pushed herself to sit.

"Confessional time." Deja stepped back from the bed, giving Linda enough space to stand, to dress, to follow.

AS THEY WALKED the manor's halls, Linda recognized the path. She had taken it with Charity the night before. A cold sweat erupted in her armpits as she thought over the implication. If Deja was leading her to the nursery, did that mean she knew about her and Charity and their almost-kiss—and worse, their sex in the shower? The floor creaked behind them

Deja glanced over her shoulder. "You're going to love this place." Her voice echoed in the otherwise empty passage. "I wanted to bring you somewhere you'd be comfortable."

"What is it?" Linda hoped her voice didn't register too high, like the voice of a liar.

"You'll see." Deja gestured for Linda to speed up. "We don't have all night."

Linda kept pace with Deja. Together, they entered the secret stretch. They moved, shadow joining with shadow, through the doors, up the little stairwell, and finally, to the threshold between the hall and the nursery. Deja's flat expression didn't change as she aimed the camera on Linda.

"Open the door," Deja said. "Turn on the light."

Linda did as she was told. She touched the brass knob, and it was warm to the touch, as though licked by fire. She turned it. The door opened.

When Linda flipped on the light, the room filled with a brightness that illuminated the life within. A bald root peeked from a yellow pot by the window, its stubby knots reaching as though to root upward instead of into the dirt. Palm fronds lined one wall, their giant rubbery leaves as wide across as human heads. In the middle of the room, brushing the wooden beams of a vaulted ceiling, a massive tree with spindly branches stretched. Its green leaves littered the floor.

Linda's gaze took in too many of the plants at first, and they were no more than a sea of leaves and trunks and stalks and dirts. She breathed a sigh of relief at so much green, her body responding to the memory of the almost-kiss as her shoulders relaxed. She breathed in the wet dirt smell, but it was lined with something fouler. In the mess of twisted limbs, hidden within the camouflage of a barren apple tree that grew from the floor and stood so tall that its giant flat leaves graced the ceiling, she saw it: a body, hung by the neck, not with rope, but with the tree's pliable branches.

The body belonged to Brandon Fuller.

CHAPTER TWENTY-SIX

LINDA

LINDA RAN FORWARD, tripping over a pair of shears on the floor as she rushed to the tree with Brandon's body dangling from it. She pulled at his arms, her hands shaking as she tried to yank him free. When his arm popped out of its socket, she let go. Up close, his skin was sallow, drained of blood. She pressed her fingers against his neck: he had no pulse. She tugged weakly at a limb, but it refused to budge.

Linda scrambled backward and grabbed the pair of shears, then hacked at the limb with the sharp edge. Deja watched, but for Linda, there was nothing but the urge to do everything she could for the man dangling by his neck. She stabbed at the root. Why a root? Why not the ugly tie that hung from his neck, or a rope? Red sap leaked from the wound onto her hand. She kept hacking until the branch snapped, and Brandon's body slumped to the floor. She knelt and felt again for his pulse. Still nothing. She pumped at his chest with both hands, then listened. She repeated the gesture until she was sure he was gone. Only then did she stop and stare at her hand, covered in red. Deja placed a hand on her shoulder. She jerked away from the touch.

Deja held a note out. "Suicide," she said, her voice as neutral as before. "Goddamn it."

Linda stared, her face slack even as her heart beat faster than she thought possible.

"Don't you want to know what it says?" Deja said.

Linda snapped back. "What does it say?" She didn't reach for it.

"It says he decided to off himself after his conversation with you. It says he realized he only had so much time before all the things he'd done got out. It says, Linda, that his suicide is all your fault."

Now Linda grabbed the note. Her eyes scanned it. Deja was right. Brandon blamed her.

"I didn't tell the man to kill himself." She swallowed hard, her brain a foggy swirl of half-thoughts. Brandon's suicide was *his* fault—or Deja's. She studied the writing, but she'd never seen anything written by Brandon. It could be his, or anyone's. Deja towered over her. She felt small trapped in her shadow.

"This isn't my fault," Linda whispered.

Deja shrugged. "Authorities might see it that way. Viewers could, if we spun it right."

Linda searched the room for Deja's camera. It lay on the floor, its red light off. Linda's stomach sunk.

"Has this happened on set before?" Linda wrapped her arms around herself, clutching the skin at her back until it caused an icepick of pain to shoot through her. "Someone…killing themselves?"

Deja rubbed her temple. " Once. A contestant. I'm not going down for this," she added. "A suicide on my watch? I've worked hard for this career."

"What do you want from me?" She felt like she might throw up. She wanted to throw up. She would aim it at Deja's feet.

"I want one thing from you. It's the thing I've wanted from the beginning: a good performance." Deja clicked the microphone at her lapel, speaking into it. "Show me the woman on edge." Her voice echoed in Linda's earpiece.

"Or else?" Linda said. "What are you dangling over my head now?"

"The blame for this has to go somewhere." Deja gave Linda a wicked half-smile.

"This is not what I signed on for." Linda moved forward on her knees, hoping the subservient position would make Deja take pity on her. It had worked with her husband, and her father before him, when she begged for him not to ground her for sneaking sips of his booze. "You promised you'd make me look good. You promised you'd give me a good future. I didn't sign up to be the woman on edge."

"Did you read your contract?" Deja stepped toward Linda, her steps heavy, as though she might stomp Linda beneath her boots. "I can make you look however I want. But Linda, I'm not a monster. If you give me what I want, I'll make this suicide note disappear. I'll put another one in its place. One that doesn't blame you."

"Let me go." Linda pictured herself running free of this place, mudslide or no. She imagined herself hiding in some hovel, living there, away from the spotlight, forever. "Let me leave."

"We're trapped," Deja said. "You saw it with your own eyes."

"I'll take my chances out there," Linda said. "I'll go through the woods, off the path. I'll walk until I can't walk anymore."

"I'm not letting you die for some stupid pride."

"So, what? We're just going to stay here with a dead body? The others are going to freak."

"The others aren't going to know." Deja knelt to meet Linda on her level. With hands too soft to belong to such a hard-ass, she wiped a tear Linda didn't realize she'd shed. Linda let her cheek graze her palm. She needed it, the hint of concern, the promise. "We're going to film like nothing happened, and this suicide thing? It's not going to come out until we're finished here. Do you understand me?"

"You want me to…lie?"

"I want you to play your part," Deja said. "And I want you to leave the truth out of it."

"And if I tell someone?"

The room stunk like new pus, soon to ripen and spread.

"Then it all comes out. Everything you've ever kept from them. What you've done. Who you are. You know the drill."

Deja wiped Linda's tear back onto Linda's night shirt, leaving behind the wet imprint of Deja's finger. "Nothing here has changed."

AS DEJA LED Linda back down the hall to her bedroom, Linda didn't walk, but forced her way through a heavy fog. She slipped into Deja's leftover footsteps. She would not step out of line. She couldn't. There was everything at stake.

When Deja stopped before her bedroom door and held it open, Linda stumbled inside. She crawled onto the bed as though it was her only choice, the final destination, a soft grave in which to die.

That night, it wasn't crying she heard, but a wail so high-pitched it might have been a ringing in her ears. But it didn't cease, and it burned her ears, the way an animal in pain hurts to hear. As the night eroded, Linda tossed and turned, and the wail transformed, amplified, until it was the howl of a coyote in heat. The shrill of cicadas dying in the heat. The crash of a summer storm outside her childhood home. The manor moaned in answer. Linda dreamt of swinging vines that scooped her up and delivered her to their mangy den.

CHAPTER TWENTY-SEVEN

SABRINA

BUZZED FROM HER picnic date with Tristan, Sabrina found herself wandering the halls as the rest of the manor dozed. They'd had such a lovely time, it left her sure that she'd be the one to stand before him as he bended knee and presented one of those network-funded rocks.

At first, she didn't know where she was walking. Like sleep-walking, love-walking was a state that possessed her and pushed her forward of its own will. She was happy to let her mind wander, and it replayed their picnic as her feet led her to her secret room, her peaceful place.

Inside the room with humming walls, she lay, legs throbbing, on the floor, letting the sound soothe her. While she had tossed and turned in bed, the hardness of the wood beneath her felt more like her stiff mattress at home. Finally, she slept and dreamt of Tristan, his boyish smile, his tickling touch. In her dream, she cried tears of happiness, not pain, and where they landed in the ground beneath her, little trees sprung through the dirt.

When she opened her eyes, her breathing had slowed. She rolled over, the sleep and love chemicals blunting her reality. She'd fallen asleep with the lights on, and it amused her, like something a child might do. As she nuzzled her own hand with her chin, her grin pressing into her palm, a movement caught her attention.

A hand reached from the wall. It reached toward her, as strong and convincing as Tristan's. She rose. She moved toward it. It needed something from her. Its presence pulled at her, asking her to lace her fingers with its fingers. It told her what to do. So, she did it.

As she took the hand, it pulled her. Her heart rate sped up as its woody skin hardened over her, and her arm sunk into the wall. She yelped, returning to her waking state. She kicked her feet, but the hand was strong. It took her into the grains, and as she screamed, the wall closed over her mouth.

She gasped for breath like a beached fish until the wall opened around her. She found herself on her knees in a womb-like entrance, a tunnel twisting around her, as pink as an intestine. It smelled like sawdust sanded from rotted wood. Someone's voice spoke on the other side. Was it her sister's? She crawled on hands and knees toward her. The wall undulated beneath her. She rode its waves, its vibrations moving through her, moving into her. As her skin hummed with them, she felt as safe as she had in Tristan's arms. She kept crawling forward and let the tunnel lead her where it wanted her to go.

WITH EVERY MAN she'd been with, Sabrina had done what they asked her to do. The tunnel was no different. She needed that direction, craved it like air.

It was direction she wanted. She needed. It was Tristan.

She crawled for what seemed like hours, time stretching into an infinite loop the way a long hospital shift might feel like three days. Her knees ached, tired of the pressure on them, yet she didn't reach an end. Her breathing came faster, and she couldn't tell if it was from a lack of oxygen or a surplus of fear. The air tasted stale, and her knees left a trail of blood behind, scratches marring the skin she worked so hard to keep soft and perfect.

Out of breath, Sabrina rested, letting her heavy lids close. The tunnel's floor settled under her, whispering against her skin as it rippled around her. The smell consumed her: earth, wet dirt and rot and a hint of decomposed green, the smell of an old antique store, dead things, the smell of old insulation. She couldn't crawl through walls. That was fact, wasn't it? They were solid, the same as her. When she let the laugh she'd been holding in escape, the sound surprised her. Her eyes shot open.

Tristan perched over her. She lay on the floor of his room, curled into a shivering ball. He wore no shirt, his chest slick from a shower, water droplets drying in the ridges of his sculpted muscles. Men shouldn't be made like this. He should be impossible.

"Sabrina," he said, frowning. "You can't come into my room whenever you want."

She hadn't. Had she? She sat up, folding her legs underneath her as the room spun.

"It's not fair to the other women."

"But—" She should argue. He'd given himself permission to sneak into her room. It hadn't been fair to her. Or to Marion, if she was honest with herself. Instead, she struggled to her shaky feet. Her knees throbbed. "I don't know what came over me." She winced. Everything she said in this moment would be permanent. "I was asleep, I think."

"You sleepwalk?" He sounded disappointed.

"A little," she lied. "Only under stress."

"You never told me that." He crossed his arms. "Dangerous to sleepwalk on a farm, you know. Just look at what you've done to your knees." He gestured to the bloody scratches. Sabrina licked a finger and tried to rub the red away, but there was too much of it.

"I haven't done it since I was a little girl." She rubbed harder, and a little more came off. "Maybe it's this haunted house?"

"I thought you didn't believe in it." He didn't either, she realized as he took an uninterested step toward his wardrobe.

"I said I did and I didn't." She wrung her stained hands. She had to turn this around. Everything had been going so well, and now... What was his problem?

"Hard to keep track." He rifled through his shirts. "Which one of these do you like?" He pulled out a blue button-down and an identical blue button-down.

Her chest ached. She pointed. He shrugged into the shirt, then modeled it for her. "I guess I can't blame you," he said, crouching to hover over her like a child. "I've showed you a lot of affection. It's easy to get confused and think you've already won. But you can't assume you're going to win, Sabrina. There are still three women in the game."

"Game?" Sabrina's stomach lurched. "This is a game?"

He stood, offering her his hand. "Not *game*. You know what I mean. *Journey.* Whatever."

Sabrina's body flamed, not from desire but from embarrassment. The two heats were nearly the same.

Tristan glanced at his bed. "I suppose we could—" His eyes traveled down her body.

She shook her head. "I'm tired." She faked a yawn, then scurried to the door. "I'm so sorry. Truly. It won't happen again."

DAY FOUR

DAY FOUR

CHAPTER TWENTY-EIGHT

SABRINA

HINTS OF LIGHT leaked from beneath the bedroom doors as Sabrina crept down the hall. Tristan was a farm boy; he woke at sunrise. She was a nurse; she kept odd hours, too. After the show, she could fix coffee with cow-fresh milk for him before sliding into her pickup and driving thirty minutes to the nearest hospital. He could shake her awake when her naps turned into post-shift comas. They could watch every sunrise over the flat Iowa farmland. But she'd fucked it up by crawling into his room in the middle of the night like an overeager whore.

She'd never done anything like that before. She hadn't been drunk. Tristan had brought mimosas to their picnic, but it was interrupted by Linda and Charity's botched escape before they drank any. When the women returned, Deja banished Sabrina to her bedroom, later delivering a dinner tray. As Sabrina pulled the tray into the room, feeling more like a prisoner than ever, Deja promised she'd given Linda a talking-to and that no more escapes would occur. Sabrina must have seemed skeptical, because Deja went on: she'd hidden the motorcycle, for one thing; and for another, Linda had learned there was no getting out until the week's end, when the roads were cleared and the bus returned.

Despite Deja's unnerving presence, her visit left Sabrina more relaxed. She tried to settle in for a nice evening alone, but her stomach didn't rumble until midnight, when she finally wolfed the cold mashed potatoes. As the moon pulsed outside her window, she turned over and over, but couldn't make herself sleep. It would have been simple enough for Deja to hide something in the food. A stimulant, a hallucinogen. Deja had missed out on evening drama, after all, and with Brandon around, she wrung her hands more than usual.

Instead of returning to her room after Tristan kicked her out, Sabrina marched to the kitchen. She opened the fridge and grabbed a plastic container of leftovers, opened it, and inhaled. It didn't smell off. Drugs would betray themselves with a bitter smell or taste, but if it were LSD or some tasteless compound, Sabrina would have no way of knowing. What she'd seen in that room, what she'd experienced, was not reality, and it had sunk her into hot water with her future husband.

"I overheard him yelling at you." Tatum's surfer voice traveled from the doorway. "He's a fuckface, Sabrina. Don't let him get to you."

"He's my boyfriend," she said, surprised at how small her voice sounded. "I love him."

"You think you do." Tatum took the container of mashed potatoes from her. "It's engineered that way. They work with psychologists, you know, to create the perfect conditions to evoke limerence. Isolation. Shared fear. Intense experience. Jealousy. Alcohol." He grabbed a fork and shoved it into the potatoes.

"Wait!" Sabrina knocked the potatoes out of his hand. They fell to the ground, white goop flying in all directions.

"The fuck did you do that for?" Tatum threw up his hands. "I'm hungry as balls."

"It's got hallucinogens in it," she said.

"Please. I ate like a whole plate of these potatoes last night. I know my hallucinogens. These are just potatoes."

Sabrina scowled, then bent at once to the floor and began scooping the potatoes with her hands, cleaning the mess she made. Tatum's hand closed around her arm. He held a towel in his other hand and draped it over the soiled floor.

"This is fine," he said. "I got this."

Sabrina leaned back on her heels and let her ass hit the floor with a painful thud.

When Tatum finished cleaning, dumping the leftover potato mush into the trash can, he offered a hand to Sabrina. She took it and stood, unsteady on her feet.

"Are you okay?" Tatum asked.

"You're wrong," Sabrina said as she let go. "Tristan is lovely."

"A DAY OFF?" Sabrina said as chewed her nails. Deja stood before her in the foyer, the afternoon sun beating through the stained glass and coloring both their skin with strips of red and blue and gold. Deja had called to her as she sat alone reading, her thoughts not on the book but on the events of the night before: the hallucination. Or the proof that there was something supernatural in the house after all. The book she'd chosen was an old anatomy textbook She carried it with her on trips away to ground herself when her sense of whimsy or fear of the unknown became too much to handle. Deja had snapped her out of her distraction, Sabrina had followed her voice to the foyer, and Deja had informed her she had the day off.

"Why?" Sabrina asked. "I haven't had a day off of filming since I began this journey." She hoped it wasn't her fault she wouldn't be on camera today.

"Tristan doesn't feel like dating right now." Deja waved her hand around. "Not until the evening, when we have to reshoot with Linda. And since Brandon got airlifted out of here this morning, we're short-staffed anyway."

"Brandon got airlifted out? Why didn't they rescue all of us?" Sabrina said. "And why didn't we hear—"

"Last I checked, we still have a show to film." Deja sighed. "He's going to let them know to get the forest service out here to clear the mudslide. In the meantime, let's finish this. But not today—not you—cause, like I said, you get a break."

Sabrina gnawed at her cuticle until she pulled a strip of skin away. Blood welled in the exposed pink space. She tasted blood as she studied Deja's face for hints.

"Is it…me? Something I did?"

Deja scrunched her forehead. "What did you do?"

But Sabrina shook her head, unwilling to give Deja any fodder. "Nothing that I know of! But I thought Tristan and I… Yesterday… The picnic…"

"Oh, he had a fine time yesterday, sure, until Linda fucked it up." Deja leaned in and whispered. "Listen, the truth is he's exasperated with Linda's behavior, and if he has to redo this scene tonight, he says he needs the day to gather himself."

"That's it?" Sabrina said.

Deja grinned. "He's not that deep, hon."

A weight lifted from her shoulders—a phantom feeling. Sabrina shrugged her shoulders back. "And he's not filming with Marion today?"

Deja shook her head. "She's still not feeling well, I'm afraid." Deja's gaze ate Sabrina up as her grin widened, Chesire-style. "I might have been wrong about your chances for winning, sweetheart."

The lifted weight became wings. Sabrina's head went airy with hope. "You think so?"

"I really do." Deja stroked Sabrina's cheek once, then pulled away. "You do this. For the smart little girls who watch this show, okay?"

Sabrina started to agree, then thought a moment more about the little girls watching. "God, I hope not *too* little. Especially this season. They might have nightmares."

"I hope so," Deja said.

SABRINA TRIED TO distract herself with her book, then a series of half-hearted sit-ups, then poring through the pantries for any type of cookie. She tried to journal about her insecurity regarding Tristan but found herself gnawing at her fingernails until her thumb was a bloody mess. Not a turn-on. Finally, she padded down the hall to Marion's room. Maybe she would have a better idea about Tristan's state of mind, and maybe Sabrina could trick Marion into telling her about it.

"Who is it?" Marion asked as Sabrina knocked. Marion's voice was weak and quiet.

"Can I come in?"

"I guess so," Marion said.

Sabrina let the door creak open. Inside, Marion had drawn the curtains and lay in her bed, her body stiff as she rolled over to take Sabrina in.

"What do you want?" Marion's lips were chalky, the paleness seeming to have taken over her whole body, even her hair, now an even lighter shade of blonde.

"Bored," Sabrina said. "Just wanted to chat."

"Not in the mood." When Marion heaved a breath, her chest hardly moved.

"Are you congested?" Sabrina asked. "Having trouble breathing?" She reached to feel Marion's forehead, but Marion let out a shriek.

"Don't touch me," she said. "I'll be fine."

"You look...off," Sabrina said. "Have they mentioned air-lifting you out like they did Brandon?"

"They airlifted Brandon?"

"This morning. They should have taken you, too. You need a hospital."

"I have no fever. No weakness in my grip or anything that happens after a stroke. I'm a little pale, and my muscles are sore? This journey has been taxing. I'm not dying."

Sabrina nodded. She didn't have the heart to ask after Tristan. But then Marion smiled, and even though her lips trembled, Sabrina understood the triumph in it.

"Of course, my being sick means Tristan's been taking care of me. All day long. All night, too."

Sabrina's excitement twisted into nausea in her gut.

"He's been with you all day?" she managed to say.

"Oh, you didn't know?" Marion moaned as she sunk deeper into her bed. The mattress creaked. "He said he couldn't just sit around while I lay in here sick as a dog. I told him not to compare me to a dog. We had a good laugh about it. I imagine he'll be back tonight, after his redo with Linda."

Sabrina stood, her eyes stinging. She wanted to retort, to be the kind of woman who would stand up even to someone as sick as Marion, but she was not that person. She never had been. She was the kind of woman who nodded, who apologized for disrupting sleep, then faded into the background. She had tried too hard to seduce Tristan, and look what happened: she appeared desperate on his floor. It was best for her to fold into herself.

"I'm sorry for bothering you," she said. She stepped back into the hall, shutting Marion's door behind her.

"That crab knows how to get to you," Charity said. She was hanging around by the wall like a creep. Sabrina jumped.

"The what?" she said as her heartbeat settled.

"Trying not to say the "B" word." Charity laughed as she smoothed forward. "It's kind of demeaning, isn't it?"

"Can be," she said. "What are you doing in the shadows?"

"Eavesdropping." Charity slouched. "I'm bored." Charity glanced at the floor, her face falling. "Linda's out there on that do-over date."

Sabrina knew the look: it was jealousy. She'd felt it several times in the manor already. She grabbed Charity by the arm, hoping that the gesture was comforting.

"Want me to distract you?" she asked.

"I'd love that." Charity winked. "What do you say we go for a forbidden stroll?"

THEY STOOD IN front of the nursery room where Charity had previously gone with Linda. Charity rattled the knob, but it wouldn't give.

"Damn it," Charity said. "It's the best room in the house. Guess they caught onto us sneaking in here."

"That's okay." Sabrina chewed her nail. She didn't necessarily want to show Charity her own secret room, but the woman stood in her same jealous shoes. If it has helped Sabrina, it might help Charity. After all, there was something soothing in the humming ceiling, and she wanted to check out the walls again after her mysterious trip through them. "I know another place."

In the empty room, Sabrina pressed a hand to the wall, testing the stability of the illusion. "It's soft enough that you can fall through it," Sabrina said. "Ask me how I know."

Charity stood beside her and pushed her hand into the wood. As it closed around her fist, she jerked back, letting out a shriek. She clutched her hand to her chest like an injured animal, but there was nothing wrong with it, no residue, not a scratch.

"What the shit?"

"Right?" Sabrina trailed her fingers along it, like she might do to a man's thigh in the dark, and ran through the visions she'd had of crawling through the wall's womb. They had not been hallucinations; the wall was the same as the first time she'd encountered it.

"Something wrong?" Charity asked.

Sabrina considered the truth, then decided against it. Her sister had taught her not to trust women too easily, and she had to remember that even as she wanted nothing more than to wrap her arms around Charity's shoulders and cry into her old black band T-shirt.

"I want to show you how they do it," Sabrina said instead, grabbing Charity by the hand, then leading her through the long, dark hall to the fake door.

"Wicked," Charity whispered as they crawled underneath, her voice the only thing that told Sabrina she was beside her. Sabrina knew the way by now. She'd walked it every time she played back the memory of her private moment with Tristan. When she crouched in front of the little door, Charity let out a wolf whistle. "Those sneaky bastards. I almost admire it."

"They put their work in." Sabrina opened the door and led the way, leaving her footprints in the dirt beneath them until they neared the platform. Halfway there, the smell hit her: something fetid, like a rotting sore.

"Holy fuck." Charity's voice was nasal, like she was pinching her nose.

It smelled like the worst dead people who got wheeled into Sabrina's ER. Like sliced ham left to mold in the fridge, a hint of old bananas and gas.

"It didn't smell like this before." Grabbing the collar of her shirt, she pulled it over her mouth and nose like a mask. Despite the smell, she moved toward the empty platform. By the time she reached it, her eyes had adjusted to the dimness.

The platform wasn't empty.

As she screamed, her shirt muffled the sound. Brandon Fuller's body sagged against the squishy wall, his tongue hanging out of his blackened mouth.

CHAPTER TWENTY-NINE

LINDA

BEFORE THE RESHOOT, the daylight that beat down on Linda was a comfort even if she knew there was no rational reason to believe horrible things only happened at night. As a little girl, each morning held the promise of a cornucopia of peaceful hours. Her father went to work before she woke, and even if breakfast consisted simply of toast sprinkled with cinnamon, she savored the way she could eat it in silence. School was easy for her in terms of the work, less so when it came to making friends, but the lonely lunch hours were manageable if it meant finishing her sandwich to a background roar of chatting children. She was a teacher's pet who always followed the rules and never spoke out of turn, and she repeated the words of praise she received every night, a lullaby to lull herself to sleep despite the voices screaming upstairs.

Night arrived with the crunch of her father's car tires. He kept vodka bottles under his seats and poured shots into a fast-food drink cup the moment he started the car, so by the time he pulled into the driveway, he was already swerving. When he walked in the door, Linda hid from the stench of his breath until dinner, when her mother forced her to the table. They learned not to speak, for her father's drunkenness kept him from understanding their conversation and led to frustrated tirades against them for being obtuse. They learned not to take him up on his offers of going out for ice cream; his driving led them more than once into a ditch. They learned not to linger too long; their presence itself burdened him.

Evening arrived at the manor the same way. Before the walk in the orchard, Deja made Linda reshoot a banal scene in which she had been eating a PowerBar during a conversation with Sabrina. Deja wanted the food to be gone and the speech to be clear, so Linda stood in the foyer talking to an orange vase while Tatum filmed her, parroting Sabrina's lines as cues. Linda finished faking a laugh as the setting sun descended through a tiny circular window, rosy and gold. She shivered.

"Don't look cold," Tatum said. "You looked warm in the other shots."

Linda progressed through the rest of her lines in a strange daze. If she thought about it rationally, she didn't believe the house was haunted, but the people in it were. Every last one of them gripped tight to their secrets, the same as her, and Deja knew the burial place of every closeted skeleton.

LINDA TORE INTO her lip with her teeth as Tatum set up the orchard for their scene. Behind the foyer's windows, it was so devoid of light that it looked like someone had hung black sheets over the elaborate stained glass. She closed her eyes, trying to rest, but Brandon's hung body, the black rings around his neck from the vine's caress, flashed beneath her lids.

Still, she could fake it with Tristan, the way she'd always done. She pressed a hand to her heart. It was chilly in the room, and in her chest. Before her arrival on the show, she hadn't realized how much she hadn't been feeling.

At the manor's front entrance, Tristan jerked open the door and offered her his arm.

"Shall we go repeat ourselves?" he said.

She forced a smile as she slipped her arm through his. They would repeat the last lines from their prior conversation, then kiss, then continue as though they had never been interrupted in the first place. They walked once more through the archway to the apple orchard, their feet crushing the cool grass. They walked that center path where Linda had told Tristan about her family and her cat. Linda tried to keep her hands from shaking as Tristan interlaced their fingers. The ornamental lights shone so bright she couldn't see the stars above.

This time, Linda didn't touch the trees' rubbery wood, but she recalled that texture, like healed wounds on fresh skin. She avoided touching the apples that dangled from the trees and lay rotting on the ground, recalling their strange insides spread out on the floor of the den.

"Thanks for being so understanding about my family," she said, as she had said that night, and she pulled at Tristan's hand, tugging him closer.

"Everyone has their demons." He bent to her, and their lips met for an instant. When he pulled back, he left his hand on her waist. It was clammy. He pulled her into a hug, using the gesture to whisper into her ear. "I would never let you win," he said.

Linda frowned. She caught herself and moved free from him, forcing that smile to return, but her stomach twisted at the idea that he still believed she wanted him. As she turned away and ran down the path, light shifted in the leaves and sent little dancing shadows like bruises across her. Her heel sunk into too-soft dirt, sending her toward the bushes between two trees, and though she caught her balance, her shoe popped off, held aloft by the soil. When she yanked it free, it made a sickening sucking sound. Tristan called after her, said her name in that twee twang. She stepped back into the brush. The terrible fruit brushed the top of her head as she knelt into the dirt. It stunk of rot. Not the rot of apples, but like pus and blood, an infected wound.

Tristan screamed. Linda heard him fall, a great thud. Then another crunch, like teeth biting into bone. He screamed harder, a shrill sound she'd not heard him make before.

"Get it off me!" he called out in his new falsetto. "Help! Someone! Get it— Not my face! *Not my face!*" Linda shook herself free from the momentary fear that had gripped her and bounded from her hiding spot to see something attacking him. Tristan pawed at whatever it was in defense, careful to protect his face at all costs. Then Deja was there with a rock in her hand, and the thing was dead on the ground within seconds. For a moment, Linda wondered if Deja might bring the rock down upon Tristan next. Her heart throbbing, she rushed forward as though to stop it. The paranoia faded as quickly as it had come.

"What the hell was that?" Linda inspected Tristan's unconscious body. "Oh, my God. Is he okay?" She started to kneel.

"Get away from him!" Deja kicked a cloud of dirt at Linda. Linda fell back onto her ass. A jolt of pain shot up her spine. "Tatum, take her inside, now!"

The cameraman offered Linda his hand. As he pulled her away, she peered back over her shoulder, angling for a final glimpse. Tristan's shoulder gushed blood despite the bunched fabric Deja pressed against it.

The dead creature sprawled on the ground was white with gray veins running through its outer surface, the sheen of its skin reflecting the spotlights above. It had rodent-like ears and a long snout. It looked like an abomination of a possum, something one might find stitched together in a curio shop, its paws and mouth bloodied with Tristan's carnage.

CHAPTER THIRTY

SABRINA

"HE DIDN'T SEEM suicidal," Charity said as they carried Brandon's body between them through the passage in the wall. Sabrina walked backward, hoping like hell she didn't trip and send Brandon's body flying. Or worse, falling on top of her. They'd considered leaving the body and telling Deja, but Sabrina feared whoever had done this to him might catch wind of their conversation and retrieve him. Or worse, that he might disappear, through the house's will or his own.

"The man had nothing," Sabrina said, talking herself down. The bruising around his neck was a common indicator of suicide, but it was also an indicator of being choked. "One-liners and platitudes and nothing else in that brain of his."

"Sure, but why would that lead him to—"

The other night, Sabrina had heard yelling in the yard between Linda and Brandon. At the time, she'd thought little of it. She even felt a sense of pride that her friend would give the creep a taste of his own toxic medicine. Now, she couldn't shake the thought that her friend might have taken it too far. It was far-fetched, but so was the situation she found herself in.

She frowned as they ducked through the tiny door, holding steady to the body even as its gases leaked and spread their filthy perfume. Kneeling on the floor, she yanked at Brandon's shoulder. A bone popped as he flew through the hole all at once, landing with a splat. Sabrina held her breath and begged herself not to barf. Beside her, Charity swallowed hard.

"Let's drag him the rest of the way," Sabrina offered, looping her arms under his pits.

"Can we?" Charity said. "I thought you'd never fucking ask."

EVEN RIGHT BEFORE she left for the show, Sabrina's house smelled like death. Her father's illness was incurable, because it was unnameable. The doctors shrugged after too many tests, claiming it had to be some sort of autoimmune disease. One recommended them to a specialist they couldn't afford, and that was the end of his medical journey.

If asked, he claimed his sickness was a curse.

As Sabrina dragged Brandon's body along the dark path, she remembered the X-rays she'd stared at as a little girl and how she promised she'd learn one day to read them. It wouldn't have mattered. Her father wouldn't believe anyone but his deceased wife. After all, it was she who swore he'd never love again as she wasted away on her deathbed.

A wave of cold flowed through her. Every night at the end, her mom recited the names of the people who had wronged her. She claimed that her voice breathed the omen of death. Her little curses, as silly as her intentions and her crystals. Only a little girl then, Sabrina longed for the rosy-smelling balms her mother would spread over Sabrina's chest to bring love, or the cardamom cookies that were supposed to translate a mother's love into the bodies of her children. Those were the memories that made Sabrina cling to her mother even when, in anger, she breathed Sabrina's name.

Their father claimed he would have left a long time ago if he could only walk out the door. He called himself powerless to their mother's energy even before he became too ill to move.

And like her mother's intentions and energies, maybe this—Brandon's death—was something supernatural. Maybe the house was at fault: for her crawling through it; for the oozes; for the nightly noises; for her mistakenly breaking into Tristan's room while under some spell cast by its walls; for everything.

But if that were true, then it was all true, and the control she once imagined she had over her life was a facade.

Sabrina tugged on the body, sweat coating her forehead as her resolve gave way.

No. Someone had done this to Brandon. Those tapes had betrayed her. This season's villain was the most dangerous in the show's history: an actual murderer, cold-blooded, the kind who pretended to be a friend.

CHAPTER THIRTY-ONE

LINDA

AS TATUM TUGGED Linda along, Deja struggled to drag Tristan across the ground into the manor. Tatum pushed at Linda's back, urging her to keep moving forward. Dazed, Linda placed one foot in front of the other along the path. Her head was floaty, fogged the way it used to get on the roughest evenings with her father. Tatum kept stride beside her, his hand clamped around her upper arm. Any other man, any other moment, she would have stomped his foot until he let go, but her knees were so weak, she appreciated the stability.

Once Linda reached the front doors, her shiver had transformed to a full-body shake. Her teeth chattered. When she glanced down to make sure she was still standing, her dress was covered in dirt.

She climbed the stairs, her legs with each step threatening to give out from under her. Tatum followed behind with his handheld camera. In her bedroom, she dressed in the casual clothes in which she'd arrived, then followed her old footsteps toward a voice in the parlor, where Marion tossed darts at the wall, her skin dull and pallid even as her stance seemed stronger.

"Where's Tristan?" Marion asked. She turned as soon as Linda entered. "You two were on a date."

Linda swallowed the lump in her throat.

"Did you see a ghost?" Marion said.

"Tristan's hurt." The words felt like a cough. "We were attacked. He's bleeding. A lot."

"Oh, my God." Marion clutched at her chest. "Where is he?"

"I don't know."

"Where is he?" She asked Tatum, who stood filming at the door.

"You should remain calm." Tatum's voice shook. "Tristan is being taken care of."

Suddenly, phantom hands pushed at Linda's back from behind. She stumbled into the parlor, her palms slapping against the floor. A sting traveled from her hands to her elbows.

"What did you do to him?" Sabrina stepped forward. Her forehead was covered in sweat, a wild energy in her movements as she advanced.

"Something bit him," Linda said as she scurried to her feet and gazed out at a knot in the distant floor, another daze coming over her. "In the orchard."

"Bullshit! He's got bruises here." Sabrina pointed to her own neck to illustrate. "You think I don't see strangling victims in the ER?"

Linda shook her head until it made her dizzy. "It came out of nowhere. Some kind of creature."

Rushing toward them, Marion grabbed Linda by the shoulders and shook her. "Where the hell is he, Linda?"

"He's in the hall," Sabrina said.

Marion let out a pained gasp as she hurried through the doorway. Her scream vibrated through Linda like a terrible orgasm. Was he—? Had he found his way to the hall, or had Deja brought him there for all to see—to catch their reactions as they absorbed this new horror? As Linda stepped out of the parlor, she lay her eyes on the lump of decaying flesh. Her hands flew to her mouth. It wasn't Tristan; it was Brandon.

"I didn't do it." Linda heard her words echo inside her, like listening to a conversation while in the first stages of sleep. In her panic, she imagined herself back in the nursery, her hand closing over Deja's mouth, her fingers around Deja's throat until Deja was slumped on the floor, no longer able to threaten her. The vision passed, and Linda gulped for new breath.

"Then who the fuck did?" Sabrina barged at Linda as though to attack, then stopped. Her face journeyed from wrinkled-brow confusion to a cocked-head morbid curiosity. "You're the one who has a violent little secret."

Charity forced herself between them. "We all have secrets."

Linda's stomach jumped. She closed her eyes, fearful that her eyes might somehow betray her, or that her mouth might speak of its own accord.

"Like what?" Sabrina said. "I'm a goddamn open book."

"I'm an actor." Charity's tone was too soft for the situation, like birdsong in a thunderstorm. "They paid me to be here."

"No fucking duh," Sabrina said.

Pieces clicked into place. Linda opened her eyes and found Charity staring, waiting for a reaction, but Linda had no emotion left inside her. She'd used it up, or pushed it down.

"He hung himself." Linda's voice came out thin. As lifeless as the man below. "Deja has the note."

"Why would he do that?" Sabrina asked.

"You're all missing the point," Marion said, her voice shaking as it broke through. "Tristan was hurt."

Sabrina turned on her heel. "What?"

"It's true." Linda flinched. "Out in the courtyard. Deja carried him off. I have no idea where."

Sabrina rushed at Tatum, a blur of fury, and pushed his camera over. He yelled out as it crashed to the ground, then knelt to gather the pieces.

"This is coming out of your paycheck," he said.

"Joke's on you," Charity said. "They don't get paid."

But Linda didn't feel like laughing. Linda didn't feel anything at all. It was just like home.

"I'm a fucking nurse." Sabrina balled her hands into fists. "You're going to tell me where he is."

CHAPTER THIRTY-TWO

SABRINA

IN THE GUEST bedroom named after birch trees, Deja had laid Tristan out on a bed, with silver sheets pulled to his waist. As the women and Tatum entered the room, Deja looked up from a chair in the corner. The room's faint light reflected off the sweat beaded all over his body. Deja had ripped away his shirt and wrapped his shoulder with a torn sheet now bloodied into a Rorschach pattern. Sabrina saw nothing in the blots but a desolate future she intended to avoid.

"Get out." Deja wrinkled her forehead.

"I'm trained for this," Sabrina said. "I'm an RN."

It was muscle memory, what came next. She scanned the room for things she might use, but it was bare of supplies, stuffed instead with pointless vases of dried flowers and an old, timeworn porcelain doll posed on the bureau, her skin cracked to reveal the hollowness inside.

Sabrina closed her eyes, mentally recreating every room, every movement of the other women since they'd arrived. She gestured at the door with her fist. "Charity, grab the hand sanitizer from the bag in your room. Linda, keep an eye out while I wash my hands."

For the first time since arriving, Sabrina was in control.

"Of course." Linda's voice was meek.

As she made her way to the bathroom, Sabrina wondered how she ever could have accused someone so small and helpless of overpowering a man like Brandon Fuller. In her nurse's mindset, she knew that it could only have been himself, or someone stronger. She let the water run over her hands, meeting her own gaze in the mirror. Tristan was ill. In *this* game, she had no competition.

Back in the birch room, Marion hurried to Tristan's side as Charity slouched against the wall. He looked pathetic and nearly dead. Sabrina pushed her sleeves to her elbows. She handed Linda the hand sanitizer.

"We need gloves," Sabrina said. "Who has some?"

"I have gloves," Charity said. "Fashion gloves. Leather. But they're freshly cleaned."

Sabrina sighed. "Better than nothing." Not by much, but she didn't want to dampen the small amount of hope in the woman's eyes. It was an emergency, and in an emergency, people who felt needed didn't overstep. She needed caution, and she needed tools. She could manufacture one and make do with substitutes for the other.

When Charity returned with the gloves, Sabrina spread hand sanitizer over them and slipped them on. They were cold to the touch, brown leather with tiny rhinestones. Sabrina's coworkers would laugh to see her now. She pulled the bloodied sheet away from Tristan's wound. The smell of decay entered the room all at once. His shoulder had caved in like a sinkhole in his brawn. Ropes of muscle and shards of bone were visible inside, like a glimpse into a pit from hell, and around the injury, the flesh had begun to knot, bulging out like infected tissue.

"What—" Sabrina muttered. She'd never seen anything like it, and she'd seen some fucked-up things.

"Can you fix him?" Marion's face was white and sickly. Sabrina should quarantine her. But first, she needed to deal with the issue at hand; the fate of the man who should be hers.

"I'm not sure what I'm looking at," Sabrina said.

"It's unfixable." Deja crossed her arms over her chest. "The process has already begun."

"What process?" Sabrina narrowed her eyes. Deja knew something more than she was telling.

"Some kind of infection. I've been trying to get cell reception." Deja held up a phone. The sight of it seemed out-of-place after so long without them. It had to be the only one on the grounds. "There's no getting through."

Tristan's lips pursed together as if in pain.

"Has he been given a painkiller?" Sabrina said.

"One thousand milligrams of Tylenol." Deja shook a bottle in her lap. "I have enough here to last through the night."

"What if we never get cell reception?" Sabrina asked. This was the way a crisis went: she formed a mental list, then checked off the questions as they were answered until the situation was reconstructed around her, revealing its solution once the picture was complete.

"The van will return in a few days," Deja said. Sabrina couldn't quite read her tone. Relieved? Resigned? Guilty? It wasn't her job to find the culprit of assault, but she sometimes sussed out clues, which the police ignored if she told them. "It's the best we can do."

"He needs help now." Sabrina thrust the bottle of hand sanitizer into Deja's chest. "Wash your hands. Get me a lighter and a knife from the kitchen. STAT."

Deja pursed her lips. Sabrina sensed her manipulative gears working, contemplating how allowing Sabrina to solve the problem might break the contract that forbade contestants from partaking in dangerous situations during filming. Sabrina didn't give a single shit about her contract, not when Tristan's life was fading like his farmer's tan under the monotone sky. She didn't care about suspected murders or ghosts or her friendships or her sister at home. She cared only for her patient.

"Do you want me to help or not?" Sabrina said, frustration edging her voice.

"Fine." Deja scowled and left the room.

"I don't want to lose him." Marion reached out as though to touch him, then stopped herself. Tristan's eyelids fluttered, but they were stiff, like a bandage stretched too tight. "Tristan? Can you hear me?" Marion squeezed his hand. "He squeezed back!"

"Don't touch him! We don't know what he's got," Sabrina snapped. The woman had sniffed too many nail salon fumes to think right—Tristan would have realized this eventually. Over in the corner of the room, Linda and Charity made eyes at one another. No one else was serious about the man's plunging heart rate.

When Deja returned with the requested materials, Sabrina wiped sanitizer over the blade, let it dry, then held the lit lighter under it, coating both sides in heat. "Better double-safe than double-sorry." Bending over Tristan, she pressed the hot blade to his flesh where the wound needed closing.

Tristan's body began to shake, like Sabrina's did when an orgasm moved through her. Where the knife touched him, smoke drifted from his skin. Sabrina coughed through it, trying to view the wound beneath the haze.

"Is that supposed to happen?" Marion pulled at her hair until a strand came off in her hand. She let it fall to the ground, too concerned with Tristan's state to care much.

His wound burst into flame.

It happened all at once, like the way paper caught on the driest days.

Sabrina screamed, and it cascaded through the room from throat to throat, an infection of throat-numbing terror. She dropped the knife. It clattered to the ground. The room smelled like a campfire, then Deja was beside Sabrina with a bucket full of water. She tossed it onto Tristan. The flame died.

"Let's wait for some professionals." Deja wiped excess water off onto her soaked pants. She grimaced as she turned away from the bed. "We could make things worse." She gestured at Tristan, who still shivered as his now-blackened wound smoldered in his shoulder. She knew this was no simple illness. This was nothing like Sabrina's mother's crystal wishes. This was something else altogether. Something summoned from Hell.

"I *am* a professional," Sabrina muttered, but this was beyond her skill set. She stared at the wilting body of the man who was supposed to be her saving grace, her ticket to unlocking everything life needed to bestow upon her.

She reached for him, her future, but she didn't dare touch.

CHAPTER THIRTY-THREE

LINDA

THE CONTESTANTS DIVVIED tasks even as Deja insisted she and Tatum had it covered: two women would watch over Tristan at a time, while two women would steal some sleep. Every few hours, Deja roamed the grounds, checking for a phone signal.

In the room, Charity's gaze remained trained on Linda. Linda felt it boring through her, insistent, worrying. Like her teachers used to be when she went half-catatonic in class.

"What?" Linda blushed to be so observed.

"Nothing." Charity's lips formed an underscore.

"You keep looking at me."

"It's just, you look like you could use a snack or something." Charity reached into the pocket of her cardigan and pulled out the smallest bar of chocolate Linda had ever seen. "Here."

"Oh." Linda unwrapped the chocolate. "Thanks." She placed it on her tongue. It was dark, with a hint of citrus, barely sweetened. The chocolate had been in Charity's pocket, warmed by her warmth, infused with her in some impossible way. It was perfect. She wanted more.

"You look zapped, too." Charity reached out as though to move a strand of hair out of Linda's face, then stopped herself. Linda offered a lazy smile, began to redo her ponytail to capture all the strands, then decided to leave another one loose enough that it would fall back down. "You should sleep first."

"What about you?" Linda asked, hoping Charity would offer to share a shift.

"I'm used to late hours, staying up until the morning."

"Aren't you a cook at a brunch place?" Sabrina said.

"Why don't you both go to sleep?" Charity said.

Linda hesitated, shifting from one foot to the other. "And Marion?"

Marion hadn't left Tristan's side, her hand as close to his without touching as she could manage. "I won't be able to sleep a wink until he's safe," Marion said.

As far as Linda was concerned, the contest should have been Marion's. It should have been finished before they came to the manor. Tristan should have dropped to one knee in front of Marion and slipped onto her finger one of those massive network-funded rocks, while generic violin notes swelled in the background. It wasn't fair that anyone else had even pretended at being a contender, that Deja had played into Sabrina's hopes. Linda swallowed.

"Well?" Sabrina said to Linda, motioning out to the hallway full of bedrooms. "You ready?"

Linda waved a tiny goodnight. As she left the room, she held Charity's gaze until the wall cut them off from each other.

LINDA AND SABRINA slipped into their pajamas and crawled under the same pink quilt in Sabrina's room. Sharing a bed was a fast pass to intimacy. Linda had experienced it with lovers, those lightheaded nights of so much talking, she stayed up until sunrise without realizing. But she kept to the edge of the mattress, her legs curled stiffly into herself. Sabrina had accused her of killing Brandon. The memory stung.

Finally, just as her eyes grew heavy, Sabrina's voice broke the silence. "Is it confessional time?" she said.

"What?" Linda's breath caught as she came alert all at once.

"What was the deal you made with Deja?" Sabrina asked.

"It's nothing," Linda said. "Just some stupid shit I did before I knew better, and she said she could get it off my record so the press wouldn't have a field day with it." It wasn't a lie, but it was about to be. "Stealing, fighting, that kind of thing." Linda forced her breath to even out. "This is stupid. You know it's Deja who sowed these seeds, right? You and me are supposed to be friends. What's with the third degree?"

Silence shivered between them before Sabrina once more broke it.

"You didn't kill Brandon, did you?" It was a whisper, barely audible.

"Of course not." Her words were a sigh of solace. "I would never."

"He killed himself?" Sabrina said, her tone failing to gain strength.

Linda sucked in a quickened breath. "I'm…not sure."

"Was it the same thing that got Tristan?"

Linda thought of the creature sprawled, dead. "Tristan was attacked by a…possum. Or something." She closed her eyes. "I think Brandon's death had something to do with Deja." As she said it, regret and relief twisted in her throat. The accusation left a sour taste on her tongue, and her heartbeat quickened. Deja was always watching. But Linda needed to unload the great weight on her chest. "It sounds crazy, right?"

"Nothing sounds crazy right now."

Linda rolled over to face her friend. "It's just, she came and got me in the middle of the night. She led me to this room, a nursery—"

"Charity tried to take me there. It was locked."

"Probably because that's where we found Brandon. She said he left a suicide note that blamed me. She said she'd release it to the public—and to y'all—if I didn't keep going with the show."

"And how did you find him?" Their words were rushed now, breathless and eager.

Linda waited for the door to burst open, for Deja to rush in and drag her away—to her death, or her public demise. When nothing happened, Linda let herself believe they were truly alone. "Hanging. From a vine."

For a while, they said nothing, the only sound their heavy breaths in the dark.

"But what if it *was* the vine?" Sabrina said, and the theory sounded so wild that they both burst into laughter.

After they once more calmed, their shared warmth and lack of surveillance lulled Linda into an unfamiliar sense of security. It was a welcome break from chaos. Even with Tristan dying a few rooms over, this was somehow nice.

"Sabrina, can I ask you a question?" Linda whispered, hoping her friend was not yet asleep.

"Yes," Sabrina said, her voice groggy.

"Have you ever been with a woman?" Linda felt taken aback at the question as soon as it left her mouth. She hadn't meant to ask, hadn't realized it was a question that lived on the tip of her tongue.

"I'm with a woman right now," Sabrina said.

"No, I mean—"

"I know what you mean." Sabrina shifted.

"I was curious. But never mind." Linda rolled over and faced the wall.

"Sorry. Yes, I've had sex with a woman. Hasn't everyone?"

"No," Linda whispered. "Not everyone."

"You're in love with her," Sabrina said.

"Excuse me?" But she did want, more than anything, to break open Charity's ribcage and know her insides in that metaphorical way she'd always assumed meant *love*. "Yeah, I guess I am."

Sabrina yawned. "Charity's a good match for you. Better than Tristan, anyway."

In the silence that followed, Linda heard Tristan's faint moaning down the hall.

"He's not a good match for anyone right now," Linda said.

The wind whistled outside the room's lone window, and the moon washed through the glass, unencumbered by the shadows of trees. Someone had ensured there were no trees within fifty feet of the property, a wise decision from an architectural standpoint, or so Linda understood from growing up in a house with foundation problems. But even without the influence of tree roots, the floors creaked all night—or maybe that was the walls. Tristan moaned again.

"He's not going to make it," Sabrina whispered, her voice catching in her throat.

"He might." Linda rolled back and wrapped her hand in Sabrina's.

Someone walked by the closed door—Deja, searching for that elusive cell signal.

"If they don't get in touch with someone soon…" Sabrina whimpered a little, and Linda realized her friend was crying.

"Hey." Linda wrapped her arms around Sabrina. Sabrina burrowed herself into Linda's chest and sobbed. As Linda's shirt grew damper, Linda knew she should be crying, too. Down the hall, a man was dying, a man she kissed not twenty-four hours ago. She swallowed. Maybe, like her mom had said to her before going into the institution, Linda was as deformed inside as that possum had been on the outside. She stroked her friend's hair. "You're going to be fine."

BY THE TIME Charity entered the bedroom, only a few fevered hours had passed. No medical professionals had arrived. It was still dark outside.

Linda's eyes fluttered open as she beamed at the woman in the half-light.

Sabrina shot up in bed. "How is he?"

"Not good," Charity said softly. "Why don't you go check on him?"

Sabrina wasted no time crawling free of the blankets and stumbling against her sleep out the door. Charity climbed beside Linda, the bed shifting to accommodate her.

"We're alone," Linda said, her palms already sweating.

"No shit." Charity groaned as she leaned into her pillow. "My back is trying to murder me." Charity glanced over at Linda. Linda shifted in the blankets. "I'm running on four hours of sleep here."

"I better get up." Linda said, staying put. She wanted something, anything, to happen. After two months of buildup with Tristan, then the terrible deaths, then the terrible thing that happened last night, then the shocked realization in the night, she teetered at the precipice of an elusive moment. The moment that would resurrect her.

"You're going to have to drag Marion to bed kicking and screaming," Charity said. "She's tired as fuck, but she's refusing to leave Tristan's side."

Tristan. He was dying, and here she was hoping for— What? Sex? She challenged her heart to hurt for the man. She challenged herself to fear for him and not for the possibility that she might never again touch Charity's mouth with her own.

"Wrestling Marion? That sounds like a job for Sabrina. Or Deja." And sure enough, down the hallway, Sabrina's pitch climbed. "Sounds like someone's trying their hand at it."

Charity sunk down further into the bed. "The man's in a bad way."

"I know." Linda risked a touch, her hand moving to rest on Charity's thigh.

Charity jumped and tried to move away, but the bed was too small for her to go far.

"You don't know me," Charity whispered. "You shouldn't get too attached."

"What? But we—" Linda chuckled nervously.

"I shouldn't have come onto you like that." Charity stretched until her back joints popped. "It was weakness. You won't like me when you get to know me. Women never do."

Linda had felt something more than a quaking orgasm in that bathroom. She had felt a splintering that extended from her neck to her feet and exposed her organs. It had been years since she fought for something, but she would kill for another touch from Charity's hands.

"We all have secrets. We all have terrible things in our pasts."

"I'm an actor," Charity said, sighing.

"You mentioned that," Linda said. "I don't care."

"You don't understand. Deja hired me to be here. To drum up drama. I don't work in a brunch place. I wait tables in a strip club, and the producers found me there. They wanted a lap dance from me, but I wasn't a stripper, and they asked me if I acted, which of course I do when I can get the work. I'd done a little in commercials and things—it was LA, after all—and so they offered me the job for a lap dance."

"Your dark secret is that you're an actor. That's nothing."

Charity huffed. "My dark secret is that women always think I'm lying to them, because I've gotten paid for lying. I go to a lot of parties that I can't take my girlfriends to, and they think I'm cheating on them. It's easier if I don't get involved with people." She frowned. "I hated Tristan, but you better believe I kissed him. I made out with him. I was going to meet his parents if it meant another paycheck."

Linda smiled as her stomach calmed. She understood what it was like to be thought of as the kind of awful person who could do horrible things. She'd lived as that person under her mother's distant watch.

"Everyone's acting at least part of the time," Linda said. "That doesn't mean nothing they do is genuine." She thought of her new friend, Sabrina, and herself, the half-true lines she recited to the camera. "Besides, we're stuck in a fucked-up house where some fucked-up stuff has gone on. We're not promising one another forever." She mustered the courage to ask for what she wanted. "Just get over here and cuddle me."

Like a sped-up video, Charity scooted as close as she could get and wrapped her arms around Linda's waist, placing her head against her chest. Linda pulled Charity into her. She smelled like orange peel, and as Linda rubbed her hand up and down her arm, she prickled with goosebumps.

"Were you so unaware of me before we came here?" Charity said into the soft night as she took Linda's hand. "I caught myself staring at you all the time."

"Were you?" Linda stroked Charity's thigh with the tips of her nails. "I didn't know. I thought you—we all—were here for Tristan. You were so heated when we talked about him. You started fights with all of us."

"Actor," Charity said. "Acting." She winced against Linda, and the movement sent a shock up her spine. "Are you mad I didn't tell you earlier?"

"Why would I be mad? You were under contract. I was, too. You had your reasons for coming onto this show. We all did—do."

"Linda, I can't believe I don't know this, but… What do you do? For work, I mean."

"Oh," Linda slouched, readjusting Charity's head to her chest. "I'm between jobs." She laughed at herself. Once upon a time, she had promised herself she'd never be the kind of person who used such obvious cliché. "I'm unemployed."

"What did they make you say for your introduction?"

"Influencer."

Charity's laugh vibrated Linda's sternum. "How many followers do you have?"

"Like one hundred thousand? I helped my ex-husband found a landscaping firm. I'd post photos and how-tos for the business. He never understood that stuff, so when I quit, or was fired due to divorce or whatever, I just changed the name of the page and kept the followers, scheduled a shitload of posts. It's bullshit, but they're popular."

"There's a lot of lonely people out there."

The silence stretched between them.

"What would you do if you could do anything?" Charity said.

"I'd open a plant nursery," Linda said. She paused, considered, continued. "And open up myself."

"You seem open to me," Charity said. "You did in that bathroom, anyway, and you do now, too." Charity reached a hand between her legs.

Linda moved the hand away. "There's a lot that you don't know about me, too."

"I'm sure." Charity nuzzled her head against Linda, and Linda caught the floral smell of the old shampoo and old sweat from Charity's scalp. It was sexy, bodily, evidence of Charity as a living, breathing person. "Nap with me a while?"

"Of course." Linda breathed in deep, settling herself. "Were they really paying you to be on the show?"

"A small sum," Charity said. "I can't believe you dated Tristan for free."

"He's not the worst, if you like men," Linda said. "The bar is low, you know."

"It's just... He seems like the kind of guy whose favorite restaurant is Applebee's."

"I think it was Texas Roadhouse," Linda said.

"I rest my case," Charity said.

As they lay warmed by their embrace, Linda returned to sleep. Her father's face greeted her, a portrait covered in brown veins. As she stared into the glass, it morphed into the image of the thing from the curio shop, and Linda fell back, screaming, into a mess of eager, grabbing limbs.

THE MANOR DIDN'T allow rest. The manor didn't allow more than stolen winks behind tired eyes, and when Linda woke, no hints of morning had slithered into the sky.

Linda reluctantly swung her legs over the side of the bed, slipped on her clothes, and padded out the door, leaving Charity peaceful and alone.

In the room of the dying, Tristan's skin looked waxy, as though his beads of sweat had soaked into his skin and made him shine. Marion lay with her head against the bedspread, unmoving but for her lips, which murmured a prayer.

Sabrina paced. "I wish I had any medical tools whatsoever." Sabrina waved both her hands at Marion. "I wish this one would get some sleep. If things keep going downhill, we're going to need all hands on deck." She paused in front of the passed-out Tatum in the corner chair. "Case in fucking point."

"Where's Deja?" Linda asked. The room stunk of impending doom. Linda stood at its threshold, unwilling to enter again into the uncertain dread surrounding Tristan's condition.

"I don't know! Looking for a signal, she says."

Charity appeared in the door, bags beneath her eyes.

"Do you think there are medical supplies somewhere?" Linda asked, eager to make herself useful elsewhere.

"You could look. I could use a needle and thread for stitching. More bandages." Sabrina held up the ripped sheet they'd been using for wrapping his wound. "We're almost out." She dropped the sheet back onto the bedside table. "Medication. Antibiotics would be helpful. I'd sure love it if Deja would come back and let me know if there's any in the manor. I'll be mad if she didn't at least search a few rooms for those already. We shouldn't have slept so long." Sabrina stomped back and forth. "And alcohol. I need alcohol. Anything. Maybe a sleeping pill for this mess." She gestured again at Marion. "Maybe a Xanax for the rest of us."

"We're on it." Linda stepped back from the door into the burst of fresh hall air. Charity followed.

The exhausted cameraman stirred. He glanced back and forth, torn between his need to stay and his desire to follow Linda.

Linda backed away. "You stay here, watch over The Groom."

The cameraman sunk back into his chair, camera perched like a second head upon his shoulder.

"As if they're even going to run this train wreck," he said.

LINDA AND CHARITY searched through the drawers in each bedroom vanity. All told, there were eight bedrooms in the wing, four on each side. The contents of each weathered vanity were unexemplary: a couple of old tubes of lipstick, a dusty powder puff, a book of matches, dust, three pencils, a flashlight, and an old notebook filled with indecipherable writing. Linda pocketed the matches and the notebook but left the rest where it lay. Next, she tried the bathrooms, searching through cabinets and drawers. They had been cleaned out of all but a few half-melted candlesticks and the faint smell of mildew. The buffet in the dining room held old silver dishes, the parlor drawers a small compact mirror.

"If I keep looking, I'll have a whole beauty kit," Linda said.

"You mean, in addition to the bathroom full of the stuff upstairs," Charity said.

The kitchen contained the standard kitchen offerings: cooking utensils, pots, and pans. Old herbs. Linda bit her lip as she examined them, trying to recall any traditional folk remedies. Charity grabbed a tin of chamomile from a cabinet and shook it.

"Good for sleep," she said. "Could calm Marion down." She gestured to a bowl of garlic bulbs. "Anti-inflammatory. Couldn't hurt."

Linda squeezed one It felt firm. Nothing else looked familiar.

Linda picked at her lips with a sharp nail. She hadn't found any proper medical supplies in the parts of the house she knew well, but they had yet to search the hidden hallways, the off-limits areas they'd been forbidden from exploring.

AFTER AN HOUR of failure, Linda arrived at the last hall—the one she had stumbled upon that contained all the rooms of stacked branches. She hadn't noticed any furniture that first time, but she hadn't been looking for areas where one might hide useful supplies. She led Charity to the first door, then gave her one final glance before twisting the knob open. She clicked on her flashlight. The batteries still worked. A shaft of light poured into the hall, illuminating a floor studded with nubs of rough wood.

"They're growing," Charity said. "Like the wood in the bathroom was."

Entering the hall, Linda motioned Charity to follow. As her feet pressed against the knots, they seemed to sink back into the wood, then rise again.

At the first door, Linda took a deep breath and pushed it open. She shined the light inside. Whereas before she had believed the room was filled with cut branches, now she saw the truth: the branches had grown from the floor. They reached to the ceiling and twisted together as they climbed, a tangle of insistent limbs. Linda shivered, remembering the way the vine had wrapped around Brandon's neck.

Linda passed the flashlight to Charity.

"Wow." Charity peered in, her voice shaking. "This can't be real."

"Maybe not," Linda said. Money could buy tricks as good as this.

Inside the next rooms, more branches had grown from what should have been a dead wood floor. In the third room, the branches had panicked to reach the top, the end-of-the-line, and had bent back on themselves in an orgy of limbs. The ceiling had cracked in several directions like a parched forest floor.

"This is going to bring the house down eventually," Charity said. "Why wouldn't the network fix this?"

"This?"

"Filing the limbs down."

"Why does the network do or not do anything?" Linda said. "Money? A misguided sense of priorities?" Linda chewed her lip as she told Charity the only information she knew. "Brandon said Deja brought the house to the network's attention. That it was her distant family who built it."

"Then she's to blame." Charity shoved her hands in her pockets. "The next room?"

Linda opened that door. Before them, the braided tangle reached. She started to hand off the flashlight when a movement caught her eye. She frowned and paused the sway of the beam on a limb. She squinted. Between the twigs and the branches, new shoots had erupted in strange shapes. Linda knelt to get closer to one nearest the door. She shined the light. That strange familiarity returned to her, an uncanniness that made her feel sick to her stomach. The new shoot was not wood, but an arm covered in flesh ridged like bark, and at the end of the shoot was a fist.

The fist opened, and Linda screamed louder than she should have—surely the sound traveled upstairs—but she couldn't help it. The hand's fingers wriggled toward her. They were gruesome in their thinness. There were no nails, only more soft, fleshy bark.

Charity yanked Linda back by the shoulder. She knelt on the floor and met her knee-to-knee. "Are you okay?"

"Look." Linda gestured.

Charity peered inside, and as she noticed the strange appendages shooting off from the branches, she jumped back and shut the door.

"Whose hands are those?" she whispered.

Linda's balance returned. Standing, she marched with purpose to the last door and flung it open. This time, she didn't scream. The whole room was filled with hands, and as she shone her light upon them, they flexed and turned toward her. They moved their fingers as though trying to grasp whatever humanity she had to give.

THEY SAT ON the floor outside the hall, their breath hurried and desperate as they pressed closed the door that led to such monstrosities.

"I want to get out of here," Charity said. It was the first time Linda had heard her sound frightened.

"I do, too." And she had since the threats, the first death, the kiss in the room that was then tainted by a swinging body. All lovely things did rot. But for once, she longed to outrun the decay.

"But also—" Charity chuckled, though there was little levity to the sound. "I'm happier right now than I've ever been before. It's like…this weird contradiction of emotions. I don't know. That doesn't make any sense."

"It's like a funeral." Linda's father's face appeared again in the dark.

"I haven't been to many," Charity said. "And not since I was a kid."

"I went to my father's," Linda said. She'd never talked about it before. The words burned her throat like vodka coming back up after a bad night. "It seemed like everyone we'd ever known was there. All the people who either cared about me or claimed to. They asked me how I was. They hugged me, fetched me plates of food at the wake. At school, a counselor called me into her office once a week for three weeks, until my mom got sick, and they moved me to the foster, who homeschooled me and didn't pay too much attention. But the funeral? After the funeral, I felt so full inside. Like, death had reaffirmed all that I'd ever heard was good about life. Love, care, affection. For a couple of days, before it became apparent my mom had disappeared mentally, I felt like I understood profound sadness and happiness at the same time."

Charity squeezed Linda's upper thigh with her trembling hand. "I wish I could have been there for you."

"That's impossible."

"But imagine. There you are. The people who claimed to care have gone. Your mom is away. You think you're alone. But you're not alone. I'm with you. You need me. I wrap you up. I'm there, in your room, whenever you call. Can you see it?"

Tears formed in Linda's eyes, but they didn't release. Instead, that crack inside widened, and she imagined its yawning maw there to eat her alive. "I see it," she said, and the thought was a remedy and a fear.

"Any time you think about those times, remember me. I'm there now. We're going to get out of this together. It's going to be better than a funeral. We're going to try our hand at this thing. It's going to be all the good stuff, and hardly any of the bad."

Linda laughed, but her heart wasn't in it. "It's never without all the bad."

"That's true," Charity admitted. "But it can be close. We have to believe that we—me and you—can get close." Charity heaved a huge sigh. "Besides, those rooms? They were tricks anyway. Right?"

"Right," Linda said, stepping again into an uncertain conclusion. "Just tricks."

CHAPTER THIRTY-FOUR

SABRINA

AS SABRINA WATCHED over Tristan, her eyes watered from how wide she kept them as she studied his fading form. He had stopped shaking and was sprawled out, still and silent. Sabrina and Marion sat on either side of the frame while Deja paced at the foot. Overnight, his hair had grown and knotted into hardened dreadlocks. Sabrina had never seen an infection that affected hair, but she assumed there was precedent somewhere outside her medical textbooks. The infection seemed to have traveled through him. His veins had darkened into brown rivers that showed through his waxen skin.

"He looks fucked up," Linda said as she and Charity stepped back inside. Their hands were empty.

Sabrina looked up. Her face was streaked with tears, and her chest burned angry to see them empty-handed. "Did you find anything?"

Linda reached into her pocket and pulled out the chamomile and garlic.

Sabrina took the root. It would be useless—his inflammation was beyond the folk remedies her mother used to push—but she didn't want to cause panic. Marion was clearly on the verge of a breakdown, mental or physical. "Marion, make yourself useful and go grab a cup of hot water—and a mortar and pestle."

"Mortar and pestle?" Marion's speech betrayed the dryness of her mouth.

"I'll get it." Charity glanced at Marion. "It's the thing witches use to mash herbs in movies."

"That bitch has got some skeletons in her closet," Marion muttered.

Skeletons lived in bodies, not closets. Sabrina had always understood that. If you wanted to get at the root of a person, check their skin and bone, not the place they kept their clothes. One reason she loved Tristan was that his body matched his words. He hid little. Sabrina needed to touch him, to experience the transparency of him once more. To hold him and know she was touching truth, when so much truth was falling away minute by minute. She took his hand in hers, despite her prior warnings. What was there to lose now? She squeezed him. His skin didn't give to her pressure.

"His hands feel hard." Sabrina squeezed it again with her gloved hand. "Like he's got lumps under his skin. Like cancer."

Charity returned and handed the items over. Sabrina pretended to smile, then unwrapped the garlic bulb, separating each wedge from its casing. She let the skin flutter to the ground, dropping the meaty hunks into the mortar. She pushed the pestle into the cloves, twisting it as her mother had done while she watched, an eager child, until the scent of garlic overwhelmed the smell of impending demise. The scent reminded her of home. She couldn't go back empty-handed.

Sabrina took a fingerful of crushed garlic clove. She wasn't sure what to do with it, but she had to do something, anything, to keep the women from losing their minds. She pressed the crushed garlic into Tristan's mouth, remembering the softness of his tongue on her fingers, on her belly. She pushed it deep into him, her finger brushing his tonsils. He didn't even stir. His lips brushed against her gloves, and she wished her hands were bare so she could feel his mouth once more. His teeth caught on the glove as she pulled free her fist. She tugged harder. Still, he didn't stir.

She cupped her hand against his chin to close his lips, then massaged his throat. His Adam's apple refused to move at her insistence. "He's not swallowing." She moved her hands from his face, then fished the garlic pieces out of his mouth with one finger. She couldn't make even a hopeless remedy look encouraging. She'd look for supplies herself.

As Sabrina stood, Marion let out a confused yelp. "But the hot water?"

"The water is for you." Sabrina opened the can of chamomile flowers and dumped several into the water. She handed Marion the mug. "Drink this down." Sabrina bent to the level of Marion's eyes, like a doctor might do for a troubled patient. "You need to sleep. When we get back, you're going to the bedroom, like it or not."

Her chest lifted at being allowed to boss Marion around, even for one measly moment. Marion scowled, but she held the hot mug between her hands regardless. As the other women left the room, Sabrina caught her sniffing the sweet brew.

AS SABRINA MARCHED down the long hall to the only room Linda didn't check, the wood walls and floor creaked around her like an echo as she passed each strange portrait. At Deja's closed door, she wrapped her clammy hand around the knob. She pushed the door open.

Deja's room was similar to the others. The theme was "Joshua Tree," and the color scheme was a deep hunter-green, expressed in the quilt stretched over her bed, the stain of the bed frame built of sturdy lumber, and the seaweed-colored wallpaper. Sabrina's heart hammered as she slid open the drawer in the dresser. Inside, she found pages stacked on pages, yellowed with time. She shuffled through them to discover the many artworks of a child. She pulled out a couple of sheets. One portrayed a giant tree with a grandmotherly face, the ridges of its bark the woman's wrinkles. Another showed the manor. In an upper window, a little girl screamed at the window.

"Yikes," Sabrina muttered. Down the hall, the floor whispered. Sabrina checked quickly each drawer and cranny, but found nothing more of note. Finally, in desperation, she pounded her fist deep into the bottom of a drawer. The bottom snapped in half. Scowling, she broke free several planks of board, revealing the true bottom. Her hands closed upon a thick book. It felt like something Deja would take from her if she saw it, so Sabrina slipped quietly from the room. Linda and Charity were walking toward her. She grabbed Linda's arm and pulled her into an empty room. Its bed was covered in old sheets that looked so brittle, they may crumble if touched. Charity followed.

"I found something," Sabrina whispered. She slid to the floor, blocking the closed door from the inside. As she propped the journal open in her lap, Linda and Charity joined her. Scratchy cursive dripped down the pages. Sabrina couldn't make it out no matter how much she squinted. Charity and Linda scooted to either side of her, leaning over the notebook and blocking the light from the lone window. Sabrina shot them a single irritated glance.

"Is this Deja's?" Linda asked.

Sabrina shrugged. "Now, how on earth would I know that?" Sabrina handed the journal over. "It was in an old dresser. Could be Deja's. Could be some previous occupant's."

Linda thumbed through until she came to a page of diagrams, then drawings of trees with cut lines down the middle of their trunks.

"Huh." Linda studied the drawings. "This is weird as shit."

"They were millers, remember?" Charity said, straining her neck to peep.

"Yeah, but look at this." Linda traced an illustration on the right side, which showed some sort of burial rite: a prone body with its arms crossed over its chest being injected with a needle and syringe. "I can't read any of this."

"It looks like English, but some sort of bastardization," Charity said. Linda raised an eyebrow. "Lit major. Dropped out."

Sabrina peered around the room with its obscure tree theme. "These people were obsessed with the forest," she said.

"Wouldn't you be? If you were surrounded by it and nothing else?" Charity said.

"And if you lived in a house built with living fucking lumber," Linda said.

"Wait, what?" Sabrina wrinkled her forehead. What Linda had told her about the vine wrapping Brandon's neck had stuck. The mention of living lumber was altogether new.

Charity and Linda exchanged glances. Linda filled Sabrina in on the weird fact Deja had unloaded on them after their shower: that the forest's roots kept the lumber in the house alive.

"Is that even possible?" Sabrina said.

"Is any of what we've seen possible?" Charity said.

The house groaned like an answer.

"If it's alive, it's grumpy as fuck," Sabrina said, and the women chuckled.

"What's so funny?"

They stopped and looked toward the voice. Marion stood at the door, which she'd opened out into the hallway. "I'm bored to tears, y'all," she said. "Please tell me what's funny."

Charity rubbed her eyes. "It wasn't even that funny. We're playing truth or dare," she lied.

Marion's eyes brightened, but it was the only part of her that didn't look worn. Her usually bright skin was dull and thick with eruptions. Her white gown brushed the floor.

"Marion, truth or dare?" Linda said.

"I want to ask," Marion said, looming over them. "Charity, a truth: does Tristan know you're a faker?"

Charity tilted her head. "Yes. I was supposed to freak out and leave, or be eliminated."

Marion frowned. "I don't believe you. Why would he keep you around?"

"Two words." Charity held up two fingers. As she spoke each word, she folded them down. "Producers'. Decision."

"Fine." Marion crossed her arms. "Sabrina, truth: why pretend you're willing to move to Iowa for a man you don't even love?"

Sabrina let out an involuntary, *ugh*. She would have gone anywhere for Tristan. Beyond Iowa. She would have moved to the Appalachians if he'd asked. "I love him more than you do."

"That's not true," Marion extended her hand, pointing a crooked finger. Her long nails had grown, their tips pointed, nearly curving in on themselves. Sabrina's eyes widened. She hadn't noticed them in the night. "I love him the most." Tears formed in Marion's eyes, but they didn't fall. Instead, they collected like a thick syrup across her lens.

Sabrina reached up to grab Marion's hand, but Marion pulled away. Sabrina answered, her voice frantic as she watched the otherworldly tears collect. Marion scooted back, away from the women. Her eyes were clouded by the thick liquid. Panic remained on Sabrina's face.

"Truth, for Linda: why try to steal another man when you already had your chance at love?"

Linda inhaled sharply.

The syrup was so thick in Marion's eyes that she looked like she had no eyes beneath it. Standing, Sabrina grabbed Marion by the shoulders. Marion thrashed, trying to get away, but Sabrina held and examined her.

"Marion, can you see?"

"I can see fine," Marion yelled, though they were all within a whisper's distance. "I see how phony you all are. I see perfectly clear."

Linda jumped up and rushed to the bathroom, returning with a wet washrag.

"Here." Linda tried to hand the rag to Sabrina, but Sabrina shook her head as she forced Marion to a kneeling position on the floor.

"You'll have to do it. Try to wipe this gunk from her eye. If I let go, she'll run."

Linda's hands shook as she stooped and leaned toward Marion. Marion tried to jerk back, but Sabrina had her. Linda wrapped one hand behind Marion's head and wiped the washrag against the thick goop. As she pulled the rag away, a string of syrup stretched from Marion's face to the rag, then broke, a strand dropping down Marion's face. It stuck to the skin from eye to cheek.

Sabrina gagged as Linda opened the rag in her hand. It looked and smelled like the maple syrup her mother used to serve on pancakes for birthday breakfasts.

"What is it?" Charity said.

"I don't know," Linda said.

"Try wiping it all off," Sabrina said, and Linda went to work again. By the time she finished wiping the bulk of it away, her rag was covered in the sticky substance, and there was no clean surface of the rag for Linda to hold.

"Marion, can you see?" Sabrina said.

"I could see the whole time." She stopped thrashing, her shoulders relaxing into Sabrina's chest. "I'm tired."

"Maybe it's best if you go back to sleep?" Sabrina said. "Can you close your eyes?"

As Marion blinked, the last goo squeezed out of the corner of her eye like super glue from a tube. She opened her eyes sleepily, slowly, stickily.

"I'd like to sleep now." She yawned.

Sabrina helped Marion stand, led her back into her bedroom, eased her into bed, and pulled the blankets to her chin. When she returned to the hall, Linda and Charity were paler than usual, their bodies small and weak against the house's reaching barriers.

"What the everlasting fuck?" Charity said. "Did she like, swallow a bunch of sap?"

"I think we need to take watch shifts for Marion and Tristan both."

"Nonsense." Charity handed Sabrina the rag. Sabrina screwed up her mouth in disgust as she took the sticky thing. "I'll get enough pillows and blankets for us. Like a slumber party."

"It's technically morning," Linda said. "Even if the sun isn't up."

Sabrina didn't respond, her attention captured by the gooey rag. She'd never seen anything like it in all her years of weird bodily fluids and medical books. There was a lot of that going on, and the joke she'd told in bed with Linda—*it's the trees*—felt less like humor as the evidence stacked in favor of the theory. As she puzzled over the substance, her friends dragged blankets, sheets, and six pillows from nearby rooms. They made a pallet on the ground as Sabrina tucked the rag into a bathroom cabinet and scrubbed the shit out of her hands.

"Well?" Charity said when Sabrina came back. "Any idea what kind of infection that is?"

Sabrina shook her head as she slid into the blankets. "I'm beginning to believe..." She trailed off. Was she really about to admit—? "This isn't an infection. Tristan, Marion. Brandon. Something has to connect them."

"You're not giving into the haunted house theory?" Linda scoffed, but Sabrina was starting to get better reads on her friend's faked emotions, and there was something scared in Linda's questions.

"Not exactly," Sabrina said. "But something outside the realm of science." She sucked in a gasp as her heartbeat skipped, a normal palpitation, a result of stress on her body.

"That's ridiculous." Charity groaned. "Remember who brought us here."

Deja, who had to know more than she let on. Sabrina ran her hands along the journal she'd stuffed into the lip of her shorts. She tore at the last remaining polish on her nails as she put herself in the shoes of her sleeping companions. They would never believe her. She let the situation unfold around her. Her body would give in if she didn't care for it. If the house was haunted, if the woods were vengeful, she'd need to save her energy for something more crucial than talking them into it. Plus, her mind would work better after a few hours shut-eye.

"I need to sleep," she said. "That's all."

"Sleep's like time travel." Linda turned down the hall lights, and the three women rested outside Marion's door. Sabrina hoped she would hear Marion should she leave in the night. In a freshly bitter way, she also hoped Marion would wake with her lips stuck together, unable to speak again. She tossed and turned until she drifted into some kind of slumber, her mind moving in a hundred strange directions. The house creaked and moaned beneath them, and for moments at a time, Sabrina felt as though she slept not on wood but atop undulating pillows of flesh. Then she would wake a little, and the wood would go hard beneath her again.

SABRINA WOKE COATED in sweat so thick it was like she'd been swimming. And as she shook the wet droplets off her hands, she rose from the soaked-down blankets. She shivered as the cool hall air caressed her. She touched a fixture to test if the metal felt weird on her skin—a sign of fever—but she noted nothing out of the ordinary.

In Marion's room, she pressed two fingers into the skin at her wrists, but she caught only the faintest pulse. When she pressed the same fingers into Marion's neck instead, the woman groaned and swatted.

"I'm trying to help you," Sabrina said.

Marion grabbed her wrist as Sabrina tried to count the beats of her rival's heart.

"I knew you'd come back for me." She rubbed her cheek against Sabrina's hand. "I knew you'd be well again."

Frowning, Sabrina pulled away. Marion's pulse was slow, but she was a fit woman. It didn't yet worry her. While Tristan was running a fever, Marion was cold to the touch. Their illnesses might be connected, but Sabrina didn't understand how.

In Tristan's room, lying still and hot, he seemed more helpless than he'd ever been with her. But it was she who was helpless, with no medical supplies, no way to carry him to safety. Even knowing the risk of contamination, she stretched beside him, pretending it was the end. It was over. She'd won.

DAY FIVE

DAY FIVE

CHAPTER THIRTY-FIVE

LINDA

CHARITY AND LINDA napped unsoundly. When Charity nuzzled her head on Linda's shoulder, Linda stroked her hair, and they drifted in and out of the world controlled by dreams. Even knowing she should be horrified at the events unfolding, Linda thrilled to touch the woman. The last few days had been long and terrible, but like Charity had admitted, they had been excellent, too.

Once her legs ached from the hard floor, she shrugged out of the makeshift sleeping bag and ventured downstairs for breakfast. Through the foyer windows, the first sunrise painted the sky like a still-life of egg and smoke. As seconds passed, the manor danced with color. It was an odd hour, but time meant nothing—only the day, number five, which told her they had two days to go before rescue.

In the dining room, Sabrina hunched over a bowl of dry oats.

"Those taste better if you heat them, you know." Linda slid into the chair beside her. "Preferably, with some water. Or milk."

"Too much work."

Linda slipped the bowl from under Sabrina's nose. She took it to the stove. She filled a pot with water and set it to boil. She waited. The silence was kind now. It seemed like forever since it was tense. When Linda finished cooking the oats, she poured the porridge back into the bowl and presented it to Sabrina, but Sabrina didn't take a bite. Instead, her chest folded onto the table, knocking the oatmeal to the ground.

"You really never wanted Tristan?" Sabrina said.

"I never did." Linda went to the counter and uncorked an old bottle of wine, then poured it into two orange juice glasses. She set one beneath Sabrina's nose. "But I want him to get better."

Sabrina nodded and tilted her glass against her lips, letting the wine drain down her throat.

"Hey, question: why do you want Tristan so much?" Linda said. "The real reason."

Sabrina breathed in deep and set her empty glass down. "It's what I was born to do."

"Girl, what?" Linda leaned in. "You weren't born to be on reality TV."

Sabrina nodded. "My mother wished so hard for me to marry rich and well, to save the family through my looks alone, that it had to come true one day. It was her intention. It was what we both wanted."

"Intention? You sound like you took *The Secret* to heart."

"She wasn't a new-age faker. She put her energy into the world, and it came back to her."

"Good things just happen. So do bad things. It's not energy and intentions." Linda shook her head. Back at The Groom mansion, Linda's new nurse friend was rational, a woman who came on the show because she was having trouble meeting a man. A professional woman with a good head on her shoulders. The house wasn't haunted, but it had possessed Sabrina. "The world is founded on rational explanations."

"Then what's happening here?" Sabrina knocked against the wall. "That goo that came out of the walls, the noises, Brandon hanging himself, Tristan?"

"Honestly, those things aren't what scare me the most."

"Then what scares you?"

"You."

Sabrina's forehead creased. "Why me?"

Linda took Sabrina's hand. Sabrina tried to let go, but Linda held tight. "This place has done something to you. You're not destined to wed Tristan because your mom wanted you to get married someday."

Sabrina shook her head. "Back in the mansion, I could pretend I might not make it to the end. That my sister's vision for me could have been a mistake. Now, I'm here, and around every corner, I'm reminded of the existence of worlds outside the one everyone knows. It hasn't done anything to me but confirmed my purpose."

Linda let go of Sabrina's hand. "Sabrina, that's insane. That's some fairy tale bullshit. You have to realize that cannot possibly be real."

"Then why am I here?"

"You're here because you're a strong, gorgeous woman, who plays well on TV. You're here because Tristan isn't a complete boil and knew you'd make a good partner for his spotlight. You weren't destined for anything. If that's what's driving you? Then you need to take another look around. Seize control for yourself."

Sabrina shook her head, but the words reached inside Linda, too. She wasn't in control. She never would be. Not while Deja pulled her strings.

AS THE SUNRISE died, morphing into the leaden monotone of another misty day, Deja came for Linda. "Confessional," she said as she gripped Linda around the arm.

"Is that necessary anymore?" Linda jerked away, but when Deja beckoned her into the den, she went.

Deja pushed her into a chair. The red recording light was already on. "I'm checking in on everyone's mental state," she said. "With the two accidents and all."

"Accidents, right." Linda folded her hands in her lap and tried not to let her voice give away discomfort; Deja would use it against her.

"Do you have an opinion on that?"

"On what?"

"On the nature of the accidents. Two in two days."

"You tell me. You're the producer. Aren't you in control of everything?"

Pulling over a chair, Deja straddled it backwards, facing Linda on her level. "You know something about accidents, don't you?"

Linda pursed her lips. "I know nothing about accidents. But you do, don't you?"

Deja's laugh was cold and short. "Your father died in an accident, didn't he? A camping accident?"

"You know how my father died."

"We can sit here all night. This is for your own mental health, Linda. You need to open up. Unburden yourself from your feelings. Seeing a dying man reminded you of your father's death. That happens. It's normal."

Anger unspooled in Linda's stomach. She clenched her fists. "I won't be manipulated."

Deja smirked. "You think you haven't been manipulated?"

Linda closed her eyes and imagined something swooping from the sky, breaking through the roof, and carrying her to safety: an eagle, a hot air balloon, even Tristan in the cockpit of his plane. But no—there was no way to call for help. Or was there?

As Linda lunged forward, Deja startled out of the way.

"What the fuck?" Deja yelled.

"Give me the goddamn phone."

Linda lunged again, knocking down the cameras and pinning Deja against the wall. Deja tripped backward, then slid onto the floor like a snake. She tried to crawl through Linda's legs, but Linda put all her weight into trapping her.

"Where's the phone?" Linda said.

Deja said nothing, and Linda ran her hand across Deja's back pockets. She felt the phone's shape in the front of Deja's jeans. She pulled it free.

"There's no signal," Deja said. "What are you going to do with a phone that doesn't work?"

Linda turned on the screen and checked the bars. Deja wasn't lying.

"You can have the damn phone," Deja said. "It's useless."

Linda held it to Deja's face to open the screen, then swiped through. The first screen was overfull with apps: calendar, music, video editing, a fitness tracker, a reader, music, some silly romance game, phone, and messaging. Linda checked the record, but there were no calls placed since they'd arrived. She opened messaging. Nothing. No one.

Outside, feet stomped toward the door. As Linda leapt up, Deja scrambled to her feet. The door burst open: Sabrina, wild-eyed, on the other side.

"You said it was a possum," she said. "But there's something else going on here, and we need to get to the bottom of it."

CHAPTER THIRTY-SIX
SABRINA

THE HAUNTED PLACE had reached into her and twisted her against herself. She had a friend. Her friend wasn't capable of murder. She knew that much if she knew anything. But Linda was wrong about one thing: there was something fucked-up about this place, something as yet unexplainable. If Sabrina were going to save Tristan, she needed to uncover the truth.

Deja shrugged. "What do I know about wildlife?"

"It wasn't an ordinary possum." Linda shivered. "It looked... monstrous."

"Where is it now?" Sabrina said. "The creature's body."

"I threw it in the trash," Deja said. "What else would I do with a dead animal?"

"Which trash can?"

Deja led the women through the manor's labyrinth and out the back door to a metal trash can pressed against the stone. She opened the lid. The fetid smell that rose to greet them was becoming familiar. Sabrina didn't even gag.

Sabrina reached with gloved hands into the bin until her hands closed around the creature's body. She pulled out the dead possum by its tail, which was thick and rigid. It cracked as she pulled, but it didn't break under its heavy weight. Its skin was smooth, as seen by the anemic sunlight that stabbed through the cloud cover and washed over it. Its veins were black and visible. Like Tristan's.

"Whatever infected this thing, it's got Tristan, too." Sabrina ran through the sensible possibilities: rabies, roundworm, blastomycosis. But it wasn't those things. It was simpler: some kind of evil.

"What do we do?" Linda said.

To find a cure, she would usually need blood work, a lab, internet for research, a phone to call colleagues who might know more than she did. Sabrina shook her head. Science was failing her here, and she flashed back to her mother's lessons. Sometimes, finding the answer was about embracing the unknowable.

"I'm not a vet." Sabrina frowned. "But we should dissect it. See if that gives us any clues."

"Don't get your hands dirty, girls," Deja said. "Your contract states I'm not to let you come to any harm."

They kept talking, and talking, and meanwhile, Tristan was fading. He hadn't signed on for that when Deja coaxed him into this "date." He'd signed on to find someone to take home, to introduce to his doting parents, to love.

"It's better than sitting around and doing nothing!" she yelled. Linda startled. "Aren't you supposed to be checking for cell signal?"

Linda held the phone out. "Still nothing."

"And you're not at all worried about that, Deja?" As Sabrina kicked the trash can, the creature swung in her grasp. She wanted to kick it toward Deja, to watch Deja crushed beneath it, but she stepped toward Deja instead, thrusting the dead creature at her.

"I'm worried!" Deja raised her voice and jumped away. She pulled something from her pocket: a taser, electricity sparking at its tip. Sabrina stopped her advance and pulled back the creature. "I understand the value of keeping calm. Unlike you people, I understand the value of minimizing drama, not exacerbating it. I've been around girls like you all for ten years now. It's all the same, and guess what? Freaking out has never solved any problem." Deja took a ragged breath.

Linda held out both palms. "This isn't helping in any way, shape, or form." She gestured at the creature and its crooked tail.

When Sabrina exhaled, the breath calmed her down. "You're right. Let's get this thing inside and take a look."

Deja waved them off as she ventured in the opposite direction. "I'm getting the fuck away from you two."

Sabrina held the creature out far in front of her as they made their way inside. In the kitchen, Sabrina searched the cabinets until she found cooking implements. "I never asked: why did you come on the show if not for Tristan?" She unrolled a silicone baking sheet and set the creature's heavy body on top of it, belly-up. Its arms and legs flopped open.

"I wanted to find love," Linda said. The creature smelled like mold, fungus, a dank forest infested with decomposition.

Sabrina searched the drawers for the sharpest knives, testing them against the counter as she went, leaving minor scars for the terrible house to remember her by. "You're not in front of cameras right now," she said. "We can speak freely." She chose three blades. She laid them out beside the creature as though for surgery.

Linda breathed in. "I wanted something to open me up."

Sabrina held the knife point to the skin at the creature's throat. "When I got divorced…" Linda paused as Sabrina pressed the blade into the skin—or tried to, at least. The skin hardly gave, and only the tip of the blade slipped into the creature. "No, before that. I was closed up from a young age. Bad family. I had to be. But I always had this hope that some grand gesture, somewhere in my future, would give me a reason to be…me. And that other people would see me, all of me. That I'd be okay, and that they would know I was okay…inside."

Sabrina paused. "I feel you. And Linda?" She pushed against the end of the blade. Finally, it slid into the creature's skin, which split from throat to belly in one long crack. The rancid smell of guts and goo wafted as she peered into the void of the creature's innards. *Bad family,* Linda had said. And family was everything: blood, guts, skin, skeleton. It was all family, when you thought about it. "I don't think you're the only one."

Linda leaned in, and together, the two women took in the thing in front of them. The creature's smooth skin was oddly a couple of inches thick, but its insides looked, at first, like a typical rodent's might: lungs, intestines, heart. Sabrina reached inside and removed each organ, laying them onto the silicone mat. They were hard and uncanny in her hands, like Tristan's skin was becoming.

"They don't feel right," Sabrina said. A chill shot through her body.

"That's the thing that got him?" Marion appeared in the doorway. "That's the thing that fucked Tristan up?"

Sabrina moved to stand in front of the creature, overcome with the sudden urge to guard their findings.

"Let me see." Marion took a step forward.

"You need to rest," Sabrina said. "You're going to make yourself sicker."

"Let me see." Marion stepped closer.

Sabrina tried to grab Marion's arm and lead her away from the strange thing. For some reason, she had the distinct impression that Marion, in her weakened state, wouldn't be able to handle seeing the mockery of nature that lay exposed on the island. But Marion shoved Sabrina away. Stunned, Sabrina stumbled across the kitchen. She tripped over the uneven wood and landed on her ass, screwing up her face in pain. Marion gripped the edge of the island in both hands and stared down at the thing, her lips curved in a snarl not unlike the snarl frozen in death on the creature's face. She reached out, and before Sabrina or Linda stopped her, grabbed hold of the creature's neck. She squeezed tight, and the veins in her hands bulged against the inflexibility of its skin. But skin wasn't the right word. Sabrina reconfigured the language: shell, outer covering, trunk, bark. It was more like bark than skin.

Sabrina rose to her feet and grabbed at Marion's hands, attempting to pry them from the animal. "You're going to hurt yourself!" she cried out, but Marion wouldn't let go.

Linda spoke up from the wall she'd pressed herself against. "Shouldn't we check in on Tristan?"

With that, Marion relaxed her grip. "Tristan, yes," she said. "Tristan's all alone."

"Charity's up there," Sabrina said.

"She doesn't care about Tristan." Marion turned and ambled out of the kitchen. Finally, they heard her footsteps on the stairs.

The creature still lay on the island, insides exposed, no longer a danger to them, but still a threat to the order of the world and its known equations. Sabrina shook her head and swept it into an open trash can. She had no more desire to pretend she'd ever figure out what was wrong with it, and what was wrong with Tristan.

"Nothing gained from that dissection." She ripped off her gloves over the sink, leaving them crumpled in the drain, and washed her hands, scrubbing too hard. Her skin was red when she heard the shrill scream.

Sabrina and Linda shared one brief glance, then rushed the long stairwell. In Tristan's room, Marion splayed her body over Tristan, wracked with sobs. Charity stood wide-eyed by the door. Sabrina trod forward to pull Marion away from the diseased corpse, then stopped herself.

"What the hell happened?" she said.

"It's Tristan," Charity said. "He's dead."

CHAPTER THIRTY-SEVEN

SABRINA

LINDA APPROACHED THE bed in a state of extended déjà vu, each step premeditated along a path she'd already walked. Somehow, she'd already seen Sabrina examine his lifeless body before she pried Marion away and lay two fingers against his well-sunned neck, now darkened and rough.

"It's hard," Sabrina said. "Like the thing downstairs."

Seconds passed like hours, and Deja arrived, stood at the bedside, and sighed as though confronting traffic, not extraordinary death. As Linda, Sabrina, and Charity watched, Deja pressed her fingers against the man's eyelids and pulled them down. They jammed back open. His big, round gaze remained focused on the ceiling. Deja heaved Marion off the floor and set her in the chair in the corner, arranging her limbs in repose across her chest. Then Deja examined each woman by placing one hand upon their foreheads.

"Marion, you feel ill," she said when she was finished. "I've said this before. I won't say it again. Get to a bed and stay there."

When Marion failed to answer, Deja ordered Tatum to carry her into a bedroom. After they left the room, Deja turned toward the other three women.

"You three look half-dead as well. Though I suspect I shouldn't use that phrasing after—" She gestured at Tristan. "I suggest everyone here takes a long rest in their rooms."

"And then what?" Linda said.

"Excuse me?" Deja said.

"A good long rest, and then what? What are we going to do with…him?" Linda gesticulated at the corpse. "Do we go home now?"

"I sent Tatum out this morning. The road's still blocked." Deja scowled. "We wait until the bus comes and realizes we're trapped. Then it's only a matter of hours before they get the forest service up here."

"The body'll begin its decomposition within twenty-four to seventy-two hours," Sabrina said. "In other words, we could risk it, if we wanted the whole manor to smell like Cadaverine."

"Which means?" Charity said.

"One of the chemicals a dead body gives off. Have you smelled a dead thing before?"

"I have," Linda said, and the memory came back to her at once, but she caught herself before she said more. "In the walls. Rats. They used to crawl in there and die. At my parents' place."

"Lovely, yes." Deja's gaze slid, boring into her. "What do you suggest we do about him?"

"We need to at least move him outside," Sabrina said.

"If, or when, the show bus comes to get us in…forty-eight hours. We can inform them we have a dead body on our hands, see what the network wants." Sabrina said. "But if we want to keep from getting sick ourselves, from the smell, from any—" She paused as though searching for the words that Linda and the others would accept. "Infectious disease he may have gotten from that rodent, we need to take him into the fresh air, away from our air."

"Wait. He could be contagious?" Charity wrapped her arms around herself.

"We don't know that for sure." Sabrina seemed to consider saying something more. She didn't. Linda wondered if she was going to tell Deja her suspicions regarding Marion, and what her reasons could be for withholding the information. Maybe Sabrina no longer trusted Deja, or maybe Sabrina no longer trusted her own impression of Marion. "I suggest we take proper precautions before we move the body."

Linda marveled at the professional demeanor that had descended upon Sabrina over the past day and night. The behavior continued as Sabrina gathered several black trash bags from the kitchen, cut holes into them, and instructed everyone who would help move the body to slip on the black bags like makeshift scrubs—Charity, then Linda, volunteered. Sabrina returned Charity's gloves, and Charity passed them to Linda. As Linda held them, astonished at the gift, Charity slipped on two oven mitts. They all tied Tatum's bandannas around their mouths for masks.

Linda had indeed smelled death, though she had lied about the source. The dead body Linda had smelled was her father's. He passed on a camping retreat, up a mountain that took a solid eight hours to ascend. It was night when Linda's mother discovered him dead in their tent. Linda's mother was unsure how long she had slept beside a dead man, but the horror would have been no more or less had she been aware. Linda and her sister awoke to their mother's screaming, and when they rushed to the tent to check on her, they saw their father's sallow skin under the glow of flashlights. His eyes were closed like he was sleeping, but no amount of shaking roused him.

At the time, they had no cell phone. Instead, they sent Linda's older sister down the mountain to locate an authority figure. Linda and her mother waited outside the tent, but as the hours passed, the open flap let enough of her father's worsening odor out that the memory of the scent of death never left her.

Tristan's heft groaned as Charity grabbed his feet, Linda grabbed his head, and they lifted him. *Light as a feather.* They carried the man down the stairs, Charity moving backward. *Stiff as a board.* Linda tripped over her feet despite being blessed to move forward. They lugged him out the manor's front door and a few steps farther. They found a space beneath the awning and left the man they had all tried to woo in the dirt.

"Should we—I don't know—cross his arms over his chest?" Charity said. "Or sit him up?"

"He looks like he's guarding the place," Linda said.

"He's fine as is," Sabrina said. "It's important, in the situation we're in, not to get attached to the body. He's not the body. The man, he's gone. The shell is all that remains."

"You didn't mention to Deja that you think Marion might have been infected," Linda said. "Why not?"

Sabrina frowned. "I don't know. I... What if Deja did something to her?"

"What do you mean?" Charity said. "You don't trust Deja?"

Sabrina motioned around them. "Where is she right now? Where has been throughout all of this? Where are the crew members who disappeared?"

The three women stood in silence, the carcass of Tristan their only witness, and stared out at the distant expanse of the yard and the trees. Linda went to scratch her nose, then remembered the bags. The smell of her father's dead flesh had been worse than the possum's, worse than Tristan's, worse than any smell she had ever smelled. Would the bodies keep piling until there were none of them left?

"I'm going to check on Marion," Linda said. She needed to feel something, a reminder that even a broken heart could keep pumping in the wake of losing it all.

MARION WAS WHERE she was supposed to be, curled into the shape of a question mark in her bed while Tatum guarded her closed door. The meaty remains of the orchard's strange apples covered her vanity. She didn't stir when they crossed the threshold, nor when Linda lay her palm against Marion's forehead to check for fever. There was none now. She didn't feel like Tristan had felt. Her skin was softer, more pliable, more living, but there was no escaping the fact she wasn't herself. The surface of her face felt blemished, rough, as though she'd broken out overnight. When she breathed, her breath rattled.

"Sabrina was right," Linda said. "Marion's ill, too."

"Like Tristan?" Charity said, unwilling to touch her.

"No," Linda admitted. "This feels like something different."

The two women slid down the wall and onto the floor. They sat side by side, knees touching. Linda pitied Marion even though she'd made Linda feel like a monster. Behind her own eyes, Linda saw flashes: the creature in the curio shop, her father's wan death face, her ex-husband's trembling lips, Tristan's gentle smile, the creature in the curio shop, her father, the creature. She was not a monster because of her divorce. But for other reasons, she could be.

"You're not broken, you know," Charity whispered. Linda was shocked by the words. It was as though Charity could read her mind, even in the chaos. How had she understood all that Linda didn't say from the few conversations they had? She read between the lines, and Linda had never experienced affection from someone who paid attention not only to her words but also to the in-betweens. There was so much the men she had known didn't understand about her, and Linda felt sure Charity would make it a point to learn, to grow, to change alongside her.

She and Charity stayed for a while more, sharing stale breaths, until Linda could no longer stand the reek of death on her body.

ONCE THEY WERE clean, the women couldn't avoid the cloud of death, so planted themselves in Tristan's room as though basking in the space his body had left might bring them solace. But Linda felt shock more than sadness, and the sudden turn of events hadn't yet appeared on Sabrina's or Charity's face.

"He was just *fine*," Charity said. "He was average."

"Date a lot of men?" Sabrina said. "I'm inclined to disagree."

"Most marriages end in divorce," Charity said. "You and Marion are better off."

"The other half end in death," Linda said.

CHAPTER THIRTY-EIGHT

SABRINA

WHEN SABRINA HAD slipped the journal from Deja's room into her shorts, she didn't know what she would do with it.

After Tristan's death, Sabrina excused herself outside, where she crouched against the back wall of the manor and pored over the pages. One page had been covered in sketches of spiral arrangements of various seeds. Another page showed an illustration of a woman with pins stuck in her skin. Finally, Sabrina reached a page that struck her less vividly, but it was familiar: a seance.

Her mother had used one like it to summon the dead.

It was after the death of her grandmother, her mother's mother, a complex woman Sabrina's mother had wanted to ruin. No matter how many intentions, curses, and bad omen crystals her mother used, Sabrina's grandmother flourished. She hoarded her luck until her death, willing none of her earthly possessions to Sabrina's mother. Sabrina's mother wouldn't rest until her curse succeeded at damning her mother to a hellish afterlife.

The illustration showed several spirits standing before a woman with a bowl. Behind her, English letters decorated the air. She bled from a single spot on her wrist, and one hungry spirit lapped at the blood like a drip from a faucet. Sabrina had blocked this one out precisely because it had frightened her as a child. She snuck through the halls of the bottom floor, searching behind each closed door until she found the quiet room with electric lights. She turned them on and sat in the middle of the floor, studying the diagram.

Sabrina took a deep breath. She did as the diagram reminded her, psyching herself up for the pricking of her finger. She'd never been frightened of needles, and she had taken so much blood, the sight of it made her weary instead of weak. But she hadn't cleaned the knife, and she had no idea what it may have been used for. She closed her eyes and let her rationality press against the task at hand, her thoughts running in circles. She could get an infected finger, and trapped as they were, that infection could fester. But if she met spirits, they could tell her how to leave, or if she even should, or if her destiny was something else, *someone* else. She was supposed to dazzle the world with her good looks, but maybe it hadn't been Tristan who was supposed to fall for them. She shivered. The spirits would tell her. But she wasn't so sure she wanted to meet the dead returned.

If the seance didn't work, she could put to rest her fears of the haunting. She could approach this place like the Sabrina who had enrolled in nursing school against her sister's wishes, the only time she'd followed her own direction. She'd felt it was right to go, that it was the path she was supposed to follow—and wasn't that the whole thing about destiny?

Sabrina dug the blade into the tip of her middle finger. It slid in easy, and she squeezed at her finger until three tiny drops of blood fell into a bowl at her feet. Then, she waited.

For what felt like a long while, nothing happened. Sabrina sat in the middle of that floor, letting flickering shadows dance over her. She allowed herself to hope, and to worry. These two competing desires—to be right and to be wrong—they warred inside her. She smiled to herself as nothing happened. The house groaned. The wind. Old houses. A natural shifting in the foundations. Pedestrian.

Then, Sabrina lost the feeling in her hands. Her head fogged, a lightness that drew her deep into herself. She closed her eyes, resigned finally to the awful truth. She waited for the spirits to come.

WHEN SHE WOKE, she found herself in that familiar place, the portal in the wall she had crawled through on the morning she wound up in Tristan's bedroom. The portal flexed on her, squeezing her inside. She pressed at the spongy brain-like texture until it expanded, allowing her to shape it. She made enough space for her to stand, then stretched the wall out more and more, until she had formed a circular room. She took in the smell, like wet guts, and called out to no one.

Slowly, the women forced their way through. First, the rejected contestants, dolled up, as though they were on their way to the final ceremonies. Their names had escaped her, except Amy, the tortured beauty who flung herself at Tristan's feet. Sabrina had pitied her, but then, she had done the same, crawling from this space to Tristan's feet, begging him to choose her over Marion. Had she let the house take hold of her? It had been easier to keep her rational mind in charge when she wasn't kept awake by the whispering of wood shifting. Amy's sparkling black dress dragged the ground as she entered and perched on a chair formed of plushy pink membrane. She crossed her dainty ankles and leveled her squinting gaze at Sabrina.

"You're here for the fab-gab?" Amy asked.

Sabrina's brow furrowed. Only eliminated women did the fab-gab, a live episode where all the former contestants talked out the drama, then hashed it out with The Groom himself.

"I knew you wouldn't make it."

The other women giggled.

"She made it far enough," one said.

"I'm not eliminated," Sabrina said. "At least, I don't think so."

"I'd remember," Brandon Fuller said as he pried apart the wall and stepped inside. He wore a bright pink suit that nearly blended with the organ in which they stood. He grinned with half his mouth. Around his neck, rope marks throbbed in the half-light. "You were there when I went home."

Amy laughed. "Brandon, you can't get eliminated! You're the host."

"And what a host I've been!" As he swept closer to Sabrina, a stage rose from beneath his feet. "Welcome to our live audience tonight, on this, our most dramatic fab-gab to date!"

Sabrina tried to pull herself together, to recall the moment she must have been sent home.

"Sabrina, please take your seat. You know you're not the star of this show."

Sabrina's stomach flipped, embarrassed to have forgotten. "I'm so sorry." She sat, and the floor rose to meet her, a toadstool of a chair forming to accept her. "I'm a little confused."

"We all are, tonight!" Brandon said as the other women laughed as one. "We're confused to see the faces of so many worthy women! Does our Groom Tristan regret any of his decisions? We'll find out soon, on this passionate episode of this season's fab-gab!"

All at once, the other women chanted: "Tristan, Tristan, Tristan!"

"And without further ado, this year's Groom, our Iowan prince himself... Tristan!"

Sabrina searched the group and the room, but she didn't see Tristan pushing his way through.

"Oh, that's right, ladies! Your dear Tristan...is dead!"

The women gasped.

"But he's come all the way from the afterlife to talk to us anyway. That's how much of a gentleman he is, ladies!"

The ground flexed, sending Sabrina's feet rocking as waves tremored across it. She pulled her legs to her chest, her belly tensing with nausea as she tried to look away from the moving floor. The shape of a face pressed through, like it had that prior night in the wall, but this time, it was followed by two hands, two feet, then a body pressing up, trying to come through also. Finally, a blade poked through and tore until the shape was sliced from head to toe, and Tristan crawled out. As he emerged, the floor sealed itself. He trembled to his feet, his body slick and gray, his hair that knotted mess he had worn on his deathbed. Sabrina slowly stood, her hand moving to her mouth.

"Tristan?" she said.

"Quiet, now!" Brandon called out. "You'll have your turn, the same as anyone."

Tristan turned to her and issued a quick wink before taking Brandon's hand and letting himself be escorted onto the stage's platform. He sat upon his own pink toadstool as Brandon sat across from him, leaning forward conspiratorially.

"So, Tristan, any regrets?"

"Well, dying wasn't too fun."

Mouthless laughs echoed around them as the contestants beamed at him. Amy laughed behind her hand. Tristan tried to grin, but his hardened mouth would no longer budge.

"And what about the ladies remaining when you passed?" Brandon asked. "Any main contenders?"

Tristan turned his whole body to look at Sabrina. Her body warmed at the attention. "A gentleman never gives away his secrets," he said.

Brandon winked, seemingly at himself. "No, he doesn't, does he?" He leaned in deeper. "But between you and me?"

"Everyone here could see it, right? Marion was everything I've ever wanted in a wife, but I'll be the first to admit Sabrina here also rocked my world."

"Sabrina?" Brandon's smile faded. "Then why send her home?"

Tristan shook his head. "I didn't."

"Then what's she doing here?"

Tristan tried to shrug, but his whole figure was as rigid as his mouth.

"She's here because I have a message for her." When he stood, his limbs lifted out like a martyr's, forming a cross of himself, but then they grew longer and thinner until one of his spindly fingers swayed right in front of her. She tried to move away from him, no longer sure of her affection or her destiny, no longer certain of her status as a living person, but she was paralyzed, her ass and legs melded to the membranes. When his finger traced her chin, she shivered to be touched by him again.

"Don't give up on us."

As he drew her to her stand, she balanced on top of what should have been his feet. She tipped, unbalanced, and when she looked down, she saw his legs had fused. Now they ended in a dirty mess of rhizome and root.

AS THE CHAMBER fell away, Sabrina woke. She lay on the floor of the empty room, vomit pooled around her head. She sat up, letting her senses return to her. She remembered everything. She understood how to meet her destiny face-to-face.

CHAPTER THIRTY-NINE

LINDA

THE CHOICE BETWEEN remaining inside the stifling manor or capturing their own breaths of fresh air was easy. Even eerie woods were more comforting than floors that seemed to live and breathe.

They weaved through the groaning trees. The forest was noisier than the day they arrived.

"Hey." Charity was squeezing her hand and trailing behind. Linda tripped forward as Charity yanked her back. "You okay?"

Linda frowned. "Yeah—" *But why was she lying?* "No. I'm not."

"Do you want to turn back?"

They were deep enough in the forest that *back* was an abstract concept.

"Let's keep walking," she said.

Dark green light filtered through the leaves and cast the forest in camouflage as limbs shifted in the breeze like grabby men. Linda intended to survive this place. She intended to take Charity to some hotel somewhere and have an excellent night's sleep, then fuck all morning, then eat continental breakfast. She planned to figure out how to make this new thing work, how to absorb the kindness Charity exuded. She intended to change. She intended, finally, as she had hoped to do at the start of this journey, this TV show, whatever you wanted to call it, to open up, to experience, to love for maybe the first time since she was an adolescent.

Charity halted ahead, frozen in place, one hand cupped against her mouth. Linda followed her gaze to the treetops, where Becca hung like a holiday ornament, speared by a limb.

Gore dangled from her belly, a mess of red spilling out of a hole the size of a volleyball. Blood dripped along a long string of intestine to the forest floor, where it pooled on the fallen leaves. Before death, she had squeezed her eyes tight as though expecting the mutilation. As though someone had chased her there, then pushed her out onto the sharpened bough.

"Who did this to her?" Charity muttered. "Who the hell would do this to someone?"

Linda let out a strangled cry. She felt sick to her stomach. She had thought death so far behind her, and here it was again and again and again. Had she brought it with her to the manor? Was it her payback? She stared at her hands. Was it her?

"No," Charity said. "There's more."

"More?" Linda squinted into the branches.

Charity threw her arm across Linda's chest. She pointed ahead. "There," Charity said. "No, lower. The ground. It's Leo."

The scene crystallized like an optical illusion, the sea of red dots that became a sunken homestead if someone stared long enough. Leo's body no longer resembled a human form; the trees' roots had wrapped and squeezed him until he popped. Fragments of bone and flesh and gut lay in a king-rat of roots. As Linda breathed in deep, the smell of blood filled her nose. She bent over and gagged, her hands on her thighs.

The scene repulsed and confused her. Something about it wasn't correct. She puzzled at the information, trying to make sense of what she was seeing: death, dismemberment, the annihilation of a whole man's soul by the roots of a tree. The roots of a tree had done this, and Linda's wildest fears, the ones she had pushed away because of their unlikelihood, flooded her. Linda wasn't scared of ordinary things. She wasn't afraid of snakes, or heights, or the dark, or clowns.

She didn't succumb to jump scares, and she kept a level head regarding other people's terrible driving on the road around her. This manor, and the woods surrounding it, terrified her to the bone.

"There's no blood," Charity muttered, almost a whisper.

No blood. That was it, the unsettling thing beyond the impossibility of it all. The death was gruesome, and it suggested truths about the world and the manor that broke Linda's conceptions of reality, but the uncanniest fact? There was no blood, despite the man's body having been ripped wide open. And she had smelled that copper perfume.

She frowned. She stepped forward, scanning the trees. She heard a faint beat. She stepped closer to the trees. She could see they had a red tint. She stepped over the edge of the root pile, and the beating grew stronger. She stumbled and fell face-first into the leaves, landing with her hands in front of her face. They pressed into something soggy and cold, a pink goo that coated her palm. It was part of his intestine. As a reflex, she wiped her hand against the closest rough thing: the bark of the nearest tree. She felt it beat beneath her touch, and she heard a sound then like the rushing of blood in her head, but all around her. It was the trees, and the bark felt soft and muscular like the back of Charity's thigh as Linda knelt between her legs and grabbed hold of the meaty flesh. She pulled back, and through a hole in the trunk, she found Jazz's calf, her music-note tattoo wrapped around the purple skin.

AS CHARITY DESCRIBED the scene to Sabrina, Linda saw it once more. Guts. Blood in the trees. Muscle. Bone. A slip of intestine against her palm. She felt woozy again. Death was a thing no one escaped.

"It's the trees," Linda whispered. "You were right."

"What?" Sabrina said.

"It's the trees," Charity repeated.

"Marion's disappeared." Deja swept into the parlor where the final women sat soaking in the horror of the day. "None of us should be alone. It's not safe, and we can't let any violent acts go unseen from here on out."

"More?" Linda frowned. "You know we just found *three* bodies in the woods, right?" Every time she blinked, the images floated like sunspots.

"Whose bodies?" Deja pressed a hand to the wall. "Tristan's? Brandon's?"

"Becca. Leo. Jazz." Linda shivered. Charity reached for her. "Can you tell us what happened to them?" She didn't mean to let the accusatory tone in her voice through, but she couldn't help it.

Deja smirked. "I don't know, Linda. Do I look omnipotent? I can't call my psychic, you know. "

"But you know some things. There's some weird shit going on," Charity said. "Brandon, Tristan, Marion. What happened to Becca, Deja? She was speared by a limb."

"And the others—" Linda shuddered again as she described them. "You know what did it, don't you?"

"Goddamn this fucking house. How the hell could this have happened?" Deja's face drained of its vibrancy. "Speared on a limb? The only thing I can guess is she was climbing the tree, and she slipped, and the limb—"

"And what about all the weird rooms full of body parts, and the wood floor in the bathroom growing?" Linda said.

"And the womb wall," Sabrina said.

Linda and Sabrina shared a confused glance, but there wasn't time to get into that now.

"There's nothing in these old rooms but wood. Now quit being naive and paranoid and help me find Marion."

"Paranoid?" Charity stood to face Deja. "Half the people who came here are dead. You're untrustworthy as shit, Deja, and we're onto you. You act like you're in charge still. Like you still own our time, our emotions. That shit ended the moment Tristan kicked the bucket. No Groom, no brides-in-waiting. We're equals now, motherfucker."

Deja's eyes flashed as she moved away from the door, resolve forcing her mouth into a thin line.

"And what about Marion? She's sick! And now she's also missing? If we go back into those woods, are we going to find her dead, too?" Sabrina stood. Linda joined her. They all crossed their arms across their chests like a monster movie girl gang. Pride surged in Linda, a tremor in her chest.

"The truth?" Deja raised her eyebrows. "She's infected with the spirit of the woods."

"What the fuck does that mean?" Sabrina said, but Deja pressed a finger to her lip.

"I grew up in this house. I'm sure you've heard that by now, as loose as your lips are. Trust me when I say you won't ever understand this place. Not like I do." Deja's voice shook for a second before she swallowed, continuing as evenly as ever. "I didn't mean for it to happen this way, but we don't have time to chat. We need to find Marion."

"Let's say she *is* infected." Sabrina's tone was a lazy river weary of flowing. "How do you suggest we cure her?"

"There's no cure," Deja said. "Only death."

The room pulsed in sync with the palpitation of Linda's heartbeat.

"Death?" Linda's throat constricted. Years ago, she had wished her father dead, and he had died. She had dreamed of wrapping her hands around his throat, and he had breathed his last breath. Now, Deja was speaking death to Marion, and Linda recognized the desperate gleam in her.

Linda understood the importance of her next lines, unscripted in that famous reality TV way. If she said the wrong thing, they would reshoot again and again until she got it right—or she'd find herself punished.

"Let's find Marion," she lied. She'd gotten so good at lying. "Tell us what to do. We'll do it."

CHAPTER FORTY

LINDA

DEJA TOOK THE bait. She assigned each woman a wing of the manor to search. "If you find her, don't engage," she said. "Come find me."

"Why not?" Sabrina asked, causing Deja to narrow her sharp gaze.

"Because she's strong, ladies. It's as simple as that." She handed over Linda's earpiece, her brows knitted. "Linda, use this to tell me where she is. You, especially: *Do. Not. Engage.*"

Linda swallowed as she pressed the piece into her ear. She was glad that Sabrina didn't ask *why her specifically*, but Linda understood: because she, too, was dangerous. As Deja scurried off, Linda ripped the earpiece out, turned it off, and shoved it into her pocket. She was done being dangerous for Deja.

"We'll need supplies," Linda said, shoving her hands in the pockets. "To get the fuck out of here."

"Where can we even go?" Sabrina grimaced. "It's a ghost town down there. The nearest town is what? An hour away by car? And it's a tiny two-building place, at that."

"Where there's a town, there's got to be cell reception." Charity steepled her hands. "Once we get there, we can call for help!"

"Right, it's not the dark ages." Linda nodded, allowing hope inside for the first time in days.

"Or, you know, maybe they have a landline." Charity managed a little jump, flinching as her twisted ankle landed hard. When Sabrina scowled at the expression, Charity waved away her concern. "I can walk on it. I just shouldn't jump around. I forgot."

Sabrina picked at the cuticle around her nail, wincing as she tore a strip of skin. "But we're bringing a lot of supplies, okay? This could be a several-day hike."

"And Tatum?" Linda said. "He didn't do anything wrong. He doesn't deserve to get left behind." Charity nodded. But they were limited in their time, and their cursory search of the manor turned up neither Tatum nor Marion, so the three women stuffed backpacks full of energy bars, peanut butter, spoons, a first aid kit, plastic water bottles, tins of beans, and a can opener. They rolled up one blanket each, grabbed a single roll of toilet paper and a small blade, and changed into tennis shoes. Linda slipped on a jacket. Once their bags were stuffed, they made their way outside.

They scanned the yard for any signs of Deja or other trouble, but she was nowhere to be seen. Tristan's body was missing from his resting place as they strolled through the yard to the orchard, playing it casual in case Deja caught sight of them and guessed that they were running.

"Neither of you have been here before, have you?" Linda asked as they crossed into the bizarre grove. The trees were bursting with fruit, their pungent ripeness filling the air. Linda stepped onto one as they marched down the center path. When she bent to examine it, it didn't feel as abnormal in her grasp as it had that first night. Linda breathed in the orchard's aroma, reaching into her pocket and fingering the acorn she kept there.

They continued, silent in the presence of the grove's flowering beauty. It *was* beautiful, the same way a shock of scum in a pond was beautiful: unexpected, a new sight for eyes fatigued with concrete and metal. Finally, Charity gripped her hand. "Keep up," she said. Linda realized she'd been lagging.

After that, she met Charity step for step. At the end of the orchard, the path faded into dirt. The three women stepped from the crushed granite to the dry earth, and Linda breathed out what felt like a lifetime of anxious wonder.

"It is a gorgeous orchard." Charity squeezed Linda's hand, her fingers trembling so lightly it was almost unnoticeable.

"I wish Tristan would have gotten the chance to walk me through." Sabrina kicked at some dirt.

"I wish I would have gotten the chance to tell him I was gay for one of his girls," said Charity. She laughed, and Linda blushed. "Sucks, too, cause it would have done killer ratings."

They reached the hulking gate. Linda wrapped her hand around one of the bars, built tightly against the others. There was no place for people to walk through, only the swinging entrance through which vehicles might pass, which was closed. She pulled at it. It didn't budge.

But Linda remembered seeing a trail that seemed to lead up the mountain and through the trees. They could hike in the opposite direction and meet road. When she squinted into the woods, all she could make out was a confusion of growth: branches and trunks blending into each other for eternity.

"We have to go through." She would have crossed herself if she'd been religious. As it was, she focused on the warmth of Charity's palm against hers, a religion of her making.

"Fuck that. I'm climbing," said Charity. She let go, leaving Linda to cradle her own hand. She grabbed hold of a horizontal bar, stuck one foot on a vertical, and craned back her head to peer at the top, her destination, ornamented with pointed black diamonds. The whole barrier stretched for at least ten feet over the top of her head.

"How are you going to climb straight-ass poles?" Sabrina crossed her arms. "We're wasting time here."

"I've danced a pole before. Filled in for women at the club where I worked." She grabbed one of the bars; it was thin, and she grunted as she struggled to lift herself. She tried to jump upwards, scrambling for purchase, but she fell back onto her ass, dirt clouding around her like an aura. Still on the ground, she kicked the fence, hollering and sweating, but all it did was rattle. Charity clenched her fists. "Through the woods it is."

LINDA INHALED AT the edge of the woods, then with a deliberate exhale, stepped into the curious expanse of green light. Her companions followed. Guided by the compass app on Deja's phone, Linda crept on her tip-toes until her calves burned, forcing her to press her feet flat into the forest floor. As an old leaf crunched, she winced. The thicket was silent, eerily so, as though the breeze had taken a vacation. Linda repeated to herself, like a girl on a movie date chewing popcorn in the quiet part, *please be silent, please be silent.*

The trees, colossal and ancient, must have borne hundreds of rings inside them. Beneath, their roots stretched for miles, tangles of ropes. If reality were really as broken as it seemed, they were worthy adversaries. The kind of monsters capable of taking Linda and the others out one by one—or all at once, like they'd done to the fleeing throuple.

A branch brushed Linda's shoulder. She jumped, screamed. Charity rushed forward, but Linda caught her breath before Charity's arms wrapped around her.

"I just brushed it. I'm fine."

They continued. When a creature leapt into their path, Sabrina threw both her hands across their bodies to push them away, but it was a baby raccoon that didn't seem afflicted with disease.

Linda eyed the near distance with confusion. In the limbs, a swaying maze suspended by ropes ran parallel to them, blurred into the background. "What is that?" she whispered.

Charity squinted then let out the slightest sigh. "Ropes course. Probably installed for a show challenge."

"Thank God we missed out on that." Linda forced a small laugh.

Deeper in, the foliage darkened and the trees closed their gaps. The ropes course continued, integrated into the crowded mass of pine. They threaded themselves among the dense clusters, careful not to touch. Finally, they arrived at a clearing in the middle of it all, but their relief was brief. Stumps formed a circle around a circle of rusty red dirt, cleared of leaves. Someone had been there, and not so long ago.

No one said a word. For Linda, the experience, *the journey*, shifted around this silent half-belief. If she spoke of the things they encountered, those phenomena would cement themselves in reality. Perhaps some cascading effect would begin, like the push of an arranged domino. But she was confident the other women noticed the space, that they, too, had diagnosed its purpose. It looked like the kind of place where someone once performed sacrifice. Linda shuddered as they resumed their path.

Now and again, they hiked through a patch of poison ivy to avoid a tangle of roots. Linda kept her fear of allergy to herself, but as the toxic chemical brushed against her jeans, she uttered little prayers to no one that the oils would not seep through. From experience, she understood the result of a trespass: a gnarly rash that would coat her tender skin. But the plant wouldn't kill her. Not unless she swallowed it.

Peering through the density, Linda sought a glimpse of sky. When the first hint of blue appeared on her horizon, a shift of light like hope before them, she waved to her friends, too wary to speak aloud now that they seemed so close to the end. She ran toward the exit, despite her screaming thighs.

Linda's heart sped as she neared the exit, soft on her feet as she bounded forward. As she broke into the open air, she let out a whoop of relief. Sabrina laughed beside her, a welcome noise after the strained silence. Linda turned, ready to bring Charity into her embrace, when the shriek rang out. A root reached from the woods like a hand from hell, wrapped around Charity's weakened ankle, and jerked her to the ground.

Charity landed on her face, her nails digging into the dirt as the snare dragged her back inside. For an instant, as

Linda bounded to her, she disappeared into some blacked-out place. Her fingers finished their resistance as her eyes dulled, then closed. But when Linda flung herself beside Charity and grabbed at the root that held her, Charity came to. She kicked her leg, trying to dislodge the tree's grip, but the grip tightened, like a snake around a throat.

Linda dropped her bag. She dumped the contents free and rooted through them as the tree pulled Charity inch by crawling inch. Her hands closed around the blade. She surged forward again. Charity's fingers clawed at the inside of the root as she whimpered, her body twisted into thrashing. Then Sabrina was there, too, root-side and holding the only sharp thing she'd carried: the can opener with its small, circular blade. Linda and Sabrina stabbed and sliced at the root. Chips of wood flew into Linda's eyes, but she kept chopping, imagining some other face—a man's, maybe—and, finally, the root unwrapped Charity and slithered back into the murky mass.

Linda sighed from the back of her throat, a guttural, primal sound that made her feel alive.

"What the fuck just happened?" Sabrina panted.

"I stepped on a goddamn root." Sprawled in the dirt, Charity pulled her leg to her chest. Tears gathered in her eyes as she inspected her torn pants. "I—it's—something's wrong."

Sabrina's thin work-lip returned. "Let go of it." She grabbed Linda's blade. Swiftly, she sliced off the bottom of Charity's pant and frowned at what she uncovered. The root had squeezed so hard it had broken the bone, which now peeked through the skin in a mess of blood and torn sinew. "It's broken," she said. "We'll have to carry her back."

"Back? There is no back!" Charity shook her head over and over. "Didn't you just see what happened? One wrong step, and that tree was going to juice me!"

Linda placed two hands on either side of Charity's face, stilling her. It was all she could do, her voice frozen in her mouth as she drifted away from herself, letting Sabrina's words drift across her skin, a dream. A nightmare.

"And what's the other option?" Sabrina paced. "We're going to carry you all the way to the nearest town? Across mudslides and down mountains? Turn a two-day journey into two weeks? On the amount of supplies we brought?" Sabrina threw up her hands. "Mission aborted. We're going back."

"No!" Charity pushed Linda away as she tried to stand, but as the ankle took weight, it folded beneath her with a loud pop. She screeched. Linda fell back onto the ground, and there she remained, dust coating her clothes.

"And you've just completed the break." Sabrina ripped a strip of fabric from her shirt and bent back down, wrapping it around the wound. "You're going to need surgery, which I can't provide. You're going to need antibiotics. And you're going to need crutches, which I can make for you, but we need to get back to the manor before you go into shock or pass out. This is not some sprain, Charity."

"Your bone," Linda said. It was all she could say. She wanted to absorb Charity's pain, but had no room. Despair had settled within her, again after all these years. Down the mountain, a clear trail led to land cleared of trees. A road, made from concrete, manufactured to keep the natural world away. An end to the journey.

"We have to carry her back." Sabrina snapped in Linda's face. Linda jerked back to life. The *end* was gone. This journey was *endless*. "Can you handle that?"

"Fuck." Charity cried. "I fucked it all up."

"Nonsense." Linda wanted to console her, but the words— she was choking on their absence. Her heart hammered as she tried. This woman she had come to know, to love, was crying, and Linda should console her. She swallowed a breath. The words scratched her throat. "It's not your fault." Linda patted Charity on the back, the gesture stiff and false. Charity let out another wracking sob.

Standing, Sabrina examined the woods with her hands on her hips.

"I'm a phony," Charity said. "I lied to everyone here. Now I'm paying for being a goddamn fake."

"No." And it was true. Linda broke open. She leaned in, gathered Charity in her arms, and absorbed her cries into the fabric of her shirt. As she pulled back, she kissed each wet spot from Charity's face. "We're going to get back. We're going to get the hell out of this place, one way or another."

Or another. Linda imagined her father's dead face, the face of the creature in the curio shop, the face of her ex-husband, the face of Deja, the final closing of her eyes.

"We're just going to have to go right back the way we came." Sabrina hefted her back over her shoulders. "We'll carry her. We'll walk as gently as we can. The trees didn't seem to notice us until Charity stepped on one of their roots." She gestured at the women huddled in a heap. "Let's do this." She slid one arm under Charity's, and Linda repeated the movement. "On three," Sabrina said, then counted, and on the third beat, they stood. Charity yelped as her ankle adjusted to the new orientation of her body, then went silent. Her face turned green with pain. She was gorgeous even when she was ugly.

"It's going to be okay," Linda whispered as she and Sabrina ambled as a five-legged beast. Once they reached the edge of the forest, they stopped, frozen, and peered back the way they'd come.

The ground was roots as far as the eye could see.

CHAPTER FORTY-ONE

SABRINA

HER NUMBER ONE goal was to escape the manor, to leave the experience in one piece.

The half of her who had emerged inside the manor's confines, the woman who promised the cameras she'd do whatever it took to survive until the bitter end, to make no friends, to win the man's heart at any cost, that part stared out at the path that led to freedom, her legs itching to run and never look back.

But the other half, the one who daily risked her health to care for other people, the half who had come to call these women friends, couldn't leave Charity wounded, to die in the grass, bleeding out, with no supplies. She had never given up on a patient. She was not about to start now.

"So much for that plan." Linda regarded the roots, but Sabrina's focus centered on a blurry chaos of rope a mile in the distance.

"The ropes course," she said. Charity groaned as her body sunk between them. "It's the only way."

THE ROPE WAS a Giant's Ladder, which was exactly what it sounded like: a series of ropes and wooden rungs spaced one average-size person apart. A teamwork exercise from Hell, the kind of activity twisted camp counselors required unruly teenagers to do. It dangled from two tree limbs that led to a platform at the top. There was no other way up.

"I've seen these on the show," Sabrina said. Her sister had forced her to watch every episode of every season, then every spin-off and copycat. "You have to work together to get up them."

"And usually with two pairs of working legs," Charity said, slumping between them.

"We've got two pairs of working legs." Sabrina used all her strength to adjust Charity's body weight against hers, a proof of capability to soothe the wounded. "We'll make do."

They stood at the bottom of the ladder, considering their first move, Sabrina's hands shaking as she counted down the seconds until something weird happened. Together, they formulated a plan. Linda and Sabrina lifted Charity, their hands cupping her by the pits, high enough to grab hold of the first rung. She pulled herself up and straddled it, swaying back and forth as she clutched the rope.

"I don't have that upper body strength," Linda admitted. "I'll need to be pulled up there."

Sabrina had built her body to keep its strength hidden beneath her curves, a careful balance of obsessive weight-lifting, dance-style aerobics, and macro-counting that resulted in a thorough knowledge of the muscles beneath her skin and the careful ability to control them. She knelt, allowing Linda to climb onto her shoulders. As Sabrina stood, hands clamped around Linda's ankles, Linda wobbled forward, forcing Sabrina to step forward and adjust her footing.

"Grab her!" she cried out, and Linda's outstretched fingers wrapped with Charity's. Clinging to the ropes, Charity pulled while Linda lifted herself. Once she hung high enough, Linda swung her legs over. They faced one another across the ladder, veering back and forth with the force of Linda's arrival.

"My turn," Sabrina said.

Linda and Charity broke eye contact, reached two hands down, and pulled her up. Her torso aching, Sabrina held one arm out, finding her balance.

"Goddamn third wheel," Sabrina muttered. "Now..." She chewed her nail, examining the possibilities. "Linda, I think you have to stand first."

Sabrina was surprised at how easily Linda followed her instructions when once they had been rivals. If Linda had known what thoughts moved through Sabrina, what revelations she had found in the walls of the manor, she might not agree so readily to put her life into Sabrina's hands. But Linda seized hold of the rope at her side with both hands. The ladder tottered wildly beneath them. Sabrina ducked and wrapped her arms around the rung, twisting to stay upright as Linda steadied herself into a standing position.

"Shit, I should have gone on the outside." Sabrina eyed Charity's twisted leg dangling into the open air. "We'll have to make do." Sabrina scooted her body until she was as close to Linda as possible, then moved her knees to the beam, crossing her ankles over one another. "Step on my back."

Linda obliged.

"Hold to the beam above you." Sabrina scooted forward, grasped the rope, and rose, lifting Linda high enough to pull up.

Once Linda arrived at the next rung, she clutched it as Sabrina instructed Charity to do the same. Then they lifted Sabrina and waited for the swinging to stop before attempting the next climb.

"How are you doing over there?" Sabrina called to Charity as they neared the top platform.

"It's high," Charity said, but Sabrina guessed it wasn't the height giving Charity's voice a fatigued quaver. Her body should be going into shock, trying to shut down, to rest, to protect her from further damage to herself. Sabrina hoped it wouldn't happen until they were far away from here.

"Almost there," Linda said, and they performed their climbing dance.

When Sabrina's knees pressed against the hard, stable surface, she let out a sigh of desperate relief. As they pulled Linda onto the platform, Sabrina searched Charity's face; she was pale and trembling. Sabrina examined the rest of the course: a zip line stretched from their platform to the next, followed by a hanging bridge. Sabrina peered down. The forest floor was a mass of roots, slithering like snakes in all directions.

"She can't zip-line by herself," Sabrina said. The next challenge. It was just like the hospital. She needed to take it one step at a time. "One of us will have to wear her as a backpack."

"I've never zip-lined before." Linda swallowed, her throat bobbing. "You have to take her."

Even losing herself to shock or blood-loss or both, Charity's face fell. But it was no time for hurt feelings.

"Good call." Sabrina hacked a second harness from the line and shoved it into Linda's hands, then knelt in front of Charity. "Help me lift her up here, tie her onto me, and get us both into this remaining harness."

As Linda lifted a woozy Charity and strapped her to Sabrina, Sabrina noted with a sharp pain to her chest that the zip line was intended for use by a couple: Tristan and his chosen contestant. It should have been her here, in another timeline. A harsh wind blew the thought away, forcing her hair into her face. The air stunk like mold and puss.

She dared to glance back.

Behind, the branches were waking. They stretched and rattled infinitely forward, like the arms of giants.

"You better go," Linda cried out.

No time to hesitate. Sabrina let her and Charity fall into the zip-line's embrace. As she zoomed across the line, she felt a conflict of feelings: relieved she and her patient were safe, but also happy that her rival was still stuck behind them.

As her feet touched down on the platform, she stared at the zip line harness in her hand. She glanced across the expanse at Linda's waiting stance, and as the boughs bent in an unearthly way, a storm surging to sweep Linda into its turmoil, Sabrina pushed the harness back.

CHAPTER FORTY-TWO

LINDA

FIRST CAME THE scent of wounds and rot. Then it was the stench of her father's last drink, the one she fixed for him: alcohol, sugar syrup, mint, and that secret ingredient.

Linda's hand shone with blood—Charity's. She wiped it away and strapped herself into the harness, and as she let herself drop forward, a hand held her back.

Screaming, she reached back and clawed at the appendage. Her fingers gripped at wood. She pried at the hardened hand until it broke, then jumped. Her stomach dropped as she flew along the line, kicking her feet to speed her through. As she landed on the platform, she chucked the hand at Sabrina's feet. It had stopped moving, splintered at the wrist.

"What the hell?" Sabrina kicked it over the side, eyes widening.

She'd once read that trees, when attacked by insects, sent pheromones on the wind to warn the rest of the forest.

"Let's finish this," Linda said, imagining a whole woodland awakening.

Charity groaned. Sabrina had set her to rest against the platform. Her mangled leg stuck out at a wrong angle, and the rest quivered as she struggled to hold onto consciousness.

"How are you feeling?" Sabrina crouched, checking her forehead. "We're almost there. Almost there."

"I can make it," Charity croaked, but an image flashed behind Linda's eyes: her father's face. Not in death—not this time—but pushing away her mother as he climbed the trail to the mountain's top. Telling her he could make it. She had wished her father dead. She couldn't lose Charity, not yet, not when she hoped she never would.

Linda pulled Charity up, forcing her to sit without support. Charity had bit her lip in pain until it bled down her chin. The dried blood gave her the appearance of some bloodsucker caught in the act. Sometimes, controlling a pain made the uncontrolled hurting lessen. Linda understood that.

"We have to cross this bridge now," Linda said. "I'm going to carry you." Linda looped her arms around Charity's legs. "Hold onto me for a few more minutes. Don't you dare let go."

Charity's drunken smile might have been endearing in some other circumstance—the kind of party they might never see together. She wrapped her arms around Linda's neck. Linda barely breathed. Fear that gripped her as she stood with Charity clinging to her back. She was responsible for Charity now. She had never been responsible for *life* before. Sabrina tied them together with the harness, then gestured them forward as a shadow stirred, covering their bodies with the amber dark of the night-blooming woods.

"Get," she said.

Linda did, stepping one foot onto the first rickety pipe that made up the bridge.

Her foot slipped.

She caught herself, grabbing the rope bridge. Charity squeezed her legs around Linda's waist, but the grip lost strength with each passing second. Linda moved to the next step, then the next, until she felt at ease with the balancing act. She didn't look down into the roots, only forward, toward that final platform. If she slipped, she would save Charity before herself. She would pay that price. There was no question, when she had once given so much more for those she loved.

And she did love Charity. It seemed too soon to say it, or so she had been told by romantic comedies, but though they had only loved one another's secret places once, they had shared more than she had ever shared with her ex, with any other. The woman pushed her, and she hoped to be the kind of person who could one day push back.

Besides, she wondered, as they navigated the pipe bridge, *why are we so scared of love that we forbid it in romance's earliest stages?* Maybe if we allowed love, if her family had allowed love, if she had permitted love, then she would have sprung open and taken root like a resistant bulb. Maybe she wouldn't have had to do what she did all those years ago. And maybe, in her adulthood, she wouldn't have moved through life like a zombie.

"Linda!" Sabrina yelled as Linda's thoughts fled like frightened roaches. Two branches swept down like salad tongs. She stood at the edge of the final platform, one step from the next victory. She bowed forward, sending Charity flying onto it as the branch yanked her into the air.

The tree suspended Linda, dangling her like a panther dangles its fresh rat-kill. Twisting in the air, she searched frantically for a way down, but Sabrina screeched across the bridge. Linda turned her head. The tree had lifted a third limb, sharpened to a point and poised above like a snake ready to strike.

"Get back!" Linda screamed to Charity on the platform, but Charity leaned over, staring up at Linda and her captor.

Sabrina jumped across the bridge's final threshold. She pulled Charity into her lap and pushed something into her hand: the harness-end of a free-fall pulley. Sabrina positioned Charity's grip on the pulley and pushed her to the edge. "Hold tight," she yelled as she shoved her down into the sinking light outside.

The limb bent at odd, animal angles, as though bones and joints moved within its bark façade. It thrust toward Linda. She twisted away, and as her body untangled, she fell to the ground.

With a thud, she landed on her back, the breath leaving her body in a *WHOOMPH*. Something cracked as she gasped, struggling to inhale. Once her breath returned, there was no time to process pain. She sprung to her feet and darted further into the safety of the sunset-lit yard, where Sabrina tended to a crumpled Charity in the grass.

"How can I help?" Linda winced. It hurt to speak.

"I'm okay," Charity said as her face drained of its last hints of color.

The forest moaned. The limbs at its perimeter stirred as if in a breeze, like the creaking moan of the manor's floors, and the ground under their bodies throbbed like the floor that had pounded their first night during dinner.

"Are you okay?" Sabrina asked. "Linda, I'm talking to you."

"Oh!" She ran her hand down her body. "I don't think anything's broken." She took stock of her ache, but it consumed her entirely, impossible to categorize. "I heard a crack, but—" When she checked her pocket, something sliced into her finger. "Ouch!" She pulled free her hand and wiped away a line of blood.

"Do you have the goddamn knife in your pocket?" Sabrina said.

Linda reached back in, more carefully now, and pulled out the giant acorn she had pocketed their first day. It was cracked in several places.

Linda peeled at the acorn's shell, tossing the remains. Inside the acorn, a tangle of pink roots wriggled like worms. There was something nestled even further in. Linda tore at the roots. They were juicy, like veins torn from a body. In their center, sat a single eye as large as a golf ball, the roots attached like optic nerves. Linda screamed as she realized what she held. She dropped the eye. In the grass, its pupil moved until it found an opening. It gaped at the women staring back at it.

Wordlessly, Sabrina and Linda scooped Charity up and carried her through the yard, moving as fast as they could. This time, they didn't give a damn if Deja saw. There were uglier things afoot. Finally they reached the inside of the manor, and within its relative safety, they slumped against a wall. Linda held back the impulse to vomit; she wasn't the one who needed medical attention.

When they returned to themselves, their fear not resolved so much as pushed deep into their bellies, they snuck into the bathroom, where Sabrina disinfected Charity's ankle.

"If we can't get out of here right now, I'll have to splint this without proper tools."

Charity nodded. "I understand."

"I don't." Linda scrubbed her hands, struggling not to inspect her reflection in the mirror. "What the fuck is going on here?"

"We can't think about that." Sabrina frowned at the protrusion of bone. "Our first step should be trying to get out of here. Get you to a hospital, where they can operate and re-set the bone in a proper medical setting. For now, you aren't to put weight on it. Ordinarily, I would try to make you a set of crutches from old branches, but—"

"I understand," Charity repeated.

Sabrina chewed her lip. "The motorcycle," she said. "Where did they put Brendan's motorcycle?"

CARRYING CHARITY, THEY crept along the manor wall until they rounded the corner of the building. The old barn beckoned, its cracking white paint out of its element beside the manor's stained glass and woodwork. It was a massive barn, with big rolling doors and enough space to hold a motorcycle.

The barn doors slid easily along their track. Charity let out a happy gasp.

"Is it…?" Sabrina said, panting, as she peered inside.

The motorcycle had been parked in the middle of the otherwise empty area. It was covered with a tan blanket and sprinkled with hay, like Deja had tried to camouflage it. Linda scoffed. How stupid did she assume the contestants were? Linda yanked the blanket off the bike, and Sabrina ran her hand down the one seat.

Charity's smile faded. "Shit."

Sabrina reached into the saddlebag and grabbed the keys. "Someone was ready for a quick getaway," she said. "My guess is Deja." Something else rattled near her hand: a bottle of pills. "Doxycycline."

"Antibiotics?" Linda asked.

Sabrina passed a pill to Charity.

"What was wrong with him?" Charity asked as she dry-swallowed.

Sabrina read the bottle: "Twice daily for treatment of chlamydia."

Linda eyed the one seat. "Obviously, you two should go," she said, her heart sinking even as she understood it was the only choice.

"If you think I'm going without you, you're mad," Charity said.

Linda crossed her arms and tried not to let her voice betray her disappointment. "You'll come back for me."

Charity slammed her fist into the dirt. "I'll do no such thing."

Linda chewed her lip. "I can't go with you. I…can't drive."

After her father died, after her mother blamed her, after everything, Linda wasn't allowed by her foster parents to learn. Unlike her peers, she relied on the kindness of men, who wanted to get into her pants, to attend school dances, football games, after-school hijinks. As soon as she could, she moved to a city big enough to have buses—uncommon in Texas—and rarely left the comfort of the city until her husband moved her to the suburbs, after which, he drove them everywhere they needed to go.

Sabrina massaged her temple. "Listen. There's still an impassable mudslide, so this is going to be a rough ride down the mountain, okay? And you're telling me you're going to make me go just because I'm the only one who knows how to drive and is uninjured enough. And you're making me to go *alone* because you two don't want to be separated?"

"That's a perfect analysis of the situation," said Linda. She peered down at the crestfallen Charity, the old barn's spectral light streaked across her skin.

"I'm not going to stand here and argue," Sabrina said. "I value my life." She spoke as though she thought Linda and Charity were children. "I'm leaving. There's no second chance for you. I'll bring help, but who knows—" Sabrina choked on the words. "Who knows what could happen between now and then."

Linda slid into the dirt beside Charity and took her hand.

"We're staying," Linda said.

"You're staying." Sabrina huffed. "Give me one of the bags there."

As Linda pushed an old potato sack through the dirt, dust billowed.

"Now listen. Here's what Charity needs to be comfortable." Sabrina rattled off the instructions for Charity's care, while Linda nodded at each new task Sabrina mentioned. Sabrina reached into the saddlebag and pulled out a clicker: the key to the gate. She started the bike and flipped on the handlebar speakers. "*She's a maniac, maniac...*" the music blared. "Out of my way, Thelma and Louise," Sabrina said.

"Be safe," Linda said.

"Enjoy freedom," Charity said.

"You two are ridiculous." Sabrina inched forward, then stopped. "But you need to be the safe ones." As she drove out of the barn, through the yard, Linda helped Charity forward and through the barn doors, where they watched Sabrina disappear onto the drive. After a few minutes, the gates opened for her.

Linda shivered. "What have we done?" She imagined herself in the seat beside Sabrina, then shivered again as she realized what that would mean: leaving a wounded Charity to her own devices.

"What do we do now?" Charity asked.

Linda pursed her lips, settling into her new script. "Survive," she said.

CHAPTER FORTY-THREE

LINDA

THEIR SURVIVAL PLAN was to hide. They would lock themselves inside a bedroom, bar the door with heavy furniture, and whittle the days away until Sabrina or the production team sent help.

The irony that they could feel safe trapped inside a haunted house didn't escape them. The house's quakes and moans were less terrifying than the trees, or rabid creatures, or Deja's secrets. Whatever her true intentions were, Linda didn't care to find out. As they slipped on their backpacks, Linda led Charity back along the shaded outer wall of the manor. At the front door, Linda surveyed their surroundings. No signs of Deja or Marion.

From the other bedrooms, Linda gathered the medical supplies Sabrina had prescribed. In their bedroom, Linda pushed an antique vanity against the door. Its mirror reflected a dirtied mess, her face and body covered in a thin layer of filth. She cleaned her hands and went to work sanitizing Charity's wound.

The blood around the break had dried. Charity winced as Linda rubbed the old blood away. Her bone still stuck out from the skin. It was grotesque, but Linda had seen death close up, and a little bone didn't bother her. When Charity yelped, Linda offered her arm, letting Charity bite on the flesh.

Charity squeezed Linda's bicep as Linda finished. After Linda had covered it in a torn and tied cloth, Linda crawled into bed beside her.

"I need to rest," Charity said. "Sabrina willed it."

"You're right." Linda kissed her. "Doctor's orders."

Their kiss deepened until Charity pulled away and snatched a clean cloth from the nightstand. She wet it with water from a bottle. Charity removed Linda's jacket, then her shirt, her shorts, telling her when to move, so Charity could reach without moving her injured leg. The pop of the button on Linda's shorts was harsh against Linda's skin, and Charity cleaned first the indentation it left pressed into her fat. She wiped Linda's arms, smoothing the hair in its proper direction, then the shoulders. Linda ached underneath in both ways: the good and the bad. Charity washed her belly and her legs, pausing at her knees so Linda could suppress her tickled giggling. All this she did sitting with legs out-stretched, propped against the back of the bed board, while Linda moved only when Charity told her to.

After Linda was clean, Charity ran her finger down Linda's body. Linda trembled not from cold but from the softness of Charity's touch.

"Kneel over my face," Charity demanded. "I want a distraction."

Linda straddled Charity's chest, her foot passing accidentally over the bone that stuck free. As Linda winced, Charity let out a strangled moan.

"I'm sorry," Linda said, frantic.

"No, it felt... good. Touch me there. It's like you're touching me inside. Somewhere no one ever has before."

"Are you sure?" Linda said.

"I'm sure." Charity reached around and cupped Linda's ass in her hands, pulling her forward. Linda inched on her knees until her cunt was positioned at Charity's mouth. She leaned forward, her fingers caressing the tip of the break as Charity's tongue swept along the crease between Linda's legs. Linda gasped as her whole body jumped. She gave herself to Charity without regret.

AFTERWARD, THEY RESTED, spent and sore with the day's demands. Time passed, and they woke only to peer for a moment out the window as though they might judge the passing of the hours by the amount of light that shone or failed to shine through the pastel curtains. The truth was they were encased in the fogs of several states: the state of new love, of fear with no end, of surviving near-death, the state of reality having been crushed beneath their fleeing feet. The house's moans grew more frenzied, and the bed shook as the floor below it shuddered. Charity's moans harmonized with the rest. By the time Linda woke enough to hone in on the sounds, she realized Charity was unwell.

When she inspected the ankle beneath the blankets, the smell that met her was fierce and terrible. The wound was fighting infection. Linda poured two more pills out from the bottle and fed them to Charity, then went to the window and yanked it open, gulping the fresh air.

Below, Deja marched toward the woods, a body dragging behind her.

Linda's stomach dropped. Deja knew everything, and learning what she knew was the only way out.

Linda kissed Charity on both cheeks, tucked her in, and slid a knife into the pocket of her own jacket. The jacket smelled like shit from its constant wear, stained now with the memory of the acorn that had lived inside. She ventured through the halls, the foyer, out the front door, and into the yard. She marched with a fresh determination into the forest, following the path she saw Deja travel.

This time, Linda walked more carefully, tottering on tiptoes across any hint of root. With each rustle of the leaves or creaking of a limb, she paused. She followed any hints of footsteps and listened, over and over, until finally, she heard: a haunting whistle. Deja's voice. She followed the sound until she arrived at the edge of a clearing, like the one they passed on their attempted escape.

Deja held a giant blade. With grim determination, she slashed at a tree. A pile of stripped bark gathered as she slid the knife into the tree's core and hummed. Beside her lay the body of Becca, covered in grime, her face contorted and frozen at the moment of death. Behind Deja, another tree had been de-barked. It bore a wound down the center that had been stitched shut with black string.

The stitched-up tree was changing: its remaining bark was fading like a leaf in autumn, brown to orange to tan. The ridges in the bark smoothed to resemble folds in fatty flesh. The change moved from trunk to crown, and the tree shivered in one fluid motion before it shook like a frightened animal in danger.

Deja sliced a final time into the unstitched tree. The bark opened with a hiss. Deja stuck her hands inside the crack and pushed it open wide. The tree parted at her command. Linda covered her mouth. Deja bent, took her knife, and pricked Becca's skin from head to toe, a hundred little piercings until she looked like she'd sweated blood. Then, Deja hoisted the body over her shoulder, smearing blood all over, and pressed the dying woman into the fissure. Deja pushed at the tree's wound. The tree moaned as it closed. Deja reached into her clothes, pulled out a needle and thick black thread, and sewed.

As the horror caught up with Linda, she forgot herself in the forest's dark truth. She screamed, then turned and ran as fast as she could.

She felt something at her back. She fell into the dirt, the weight of a woman on top of her. Deja had caught her and taken her down.

CHAPTER FORTY-FOUR

LINDA

LINDA WOKE, TIED to a tree with a camera's charging cord. Deja was finishing sewing shut the wound she had inflicted on the tree. Her belt was strung with tools: knife, walkie talkie, coiled cords, and a spool of thick black thread, and they bobbed as Deja moved against the bark. Deja hummed a song that wormed its way inside Linda, lulling and beautiful, like the woods.

"What are you doing?" Linda whispered.

Deja turned to face her. "Making sure I have a life outside this place when all is said and done." She sighed. "Cleaning up other people's messes, like I've always done."

The tree behind them had stopped shaking and swayed, bending as no tree should.

"And who's in that one?" Linda racked her brain. "Marion? Tatum?"

"Brandon. Pink suit and all." She pursed her lips. "You must think I'm a monster. Is that what you think?" Deja moved away from the half-stitched tree and peered at Linda's wilting body. "But you're the one who killed her own father."

"It's not like there's only one monster in the world," Linda said. "They're everywhere." Linda tried to move her hands, but they were tied tight.

"You think your father was bad because he drank a little? You don't know anything about bad fathers." Deja knelt in front of Linda and gestured around her. "Linda, I'd like you to meet my family."

"Your family?"

"These woods here, they're the men of the house. Plus my recent additions. The women occupy an ornamental grove. The sexes must be separated, after all. Isn't that what makes good boys and girls?" Sarcasm dripped from her words as she returned to the wound. She took the needle once more and sewed the final stitches. Behind her, her first creation stopped bending and settled into its slowed reality. Still, every time Linda blinked, the tree had moved an inch closer to Deja.

"Let us go," Linda said. "I'll carry her out. We won't tell anyone about any of this. We signed contracts, remember?"

Deja frowned. She finished her stitching.

"You know my past?" Linda said, struggling at the cord around her wrists. "Then you know I can keep a secret. I won't tell anyone what happened here."

As Deja pulled through her final stitch, she stepped back. The seams sealed, and the transformation began. Linda remained silent, and in that silence she heard—at such a high frequency it was nearly inaudible—screaming.

"You know what it's like to be haunted," Deja said. "I tried to leave, just like you left your mother. Your husband. Family has a way of calling you back." Deja's voice caught. "I wake every night to my sister's face. I hear her screaming as they sewed her in. I'm as haunted as you are."

"What are you talking about, you crazy bitch?" Linda said. "Everyone's haunted by something. Let me go."

Deja wrung her hands. "I'm afraid I can't."

"And why not?" Linda begged.

"Because I'm the winner of this season," she said. "There can't be two women walking out of here. Not when you've seen what you've seen."

"Deja, I don't even know what I've seen."

"You know enough."

Deja patted the bark as it shifted to skin. She ran a hand along Linda's jaw. "You remind me of me. We both thought we could evade being what our families made us." Deja's eyes sparked with despair. "I was going to lose my job, you know. Everything I built. This franchise. They were going to blame me for the numbers falling, but I gave my whole life to this show. I understood that it was a risk to bring you all here, but it was the only thing I could think of. They drained me, you see."

"Your family?" Linda wanted to keep her talking, to keep her rationalizing until she realized the error of her ways.

"This show. The well of ideas was dry. I swore I wouldn't come back here, not after what they did to my sister. But a haunted excursion? A paranormal season? It was too good an idea to pass up."

"You brought us here knowing?" Linda scrunched her face. "All those people…"

Deja closed her eyes. "It was a mistake. And it was the last mistake I'll be making." She pulled out a lighter. "I'm so sorry." Linda's eyes darted, looking for any escape she might settle on. And that's when she glimpsed the gas can Deja had dragged with her. Deja picked it up, tipped it over, and poured.

LINDA TRIED TO rub the cord that bound her against the bark, but the plastic wouldn't catch. She screamed, but there was no one there to hear her.

A presence surfaced behind her. She didn't dare scream again. She tried to turn her head, but she couldn't catch sight of whatever was making its way to her.

Then she smelled Charity's mix of sweetness and sour infection.

"How did you get out here?" Linda said, relief flooding her.

"I hopped on one foot," she said. "I won't lie. I fucked up my good foot, and I fell about a hundred times." Reaching into her pocket, she pulled out the earpiece. "When I realized you were gone, I had this hunch. So I turned this thing on. And sure enough, Deja had hers on, and I heard you. Took me a minute, but I got here."

"Jacket pocket," Linda said.

Charity grabbed the blade from Linda. She sawed at the cord until it broke. Linda's hands sprung free. She pressed her lips against Charity's, holding Charity against her, and when they broke free, she didn't let go.

"I love you," Linda said.

When Charity smiled, it was everything. "I love you."

"I've learned a lot."

"I heard some of it." Charity chucked the earpiece. "Let's do whatever we're going to do."

Linda struggled to her feet. Charity's exposed ankle was covered in dirt. Linda helped Charity stand, and together they followed the smell of gasoline. At the border, they found Deja. As she caught sight of them, her forehead wrinkled as her eyebrows frowned.

"Goddamn it." Deja grabbed a leaf from the ground and flicked the flame onto its brittle surface.

A monstrous hand sprung from the murk of the woods and grabbed Deja by the neck. Its long fingers were pointed at the end, covered in thick flesh. It closed its massive fingers around Deja and lifted her. The creature surged forward: it was Marion. She was half-human, half-creature of the woods, her skin as ridged as bark, her eyes two knots in a long trunk, her mouth grown over. Her arms were branches while her feet remained the same. She was terrible in her mockery of nature and humanity, and Charity's grip on Linda tightened.

Marion advanced as Deja dangled from her grip. The leaf the producer was holding dropped, and the fire crept, leaf by leaf. Linda let go of Charity and ran forward, stomping out the fire. Marion turned her whole body to look at Linda, then reached with her other hand to grab at her. Linda dropped to the charred ground. She rolled away from Marion. With all the energy she had left, she swooped Charity up, and they hobbled off inch by inch.

Marion trailed them, her steps meandering, but she gained on them. Deja banged her hands against the trunk that was now Marion's body.

"Here, catch!" Tatum scrambled in front of them, tossing them one of the ballgowns from the elimination ceremonies. It soared heavily through the ground and landed at their feet, gas fumes wafting up into their nostrils.

Linda set Charity onto the ground and lifted the dress. Charity moved backward on hands and her one good leg, away. Linda didn't have time to think about what might happen. She wadded the dress and tossed it. Marion was close enough that the dress snagged on her ridged limb.

"There's no goddamn fire, Tatum!" Linda yelled.

She dragged Charity, panting hard, as Marion closed in.

"We have to get inside," Charity wheezed.

"Fuck. Shit." Tatum pulled a lighter from his pocket. "Hey, Deja! I quit!" He ran, screaming, and as he neared Marion, readying himself to jump, flame flickering in his hand, Marion raised her trunk of a foot and brought it down on top of him. The flame died as Tatum's bones broke with a sickening crunch, his guts flowing out in all directions like a squashed roach.

Deja let out an unexpected cry.

Linda glanced across the vast expanse of yard. The woods seemed closer to the manor with each minute. And who was to say Marion wouldn't brute her way indoors? But Linda followed Charity's request. It was the best she could do.

Marion groaned, and though Linda didn't look back, she smelled the reek of gas and old wounds and fresh bark and rotting flesh. A lighter clicked in the background. A great *whoosh*. Linda dove, pushing Charity farther into the grass. Marion lunged with one final shriek. The rip of tearing clothes preceded an amalgamation of screaming, then groaning, then fire erupting. Linda dared to turn, still scurrying backward: Marion's hands were wrapped around Deja's body, shredding with abandon as Deja clung to the fiery gown with one hand and to Marion's thick neck with her other. Marion freed herself from Deja and tossed her out, but it was too late. The fire had caught on Marion's woody exterior, and as they watched, she burst into flame.

Deja rolled away, extinguishing the flames engulfing her own body, then lay, broken and bleeding. Marion's body stilled as she shrieked, the flames licking her from crown to toe. She burned black, the radiating heat warming Linda in the chill air. Charity collapsed. Sweat beaded on her forehead from the heat and the infection. When Linda pressed the back of her palm against the skin there, it burned to the touch.

"Deja, please help me," Linda called out. But Deja was worse off than Linda had realized. She could barely move from the burns that marred her body. What wasn't burnt, leaked blood from gashes Marion had inflicted. Linda crawled to Deja as Marion's trunk broke down, small chunks falling into a pile of coals and ash.

"I'll patch you up," Linda said. "You'll be good as new."

But Linda knew it was a lie even as she spun it.

Deja's laugh became a cough that wracked her fragile body.

"It's too late for me, but you... You can get away from them," Deja said. And Linda understood Deja didn't mean from the woods or the haunted house, but from the wounds of her family.

"I'll keep them at bay," Deja said, "if you sew me into a tree."

Linda pulled back, a wave of horror stirring through her. "But you tried to burn down the woods. Now you want me to make you one of them?"

"I want you to let me destroy them from the inside out," Deja said.

Linda glanced back at her girlfriend shaking in the dying grass.

"And you'll keep them from killing us?"

Deja tried to lift her hands only to yelp and let them drop. "Cross my wicked heart."

CHAPTER FORTY-FIVE

LINDA

THE MOMENTS LINDA remembered best from childhood: her father's vodka breath when he picked her up, her father's open mouth as he drunkenly dozed on the couch each night, her father's inconsistent anger, her mother's tears behind a closed bathroom door. As a little girl, she never knew whether an errant word from her might set him off, and so she remained, for the most part, silent. She wanted to stick up for herself, for her mother, for their lives, but she was seven years old, and she quickly learned she was not allowed, by the laws of parenthood, to fight back against her father's injustices. Childhood demanded she accept what she had been given or face the loud whip of a belt against her bare ass. Childhood demanded she ignore her mother's dark circles or else call the wrath of her father's insults down upon them both. She was "a smart aleck," "nosy bones," or even, when she tried to wrap her arms around her mother's leg, trying with all the power of her thoughts to protect the woman, "a rotten brown-noser."

Other days, her father was precious to her. His terrible moods made her all the more thankful for his loving ones, and so when he offered to toss a ball with her in the front yard, or play diving games with her in the pool, or teach her a poker game that held all the allure of adult things, she rushed to his side and soaked up every kind word he offered, like parched dirt in a summer shower. Some days, she even thought she might love him the most, out of her two parents. The way her love for him ebbed then surged couldn't compete with the steady admiration and adoration she held for her mother and her sister.

As she grew old enough to know better, she understood that other children's parents didn't drink until they couldn't walk or talk. They didn't drink until they could no longer understand language itself. Her father's drink infused him with irritation; he became more frustrated with the conversation that passed around him among Linda, her mother, and her sister. They were always forced to contend with his needless confusion. As a result, their conversations were muddled with constant re-explanations, responses to his repeated *what*'s, and angry sighs from every mouth. The family grew apart more and more, unable to focus on anything but the man of the house and his constant need for attention, for care, for pity. If they had allowed each other to speak their emotions, they would have, all of them, fallen to pieces. And who would have cared for the man who fell down the stairs and broke his arm one sloppy morning?

During her turbulent adolescence, Linda needed more than anything to be wrapped in the loving arms of family and assured that the roiling fear and anger and sadness inside her would calm, would become manageable. She needed more than anything for her family to notice her daily breakdowns and get her help. She needed something, anything, to lead her through the rage that descended upon her without warning.

Instead, she was advised to suck up her emotions and to let go of what couldn't possibly be that bad, considering her age. She was ignored for the sake of her father's errant moods, which were assigned more importance than hers for no reason but that he had earned them, with his years and the priority that all men were given over girls.

They had one cell phone, and it was her parents, an early flip-phone model, thin and fragile. Her mother planned the camping trip. When Linda's mother and father were younger, they had enjoyed similar camping trips. They had hiked. He drank as much then, too, but it didn't weigh on his body as it did by the time he became a father. Linda's mother wanted to bring the phone along, in case of emergency; motherhood had made her more cautious. But Linda's father worried about the phone's fragility. Linda heard them arguing as they packed for the trip.

"We're going to the top of a mountain, Sam," she said.

"Yeah, and we've done it before. Before cell phones. Before there were even as many rangers stationed about. We're leaving the phone," he said.

"What if something happens to one of us?" Linda's mother asked.

"We're going to be fine. You're being paranoid."

But Linda understood the worry. What if something happened to her father, to Sam? What if he fell down a mountain as he had fallen down the stairs? At the thought, Linda couldn't help but smile. The smile disturbed her, and she dropped it from her face. She closed herself in her room. She had wished, for a moment, for her father's death. She examined the emotion, a coping mechanism she taught to herself. If her father died, she would be sad. She would remember the good things he had done. She would remember the bad. She would cry at his funeral. She would be relieved. She could process his memory in a way that she failed to process during the living nightmare of his daily presence.

Linda took a walk through the woods that surrounded their house. She tried not to let herself cry, but she couldn't help it. She navigated the trails, despite the hazy vision caused by a deluge of tears. She pushed through great walloping sobs. She was full of hormones, and she understood that, but she also understood that her mother and her sister were past their adolescence and still they cried for her father. If he died, they could move on, the three of them, and live a happy life. Her mother would never leave him because of her own medical issues and her subsequent inability to work, but if he was dead, she'd have no choice, and her daughters could take care of her. She never discussed her medical issues openly, but even as a child, Linda understood them to be of a mental variety that required extensive medication. Linda's mother had birthed herself a cage, with daughter-shaped bars and a lock shaped like a husband who would never, ever open up and set her free.

On the trail, Linda stopped in her tracks. She'd come to a patch of bright green, three-leafed, woody plants. She blinked her tears away and knelt in front of them. When she was little, she had picked a bouquet of these flowers and these plants, her first time encountering them, and brought them inside to her father. He had yelled when he saw them. *Was she trying to kill him?* he asked. Her mother heard the commotion and came to explain to the young Linda, these were poison ivy. *Leaves of three, let it be.* Linda's father was allergic. Linda might be allergic, too, though the allergy had spared Linda's mother and sister. Linda's mother took the bouquet and threw the whole thing far away in the yard.

Linda had stumbled into the plant several times throughout her childhood. She had been upset to discover she shared her father's allergy. Often, when she accidentally encountered the plant, she developed such an intense rash all over her arms, legs, and face, that she was forced to stay home from school.

On the trail, Linda thanked a God she didn't believe in that she hadn't stepped into the poison ivy. She took a deep breath. She moved on down the trail.

Later, on her way up the mountain with her family, she noted the prevalence of poison ivy over the trails they walked. She remembered her father's fear. He had accused her as a child of trying to kill him when she had wanted only to impress him. Now, she felt a thing growing inside her that may have been planted all those years ago, a dark urge in her belly. She *did* want to kill him. More than anything. As she watched him struggle, panting in his ill health, up the side of the mountain, she wanted him to meet his end.

Once they set up camp, Linda's mother began cooking hot dogs and burgers over the campfire Linda's sister built. Linda excused herself to a bathroom trip in the brush and took with her gloves, a shovel, and a plastic bag. She gathered as many bunches of poison ivy as she could within a period that wouldn't arouse questions about her whereabouts. She placed them in the bag and tied it. She stomped on it until she was sure the poison ivy had been crushed. She returned to the campfire, to her father dozing drunk in his camp chair while her mother finished cooking. Linda's mother finished the food and asked Linda to shake her father awake.

He came to as though from ages of sleep. "What...?" he said. "Where...?"

"Dinner's ready," Linda said, and reality dawned on him.

"Will you fix your dad a drink?" he asked as he stretched and gathered his strength, though Linda knew her mother would fix his plate for him and place it right into his lap, no movement on his part required.

Linda dug around in the cooler and found his vodka arranged with Linda's juice boxes, her mother's whiskey, mint leaves, seltzer for the mint juleps she drank on weekends, and several cans of Mountain Dew for Linda's sister. Linda grabbed a red Solo cup from the baggie beside the cooler. She poured in a fair amount of vodka with half a can of Mountain Dew, then she crushed several mint leaves in her hand and dropped those in the drink as well. The sun had set, and Linda's deeds were covered by night, her mother's fussing over her father's dinner, and her father's loud complaining about how sick he felt from a day of sun and hiking. Linda dumped in as many poison ivy leaves as she could get away with, then rubbed the inside part of the baggie against the rim of the cup.

"I made up a cocktail," she said as she presented the drink to her father.

Linda's mother paused in her meal and looked at Linda and her father, a frown forming on her face.

"Well, look at that!" Her father took the Solo cup from Linda's hands. "My own little bartender!" He laughed. Linda's mother chuckled. Linda's sister said nothing. "Like father, like daughter!" And he took his first sip of the drink.

Linda watched for his reaction. He turned up his lip at the taste, but he tried not to show his disgust with her creation.

"What do you call this drink, Lin?" he said.

"Mountain Mystery," she said.

"I think you've got a solid future in beverage concoction," he said, and he drained the cup and handed it back to her. "Mind if I just have a standard vodka on the rocks this time, bartender? No offense to your special creation."

Linda nodded and fixed her father a vodka and ice. He drained it, too, and the drinks just kept on coming.

IN THE MIDDLE of nowhere, in a ghost town, in the haunted manor, Linda found herself contending once more with dead and dying bodies. In the grass lay Deja, her skin shredded with the mark of Marion's claws, her breath a wisp. At the edge of the wood lay Marion in her final charred form. And in her own arms lay the woman Linda had come to love.

Deja had asked Linda to kill her, to open an uninhabited tree and to sew Deja inside. Linda had done it once, ended a life. She had poisoned her father to save her mother, to save her sister, to save herself. Self-preservation was a quality all living things possessed. Even Deja, now begging Linda to not kill her. To preserve her. Indefinitely. To help her become something else. To save Linda and Charity. But Linda had learned a lesson in her young age: sometimes, when you saved someone, you lost them.

Linda's mother's meds hadn't been a question of money. Her father's life insurance policy had paid out, after all, and Linda's mother had enough supply to last her for a long while. It was a question of serving someone. Linda's mother had aimed, her whole life, to serve Linda's father. To serve a man. To be a mother was in service of his being a father. To be a woman was in service of his needs, his wants. And Linda's mother couldn't transition from a need to serve her husband to a need to serve her children. She hadn't been trained her whole life for that. She stopped taking her medicine, and neither child understood that it wasn't their duty to force her. They tried bringing it to her each morning, slipping it into her food. She stopped eating, as though she could smell their attempts nestled in thick slices of bread or melted in chicken noodle soup warmed from a can.

Their mother descended into a black hole, and soon, she refused even to leave her bed. The kids missed school. The state came calling. They hauled Linda's mother away and placed the children in foster care. Linda's sister lasted a week before she fled with one of the foster boys, never to return. The foster family blamed Linda for the loss of two of their children, and the money they could claim to host them, and the trouble that rained down on them for not being able to keep them from running.

Linda had tried to save someone, and instead, she dug herself deeper into the grave of her misfortune. Now, to save Charity, she once more had to commit a terrible act.

Linda laughed at the way it sounded. To think it made her feel mad. But she didn't feel like her adolescent self had felt. The same desperation hummed in her, but now she *needed* to complete the monstrous act, to become the wicked creature, to save a love that flowed both ways, not to create that love from nothing.

Deja explained how her journals showed every step of the ritual and every word that need be spoken. The simple ritual required a kind hand, a soft song, and a few specific actions.

Seeing Deja perform part of it had helped. Linda recalled, with the same picture-perfect accuracy she displayed when recalling her father's face, the way Deja had taken a blade and pricked the cameraman's naked body from head to toe, bringing out tiny drops of blood that shone in the shifting light like little bulbs on a Christmas tree.

Linda grabbed Deja's feet and dragged her through the woods until she reached a clearing. As she dropped her, Deja moaned, her eyes fluttering with near-death.

"I'm close to going," she whispered, her voice scratched and deep like the gashes in her neck. "I'm on my way."

Linda breathed. She closed her eyes, recalling the tune of the song Deja had hummed. Pulling it forth, she let it dance across her tongue as she placed a palm against each tree. One hummed back. She lay her cheek against the bark, an apology of skin on what would become skin.

Then, she pried the bark away, tossing each piece to the ground until she exposed an area large enough to fit a folded-up person. With her blade, she hacked the naked wood. Her forearms ached with each nick. She hummed until her throat was sore. She tried her best to ignore Deja's dying moans, but they wormed into her, and the buzz that floated from her mouth dripped with pain. Finally, the tree spread itself with a hiss, and Linda gasped as she gazed at its eager inner core.

Clinging to her knife, Linda knelt beside Deja. She started at her feet. She skirted around the copious wounds, coaxing dots of blood to the surface.

"I wonder what I'll be like," Deja whispered.

"What do you mean?" Linda reached Deja's naked belly.

"The Williams weren't always like this, you know. They became the monsters people said they were."

When Linda poked into Deja's breastbone, Deja didn't flinch.

"And here you are, doing it again," Deja said. "Becoming the monster."

Linda stopped. She frowned. Once, she would have agreed with Deja. She would have prostrated herself on the altar of evil. Now, she shook her head. From the corner of her eye, she glimpsed the green gleam of poison ivy. "You asked me to do this." And she ripped the plant from the ground and stuffed it into Deja's mouth, muffling her words. "You've said enough. No more guilt."

With that, she grasped Deja by the neck and pierced twenty holes in her face as she sputtered, trying to spit out the ivy. Linda hoisted the woman over her shoulder. Breathing hard, she carried her to the tree and thrust her inside as Deja's attempts to speak faded into guttural moans. Deja folded her arms across her chest, resigned to the fate that had always awaited her.

"Ready?" Linda said, but she didn't wait for a reply before pushing closed the gash. The wood fibers grabbed at one another, and Linda sewed shut the wound, moving each stitch through with all the effort that remained.

When she finished, the tree shuddered as the bark transformed.

"Do good by us," Linda said. "Or else, we're dead as you."

CHAPTER FORTY-SIX

LINDA

THE FOOD SUPPLIES were thin. Linda cursed Deja even as she heard the once-producer groaning outside the windows, doing her best to manage the movements of the woods the way she had managed her contestants' actions.

The day the crew was to arrive was still two days away.

Early in the morning, Linda trekked out to check the road and found it blocked, with no sign of Sabrina's escape, save a trampled path down the mountainside that might have been her friend—or a mountain lion. Linda worried that their two days would extend into a week or more. Maybe help would never come.

Charity begged for release, so in the AM, they made careful love beneath the blanket. Linda's skin buzzed when she thought over the map of Charity's pleasure. Charity's skin prickled when Linda sucked on her earlobe. Charity's left leg twitched when Linda ran her hand along the back of her knee. And Charity was never satisfied before a total of three orgasms had wracked her breathless.

Charity was a fast learner when it came to Linda, too. Linda hadn't needed to tell her that she liked her nipples sucked to a hard point then flicked, or that she needed sweet words whispered into her ear to climax. Best of all, Linda didn't have to instruct Charity in the art of making her feel beautiful. Charity's admiration was apparent in the way she looked at Linda in the faint morning light, the way she said "Morning, love." The way Linda caught Charity throughout the day staring when Linda rested her eyes.

After making love, Linda carried Charity downstairs like an old bride, and they returned to wakefulness with two cups of old Earl Grey tea. They waited as long as they were able to have a breakfast of old jerky, rationed for their remaining days and a few beyond. They spent their afternoon in a daze, both from the love chemicals that lit their brains and from the hunger that rumbled their stomachs. Lunch was hearty: a protein bar from Deja's stash. They snacked on the few remaining grocery items in the fridge: hard pretzels with leftover mustard, thin slices of lunch meat, the rest of the potatoes.

For dinner, Linda picked wild onions and mushrooms from the front flower beds and brought them to Charity at the dining room table, where Charity picked through and eliminated the toxic varieties, then instructed Linda in which spices to use before Linda cooked them into a dinner broth.

"Thanks for helping with the food," Linda said as they sipped it down.

"You're welcome," Charity said.

"It's lovely."

"You're nice to me."

"You're nice," Linda said. "To everyone."

Charity squeezed Linda's hand. They sipped in silence.

"We'll get out of here," Charity said. "Together. And then we'll go away, me and you. We'll go get our little house in a medium-sized town."

"How do you feel about cats?" Linda asked, suddenly aware she had never asked.

"I love them," Charity said. "What's your cat's name?"

"His name is—"

Deep inside the manor, glass shattered, a window broken somewhere. Linda jumped from the table and ran into the foyer. The stained scene littered the floor, sharp shards that kept Linda from stepping too far into the room. But from where she stood in the entryway, she saw enough. A darkness had descended on the manor, and it wasn't a storm. A branch quivered through the hole in the pane, its twigs flexing like fingers. Outside, the forest had advanced to the manor's walls.

In every room, branches tapped as though asking for her to let them in.

Linda didn't have to tell Charity what she'd found. Instead, she offered her girlfriend a hand, and together they fled through the manor to the stairwell made of stone. There, they hid from the trees' assault.

"Our little house." Linda laughed through the tears that snuck down her face. "Tell me more about what you'll cook for me."

"I'll cook the world for you," Charity said. "Bulgogi, with meat fresh from a local butcher shop. Chili on the first cold day of the year. You can give me your recipe. Soft Tofu stew on the second cold day. I'll bake you birthday cakes, any flavor."

"Vanilla, with chocolate icing."

"Vanilla with chocolate icing. Sponge as soft as you've ever tasted."

"Like a cloud."

Charity grasped her hand.

"Like a cloud, of course. I'll make you patbingsu. And ice cream, with basil and blackberries from my garden. A feast of sugar."

The walls groaned.

"I would kill for some sugar right now," Linda said.

Outside, a branch crept against more glass, the sound of its scratching like a nail down a chalkboard. They didn't pause to guess if the creature that Deja had become could hold this one back.

"We may have to—" Charity said.

"Tell me more," Linda said.

"I'll make you jerky from scratch. Fresh salads, with fresh tomatoes and arugula and snap peas. I'll make our bed every morning. I'll make you a garden with flowers that die every winter. I'll make you a life, Linda Meadows."

"I'd like that," Linda said. "I'd like that very much."

CHAPTER FORTY-SEVEN

SABRINA

SABRINA WAS THROUGH being selfless.

As she rode away from the manor and its stench of death, navigating the motorcycle down the dangerous mountainside and through muddied paths, she thought of her mother. It was the only way she could keep going once the adrenaline faded: remembering her mother's gift to her, the resolve Sabrina had felt when wrapped in Tristan's arms. His words to her in the walls.

In the general store parking lot, she dismounted and hobbled inside, ignoring the look of shock on the cashier's face.

"I need a ride," Sabrina said. "To California."

The man recognized the wild expression and the injured posture and offered the woman an ambulance instead. "You need some medical assistance, hon," he said, his rural Oregon accent muddling his words.

"I need a goddamn ride," she said.

Finally, he offered to take her, and she instructed him to take her to the nearest police station. In the stranger's backseat, she dozed, dreaming of Tristan's face in the manor walls, of his drawl as he told her that it was her he wanted, not Marion. When she arrived at the police station, she informed the officers that Charity and Linda were trapped at Matrimony Manor, and that there had been murders on the premises. The sheriff scanned her up and down and smirked.

"Sure thing, sweetie," he said.

She pulled out a laptop with some dailies, which she'd snuck into her bag before departing.

"I've got proof. These are the dailies from our production."

Frowning, the sheriff handed the laptop to his junior and instructed the man to have a look.

"You famous or something?" he drawled.

"Ever heard of a reality show called The Groom?" she asked.

"I have," he said. "You win it?"

"I intend to," she said.

SHE WAITED IN a holding cell for the sheriff and his junior to return. Though she insisted on going with them, they refused to let her into the forest service's helicopter when it tornadoed into the field across the station. They assured her she "wasn't in no trouble," their words exactly, but as Sabrina grasped the bars and peered out at the varsity football captain in charge of watching over her, she doubted they were telling the truth.

The guy looked like the kind of generic cop who made jokes about Mondays. He reminded her of Tristan. She laughed. If only they knew what kind of man she belonged to. They wouldn't force her to wait behind bars.

When the sheriff returned, he let her out and handed her the laptop.

"My friends?" she said.

"Ma'am, there ain't no one out there at that manor," he said. "And it's overgrown to shit. Doesn't look like anyone's been out there for a dozen years." He held up a photo on his phone, showing a rundown building squeezed half-to-death by trees.

"Then, they were murdered, too," she said.

"There's no evidence of murders," he said.

"But... I..." The room spun around her. "I saw it."

"Are you sure?" The man pressed his hand to her shoulder, forcing her to sit down on the cot at the room's back wall. "I know a little something about these shows. They're designed to make the contestants crazy. That's why they cut off your connection with the outside world. They don't let you exercise, or watch TV, or read. It's to make you nuts, so you act nuts."

Sabrina ran through what she'd seen: Brandon's body; Tristan's body; the three camera operators in the woods (though, she hadn't seen them with her own eyes); and she'd found that trick wall. Maybe he was right.

"Here." The sheriff opened the laptop in her lap and pressed play. "You'll see."

He was right. There was nothing on the dailies but drama. The files showed nothing of the weird shit she'd witnessed.

"We're going to get you home," he said. "We've already called your sister, and she's so happy you're safe and well."

BACK HOME, SABRINA tried to reconcile what she'd seen with the home she'd left. She sat in her first bath in weeks and stared at her hands as she tried to separate reality from the fantasy, but it left her head in a constant spin cycle until her sister stepped through the bathroom door.

"I locked that," Sabrina said.

Morgan held up her pinkie. "Fingernail trick."

"I want to be alone."

Morgan sat on the toilet and scanned Sabrina's naked body. "You need help."

"I need space," Sabrina said.

"Dad has to go in for another surgery," she said. "I maxed out our credit cards while you were gone. So you didn't win *The Groom*? Fine. We'll get you on the next dating show. We'll find some way to get ourselves invited to some rich parties and find a CEO."

Morgan grabbed a pair of tweezers and knelt at the side of the tub. She plucked several hairs from Sabrina's brows, washing them off into the water. Sabrina watched them float to the sides and stick to the bath.

"I loved Tristan," she said.

"You didn't," Morgan said, plucking a hair from Sabrina's chin. She pinched the skin. Sabrina yelped.

"I did!" she said, then caught herself and lowered her voice. "I don't want someone else."

"You have to," Morgan said. "It's what Mom gave you." She moved down to Sabrina's nipples, tweezing a dark hair around the areola.

Sabrina had always been self-conscious about the hair on her chest, but when she'd expressed that to Tristan, he'd kissed her there and grinned. *"I'll let you in on a little secret,"* he said. *"I didn't even notice."*

Bringing her hand down, she knocked the tweezers from Morgan's hand. They plunked into the water.

"What the fuck?" Morgan said as Sabrina rose out of the bath.

"Tristan wouldn't have faked his death," she said. "He wanted me. He needed me."

Morgan scowled. "Get back in there. You're not clean yet."

But Sabrina emerged from the tub, dripping onto the floor below. Water pooled out from her feet, and as she marched into the living room, naked as Lady Godiva, she left wet steps behind, like the footprints of a ghost.

In her mother's bedroom, Sabrina pulled a giant pink bag out of the closet. As she unzipped it, white taffeta sprung free. The smell of old lace wafted into her as she dissected the dress bag and revealed her mother's wedding gown. Carefully, she stepped into the graceful bulk, zipped it up as far as she could by herself, gathered her mother's crystals, and left.

THE FOREST SERVICE had cleared the mudslide, and Sabrina maneuvered her rented red Jeep around the twisting roads with ease. Her dress cupcaked around her waist, taking up both front seats, but she wouldn't dream of returning to Matrimony Manor in anything but the gown in which she'd be wed.

The sheriff hadn't doctored the photographs. As the gates opened up before her, she saw that the forest had closed in, but she wasn't afraid of the trees anymore. She was supposed to be here. She was more certain than she had been of anything in her whole life. It was like coming home.

First, she double-checked the mansion for Linda and Charity, but the sheriff had told the truth about that, too. They weren't there, and Sabrina found no sign of their bodies, nor their escape, as she explored, taking care to step around the carpets of glass. At the dining table, she found their bowls and silverware, as though abandoned in the middle of a romantic evening.

Good for them, wherever they were. She hoped they were safe, but their well-being was not the reason she had come.

Outside, she searched the ground for the hints she'd left herself: the strips of bright ribbon, shredded and spread, that led into the glade. A path. Like Hansel and Gretel, she searched for hours for each patch, ground as they were into the dirt, until she found herself, finally, face to face with the prize she planted.

Tristan's body had morphed even more since she'd dug a hole and set his dead body upright into it, making sure to cover his fused and rooted feet with enough dirt to keep the tender tendrils safe. His skin was white bark now, mottled with pretty patches of well-sunned red, but there was no denying it was him. Even budding at the far lengths of his limbs, even twisting where his torso became chest became neck, Sabrina recognized him. Where his mouth once was, a knotty growth remained. She had kissed those lips enough to know them anywhere.

Her wedding dressed bunched around her as she leaned forward and rested her forehead against him. She wrapped her arms around his trunk. He was her happily-ever-after, and she would do everything she could to bring him back.

"Will you accept this ribbon?" she said as she tied her white sash around him.

The canopy seemed to whisper, *yes.*

ACKNOWLEDGMENTS

HOLY SMOKES. WOW. There are so many people I want to thank for following me and the show on this journey toward true love.

Thank you first of all to the producers: agent Kristopher O'Higgins at Scribe; editor Rob Carroll and PR expert Samantha Carroll at Dark Matter INK; and marketing guru D. L. Young. Thank you for helping to make this story and its release be all that it could be.

Thank you to the wonderful cast whose presence helped shape this beast: Chris Panatier, first reader; my inspiring DSOP friends; my Stonecoast teachers Liz, Caro, Dora, David, Jim; my Stonecoast bestie, Katie; and all my writer friends at all the writer cons. You're all fan favorites, deserving of every happy ending headed your way.

Thanks—*so* many thanks—to those who work behind the scenes, the crew: Emily, Drew, Cera, Jacob, Andrew, Fran, Kim, Fabian, Alicia, Melissa, Becca. All the work you do, all the daily frights you've given, have inspired me in every way.

And thank you to my family. Without your chaotic energy, and support, I wouldn't be the person I am today: Mom, Dad, Rachel, Tommy, Carolyn, and Bob. Ian and Silas: don't read this until you're older.

And thanks most of all to William. As always, my muse. My one. You're always here for the right reasons.

—Bonnie Jo Stufflebeam

ABOUT THE AUTHOR

 **BONNIE JO STUFFLEBEAM** is the author of the collection Where You Linger and the novella Glorious Fiends. Her short fiction has appeared in over ninety publications, including Popular Science and LeVar Burton Reads, and has been nominated twice for the Nebula Award. By day, she writes for video games. By night, she tries to dodge the chaotic parkour performed by her needy cats, Ichabod and Wednesday.

Also Available or Coming Soon from Dark Matter INK

Human Monsters: A Horror Anthology
Edited by Sadie Hartmann & Ashley Saywers
ISBN 978-1-958598-00-9

Zero Dark Thirty: The 30 Darkest Stories from Dark Matter Magazine, 2021–'22 Edited by Rob Carroll
ISBN 978-1-958598-16-0

Linghun by Ai Jiang
ISBN 978-1-958598-02-3

Monstrous Futures: A Sci-Fi Horror Anthology
Edited by Alex Woodroe
ISBN 978-1-958598-07-8

Our Love Will Devour Us by R. L. Meza
ISBN 978-1-958598-17-7

Haunted Reels: Stories from the Minds of Professional Filmmakers Curated by David Lawson
ISBN 978-1-958598-13-9

The Vein by Steph Nelson
ISBN 978-1-958598-15-3

Other Minds by Eliane Boey
ISBN 978-1-958598-19-1

Monster Lairs: A Dark Fantasy Horror Anthology
Edited by Anna Madden
ISBN 978-1-958598-08-5

Frost Bite by Angela Sylvaine
ISBN 978-1-958598-03-0

Free Burn by Drew Huff
ISBN 978-1-958598-26-9

The House at the End of Lacelean Street
by Catherine McCarthy
ISBN 978-1-958598-23-8

When the Gods Are Away by Robert E. Harpold
ISBN 978-1-958598-47-4

The Dead Spot: Stories of Lost Girls
by Angela Sylvaine
ISBN 978-1-958598-27-6

The Bleed by Stephen S. Schreffler
ISBN 978-1-958598-11-5

Voracious by Belicia Rhea
ISBN 978-1-958598-25-2

Beautiful Ways We Break Each Other Open
by Angela Liu
ISBN 978-1-958598-60-3

Chopping Spree by Angela Sylvaine
ISBN 978-1-958598-31-3

The Off-Season: An Anthology of Coastal New Weird
Edited by Marissa van Uden
ISBN 978-1-958598-24-5

The Threshing Floor by Steph Nelson
ISBN 978-1-958598-49-8

Club Contango by Eliane Boey
ISBN 978-1-958598-57-3

The Divine Flesh by Drew Huff
ISBN 978-1-958598-59-7

Psychopomp by Maria Dong
ISBN 978-1-958598-52-8

Darkly Through the Glass Place by Kirk Bueckert
ISBN 978-1-958598-48-1

Disgraced Return of the Kap's Needle by Renan Bernardo
ISBN 978-1-958598-74-0

Soul Couriers by Caleb Stephens
ISBN 978-1-958598-76-4

Abducted by Patrick Barb
ISBN 978-1-958598-37-5

Little Red Flags: Stories of Cults, Cons, and Control
Edited by Noelle W. Ihli & Steph Nelson
ISBN 978-1-958598-54-2

Frost Bite 2 by Angela Sylvaine
ISBN 978-1-958598-55-9

Dark Matter Presents: Fear City
ISBN 978-1-958598-90-0

Part of the Dark Hart Collection

Rootwork by Tracy Cross
ISBN 978-1-958598-01-6

Mosaic by Catherine McCarthy
ISBN 978-1-958598-06-1

Apparitions by Adam Pottle
ISBN 978-1-958598-18-4

I Can See Your Lies by Izzy Lee
ISBN 978-1-958598-28-3

A Gathering of Weapons by Tracy Cross
ISBN 978-1-958598-38-2